PRAISE
NICK RENNISON'S

'An intriguing anthology' – *Mail on Sunday*

'These 15 sanguinary spine-tinglers… deliver delicious chills'
– **Christopher Hirst,** *Independent*

'A book which will delight fans of crime fiction'
– *Verbal Magazine*

'It's good to see that Mr Rennison has also selected some rarer
pieces – and rarer detectives, such as November Joe, Sebastian
Zambra, Cecil Thorold and Lois Cayley' – **Roger Johnson,**
*The District Messenger (Newsletter of the Sherlock Holmes
Society of London)*

'A gloriously Gothic collection of heroes fighting against
maidens with bone-white skin, glittering eyes and blood-
thirsty intentions' – **Lizzie Hayes,** *Promoting Crime Fiction*

'Nick Rennison's *The Rivals of Dracula* shows that many
Victorian and Edwardian novelists tried their hand at this staple
of Gothic horror' – **Andrew Taylor,** *Spectator*

'*The Rivals of Dracula* is a fantastic collection of classic tales to
chill the blood and tingle the spine. Grab a copy and curl up
somewhere cosy for a night in' – *Citizen Homme Magazine*

ALSO BY NICK RENNISON

Freud and Psychoanalysis
Peter Mark Roget – The Man Who Became a Book
Robin Hood – Myth, History & Culture
A Short History of Polar Exploration
Bohemian London

The Rivals of Sherlock Holmes
The Rivals of Dracula
Supernatural Sherlocks
More Rivals of Sherlock Holmes

SHERLOCK'S SISTERS

Stories from

THE GOLDEN AGE OF THE FEMALE DETECTIVE

edited and introduced by

NICK RENNISON

NO EXIT PRESS

First published in 2020 by No Exit Press,
an imprint of Oldcastle Books Ltd,
Harpenden, UK
noexit.co.uk

Editorial comment © Nick Rennison, 2020

ISBN
978-0-85730-398-1 (print)
978-0-85730-399-8 (epub)

2 4 6 8 10 9 7 5 3 1

Typeset in 11.25pt Bembo
by Avocet Typeset, Bideford, Devon, EX39 2BP
Printed and bound in Great Britain by Clays Ltd, Elcograf S.p.A.

To my mother, Eileen Rennison,
who enjoys a good crime story.

Contents

CONTENTS

INTRODUCTION

Female detectives make their first appearances surprisingly early in the history of crime fiction. The 1860s was not a decade in which women in real life had much scope to forge independent careers for themselves, particularly in the field of law enforcement, but, in the pages of novels and short stories, they were already busy solving crimes and bringing villains to justice. Andrew Forrester's 1864 book *The Female Detective* (recently republished by the British Library) introduced readers to the mysterious 'G', a woman enquiry agent employed by the police who sometimes goes by the name of 'Miss Gladden'. There had been women who turned detective in fiction before. Wilkie Collins's short story entitled 'The Diary of Anne Rodway', for example, was published in 1856 in Dickens's magazine *Household Words*, and has a heroine who investigates the suspicious circumstances of a friend's death. However, Forrester's character seems to have been the first professional female detective in British fiction. Like 'Miss Gladden', 'Andrew Forrester' was a pseudonym. The author's real name was James Redding Ware (1832-1909), a novelist, dramatist and writer for hire in Victorian London who produced books on a wide variety of subjects from card games and English slang to dreams of famous people and the lives of centenarians. *The Female Detective* consists of a number of 'G''s cases, narrated by herself, in which she deploys her deductive and logical skills to reveal the truth.

The Female Detective, and other titles such as WS Hayward's *Revelations of a Lady Detective* which appeared at about the same time, were published as 'yellowbacks'. These were cheaply produced books, so called because of their covers which often had bright yellow borders. They were sold mostly at the bookstalls which had recently sprung up at railway stations across the country, and were intended as easy, disposable reads for train journeys.

For nearly twenty-five years, Miss Gladden and Mrs Paschal, the heroine of Hayward's book, had no real successors in English fiction. The third woman detective did not put in an appearance until 1888 when Leonard Merrick (1864-1939) made Miriam Lea, a former governess turned private investigator, into the central character of his short novel *Mr Bazalgette's Agent*. Employed by Mr Bazalgette's detective agency, Miriam pursues an embezzler halfway across Europe in what is a charming, skilfully written narrative. Unfortunately her creator, Leonard Merrick, who was in his early twenties when he wrote *Mr Bazalgette's Agent*, came to hate it. He went on to become a well-respected novelist whose admirers included HG Wells, JM Barrie and GK Chesterton. George Orwell enjoyed his novels and wrote a foreword to a new edition of one of them. In later life Merrick clearly saw his detective story as an embarrassment – 'the worst thing I wrote', he called it – and made every effort to cover up its existence. He took to buying up copies of the book and destroying them which explains why only a handful now remains in existence. Luckily, the British Library republished it in their 'Crime Classics' series in 2013 so readers today can see that Merrick was unjustly severe on his own work.

By 1890 there had only been a very small number of pioneering women detectives in crime fiction but that was about to change. Two phenomena dictated that change. One was the astonishing increase in the number of magazines and periodicals in the last decade of the nineteenth century. Between 1875 and 1903, that number nearly quadrupled from just short of 700 to more than 2,500. Not all of them, of course, carried crime stories but a significant proportion did. The market for all kinds of what would later be called 'genre' fiction, but especially crime stories, grew exponentially.

The other factor was the advent of Sherlock Holmes. The great detective's debut in *A Study in Scarlet*, published in *Beeton's Christmas Annual* for 1887, did not immediately start the Holmes craze. It was only when *The Strand Magazine* began to publish the short stories featuring Holmes and Dr Watson four years later that the public took the characters to its collective heart and worldwide fame beckoned. The success of the Holmes stories was so startling that soon every fiction magazine was looking to duplicate it and writers of all kinds were hoping to come up with a detective as appealing.

Between 1891 and the outbreak of the First World War, dozens and dozens of crime-fighting characters made their bow in the periodical press. Each writer strove to make his detective stand out from the crowd. Provide your creation with some kind of USP and you might, at least in your dreams, attain the kind of success Conan Doyle had done. So a blind detective (Ernest Bramah's Max Carrados), a detective who was a Canadian woodsman (Hesketh Prichard's November Joe), a Hindu from a remote Indian village (Headon Hill's Kala Persad), and many more with a bewildering variety of talents, characteristics and geographical origins were sent out into the world to attract potential readers.

Among all the competing sleuths, a significant number were women. These female detectives were almost as diverse as their male counterparts. Some had special talents which helped them in their work. Richard Marsh's Judith Lee, who appeared in a series of stories published in *The Strand Magazine* in 1911, was a lip-reader who was forever spotting crooks discussing their nefarious plans. Diana Marburg, the so-called 'Oracle of Maddox Street', who was created by the writing partnership of LT Meade and Robert Eustace, was a palm-reader, although she solved her cases more through the application of observation and common sense than through her skill at interpreting lines on the hand. Several of the women detectives, most notably George R Sims's Dorcas Dene, had been actresses and their stage experience came in handy when they were donning disguises to pursue villains.

Many of the female detectives from the late Victorian and Edwardian periods were women obliged, for a variety of reasons, to make their own way in the world without the support of husband or family. They were resourceful and swift to adapt themselves to new circumstances. Catherine Louisa Pirkis's Loveday Brooke had been 'thrown upon the world penniless and almost friendless' by 'a jerk of Fortune's wheel' but she becomes the leading light in Ebenezer Dyer's detective agency. 'She has so much common sense that it amounts to genius,' her boss remarks. Mollie Delamere, the heroine of Beatrice Heron-Maxwell's 1899 book, *The Adventures of a Lady Pearl-Broker*, is a young widow who has no assured income. 'People seem to think it a disgrace that one's husband should not leave one enough to live on,' she wryly comments. She takes a job as an agent for pearl merchant Mr Leighton. This exposes her to many dangers and adventures, all of which she takes in her stride.

The 1890s and 1900s were an era in which feminism was on the rise. Educational opportunities were increasing. More and more women were demanding access to professions like medicine and journalism. They wanted to challenge men in what had previously been exclusively masculine domains. It is no surprise that the crime fiction of the time provided plenty of examples of what was called 'The New Woman' in action. Grant Allen's Lois Cayley is a graduate of Girton College, Cambridge. In the course of her globe-trotting adventures, she wins a bicycle race, exposes the charlatanry of a quack doctor, rescues a kidnapped woman and kills a tiger. By doing so she amply proves herself to be a match in spirit and intelligence for any man. The eponymous protagonist of M McDonnell Bodkin's *Dora Myrl: The Lady Detective* is a brilliant mathematician with a medical degree. Unable to get a practice, she has tried various jobs (including journalism) before she falls into detective work. There her gifts and personality finally come into their own. Bodkin was a prolific writer whose earlier creations had included a male detective named Paul Beck. In a later book, Beck and Dora work together and eventually marry.

Like Dora Myrl, many of the female detectives from the decades before the First World War were created by men. This was largely a simple reflection of the fact that the majority of the stories of all kinds in the periodical press were written by men.

However, there were plenty of women writers publishing stories in magazines like *The Strand*, *Pearson's Magazine*, *The Idler* and the dozens of competing titles which could be found in newsagents and on railway bookstalls. Possibly the best example of such a woman is LT Meade who, with her regular collaborator Robert Eustace, makes two appearances in this anthology. Miss Florence Cusack and Diana Marburg, the 'Oracle of Maddox Street', are among many series characters that the immensely productive Meade created, both with and without the assistance of other writers.

In America, women writers such as Anna Katharine Green produced early examples of detective fiction but women detectives were few and far between before 1900. Those that did appear were mostly published in so-called 'dime novels', the transatlantic equivalents of the 'yellowbacks' and cheap railway formats which, in Britain, had provided a home for Miss Gladden and Mrs Paschal. Characters such as the heroine of *Madeline Payne, the Detective's Daughter*, published in 1884, Mignon Lawrence, a feisty New Yorker sent west in pursuit of a bad guy, and Caroline 'Cad' Metti, a beautiful Italian-American who took centre stage in several stories in the 1890s, were the chief protagonists of entertaining potboilers with little pretension to literary merit.

In the first two decades of the twentieth century the woman detective migrated from the pages of the dime novel to more respectable literature. Anna Katharine Green was the author of *The Leavenworth Case*, an 1878 novel which introduced the detective Ebenezer Gryce to American readers. Twenty years later, Green created Amelia Butterworth, a high-society spinster with a taste for poking her nose into other people's misfortunes, who joined forces with Gryce to solve crimes in three novels, beginning with *That Affair Next Door* (1897). In 1915, nearly forty years after her first detective novel, Green published a series of short stories featuring Violet Strange, a young woman from a wealthy New York family who earns her pin money working for a detective agency. One of these is included in this anthology. Arthur B Reeve's Constance Dunlap is another young woman who makes a living from fighting crime. Reeve is best known for creating the 'scientific detective' Craig Kennedy who appeared in dozens of short stories, more than twenty novels, several films and a 1950s TV series. He was a much less sophisticated writer than, say, Anna Katharine Green, and both his Craig Kennedy stories and his tales of Constance Dunlap reflect that, but they retain their charm and are full of fascinating period detail. 'The Dope Fiends', the story I have included in this anthology, reveals much, both consciously and unconsciously, about attitudes to drug-taking in the 1910s.

In the several anthologies I have compiled (*The Rivals of Sherlock Holmes, More Rivals of Sherlock Holmes, The Rivals of Dracula, Supernatural Sherlocks*), my aim has always been to demonstrate the sheer range of entertaining short fiction that was produced in the late Victorian and Edwardian eras. My purpose in putting together this volume is the same. From a palm-reading society lady (Diana Marburg) to the gypsy owner of a pawnshop (Hagar Stanley), from a Scotland Yard detective (Lady Molly) solving crimes years before women in real life were even allowed to join the police force to a nurse of genius (Hilda Wade) looking to revenge the death of her father, the female detectives of this golden age of genre fiction were a gloriously mixed bunch. I hope that readers enjoy their assorted adventures as much as I do.

DORA BELL

Created by Elizabeth Burgoyne Corbett
(1846–1930)

A journalist who worked for the Newcastle Daily Chronicle, *Elizabeth Burgoyne Corbett also wrote a number of interesting genre novels.* New Amazonia: A Foretaste of the Future, *first published in 1889, is a feminist utopia in which her heroine falls asleep in the late nineteenth century and awakes in the year 2472 to find a society in which women have control. Thanks to a technique known as 'nerve-rejuvenation', these 'Amazonians' live for hundreds of years in the prime of life and have created a fairer and less corrupt world. (Although, disconcertingly for a modern reader, they do practise a form of eugenics.) Corbett was not only a pioneer of women's science fiction. She also published crime novels. In* When the Sea Gives Up Its Dead, *subtitled 'A Thrilling Detective Story', Annie Cory turns detective when her fiancé is falsely accused of stealing diamonds from the firm for which he works. Adopting a series of alternative identities and disguises (including cross-dressing as a man), Annie sets out to prove his innocence. The book was published in 1894. At about the same time, Corbett created another female detective in Dora Bell, an agent for the Bell & White Agency, who appeared in a series of stories published in provincial and colonial newspapers such as the* Leeds Mercury *and the* Adelaide Observer. *These do not seem to have been collected in book form although an earlier volume of stories by Corbett,* Secrets of a Private Enquiry Office *(1890), does include a character named Dora. The Dora Bell stories are short and uncomplicated, ideally suited to the newspaper readership at which they were aimed. They win no prizes for great originality but they remain entertaining and easy to read.*

MADAME DUCHESNE'S GARDEN PARTY

'It cost more than two hundred pounds, Miss Bell. But that is
not the worst of the matter. My aunt stipulated that I should
always wear it as a perpetual reminder of her past kindness and
her future good intentions, and if she misses it I shall lose favour
with her altogether. To lose Miss Mainwaring's favour means to
lose the splendid fortune which is hers to bequeath, so you see
how very serious the matter is for me. It is, indeed, little short
of life and death, for poverty would kill me now. For God's sake
do your best for me.'

'But surely, if Miss Mainwaring knows that you could not
possibly have foreseen your loss, she will not be unjust enough
to disinherit you?'

'Indeed she will. She believes me to be vacillating and
unreliable, because I broke off an engagement with a rich man to
whom I had but given a reluctant acceptance, and united myself
to the man of my choice. My husband was poor, and therefore
beyond the pale of forgiveness, and my own pardon is only based
on the most unswerving obedience to all my aunt's injunctions.
The pendant came from India, and the stones in it are said to
possess occult power – I wish they had the power to come back
to their rightful owner.'

The speaker heaved a sigh of desperation as she spoke, and
I glanced at her with considerable interest. She was tall, pale,
dark-eyed, and handsome, but her appearance bore certain signs
of that vacillation and carelessness of which her aunt accredited
her with the possession.

The circumstances surrounding the loss of which she
complained were peculiar. She had been spending the evening
at the house of the German Ambassador, and returning home in
Miss Mainwaring's carriage, when she became aware of the fact
that she had lost the jewelled pendant which her aunt had given
her as a token of reconciliation when she returned to her after
being suddenly widowed.

A frantic search of the carriage bore no results, and Mrs Bevan hastily told the coachman to return to the Embassy. But she prudently refrained from confiding the particulars of her loss to him, for she was not quite without hope that it might be remedied. Madame von Auerbach was, however, able to give her no comfort, for she had herself suffered in like manner with her guest.

She had lost a valuable diamond-studded watch, and when the most careful search failed to discover it, the conclusion arrived at was that some thief must have been present at the reception. It was an unpleasant conclusion to arrive at. But it was the only natural one. For the Ambassador's wife had not left her guests, or gone beyond the reception rooms, from the time she entered them, wearing the watch to the moment when, the last visitors having just gone, she thought of looking at her watch, and found that it had disappeared.

Mrs Bevan's return a few moments later with the news that her pendant had disappeared, confirmed the supposition that some professional thief must have been at work, and the police were at once communicated with. They were also strictly enjoined to keep the matter a profound secret, for various reasons.

But Mrs Bevan was too anxious to rely entirely upon the exertions of the regular force, hence her application to our firm and her urgent entreaty that I would act with the utmost despatch.

Soon after my client's departure I sought an interview with Madame von Auerbach, but could glean very little useful information. The invitations had been sent out with great care, but their exclusiveness was negatived by the fact that they were all sent to So-and-so and friend. The position of those invited by name had been considered sufficient guarantee of the perfect suitability of the friends whom they might select to accompany them to the Embassy, and at least a score of people had been present of whom the hostess barely heard even their names.

Of course, no one could treat any single one of these individuals as suspects without some definite suspicion to work upon, and, unfortunately for our prospects of success, there was not the slightest ground for suspecting anyone in particular.

I was about to quit Madame von Auerbach's house when a servant entered with a card upon a waiter, and upon hearing that the name inscribed thereon was that of one of the guests of the previous evening, I hastily decided to stay a little longer, and requested Madame von Auerbach to keep my vocation a secret from her visitor.

The next minute a most bewitching little woman was ushered into the room.

'Oh, my dear madame!' she exclaimed, with a charming foreign accent. 'Such an unfortunate thing! I lost my beautiful diamond clasp last night. Have your servants seen anything of it?'

Madame von Auerbach turned pale, and I looked with augmented interest at the harbinger of this new development of the previous evening's mystery. The depredations had evidently been on a large scale, and the depredators had shown remarkably good taste in the choice of their spoil. The latest victim was a French lady named Madame Duchesne, and she waxed eloquent in lamentations over her loss when it was shown to her how little hope there was of recovering her diamond clasp.

'And do you know, I feel so terribly upset,' was her pathetic protest, 'that I would give anything not to have had to go on with my own garden party tomorrow. And I don't like to say it, but it is a fact I also may have included the thief in my invitation, and it would be awful if more things were to be stolen. Whatever shall I do?'

As no practical advice seemed to be forthcoming, Madame Duchesne studied for a moment, and then announced her intention of employing a detective.

'Not a real, horrid policeman,' she averred, 'but one of those extraordinary individuals who seem able to look through and through you, and who can find anything out. Private detectives, I think they call them.'

Madame von Auerbach looked up eagerly, but I gave her a warning glance which caused her to postpone the revelation of my identity which she had felt prompted to make.

'Do you know any of these people?' was the Frenchwoman's appeal to me. 'Can you help me to the address of one?'

'There are several firms of private detectives in London, if we are to judge from their advertisements,' I answered. 'I have heard Messrs Bell and White, of Holborn, spoken of as fairly good, but, of course, there are plenty of others equally good, or probably better.'

'Bell and White, Holborn. Yes, I will try them. Thank you so much for helping me. May I ask if you live in London?'

Seizing my cue, Madame von Auerbach promptly came to my assistance.

'I am very angry with Miss Gresham,' she averred. 'Since she resigned her post as governess to the Duke of Solothurn's children, she has hardly deigned to take any notice of the numerous friends she made in Germany. But I mean to make her stay a few days with me, now that she has come to see me.'

'Then you must bring her with you to my garden party,' said Madame Duchesne, and the invitation so cleverly angled for was accepted with a faint pretence of hesitation at the idea of inflicting myself upon the hospitality of a total stranger.

After Madame Duchesne's departure I congratulated Madame von Auerbach very warmly upon her tact and presence of mind, and arranged to visit the garden party as her friend the next day.

In due course the interesting function was in full swing, and the fascinating hostess had quite a crowd of guests to look after. My guarantor had left me, at my own request, to my own devices. I wanted to look about me, and to note all that was going on, without being too much in evidence myself.

Presently Madame Duchesne approached me with a very mysterious air, and introduced a very handsome man to my notice. 'Don't be shocked,' she whispered. 'But this is the private detective, Mr Bell. I communicated with him at once after leaving Madame von Auerbach's yesterday, and he is here to watch that no pickpocket secures booty here. Isn't it too dreadful to have to take such precautions? I will never give another party in London!'

I responded to this confidential communication with due

sympathy, and gravely acknowledged the attention my new companion bestowed upon me for a few moments. And I had need of my gravity and presence of mind. For the man introduced to me was not my uncle, the detective. I knew that our firm had not been applied to by Madame Duchesne, in spite of her assertion to the contrary, and as this was certainly no one who had ever been in our office, I knew that certain suspicions that I had formed yesterday were likely to be verified. Since this stranger was certainly no detective, I concluded that he was merely posing as one for the sake of diverting suspicion from the offenders whom I was anxious to run to earth. The assumption that he was the associate and helpmate of the thieves was also a very natural one, although a glance at the lovely hostess and her dainty surroundings almost seemed to belie such a supposition.

But I knew that I was on the right track, and within the hour my vigilance was rewarded. The sham detective, whose pretended avocation had been disclosed to none but Madame von Auerbach and myself, sauntered from group to group, as if intent upon scrutinising their actions. His real object was to attach their jewellery, and I had the satisfaction of seeing him possess himself of a costly watch which Lady A was wearing in somewhat careless fashion. Instant denunciation was not my intention. I meant to probe the matter to the root, and followed Mr Bell's movements with apparent nonchalance. Presently he culled a couple of beautiful standard roses, and handed them to Madame Duchesne with a graceful compliment.

The thing was beautifully done, and none but a person keenly on guard would have noticed that the watch changed hands with the roses. This little comedy over, Madame sauntered towards the house, and, five minutes later, I came upon her, quite by accident, of course, just as she was relocking a dainty cabinet from which she had taken a fresh bottle of perfume, in the use of which she was very lavish.

There were two or three other people in Madame's charming boudoir, among them being Madame von Auerbach, by whose side I seated myself with an air of sudden weakness.

She was really startled by the development of events, but she had been previously cautioned, and played her part very well indeed, when I exclaimed that I felt dreadfully ill.

'What shall I do?' she cried. 'I hope it is not one of your old attacks.'

'Yes, it is,' I whispered, faintly. 'Do send for my uncle. He is the only one who can help me.'

I was promptly placed on the couch, and dosed with all sorts of amateur remedies, pending the arrival of my uncle, who had been sent for in hot haste, and who, entre nous, was waiting with a police officer in private clothes for the expected urgent summons. No sooner did they appear than my indisposition vanished, and I astonished the bystanders by springing vigorously to my feet.

'Arrest Madame Duchesne,' I cried, 'and her accomplice.' Pointing to the latter, I continued, 'That man has stolen Lady A's watch, and it is locked in that cabinet.'

What a scene of confusion there was immediately. Not only Lady A, but several other people discovered that they had been robbed, and the cabinet was found to contain a great quantity of stolen valuables, among them being Mrs Bevan's much-prized pendant.

My discovery was only made in the nick of time. In another twelve hours the birds would have flown, for the real Madame Duchesne, the lady from whom they had stolen the letters of introduction which had obtained them the entree to London society, had arrived in London that day. An accomplice had warned them of the fact, and as they knew that this garden party they were giving at the gorgeous house they had hired would be their last opportunity for some time, they had determined to make a large haul and decamp that same evening.

Luckily for many people, I was able to frustrate their intention. At present they are lodging in infinitely less luxurious quarters, and several members of the upper classes are much more careful than formerly as to whom they associate with by virtue of letters of introduction.

LOVEDAY BROOKE

Created by Catherine Louisa Pirkis
(1839–1910)

In 1893, the same year that Conan Doyle attempted to despatch
Sherlock Holmes by supposedly sending him over the Reichenbach Falls
(the character was, of course, to be resurrected later), a new detective
appeared in the pages of The Ludgate Monthly. Sometimes known
(slightly misleadingly) as 'the female Sherlock Holmes', Loveday Brooke
was the heroine of half a dozen stories which were subsequently gathered
together in a volume entitled The Experiences of Loveday Brooke,
Detective. She is one of the most interesting and appealing of late
Victorian female detectives. A professional who works for a Fleet Street
Detective Agency, she shows resourcefulness when she is sent under cover
(as she is in several of the stories) and confidence in her own ability to
discover the truth about the crimes she is investigating. The character,
a woman making her way successfully in a world usually the preserve
of men, was created by Catherine Louisa Pirkis, the wife of a Royal
Navy officer, who had taken up writing in her late thirties. Her first
novel, entitled Disappeared from her Home, was published in
1877 and was followed by more than a dozen others, offering readers
a mixture of melodrama, mystery and romance. She was also a regular
contributor of short stories to the periodical press. After the publication of
the tales of Loveday Brooke, Pirkis largely gave up writing in favour of
charitable work. She and her husband were active in the anti-vivisection
movement and were among the founders of the National Canine Defence
League.

CATHERINE LOUISA PIRKIS

THE REDHILL SISTERHOOD

'THEY want you at Redhill, now,' said Mr Dyer, taking a packet of papers from one of his pigeon-holes. 'The idea seems gaining ground in manly quarters that in cases of mere suspicion, women detectives are more satisfactory than men, for they are less likely to attract attention. And this Redhill affair, so far as I can make out, is one of suspicion only.'

It was a dreary November morning; every gas jet in the Lynch Court office was alight, and a yellow curtain of outside fog draped its narrow windows.

'Nevertheless, I suppose one can't afford to leave it uninvestigated at this season of the year, with country-house robberies beginning in so many quarters,' said Miss Brooke.

'No; and the circumstances in this case certainly seem to point in the direction of the country-house burglar. Two days ago a somewhat curious application was made privately, by a man giving the name of John Murray, to Inspector Gunning, of the Reigate police – Redhill, I must tell you is in the Reigate police district. Murray stated that he had been a greengrocer somewhere in South London, had sold his business there, and had, with the proceeds of the sale, bought two small houses in Redhill, intending to let the one and live in the other. These houses are situated in a blind alley, known as Paved Court, a narrow turning leading off the London and Brighton coach road. Paved Court has been known to the sanitary authorities for the past ten years as a regular fever nest, and as the houses which Murray bought – numbers 7 and 8 – stand at the very end of the blind alley, with no chance of thorough ventilation, I dare say the man got them for next to nothing. He told the Inspector that he had had great difficulty in procuring a tenant for the house he wished to let, number 8, and that consequently when, about three weeks back, a lady, dressed as a nun, made him an offer for it, he immediately closed with her. The lady gave her name simply as "Sister Monica", and stated that she was a member of an undenominational Sisterhood that had recently been founded

23

by a wealthy lady, who wished her name kept a secret. Sister Monica gave no references, but, instead, paid a quarter's rent in advance, saying that she wished to take possession of the house immediately, and open it as a home for crippled orphans.'

'Gave no references – home for cripples,' murmured Loveday, scribbling hard and fast in her notebook.

'Murray made no objection to this,' continued Mr Dyer, 'and, accordingly, the next day, Sister Monica, accompanied by three other Sisters and some sickly children, took possession of the house, which they furnished with the barest possible necessaries from cheap shops in the neighbourhood. For a time, Murray said, he thought he had secured most desirable tenants, but during the last ten days suspicions as to their real character have entered his mind, and these suspicions he thought it his duty to communicate to the police. Among their possessions, it seems, these Sisters number an old donkey and a tiny cart, and this they start daily on a sort of begging tour through the adjoining villages, bringing back every evening a perfect hoard of broken victuals and bundles of old garments. Now comes the extraordinary fact on which Murray bases his suspicions. He says, and Gunning verifies his statement, that in whatever direction those Sisters turn the wheels of their donkey-cart, burglaries, or attempts at burglaries, are sure to follow. A week ago they went along towards Horley, where, at an outlying house, they received much kindness from a wealthy gentleman. That very night an attempt was made to break into that gentleman's house – an attempt, however, that was happily frustrated by the barking of the house-dog. And so on in other instances that I need not go into. Murray suggests that it might be as well to have the daily movements of these sisters closely watched, and that extra vigilance should be exercised by the police in the districts that have had the honour of a morning call from them. Gunning coincides with this idea, and so has sent to me to secure your services.'

Loveday closed her notebook. 'I suppose Gunning will meet me somewhere and tell me where I'm to take up my quarters?' she said.

'Yes; he will get into your carriage at Merstham – the station before Redhill – if you will put your hand out of the window, with the morning paper in it. By the way, he takes it for granted that you will take the 11.05 train from Victoria. Murray, it seems, has been good enough to place his little house at the disposal of the police, but Gunning does not think espionage could be so well carried on there as from other quarters. The presence of a stranger in an alley of that sort is bound to attract attention. So he has hired a room for you in a draper's shop that immediately faces the head of the court. There is a private door to this shop of which you will have the key, and can let yourself in and out as you please. You are supposed to be a nursery governess on the lookout for a situation, and Gunning will keep you supplied with letters to give colour to the idea. He suggests that you need only occupy the room during the day, at night you will find far more comfortable quarters at Laker's Hotel, just outside the town.'

This was about the sum total of the instructions that Mr Dyer had to give.

The 11.05 train from Victoria, that carried Loveday to her work among the Surrey Hills, did not get clear of the London fog till well away on the other side of Purley. When the train halted at Merstham, in response to her signal a tall, soldier-like individual made for her carriage, and, jumping in, took the seat facing her. He introduced himself to her as Inspector Gunning, recalled to her memory a former occasion on which they had met, and then, naturally enough, turned the talk upon the present suspicious circumstances they were bent upon investigating.

'It won't do for you and me to be seen together,' he said; 'of course I am known for miles round, and anyone seen in my company will be at once set down as my coadjutor, and spied upon accordingly. I walked from Redhill to Merstham on purpose to avoid recognition on the platform at Redhill, and halfway here, to my great annoyance, found that I was being followed by a man in a workman's dress and carrying a basket of tools. I doubled, however, and gave him the slip, taking a short cut down a lane which, if he had been living in the place, he would have known as well as I did. By Jove!' this was added with a sudden start, 'there is the fellow, I declare; he has weathered me after all, and has no doubt taken good stock of us both, with the train going at this snail's pace. It was unfortunate that your face should have been turned towards that window, Miss Brooke.'

'My veil is something of a disguise, and I will put on another cloak before he has a chance of seeing me again,' said Loveday.

All she had seen in the brief glimpse that the train had allowed, was a tall, powerfully-built man walking along a siding of the line. His cap was drawn low over his eyes, and in his hand he carried a workman's basket.

Gunning seemed much annoyed at the circumstance. 'Instead of landing at Redhill,' he said, 'we'll go on to Three Bridges and wait there for a Brighton train to bring us back, that will enable you to get to your room somewhere between the lights; I don't want to have you spotted before you've so much as started your work.'

Then they went back to their discussion of the Redhill Sisterhood.

'They call themselves "undenominational", whatever that means,' said Gunning. 'They say they are connected with no religious sect whatever, they attend sometimes one place of worship, sometimes another, sometimes none at all. They refuse to give up the name of the founder of their order, and really no one has any right to demand it of them, for, as no doubt you see, up to the present moment the case is one of mere suspicion, and it may be a pure coincidence that attempts at burglary have followed their footsteps in this neighbourhood. By the way, I have heard of a man's face being enough to hang him, but until I saw Sister Monica's, I never saw a woman's face that could perform the same kind office for her. Of all the lowest criminal types of faces I have ever seen, I think hers is about the lowest and most repulsive.'

After the Sisters, they passed in review the chief families resident in the neighbourhood.

'This,' said Gunning, unfolding a paper, 'is a map I have

specially drawn up for you – it takes in the district for ten miles round Redhill, and every country house of any importance is marked with it in red ink. Here, in addition, is an index to those houses, with special notes of my own to every house.'

Loveday studied the map for a minute or so, then turned her attention to the index.

'Those four houses you've marked, I see, are those that have been already attempted. I don't think I'll run them through, but I'll mark them "doubtful"; you see the gang – for, of course, it is a gang – might follow our reasoning on the matter, and look upon those houses as our weak point. Here's one I'll run through, "house empty during winter months", that means plate and jewellery sent to the bankers. Oh! and this one may as well be crossed off, "father and four sons all athletes and sportsmen", that means firearms always handy – I don't think burglars will be likely to trouble them. Ah! now we come to something! Here's a house to be marked "tempting" in a burglar's list. "Wootton Hall, lately changed hands and rebuilt, with complicated passages and corridors. Splendid family plate in daily use and left entirely to the care of the butler". I wonder, does the master of that house trust to his "complicated passages" to preserve his plate for him? A dismissed dishonest servant would supply a dozen maps of the place for half-a-sovereign. What do these initials, "EL", against the next house in the list, North Cape, stand for?'

'Electric lighted. I think you might almost cross that house off also. I consider electric lighting one of the greatest safeguards against burglars that a man can give his house.'

'Yes, if he doesn't rely exclusively upon it; it might be a nasty trap under certain circumstances. I see this gentleman also has magnificent presentation and other plate.'

'Yes. Mr Jameson is a wealthy man and very popular in the neighbourhood; his cups and epergnes are worth looking at.'

'Is it the only house in the district that is lighted with electricity?'

'Yes; and, begging your pardon, Miss Brooke, I only wish it were not so. If electric lighting were generally in vogue it would save the police a lot of trouble on these dark winter nights.'

'The burglars would find some way of meeting such a condition of things, depend upon it; they have reached a very high development in these days. They no longer stalk about as they did fifty years ago with blunderbuss and bludgeon; they plot, plan, contrive and bring imagination and artistic resource to their aid. By the way, it often occurs to me that the popular detective stories, for which there seems too large a demand at the present day, must be, at times, uncommonly useful to the criminal classes.'

At Three Bridges they had to wait so long for a return train that it was nearly dark when Loveday got back to Redhill. Mr Gunning did not accompany her thither, having alighted at a previous station. Loveday had directed her portmanteau to be sent direct to Laker's Hotel, where she had engaged a room by telegram from Victoria Station. So, unburthened by luggage, she slipped quietly out of the Redhill Station and made her way straight for the draper's shop in the London Road. She had no difficulty in finding it, thanks to the minute directions given her by the Inspector.

Street lamps were being lighted in the sleepy little town as she went along, and as she turned into the London Road, shopkeepers were lighting up their windows on both sides of the way. A few yards down this road, a dark patch between the lighted shops showed her where Paved Court led off from the thoroughfare. A side door of one of the shops that stood at the corner of the court seemed to offer a post of observation whence she could see without being seen, and here Loveday, shrinking into the shadows, ensconced herself in order to take stock of the little alley and its inhabitants. She found it much as it had been described to her – a collection of four-roomed houses of which more than half were unlet. Numbers 7 and 8 at the head of the court presented a slightly less neglected appearance than the other tenements. Number 7 stood in total darkness, but in the upper window of number 8 there showed what seemed to be a night-light burning, so Loveday conjectured that this possibly was the room set apart as a dormitory for the little cripples.

While she stood thus surveying the home of the suspected Sisterhood, the Sisters themselves – two, at least, of them – came into view, with their donkey-cart and their cripples, in the main road. It was an odd little cortège. One Sister, habited in a nun's dress of dark blue serge, led the donkey by the bridle; another Sister, similarly attired, walked alongside the low cart, in which were seated two sickly-looking children. They were evidently returning from one of their long country circuits, and unless they had lost their way and been belated, it certainly seemed a late hour for the sickly little cripples to be abroad.

As they passed under the gas lamp at the corner of the court, Loveday caught a glimpse of the faces of the Sisters. It was easy, with Inspector Gunning's description before her mind, to identify the older and taller woman as Sister Monica, and a more coarse-featured and generally repellent face Loveday admitted to herself she had never before seen. In striking contrast to this forbidding countenance, was that of the younger Sister. Loveday could only catch a brief passing view of it, but that one brief view was enough to impress it on her memory as of unusual sadness and beauty. As the donkey stopped at the corner of the court, Loveday heard this sad-looking young woman addressed as 'Sister Anna' by one of the cripples, who asked plaintively when they were going to have something to eat.

'Now, at once,' said Sister Anna, lifting the little one, as it seemed to Loveday, tenderly out of the cart, and carrying him on her shoulder down the court to the door of number 8, which opened to them at their approach. The other Sister did the same with the other child; then both Sisters returned, unloaded the cart of sundry bundles and baskets, and, this done, led off the old donkey and trap down the road, possibly to a neighbouring costermonger's stables.

A man, coming along on a bicycle, exchanged a word of greeting with the Sisters as they passed, then swung himself off his machine at the corner of the court, and walked it along the paved way to the door of number 7. This he opened with a key, and then, pushing the machine before him, entered the house.

Loveday took it for granted that this man must be the John Murray of whom she had heard. She had closely scrutinised him as he had passed her, and had seen that he was a dark, well-featured man of about fifty years of age.

She congratulated herself on her good fortune in having seen so much in such a brief space of time, and coming forth from her sheltered corner turned her steps in the direction of the draper's shop on the other side of the road.

It was easy to find it. 'Golightly' was the singular name that figured above the shopfront, in which were displayed a variety of goods calculated to meet the wants of servants and the poorer classes generally. A tall, powerfully-built man appeared to be looking in at this window. Loveday's foot was on the doorstep of the draper's private entrance, her hand on the door-knocker, when this individual, suddenly turning, convinced her of his identity with the journeyman workman who had so disturbed Mr Gunning's equanimity. It was true he wore a bowler instead of a journeyman's cap, and he no longer carried a basket of tools, but there was no possibility for anyone, with so good an eye for an outline as Loveday possessed, not to recognise the carriage of the head and shoulders as that of the man she had seen walking along the railway siding. He gave her no time to make minute observation of his appearance, but turned quickly away, and disappeared down a by-street.

Loveday's work seemed to bristle with difficulties now. Here was she, as it were, unearthed in her own ambush; for there could be but little doubt that during the whole time she had stood watching those Sisters, that man, from a safe vantage point, had been watching her.

She found Mrs Golightly a civil and obliging person. She showed Loveday to her room above the shop, brought her the letters which Inspector Gunning had been careful to have posted to her during the day. Then she supplied her with pen and ink and, in response to Loveday's request, with some strong coffee that she said, with a little attempt at a joke, would 'keep a dormouse awake all through the winter without winking'.

While the obliging landlady busied herself about the room, Loveday had a few questions to ask about the Sisterhood who lived down the court opposite. On this head, however, Mrs Golightly could tell her no more than she already knew, beyond the fact that they started every morning on their rounds at eleven o'clock punctually, and that before that hour they were never to be seen outside their door.

Loveday's watch that night was to be a fruitless one. Although she sat, with her lamp turned out and safely screened from observation, until close upon midnight, with eyes fixed upon numbers 7 and 8 Paved Court, not so much as a door opening or shutting at either house rewarded her vigil. The lights flitted from the lower to the upper floors in both houses, and then disappeared somewhere between nine and ten in the evening; and after that, not a sign of life did either tenement show.

And all through the long hours of that watch, backwards and forwards there seemed to flit before her mind's eye, as if in some sort it were fixed upon its retina, the sweet, sad face of Sister Anna. Why it was this face should so haunt her, she found it hard to say.

'It has a mournful past and a mournful future written upon it as a hopeless whole,' she said to herself. 'It is the face of an Andromeda! "Here am I," it seems to say, "tied to my stake, helpless and hopeless."'

The church clocks were sounding the midnight hour as Loveday made her way through the dark streets to her hotel outside the town. As she passed under the railway arch that ended in the open country road, the echo of not very distant footsteps caught her ear. When she stopped they stopped, when she went on they went on, and she knew that once more she was being followed and watched, although the darkness of the arch prevented her seeing even the shadow of the man who was thus dogging her steps.

The next morning broke keen and frosty. Loveday studied her map and her country-house index over a seven o'clock breakfast, and then set off for a brisk walk along the country road. No doubt in London the streets were walled in and roofed with yellow fog; here, however, bright sunshine played in and out of the bare tree-boughs and leafless hedges on to a thousand frost spangles, turning the prosaic macadamised road into a gangway fit for Queen Titania herself and her fairy train.

Loveday turned her back on the town and set herself to follow the road as it wound away over the hill in the direction of a village called Northfield. Early as she was, she was not to have that road to herself. A team of strong horses trudged by on their way to their work in the fuller's-earth pits. A young fellow on a bicycle flashed past at a tremendous pace, considering the upward slant of the road. He looked hard at her as he passed, then slackened pace, dismounted, and awaited her coming on the brow of the hill.

'Good morning, Miss Brooke,' he said, lifting his cap as she came alongside of him. 'May I have five minutes' talk with you?'

The young man who thus accosted her had not the appearance of a gentleman. He was a handsome, bright-faced young fellow of about two-and-twenty, and was dressed in ordinary cyclists' dress; his cap was pushed back from his brow over thick, curly, fair hair, and Loveday, as she looked at him, could not repress the thought how well he would look at the head of a troop of cavalry, giving the order to charge the enemy.

He led his machine to the side of the footpath.

'You have the advantage of me,' said Loveday; 'I haven't the remotest notion who you are.'

'No,' he said; 'although I know you, you cannot possibly know me. I am a north countryman, and I was present, about a month ago, at the trial of old Mr Craven, of Troyte's Hill — in fact, I acted as reporter for one of the local papers. I watched your face so closely as you gave your evidence that I should know it anywhere, among a thousand.'

'And your name is — ?'

'George White, of Grenfell. My father is part proprietor of one of the Newcastle papers. I am a bit of a literary man myself, and sometimes figure as a reporter, sometimes as leader-writer, to that paper.' Here he gave a glance towards his side pocket, from which protruded a small volume of Tennyson's poems.

The facts he had stated did not seem to invite comment, and Loveday ejaculated merely:

'Indeed!'

The young man went back to the subject that was evidently filling his thoughts. 'I have special reasons for being glad to have met you this morning, Miss Brooke,' he went on, making his footsteps keep pace with hers. 'I am in great trouble, and I believe you are the only person in the whole world who can help me out of that trouble.'

'I am rather doubtful as to my power of helping anyone out of trouble,' said Loveday; 'so far as my experience goes, our troubles are as much a part of ourselves as our skins are of our bodies.'

'Ah, but not such trouble as mine,' said White eagerly. He broke off for a moment, then, with a sudden rush of words, told her what that trouble was. For the past year he had been engaged to be married to a young girl, who, until quite recently had been fulfilling the duties of a nursery governess in a large house in the neighbourhood of Redhill.

'Will you kindly give me the name of that house?' interrupted Loveday.

'Certainly; Wootton Hall, the place is called, and Annie Lee is my sweetheart's name. I don't care who knows it!' He threw his head back as he said this, as if he would be delighted to announce the fact to the whole world. 'Annie's mother,' he went on, 'died when she was a baby, and we both thought her father was dead also, when suddenly, about a fortnight ago, it came to her knowledge that instead of being dead, he was serving his time at Portland for some offence committed years ago.'

'Do you know how this came to Annie's knowledge?'

'Not the least in the world; I only know that I suddenly got a letter from her announcing the fact, and at the same time, breaking off her engagement with me. I tore the letter into a thousand pieces, and wrote back saying I would not allow the engagement to be broken off, but would marry her tomorrow if she would have me. To this letter she did not reply; there came instead a few lines from Mrs Copeland, the lady at Wootton Hall, saying that Annie had thrown up her engagement and joined some Sisterhood, and that she, Mrs Copeland, had pledged her word to Annie to reveal to no one the name and whereabouts of that Sisterhood.'

'And I suppose you imagine I am able to do what Mrs Copeland is pledged not to do?'

'That's just it, Miss Brooke,' cried the young man enthusiastically. 'You do such wonderful things; everyone knows you do. It seems as if, when anything is wanted to be found out, you just walk into a place, look round you and, in a moment, everything becomes clear as noonday.'

'I can't quite lay claim to such wonderful powers as that. As it happens, however, in the present instance, no particular skill is needed to find out what you wish to know, for I fancy I have already come upon the traces of Miss Annie Lee.'

'Miss Brooke!'

'Of course, I cannot say for certain, but it is a matter you can easily settle for yourself – settle, too, in a way that will confer a great obligation on me.'

'I shall be only too delighted to be of any – the slightest service to you,' cried White, enthusiastically as before.

'Thank you. I will explain. I came down here specially to watch the movements of a certain Sisterhood who have somehow aroused the suspicions of the police. Well, I find that instead of being able to do this, I am myself so closely watched – possibly by confederates of these Sisters – that unless I can do my work by deputy I may as well go back to town at once.'

'Ah! I see – you want me to be that deputy.'

'Precisely. I want you to go to the room in Redhill that I have hired, take your place at the window – screened, of course, from observation – at which I ought to be seated – watch as closely as possible the movements of these Sisters and report them to me at the hotel, where I shall remain shut in from morning till night – it is the only way in which I can throw my persistent spies off the scent. Now, in doing this for me, you will be also doing yourself a good turn, for I have little doubt but that under the blue serge hood of one of the sisters you will discover the pretty face of Miss Annie Lee.'

As they had talked they had walked, and now stood on the top of the hill at the head of the one little street that constituted the whole of the village of Northfield.

On their left hand stood the village schools and the master's house; nearly facing these, on the opposite side of the road, beneath a clump of elms, stood the village pound. Beyond this pound, on either side of the way, were two rows of small cottages with tiny squares of garden in front, and in the midst of these small cottages a swinging sign beneath a lamp announced a 'Postal and Telegraph Office'.

'Now that we have come into the land of habitations again,' said Loveday, 'it will be best for us to part. It will not do for you and me to be seen together, or my spies will be transferring their attentions from me to you, and I shall have to find another deputy. You had better start on your bicycle for Redhill at once, and I will walk back at leisurely speed. Come to me at my hotel without fail at one o'clock and report proceedings. I do not say anything definite about remuneration, but I assure you, if you carry out my instructions to the letter, your services will be amply rewarded by me and by my employers.'

There were yet a few more details to arrange. White had been, he said, only a day and night in the neighbourhood, and special directions as to the locality had to be given to him. Loveday advised him not to attract attention by going to the draper's private door, but to enter the shop as if he were a customer, and then explain matters to Mrs Golightly, who, no doubt, would be in her place behind the counter; tell her he was the brother of the Miss Smith who had hired her room, and ask permission to go through the shop to that room, as he had been commissioned by his sister to read and answer any letters that might have arrived there for her.

'Show her the key of the side door – here it is,' said Loveday; 'it will be your credentials, and tell her you did not like to make use of it without acquainting her with the fact.'

The young man took the key, endeavoured to put it in his waistcoat pocket, found the space there occupied and so transferred it to the keeping of a side pocket in his tunic.

All this time Loveday stood watching him.

'You have a capital machine there,' she said, as the young man mounted his bicycle once more, 'and I hope you will turn it to account in following the movements of these Sisters about the neighbourhood. I feel confident you will have something definite to tell me when you bring me your first report at one o'clock.'

White once more broke into a profusion of thanks, and then, lifting his cap to the lady, started his machine at a fairly good pace.

Loveday watched him out of sight down the slope of the hill, then, instead of following him as she had said she would 'at a leisurely pace', she turned her steps in the opposite direction along the village street.

It was an altogether ideal country village. Neatly-dressed chubby-faced children, now on their way to the schools, dropped quaint little curtsies, or tugged at curly locks as Loveday passed; every cottage looked the picture of cleanliness and trimness, and although so late in the year, the gardens were full of late-flowering chrysanthemums and early-flowering Christmas roses.

At the end of the village, Loveday came suddenly into view of a large, handsome, red-brick mansion. It presented a wide frontage to the road, from which it lay back amid extensive pleasure grounds. On the right hand, and a little in the rear of the house, stood what seemed to be large and commodious stables, and immediately adjoining these stables was a low-built, red-brick shed, that had evidently been recently erected.

That low-build, red-brick shed excited Loveday's curiosity.

'Is this house called North Cape?' she asked of a man, who chanced at that moment to be passing with a pickaxe and shovel.

The man answered in the affirmative, and Loveday then asked another question: could he tell her what was that small shed so close to the house – it looked like a glorified cowhouse – now what could be its use?

36

The man's face lighted up as if it were a subject on which he liked to be questioned. He explained that that small shed was the engine-house where the electricity that lighted North Cape was made and stored. Then he dwelt with pride upon the fact, as if he held a personal interest in it, that North Cape was the only house, far or near, that was thus lighted.

'I suppose the wires are carried underground to the house,' said Loveday, looking in vain for signs of them anywhere.

The man was delighted to go into details on the matter. He had helped to lay those wires, he said: they were two in number, one for supply and one for return, and were laid three feet below ground, in boxes filled with pitch. These wires were switched on to jars in the engine-house, where the electricity was stored, and, after passing underground, entered the family mansion under its flooring at its western end.

Loveday listened attentively to these details, and then took a minute and leisurely survey of the house and its surroundings. This done, she retraced her steps through the village, pausing, however, at the 'Postal and Telegraph Office' to dispatch a telegram to Inspector Gunning.

It was one to send the Inspector to his cipher-book. It ran as follows:

'Rely solely on chemist and coal-merchant throughout the day. – LB.'

After this, she quickened her pace, and in something over three-quarters of an hour was back again at her hotel.

There she found more of life stirring than when she had quitted it in the early morning. There was to be a meeting of the 'Surrey Stags', about a couple of miles off, and a good many hunting men were hanging about the entrance to the house, discussing the chances of sport after last night's frost. Loveday made her way through the throng in leisurely fashion, and not a man but what had keen scrutiny from her sharp eyes. No, there was no cause for suspicion there: they were evidently one and all just what they seemed to be – loud-voiced, hard-riding men, bent on a day's sport; but – and here Loveday's eyes travelled beyond the hotel courtyard to the other side of the road – who was that man with a bill-hook hacking at the hedge there – a thin-featured, round-shouldered old fellow, with a bent-about hat? It might be as well not to take it too rashly for granted that her spies had withdrawn, and had left her free to do her work in her own fashion.

She went upstairs to her room. It was situated on the first floor in the front of the house, and consequently commanded a good view of the high road. She stood well back from the window, and at an angle whence she could see and not be seen, took a long, steady survey of the hedger. And the longer she looked the more convinced she was that the man's real work was something other than the bill-hook seemed to imply. He worked, so to speak, with his head over his shoulder, and when Loveday supplemented her eyesight with a strong field-glass, she could see more than one stealthy glance shot from beneath his bent-about hat in the direction of her window.

There could be little doubt about it: her movements were to be as closely watched today as they had been yesterday. Now it was of first importance that she should communicate with Inspector Gunning in the course of the afternoon: the question to solve was how it was to be done?

To all appearance Loveday answered the question in extraordinary fashion. She pulled up her blind, she drew back her curtain, and seated herself, in full view, at a small table in the window recess. Then she took a pocket inkstand from her pocket, a packet of correspondence cards from her letter-case, and with rapid pen, set to work on them.

About an hour and a half afterwards, White, coming in, according to his promise, to report proceedings, found her still seated at the window, not, however, with writing materials before her, but with needle and thread in her hand with which she was mending her gloves.

'I return to town by the first train tomorrow morning,' she said as he entered, 'and I find these wretched things want no end of stitches. Now for your report.'

White appeared to be in an elated frame of mind. 'I've seen her!' he cried, 'my Annie – they've got her, those confounded Sisters; but they shan't keep her – no, not if I have to pull the house down about their ears to get her out.'

'Well, now you know where she is, you can take your time about getting her out,' said Loveday. 'I hope, however, you haven't broken faith with me, and betrayed yourself by trying to speak with her, because, if so, I shall have to look out for another deputy.'

'Honour, Miss Brooke!' answered White indignantly. 'I stuck to my duty, though it cost me something to see her hanging over those kids and tucking them into the cart, and never say a word to her, never so much as wave my hand.'

'Did she go out with the donkey-cart today?'

'No, she only tucked the kids into the cart with a blanket, and then went back to the house. Two old Sisters, ugly as sin, went out with them. I watched them from the window, jolt, jolt, jolt, round the corner, out of sight, and then I whipped down the stairs, and on to my machine, and was after them in a trice and managed to keep them well in sight for over an hour and a half.'

'And their destination today was?'

'Wootton Hall.'

'Ah, just as I expected.'

'Just as you expected?' echoed White.

'I forgot. You do not know the nature of the suspicions that are attached to this Sisterhood, and the reasons I have for thinking that Wootton Hall, at this season of the year, might have an especial attraction for them.'

White continued staring at her. 'Miss Brooke,' he said presently, in an altered tone, 'whatever suspicions may attach to the Sisterhood, I'll stake my life on it, my Annie has had no share in any wickedness of any sort.'

'Oh, quite so; it is most likely that your Annie has, in some way, been inveigled into joining these Sisters – has been taken possession of by them, in fact, just as they have taken possession of the little cripples.'

'That's it!' he cried excitedly; 'that was the idea that occurred to me when you spoke to me on the hill about them, otherwise you may be sure –'

'Did they get relief of any sort at the Hall?' interrupted Loveday.

'Yes; one of the two ugly old women stopped outside the lodge gates with the donkey-cart, and the other beauty went up to the house alone. She stayed there, I should think, about a quarter of an hour, and when she came back, was followed by a servant, carrying a bundle and a basket.'

'Ah! I've no doubt they brought away with them something else beside old garments and broken victuals.'

White stood in front of her, fixing a hard, steady gaze upon her.

'Miss Brooke,' he said presently, in a voice that matched the look on his face, 'what do you suppose was the real object of these women in going to Wootton Hall this morning?'

'Mr White, if I wished to help a gang of thieves break into Wootton Hall tonight, don't you think I should be greatly interested in procuring from them the information that the master of the house was away from home; that two of the men servants, who slept in the house, had recently been dismissed and their places had not yet been filled; also that the dogs were never unchained at night, and that their kennels were at the side of the house at which the butler's pantry is not situated? These are particulars I have gathered in this house without stirring from my chair, and I am satisfied that they are likely to be true. At the same time, if I were a professed burglar, I should not be content with information that was likely to be true, but would be careful to procure such that was certain to be true, and so would set accomplices to work at the fountain head. Now do you understand?'

White folded his arms and looked down on her.

'What are you going to do?' he asked, in short, brusque tones.

Loveday looked him full in the face. 'Communicate with

the police immediately,' she answered; 'and I should feel greatly obliged if you will at once take a note from me to Inspector Gunning at Reigate.'

'And what becomes of Annie?'

'I don't think you need have any anxiety on that head. I've no doubt that when the circumstances of her admission to the Sisterhood are investigated, it will be proved that she has been as much deceived and imposed upon as the man, John Murray, who so foolishly let his house to these women. Remember, Annie has Mrs Copeland's good word to support her integrity.'

White stood silent for a while.

'What sort of a note do you wish me to take to the Inspector?' he presently asked.

'You shall read it as I write it, if you like,' answered Loveday. She took a correspondence card from her letter case, and, with an indelible pencil, wrote as follows:

'Wooton Hall is threatened tonight – concentrate attention there. LB.'

White read the words as she wrote them with a curious expression passing over his handsome features.

'Yes,' he said, curtly as before. 'I'll deliver that, I give you my word, but I'll bring back no answer to you. I'll do no more spying for you – it's a trade that doesn't suit me. There's a straight-forward way of doing straight-forward work, and I'll take that way – no other – to get my Annie out of that den.'

He took the note, which she sealed and handed to him, and strode out of the room.

Loveday, from the window, watched him mount his bicycle. Was it her fancy, or did there pass a swift, furtive glance of recognition between him and the hedger on the other side of the way as he rode out of the courtyard?

Loveday seemed determined to make that hedger's work easy for him. The short winter's day was closing in now, and her room must consequently have been growing dim to outside observation.

She lighted the gas chandelier which hung from the ceiling and, still with blinds and curtains undrawn, took her old place at the window, spread writing materials before her and commenced a long and elaborate report to her chief at Lynch Court.

About half an hour afterwards, as she threw a casual glance across the road, she saw that the hedger had disappeared, but that two ill-looking tramps sat munching bread and cheese under the hedge to which his bill-hook had done so little service. Evidently the intention was, one way or another, not to lose sight of her so long as she remained in Redhill.

Meantime, White had delivered Loveday's note to the Inspector at Reigate, and had disappeared on his bicycle once more.

Gunning read it without a change of expression. Then he crossed the room to the fireplace and held the card as close to the bars as he could without scorching it.

'I had a telegram from her this morning,' he explained to his confidential man, 'telling me to rely upon chemicals and coals throughout the day, and that, of course, meant that she would write to me in invisible ink. No doubt this message about Wootton Hall means nothing –'

He broke off abruptly, exclaiming: 'Eh! what's this!' as, having withdrawn the card from the fire, Loveday's real message stood out in bold, clear characters between the lines of the false one.

Thus it ran:

'North Cape will be attacked tonight – a desperate gang – be prepared for a struggle. Above all, guard the electrical engine-house. On no account attempt to communicate with me; I am so closely watched that any endeavour to do so may frustrate your chance of trapping the scoundrels. LB.'

That night when the moon went down behind Reigate Hill an exciting scene was enacted at 'North Cape'. The *Surrey Gazette*, in its issue the following day, gave the subjoined account of it under the heading, 'Desperate encounter with burglars'.

'Last night, "North Cape", the residence of Mr Jameson, was

the scene of an affray between the police and a desperate gang of burglars. "North Cape" is lighted throughout with electricity, and the burglars, four in number, divided in half – two being told off to enter and rob the house, and two to remain at the engine-shed, where the electricity is stored, so that, at a given signal, should need arise, the wires might be unswitched, the inmates of the house thrown into sudden darkness and confusion, and the escape of the marauders thereby facilitated. Mr Jameson, however, had received timely warning from the police of the intended attack, and he, with his two sons, all well armed, sat in darkness in the inner hall awaiting the coming of the thieves. The police were stationed, some in the stables, some in out-buildings nearer to the house, and others in more distant parts of the grounds. The burglars effected their entrance by means of a ladder placed to a window of the servants' staircase which leads straight down to the butler's pantry and to the safe where the silver is kept. The fellows, however, had no sooner got into the house than the police, issuing from their hiding-place outside, mounted the ladder after them and thus cut off their retreat. Mr Jameson and his two sons, at the same moment, attacked them in front, and thus overwhelmed by numbers, the scoundrels were easily secured. It was at the engine-house outside that the sharpest struggle took place. The thieves had forced open the door of this engine-shed with their jimmies immediately on their arrival, under the very eyes of the police, who lay in ambush in the stables, and when one of the men, captured in the house, contrived to sound an alarm on his whistle, these outside watchers made a rush for the electrical jars, in order to unswitch the wires. Upon this the police closed upon them, and a hand-to-hand struggle followed, and if it had not been for the timely assistance of Mr Jameson and his sons, who had fortunately conjectured that their presence here might be useful, it is more than likely that one of the burglars, a powerfully-built man, would have escaped.

'The names of the captured men are John Murray, Arthur and George Lee (father and son), and a man with so many aliases that it is difficult to know which is his real name. The whole thing had been most cunningly and carefully planned. The elder Lee, lately released from penal servitude for a similar offence, appears to have been prime mover in the affair. This man had, it seems, a son and a daughter, who, through the kindness of friends, had been fairly well placed in life: the son at an electrical engineers' in London, the daughter as nursery governess at Wootton Hall. Directly this man was released from Portland, he seems to have found out his children and done his best to ruin them both. He was constantly at Wootton Hall endeavouring to induce his daughter to act as an accomplice to a robbery of the house. This so worried the girl that she threw up her situation and joined a Sisterhood that had recently been established in the neighbourhood. Upon this, Lee's thoughts turned in another direction. He induced his son, who had saved a little money, to throw up his work in London, and join him in his disreputable career. The boy is a handsome young fellow, but appears to have in him the makings of a first-class criminal. In his work as an electrical engineer he had made the acquaintance of the man John Murray, who, it is said, has been rapidly going downhill of late. Murray was the owner of the house rented by the Sisterhood that Miss Lee had joined, and the idea evidently struck the brains of these three scoundrels that this Sisterhood, whose antecedents were a little mysterious, might be utilised to draw off the attention of the police from themselves and from the especial house in the neighbourhood that they had planned to attack. With this end in view, Murray made an application to the police to have the Sisters watched, and still further to give colour to the suspicions he had endeavoured to set afloat concerning them, he and his confederates made feeble attempts at burglary upon the houses at which the Sisters had called, begging for scraps. It is a matter for congratulation that the plot, from beginning to end, has been thus successfully unearthed, and it is felt on all sides that great credit is due to Inspector Gunning and his skilled coadjutors for the vigilance and promptitude they have displayed throughout the affair.'

Loveday read aloud this report, with her feet on the fender of the Lynch Court office.

'Accurate, as far as it goes,' she said, as she laid down the paper.

'But we want to know a little more,' said Mr Dyer. 'In the first place, I would like to know what it was that diverted your suspicions from the unfortunate Sisters?'

'The way in which they handled the children,' answered Loveday promptly. 'I have seen female criminals of all kinds handling children, and I have noticed that although they may occasionally – even this is rare – treat them with a certain rough sort of kindness, of tenderness they are utterly incapable. Now Sister Monica, I must admit, is not pleasant to look at; at the same time, there was something absolutely beautiful in the way in which she lifted the little cripple out of the cart, put his tiny thin hand round her neck, and carried him into the house. By the way, I would like to ask some rapid physiognomist how he would account for Sister Monica's repulsiveness of feature as contrasted with young Lee's undoubted good looks – heredity, in this case, throws no light on the matter.'

'Another question,' said Mr Dyer, not paying much heed to Loveday's digression: 'how was it you transferred your suspicions to John Murray?'

'I did not do so immediately, although at the very first it had struck me as odd that he should be so anxious to do the work of the police for them. The chief thing I noticed concerning Murray, on the first and only occasion on which I saw him, was that he had had an accident with his bicycle, for in the right-hand corner of his lamp-glass there was a tiny star, and the lamp itself had a dent on the same side, had also lost its hook, and was fastened to the machine by a bit of electric fuse. The next morning as I was walking up the hill towards Northfield, I was accosted by a young man mounted on that self-same bicycle – not a doubt of it – star in glass, dent, fuse, all three.'

'Ah, that sounded an important keynote, and led you to connect Murray and the younger Lee immediately.'

'It did, and, of course, also at once gave the lie to his statement that he was a stranger in the place, and confirmed my opinion that there was nothing of the north-countryman in his accent.

Other details in his manner and appearance gave rise to other suspicions. For instance, he called himself a press reporter by profession, and his hands were coarse and grimy as only a mechanic's could be. He said he was a bit of a literary man, but the Tennyson that showed so obtrusively from his pocket was new, and in parts uncut, and totally unlike the well-thumbed volume of the literary student. Finally, when he tried and failed to put my latch-key into his waistcoat pocket, I saw the reason lay in the fact that the pocket was already occupied by a soft coil of electric fuse, the end of which protruded. Now, an electric fuse is what an electrical engineer might almost unconsciously carry about with him, it is so essential a part of his working tools, but it is a thing that a literary man or a press reporter could have no possible use for.'

'Exactly, exactly. And it was no doubt, that bit of electric fuse that turned your thoughts to the one house in the neighbourhood lighted by electricity, and suggested to your mind the possibility of electrical engineers turning their talents to account in that direction. Now, will you tell me, what, at that stage of your day's work, induced you to wire to Gunning that you would bring your invisible-ink bottle into use?'

'That was simply a matter or precaution; it did not compel me to the use of invisible ink, if I saw other safe methods of communication. I felt myself being hemmed in on all sides with spies, and I could not tell what emergency might arise. I don't think I have ever had a more difficult game to play. As I walked and talked with the young fellow up the hill, it became clear to me that if I wished to do my work I must lull the suspicions of the gang, and seem to walk into their trap. I saw by the persistent way in which Wootton Hall was forced on my notice that it was wished to fix my suspicions there. I accordingly, to all appearance, did so, and allowed the fellows to think they were making a fool of me.'

'Ha! ha! Capital that – the biter bit, with a vengeance! Splendid idea to make that young rascal himself deliver the letter that was to land him and his pals in jail. And he all the time laughing in his sleeve and thinking what a fool he was making of you! Ha, ha, ha!' And Mr Dyer made the office ring again with his merriment.

'The only person one is at all sorry for in this affair is poor little Sister Anna,' said Loveday pityingly; 'and yet, perhaps, all things considered, after her sorry experience of life, she may not be so badly placed in a Sisterhood where practical Christianity – not religious hysterics – is the one and only rule of the order.'

MISS FLORENCE CUSACK

Created by LT Meade (1844-1914)
and Robert Eustace (1854-1943)

The glamorous Florence Cusack – 'this handsome girl with her slender figure, her eyes of the darkest blue, her raven black hair and clear complexion' – appeared in a series of six short stories first published in The Harmsworth Magazine *between 1899 and 1901. She is obviously wealthy, lives alone in a large house in Kensington and is at home in the upper reaches of society. Yet she is also 'a power in the police courts' and 'highly respected by every detective in Scotland Yard'. Much of the legwork in the stories is done by the narrator, Dr Lonsdale, who is clearly more than a little in love with Miss Cusack, but it is she who provides the final insights and solves the crimes. She was the creation of a writing partnership which also produced several other series characters for the big-name periodicals of the day, including the palmist Diana Marburg (see page 192) LT Meade was the pseudonym of Elizabeth Thomasina Meade Smith, a very busy author in the late Victorian and Edwardian eras who was best known at the time as the author of stories for girls, often with a school setting, but is now mostly remembered for her crime stories. She collaborated regularly with Robert Eustace (real name Eustace Robert Barton), a doctor and part-time writer. Meade and Eustace may have intended to write more Florence Cusack stories than they did. There are certainly indications that the series remains unfinished. However, the stories that we have are ingenious and entertaining and their heroine often shows herself to be, as she says herself, 'the most acute and, I believe, successful lady detective in the whole of London'.*

MR BOVEY'S UNEXPECTED WILL

Amongst all my patients there were none who excited my sense of curiosity like Miss Florence Cusack. I never thought of her without a sense of baffled inquiry taking possession of me, and I never visited her without the hope that some day I should get to the bottom of the mystery which surrounded her.

Miss Cusack was a young and handsome woman. She possessed to all appearance superabundant health, her energies were extraordinary, and her life completely out of the common. She lived alone in a large house in Kensington Court Gardens, kept a good staff of servants, and went much into society. Her beauty, her sprightliness, her wealth, and, above all, her extraordinary life, caused her to be much talked about. As one glanced at this handsome girl with her slender figure, her eyes of the darkest blue, her raven black hair and clear complexion it was almost impossible to believe that she was a power in the police courts and highly respected by every detective in Scotland Yard.

I shall never forget my first visit to Miss Cusack. I had been asked by a brother doctor to see her in his absence. Strong as she was, she was subject to periodical and very acute nervous attacks. When I entered her house she came up to me eagerly.

'Pray do not ask me too many questions or look too curious, Dr Lonsdale,' she said; 'I know well that my whole condition is abnormal; but, believe me, I am forced to do what I do.'

'What is that?' I inquired.

'You see before you,' she continued, with emphasis, 'the most acute and, I believe, successful lady detective in the whole of London.'

'Why do you lead such an extraordinary life?' I asked.

'To me the life is fraught with the very deepest interest,' she answered. 'In any case,' and now the colour faded from her cheeks and her eyes grew full of emotion, 'I have no choice; I am under a promise, which I must fulfil. There are times, however, when I need help – such help as you, for instance, can give me.

I have never seen you before, but I like your face. If the time should ever come, will you give me your assistance?'

I asked her a few more questions, and finally agreed to do what she wished.

From that hour Miss Cusack and I became the staunchest friends. She constantly invited me to her house, introduced me to her friends, and gave me her confidence to a marvellous extent.

On my first visit I noticed in her study two enormous brazen bulldogs. They were splendidly cast, and made a striking feature in the arrangements of the room; but I did not pay them any special attention until she happened to mention that there was a story, and a strange one, in connection with them.

'But for these dogs,' she said, 'and the mystery attached to them, I should not be the woman I am, nor would my life be set apart for the performance of duties at once herculean and ghastly.'

When she said these words her face once more turned pale, and her eyes flashed with an ominous fire.

On a certain afternoon in November 1894, I received a telegram from Miss Cusack, asking me to put aside all other work and go to her at once. Handing my patients over to the care of my partner, I started for her house. I found her in her study and alone. She came up to me holding a newspaper in her hand.

'Do you see this?' she asked. As she spoke she pointed to the agony column. The following words met my eyes:

Send more sand and charcoal dust. Core and mould ready for casting. – JOSHUA LINKLATER.

I read these curious words twice, then glanced at the eager face of the young girl.

'I have been waiting for this,' she said, in a tone of triumph.

'But what can it mean?' I said. 'Core and mould ready for casting?'

She folded up the paper, and laid it deliberately on the table.

'I thought that Joshua Linklater would say something of

the kind,' she continued. 'I have been watching for a similar advertisement in all the dailies for the last three weeks. This may be of the utmost importance.'

'Will you explain?' I said.

'I may never have to explain, or, on the other hand, I may,' she answered. 'I have not really sent for you to point out this advertisement, but in connection with another matter. Now, pray, come into the next room with me.'

She led me into a prettily and luxuriously furnished boudoir on the same floor. Standing by the hearth was a slender fair-haired girl, looking very little more than a child.

'May I introduce you to my cousin, Letitia Ransom?' said Miss Cusack, eagerly. 'Pray sit down, Letty,' she continued, addressing the girl with a certain asperity, 'Dr Lonsdale is the man of all others we want. Now, doctor, will you give me your very best attention, for I have an extraordinary story to relate.'

At Miss Cusack's words Miss Ransom immediately seated herself. Miss Cusack favoured her with a quick glance, and then once more turned to me.

'You are much interested in queer mental phases, are you not?' she said.

'I certainly am,' I replied.

'Well, I should like to ask your opinion with regard to such a will as this.'

Once again she unfolded a newspaper, and, pointing to a paragraph, handed it to me. I read as follows:

EXTRAORDINARY TERMS OF A MISER'S WILL.

Mr Henry Bovey, who died last week at a small house at Kew, has left one of the most extraordinary wills on record. During his life his eccentricities and miserly habits were well known, but this eclipses them all, by the surprising method in which he has disposed of his property.

Mr Bovey was unmarried, and, as far as can be proved, has no near relations in the world. The small balance at his banker's is to be used for defraying fees, duties, and sundry charges, also any existing debts, but the main bulk of his securities were recently realised, and the money in sovereigns is locked in a safe in his house.

A clause in the will states that there are three claimants to this property, and that the one whose net bodily weight is nearest to the weight of these sovereigns is to become the legatee. The safe containing the property is not to be opened till the three claimants are present; the competition is then to take place, and the winner is at once to remove his fortune.

Considerable excitement has been manifested over the affair, the amount of the fortune being unknown. The date of the competition is also kept a close secret for obvious reasons.

'Well,' I said, laying the paper down, 'whoever this Mr Bovey was, there is little doubt that he must have been out of his mind. I never heard of a more crazy idea.'

'Nevertheless it is to be carried out,' replied Miss Cusack. 'Now listen, please, Dr Lonsdale. This paper is a fortnight old. It is now three weeks since the death of Mr Bovey, his will has been proved, and the time has come for the carrying out of the competition. I happen to know two of the claimants well, and intend to be present at the ceremony.'

I did not make any answer, and after a pause she continued:

'One of the gentlemen who is to be weighed against his own fortune is Edgar Wimburne. He is engaged to my cousin Letitia. If he turns out to be the successful claimant there is nothing to prevent their marrying at once; if otherwise...' – here she turned and looked full at Miss Ransom, who stood up, the colour coming and going in her cheeks – 'if otherwise, Mr Campbell Graham has to be dealt with.'

'Who is he?' I asked.

'Another claimant, a much older man than Edgar. Nay, I must tell you everything. He is a claimant in a double sense, being also a lover, and a very ardent one, of Letitia's.

'Lettie must be saved,' she said, looking at me, 'and I believe I know how to do it.'

'You spoke of three claimants,' I interrupted; 'who is the third?'

'Oh, he scarcely counts, unless indeed he carries off the prize. He is William Tyndall, Mr Bovey's servant and retainer.'

'And when, may I ask, is this momentous competition to take place?' I continued.

'Tomorrow morning at half-past nine, at Mr Bovey's house. Will you come with us tomorrow, Dr Lonsdale, and be present at the weighing?'

'I certainly will,' I answered, 'it will be a novel experience.'

'Very well; can you be at this house a little before half-past eight, and we will drive straight to Kew?'

I promised to do so, and soon after took my leave. The next day I was at Miss Cusack's house in good time. I found waiting for me Miss Cusack herself, Miss Ransom, and Edgar Wimburne.

A moment or two later we all found ourselves seated in a large landau, and in less than an hour had reached our destination. We drew up at a small dilapidated-looking house, standing in a row of prim suburban villas, and found that Mr Graham, the lawyer, and the executors had already arrived.

The room into which we had been ushered was fitted up as a sort of study. The furniture was very poor and scanty, the carpet was old, and the only ornaments on the walls were a few tattered prints yellow with age.

As soon as ever we came in, Mr Southby, the lawyer, came forward and spoke.

'We are met here today,' he said, 'as you are all of course, aware, to carry out the clause of Mr Bovey's last will and testament. What reasons prompted him to make these extraordinary conditions we do not know; we only know that we are bound to carry them out. In a safe in his bedroom there is, according to his own statement, a large sum of money in gold, which is to be the property of the one of these three gentlemen whose weight shall nearest approach to the weight of the gold. Messrs Hutchinson and Co have been kind enough to supply one of their latest weighing machines, which has been carefully checked, and now if you three gentlemen will kindly come with me into the next room we will begin the business at once. Perhaps you, Dr Lonsdale, as a medical man, will be kind enough to accompany us.'

Leaving Miss Cusack and Miss Ransom we then went into the old man's bedroom, where the three claimants undressed and were carefully weighed. I append their respective weights, which I noted down:

Graham 13 stone 9 lbs 6 oz.
Tyndall 11 stone 6 lbs 3 oz.
Wimburne 12 stone 11 lbs.

Having resumed their attire, Miss Cusack and Miss Ransom were summoned, and the lawyer, drawing out a bunch of keys, went across to a large iron safe which had been built into the wall.

We all pressed round him, everyone anxious to get the first glimpse of the old man's hoard. The lawyer turned the key, shot back the lock, and flung open the heavy doors. We found that the safe was literally packed with small canvas bags – indeed, so full was it that as the doors swung open two of the bags fell to the floor with a heavy crunching noise. Mr Southby lifted them up, and then cutting the strings of one, opened it. It was full of bright sovereigns.

An exclamation burst from us all. If all those bags contained gold there was a fine fortune awaiting the successful candidate! The business was now begun in earnest. The lawyer rapidly extracted bag after bag, untied the string, and shot the contents with a crash into the great copper scale pan, while the attendant kept adding weights to the other side to balance it, calling out the amounts as he did so. No one spoke, but our eyes were fixed as if by some strange fascination on the pile of yellow metal that rose higher and higher each moment.

As the weight reached one hundred and fifty pounds, I heard the old servant behind me utter a smothered oath. I turned and glanced at him; he was staring at the gold with a fierce expression of disappointment and avarice. He at any rate was out of the reckoning, as at eleven stone six, or one hundred and sixty pounds, he could be nowhere near the weight of the sovereigns, there being still eight more bags to untie.

The competition, therefore, now lay between Wimburne and Graham. The latter's face bore strong marks of the agitation which consumed him; the veins stood out like cords on his forehead, and his lips trembled. It would evidently be a near thing, and the suspense was almost intolerable. The lawyer continued to deliberately add to the pile. As the last bag was shot into the scale, the attendant put four ten-pound weights into the other side. It was too much. The gold rose at once. He took one off, and then the two great pans swayed slowly up and down, finally coming to a dead stop.

'Exactly one hundred and eighty pounds, gentlemen,' he cried, and a shout went up from us all. Wimburne at twelve stone eleven, or one hundred and seventy-nine pounds, had won.

I turned and shook him by the hand.

'I congratulate you most heartily,' I cried. 'Now let us calculate the amount of your fortune.'

I took a piece of paper from my pocket and made a rough calculation. Taking 56 to the pound avoirdupois, there were at least ten thousand and eighty sovereigns in the scale before us.

'I can hardly believe it,' cried Miss Ransom.

I saw her gazing down at the gold, then she looked up into her lover's face.

'Is it true?' she said, panting as she spoke.

'Yes, it is true,' he answered. Then he dropped his voice. 'It removes all difficulties,' I heard him whisper to her.

Her eyes filled with tears, and she turned aside to conceal her emotion.

'There is no doubt whatever as to your ownership of this money, Mr Wimburne,' said the lawyer, 'and now the next thing is to ensure its safe transport to the bank.'

As soon as the amount of the gold had been made known, Graham, without bidding goodbye to anyone, abruptly left the room, and I assisted the rest of the men in shovelling the sovereigns into a stout canvas bag, which we then lifted and placed in a four-wheeled cab which had arrived for the purpose of conveying the gold to the city.

'Surely someone is going to accompany Mr Wimburne?' said Miss Cusack at this juncture. 'My dear Edgar,' she continued, 'you are not going to be so mad as to go alone?'

To my surprise, Wimburne coloured, and then gave a laugh of annoyance.

'What could possibly happen to me?' he said. 'Nobody knows that I am carrying practically my own weight in gold into the city.'

'If Mr Wimburne wishes I will go with him,' said Tyndall, now coming forward. The old man had to all appearance got over his disappointment, and spoke eagerly.

'The thing is fair and square,' he added. 'I am sorry I did not win, but I'd rather you had it, sir, than Mr Graham. Yes, that I would, and I congratulate you, sir.'

'Thank you, Tyndall,' replied Wimburne, 'and if you like to come with me I shall be very glad of your company.'

The bag of sovereigns being placed in the cab, Wimburne bade us all a hasty goodbye, told Miss Ransom that he would call to see her at Miss Cusack's house that evening, and, accompanied by Tyndall, started off. As we watched the cab turn the corner I heard Miss Ransom utter a sigh.

'I do hope it will be all right,' she said, looking at me. 'Don't you think it is a risky thing to drive with so much gold through London?'

I laughed in order to reassure her.

'Oh, no, it is perfectly safe,' I answered, 'safer perhaps than if the gold were conveyed in a more pretentious vehicle. There is nothing to announce the fact that it is bearing ten thousand and eighty sovereigns to the bank.'

A moment or two later I left the two ladies and returned to my interrupted duties. The affair of the weighing, the strange clause in the will, Miss Ransom's eager pathetic face, Wimburne's manifest anxiety, had all impressed me considerably, and I could scarcely get the affair off my mind. I hoped that the young couple would now be married quickly, and I could not help being heartily glad that Graham had lost, for I had by no means taken to his appearance.

My work occupied me during the greater part of the afternoon, and I did not get back again to my own house until about six o'clock. When I did so, I was told to my utter amazement that Miss Cusack had arrived and was waiting to see me with great impatience. I went at once into my consulting room, where I found her pacing restlessly up and down.

'What is the matter?' I asked.

'Matter!' she cried; 'have you not heard? Why, it has been cried in the streets already – the money is gone, was stolen on the way to London. There was a regular highway robbery in the Richmond Road, in broad daylight too. The facts are simply these: Two men in a dogcart met the cab, shot the driver, and after a desperate struggle, in which Edgar Wimburne was badly hurt, seized the gold and drove off. The thing was planned, of course – planned to a moment.'

'But what about Tyndall?' I asked.

'He was probably in the plot. All we know is that he has escaped and has not been heard of since.'

'But what a daring thing!' I cried. 'They will be caught, of course; they cannot have gone far with the money.'

'You do not understand their tricks, Dr Lonsdale; but I do,' was her quick answer, 'and I venture to guarantee that if we do not get that money back before the morning, Edgar Wimburne has seen the last of his fortune. Now, I mean to follow up this business, all night if necessary.'

I did not reply. Her dark, bright eyes were blazing with excitement, and she began to pace up and down.

'You must come with me,' she continued, 'you promised to help me if the necessity should arise.'

'And I will keep my word,' I answered.

'That is an immense relief.' She gave a deep sigh as she spoke.

'What about Miss Ransom?' I asked.

'Oh, I have left Letty at home. She is too excited to be of the slightest use.'

'One other question,' I interrupted, 'and then I am completely at your service. You mentioned that Wimburne was hurt.'

'Yes, but I believe not seriously. He has been taken to the hospital. He has already given evidence, but it amounts to very little. The robbery took place in a lonely part of the road, and just for the moment there was no one in sight.'

'Well,' I said, as she paused, 'you have some scheme in your head, have you not?'

'I have,' she answered. 'The fact is this: from the very first I feared some such catastrophe as has really taken place. I have known Mr Graham for a long time, and – distrusted him. He has passed for a man of position and means, but I believe him to be a mere adventurer. There is little doubt that all his future depended on his getting this fortune. I saw his face when the scales declared in Edgar Wimburne's favour – but there! I must ask you to accompany me to Hammersmith immediately. On the way I will tell you more.'

'We will go in my carriage,' I said, 'it happens to be at the door.'

We started directly. As we had left the more noisy streets Miss Cusack continued –

'You remember the advertisement I showed you yesterday morning?'

I nodded.

'You naturally could make no sense of it, but to me it was fraught with much meaning. This is by no means the first advertisement which has appeared under the name of Joshua Linklater. I have observed similar advertisements, and all, strange to say, in connection with founder's work, appearing at intervals in the big dailies for the last four or five months, but my attention was never specially directed to them until a circumstance occurred of which I am about to tell you.'

'What is that?' I asked.

'Three weeks ago a certain investigation took me to

Hammersmith in order to trace a stolen necklace. It was necessary that I should go to a small pawnbroker's shop – the man's name was Higgins. In my queer work, Dr Lonsdale, I employ many disguises. That night, dressed quietly as a domestic servant on her evening out, I entered the pawnbroker's. I wore a thick veil and a plainly trimmed hat. I entered one of the little boxes where one stands to pawn goods, and waited for the man to appear.

'For the moment he was engaged, and looking through a small window in the door I saw to my astonishment that the pawnbroker was in earnest conversation with no less a person than Mr Campbell Graham. This was the last place I should have expected to see Mr Graham in, and I immediately used both my eyes and ears. I heard the pawnbroker address him as Linklater.

'Immediately the memory of the advertisements under that name flashed through my brain. From the attitude of the two men there was little doubt that they were discussing a matter of the utmost importance, and as Mr Graham, *alias* Linklater, was leaving the shop, I distinctly overheard the following words: "In all probability Bovey will die tonight. I may or may not be successful, but in order to insure against loss we must be prepared. It is not safe for me to come here often – look out for the advertisement – it will be in the agony column."

'I naturally thought such words very strange, and when I heard of Mr Bovey's death and read an account of the queer will, it seemed to me that I began to see daylight. It was also my business to look out for the advertisement, and when I saw it yesterday morning you may well imagine that my keenest suspicions were aroused. I immediately suspected foul play, but could do nothing except watch and await events. Directly I heard the details of the robbery I wired to the inspector at Hammersmith to have Higgins's house watched. You remember that Mr Wimburne left Kew in the cab at ten o'clock; the robbery must therefore have taken place some time about ten-twenty. The news reached me shortly after eleven, and my wire was sent off about eleven-fifteen. I mention these hours, as much may turn upon them. Just before I came to you I received a wire from the police station containing startling news. This was sent off about five-thirty. Here, you had better read it.'

As she spoke she took a telegram from her pocket and handed it to me. I glanced over the words it contained.

'Just heard that cart was seen at Higgins's this morning. Man and assistant arrested on suspicion. House searched. No gold there. Please come down at once.'

'So they have bolted with it?' I said.

'That we shall see,' was her reply.

Shortly afterwards we arrived at the police station. The inspector was waiting for us, and took us at once into a private room.

'I am glad you were able to come, Miss Cusack,' he said, bowing with great respect to the handsome girl.

'Pray tell me what you have done,' she answered, 'there is not a moment to spare.'

'When I received your wire,' he said, 'I immediately placed a man on duty to watch Higgins's shop, but evidently before I did this the cart must have arrived and gone – the news with regard to the cart being seen outside Higgins's shop did not reach me till four-thirty. On receiving it I immediately arrested both Higgins and his assistant, and we searched the house from attic to cellar, but have found no gold whatever. There is little doubt that the pawnbroker received the gold, and has already removed it to another quarter.'

'Did you find a furnace in the basement?' suddenly asked Miss Cusack.

'We did,' he replied, in some astonishment; 'but why do you ask?'

To my surprise Miss Cusack took out of her pocket the advertisement which she had shown me that morning and handed it to the inspector. The man read the queer words aloud in a slow and wondering voice:

Send more sand and charcoal dust. Core and mould ready for casting. – JOSHUA LINKLATER.

'I can make nothing of it, miss,' he said, glancing at Miss Cusack. 'These words seem to me to have something to do with founder's work.'

'I believe they have,' was her eager reply. 'It is also highly probable that they have something to do with the furnace in the basement of Higgins's shop.'

'I do not know what you are talking about, miss, but you have something at the back of your head which does not appear.'

'I have,' she answered, 'and in order to confirm certain suspicions I wish to search the house.'

'But the place has just been searched by us,' was the man's almost testy answer. 'It is impossible that a mass of gold should be there and be overlooked; every square inch of space has been accounted for.'

'Who is in the house now?'

'No one; the place is locked up, and one of our men is on duty.'

'What size is the furnace?'

'Unusually large,' was the inspector's answer.

Miss Cusack gave a smile which almost immediately vanished.

'We are wasting time,' she said; 'let us go there immediately.'

'I must do so, of course, if nothing else will satisfy you, miss; but I assure you –'

'Oh, don't let us waste any more time in arguing,' said Miss Cusack, her impatience now getting the better of her. 'I have a reason for what I do, and must visit the pawnbroker's immediately.'

The man hesitated no longer, but took a bunch of keys down from the wall. A blaze of light from a public house guided us to the pawnbroker's, which bore the well-known sign, the three golden balls. These were just visible through the fog above us. The inspector nodded to the man on duty, and unlocking the door we entered a narrow passage into which the swing doors of several smaller compartments opened. The inspector struck a match, and, lighting the lantern, looked at Miss Cusack, as much as to say, 'What do you propose to do now?'

'Take me to the room where the furnace is,' said the lady.

'Come this way,' he replied.

We turned at once in the direction of the stairs which led to the basement, and entered a room on the right. At the further end was an open range which had evidently been enlarged in order to allow the consumption of a great quantity of fuel, and upon it now stood an iron vessel, shaped as a chemist's crucible. Considerable heat still radiated from it. Miss Cusack peered inside, then she slowly commenced raking out the ashes with an iron rod, examining them closely and turning them over and over. Two or three white fragments she examined with peculiar care.

'One thing at least is abundantly clear,' she said at last; 'gold has been melted here, and within a very short time; whether it was the sovereigns or not we have yet to discover.'

'But surely, Miss Cusack,' said the inspector, 'no one would be rash enough to destroy sovereigns.'

'I am thinking of Joshua Linklater's advertisement,' she said.

'"Send more sand and charcoal dust." This,' she continued, once more examining the white fragments, 'is undoubtedly sand.'

She said nothing further, but went back to the ground floor and now commenced a systematic search on her own account.

At last, we reached the top floor, where the pawnbroker and his assistant had evidently slept. Here Miss Cusack walked at once to the window and flung it open. She gazed out for a minute, and then turned to face us. Her eyes looked brighter than ever, and a certain smile played about her face.

'Well, miss,' said the police inspector, 'we have now searched the whole house, and I hope you are satisfied.'

'I am,' she replied.

'The gold is not here, miss.'

'We will see,' she said. As she spoke she turned once more and bent slightly out, as if to look down through the murky air at the street below.

The inspector gave an impatient exclamation.

'If you have quite finished, miss, we must return to the station,' he said. 'I am expecting some men from Scotland Yard to go into this affair.'

'I do not think they will have much to do,' she answered, 'except, indeed, to arrest the criminal.' As she spoke she leant a little further out of the window, and then withdrawing her head said quietly, 'Yes, we may as well go back now; I have quite finished. Things are exactly as I expected to find them; we can take the gold away with us.'

Both the inspector and I stared at her in utter amazement.

'What do you mean, Miss Cusack?' I cried.

'What I say,' she answered, and now she gave a light laugh; 'the gold is here, close to us; we have only to take it away. Come,' she added, 'look out, both of you. Why, you are both gazing at it.'

I glanced round in utter astonishment. My expression of face was reproduced in that of the inspector's.

'Look,' she said, 'what do you call that?' As she spoke she pointed to the sign that hung outside – the sign of the three balls.

'Lean out and feel that lower ball,' she said to the inspector.

He stretched out his arm, and as his fingers touched it he started back.

'Why, it is hot,' he said; 'what in the world does it mean?'

'It means the lost gold,' replied Miss Cusack; 'it has been cast as that ball. I said that the advertisement would give me the necessary clue, and it has done so. Yes, the lost fortune is hanging outside the house. The gold was melted in the crucible downstairs, and cast as this ball between twelve o'clock and four-thirty today. Remember it was after four-thirty that you arrested the pawnbroker and his assistant.'

To verify her extraordinary words was the work of a few moments. Owing to its great weight, the inspector and I had some difficulty in detaching the ball from its hook. At the same time we noticed that a very strong stay, in the shape of an iron-wire rope, had been attached to the iron frame from which the three balls hung.

'You will find, I am sure,' said Miss Cusack, 'that this ball is not of solid gold; if it were, it would not be the size of the other two balls. It has probably been cast round a centre of plaster of Paris to give it the same size as the others. This explains the advertisement with regard to the charcoal and sand. A ball of that size in pure gold would weigh nearly three hundred pounds, or twenty stone.'

'Well,' said the inspector, 'of all the curious devices that I have ever seen or heard of, this beats the lot. But what did they do with the real ball? They must have put it somewhere.'

'They burnt it in the furnace, of course,' she answered; 'these balls, as you know, are only wood covered with gold paint. Yes, it was a clever idea, worthy of the brain of Mr Graham; and it might have hung there for weeks and been seen by thousands passing daily, till Mr Higgins was released from imprisonment, as nothing whatever could be proved against him.'

Owing to Miss Cusack's testimony, Graham was arrested that night, and, finding that circumstances were dead against him, he confessed the whole. For long years he was one of a gang of coiners, but managed to pass as a gentleman of position. He knew old Bovey well, and had heard him speak of the curious will he had made. Knowing of this, he determined, at any risk to secure the fortune, intending when he had obtained it, to immediately leave the country. He had discovered the exact amount of the money which he would leave behind him, and had gone carefully into the weight which such a number of sovereigns would make. He knew at once that Tyndall would be out of the reckoning, and that the competition would really be between himself and Wimburne. To provide against the contingency of Wimburne's being the lucky man, he had planned the robbery; the gold was to be melted, and made into a real golden ball, which was to hang over the pawnshop until suspicion had died away.

MOLLIE DELAMERE

Created by Beatrice Heron-Maxwell
(1859-1927)

The daughter of Edward Eastwick, a diplomat and scholar of Oriental languages who was later a Cornish MP, Beatrice Heron-Maxwell (as she became after her second marriage) took up writing after the death of her first husband left her a widow with two young children. Over a thirty-year period she produced a wide range of fiction. She was a regular contributor to the leading magazines of the day, including The Strand *(home of Sherlock Holmes),* The Idler *and* The Pall Mall Magazine. What May Happen, *published in 1901, was a collection of what were described as 'stories natural and supernatural'. One of Heron-Maxwell's uncanny stories, 'The Devil's Stone', still appears from time to time in anthologies of tales of witchcraft. She was also the author of romances, including* The Queen Regent *(1902), an addition to the sub-genre of Ruritanian adventure which had been inspired by the enormous success of Anthony Hope's 1894 novel* The Prisoner of Zenda. The Adventures of a Lady Pearl-Broker, *a collection of linked short stories, was first published in 1899. Its heroine and narrator, Mollie Delamere, is a widow in need of an income, just as her creator had once been. She meets with Mr Leighton, 'the prince of pearl merchants', a man in search of a female agent who is good-looking, intelligent, courageous and comfortable in high society. Meeting these requirements, Mollie takes the job and is soon launched on a variety of adventures including one in which she nearly finds herself kidnapped and despatched to a Maharajah's court in India and one, mentioned in the story below, in which she meets up with a mysterious Countess and a 'Society of Gentlemen Thieves'.*

THE ADVENTURES OF A LADY
PEARL-BROKER

I gave myself a holiday for a few days after my involuntary exploration of the Society of Gentlemen Thieves, and then I turned my attention steadily to work again, and accomplished a great deal of business to my own and Mr Leighton's satisfaction. It had taken me about three weeks to finish a commission entrusted to me by the head of a Bond Street firm for a necklace of pearls, three rows in graduated sizes, and I was much pleased when after matching those in the last row, over which I had had a somewhat unusual difficulty, I took them to Bond Street, and handed them to the senior partner.

'These will do nicely,' he said, 'our customer is very particular, and will criticise every pearl separately. But these are perfect.'

I was rising to go, when an assistant came in with a small ring-case, and asked for some directions as to its being sent off. The senior partner opened the case, and showed me the ring, asking me if I did not think it very nice.

'It is splendid,' I said. 'It makes me feel quite covetous.'

The five diamonds, as large as could possibly be worn in a ring, were beautifully set and of a most dazzling lustre.

'A wedding present?' I said interrogatively, as I handed it back.

'A betrothal ring,' he answered, 'sent for in a hurry. It is the lady's birthday tonight, and, as the engagement is to be announced at a dinner party, she wished to have her ring. It had to be made smaller for her.'

'I wonder if it can be Miss Somers-Brand,' I said, 'it is her birthday today, and they are giving a large dinner to which I am going. If so, I hope it is to Sir Charles Merivale.'

The senior partner smiled.

'Sir Charles is an old customer of ours, and his father and grandfather were before him,' he said. 'His bride will not need to envy anyone's jewels. We are doing up the family rubies now.'

I felt sure, though my question had received an indirect reply, that my surmise was correct. Sir Charles' devotion to Miss

Somers-Brand from the first moment of their meeting at her coming-out ball had been apparent to everyone. But though she was very pretty and charming she was undowered, and people had wondered whether such a very desirable *parti*, both as to rank, and riches, as Sir Charles Merivale would select her from the many eligible young ladies amongst whom he might have chosen.

I saw that I was right in my guess as soon as I arrived at the Brands' house that night. Amidst a group of men on the hearthrug, Mr Somers-Brand and Sir Charles Merivale stood conversing together with marked cordiality, the latter beaming with the assured and triumphant happiness of a newly-engaged man.

Nellie Brand, all pink chiffon and blushes, came forward to shake hands with me, and when I laughingly lifted her left hand and looked at the ring sparkling in all its pristine beauty on the third finger, she blushed still more, and nodded an affirmative to my unspoken question.

There were a great many people present – it was a party of twenty-four – and I was the last to arrive, so that I had not time to notice all the other guests, and almost immediately after my entrance we paired off and went downstairs.

I was taken in by the son of the house, and as he and I were friends of long standing, and had not met for some time, we were occupied at first in giving a mutual account of ourselves, and getting as it were 'up to date' with each other.

Now and then the voice of a man seated on the same side of the table as myself, and hidden from me by the intervening couples, broke in and arrested my attention. It was a familiar voice certainly, but besides that it gave me an odd feeling of anxiety.

Where had I heard it last? It was associated with some uncomfortable experience I felt sure; but when and how?

I glanced in the direction of it once or twice, but I could not catch the man's face.

At last it worried me so that I said to Tom Brand:

'Tell me who is sitting on our side of the table? There's a voice I recognise, and I cannot fit the person to it.'

He mentioned the names of the four couples, and I stopped him at the last.

'Of course,' I said, in a sort of surprise, 'Gerard Beverley! Why, dear me, he is a —'

I broke off suddenly, realising the betrayal of which I was on the verge.

Tom smiled at my apparently unnecessary excitement and confusion.

'He is a son of old Admiral Beverley,' he said, 'and he is a confounded young fool; throws all his money away on betting, and gets into no end of scrapes; but I don't know anything worse of him than that. Why do you look so horrified about him? You knew him when he was a lad down in Hampshire, didn't you?'

'Yes,' I answered, 'I knew them all quite well; I loved Mrs Beverley; she was such a sweet, gracious old lady, and so devoted to her boys. What a grief Gerard must be to her.'

Tom laughed again.

'Oh, he is only a scapegrace; he'll get over it some of these days, I expect. You seem very down on him, Mrs Delamere, which is not like you – you are generally so charitable. Has he been so unlucky as to offend you?'

'No,' I said, 'quite the contrary. But I happen to know something about him which I would greatly prefer not to know. I would not say even so much as that to you, but it just occurs to me that perhaps you could look after him a little. You know his people better even than I do. Could you manage to convey to them that he wants a very great deal of looking after, much more than they think; and that the kindest thing they could do to him, would be to pay all his debts – for I am sure he must have many – and send him out to some definite work abroad. Will you try to do this?'

'I certainly will if you are as much in earnest as you seem to be,' he replied; 'you shall tell me just what you want me to do presently when we can have a quiet talk together.'

At this moment there was a little stir, and a buzz of louder conversation.

We had reached the dessert stage, and an old friend of the family had insisted on proposing a toast – 'the engaged couple'.

We all looked and spoke our compliments to them, and Sir Charles Merivale said a word or two of thanks for himself and Nellie, and then someone asked to see her ring, and she took it off and handed it round for general inspection.

It passed Tom and me, and I handed it on to my next-door neighbour; then our attention was attracted by an exciting story of an Indian loot, told by an old general who had taken part in it, and whose recollections were aroused by the brilliance of Nellie's diamond ring.

The whole party listened to the story – a stirring one and well told – and it was not till the general had concluded, and the comments were subsiding that Nellie said with a laugh: 'Please may I have my ring back now? My finger is catching cold.'

There was a little murmur of reply, and then she said in a decisive voice:

'But I have not got it, indeed; it has never come back to me.'

Several people began looking about, moving the plates and wine glasses; one or two sitting near Nellie stopped and looked on the floor; finally, Mr Brand rang the bell for the butler, and Nellie, getting up, shook her dress, thinking it might have fallen into the folds.

But the ring was not forthcoming!

It came upon me with a sort of shock that I knew with absolute certainty where the ring was, and yet that it was impossible for me to reveal my knowledge, because such a revelation would have made me a traitor, though indirectly, towards someone who claimed my loyalty, and would – though in justice to myself, I must say this was a secondary consideration to me – have been very dangerous to me.

A complete search was made all over the room for the ring; each one saying in turn that it had been passed on to the next person at the table.

When, after an interval of ten minutes it was still invisible, a sort of hush fell over the whole party, and the extreme unpleasantness of the situation dawned on most of them.

I say most of them, because I knew that there were two people whose feelings were totally different to those of the others, and one of those two was myself.

'I don't know what to do,' said Mr Somers-Brand at last; 'it is a most extraordinary thing, and seems like magic. The ring seems to have disappeared from the face of the earth.'

He looked appealingly round at his guests; it was really a most awkward predicament. Mrs Brand seemed inclined to make a move to the drawing room.

I felt desperate; I seemed such a traitor either way.

A thought occurred to me; I spoke a few words rapidly to Tom. Fortunately I knew him well enough to feel assured that he would not misconstrue my agitation. He interposed at once between his mother and the door.

'Don't go, mother,' he said, 'stay and help us to solve this problem. Who else was in the room besides you?' he continued, turning to the butler.

'Only William, sir,' that decorous official replied, with the imperturbable demeanour which is so admirable in butlers.

'Ring for William,' said Tom.

As soon as William, the footman, had made a sheepish appearance, Tom proceeded to address the whole company.

'With my father's permission,' he said, 'I will make a suggestion, and I hope that you will all approve of it, and that you will appreciate the motives I have in making it. It is this. That the door should be locked and the key held by my father; that we should all resume our places at table; and that the lights should then be turned off. That after a minute or two they should be turned on again. I should like to say that I have a theory about the disappearance of the ring which I am anxious to prove. If this way is unsuccessful I shall suggest another. But I fully believe that when the lights are turned on the ring will be visible.

'I apologise to you all for asking you to do this, but I feel certain that you would all prefer that the ring should now be found, if possible. Do you agree to my suggestion?'

Apparently everyone did, and it was carried out in every detail.

When the electric lights flashed up again we were all dazzled for an instant, after our temporary eclipse, and looked vaguely at each other as though we expected to see the ring suspended in mid-air or lurking in some unusual place like a conjuring trick.

Then Nellie Brand gave a little glad cry, and, stooping forward, picked the ring out from the folds of yellow ribbon that meandered about amongst the flowers in the centre of the table.

'Ah!' said Tom, with an accent of relief, 'a practical joke as I thought, and very cleverly played! Now, mother, we will consent to part with you.'

He telegraphed to me a look of grateful acknowledgement as I passed out of the room; I saw him turn and go towards Gerard Beverley.

I had no need to be assured by the ghastly look on the boy's face that he was a thief, for from the moment that Tom told me to whom the voice, so oddly familiar to me, belonged, I had identified him with the Countess's impetuous champion in the Gentlemen Burglars' Club, on the memorable occasion when I was the unwilling witness of one of their meetings, and when the question of my escape with life and honour hung and trembled in the balance.

Scarcely any other subject was spoken of either in the drawing-room, or, as I heard from Tom afterwards, in the dining-room that evening.

Many were the surmises as to the perpetrator of the joke, or the theft, that had made such a sensation, but neither Tom nor I betrayed our knowledge.

When we managed to have a few quiet words together just before I left, I explained to him the suggestion I had made, and which he had adopted by saying that I had heard of it being done, and with the same successful result on a very similar occasion.

But I did not acknowledge to him, either then or later, that I knew Gerard Beverley to be a thief, for I felt that to do so might lead eventually to the discovery of the club, and that I should then have broken faith with my kind little 'Countess'.

Nevertheless, I cannot doubt that Tom guessed the real state of affairs for himself; he told me that he saw Gerard home that night, and took the opportunity of having a serious talk with him.

The wretched young fellow completely broke down, confessed he was in worse trouble than anyone imagined, and, only after immense persuasion, consented to make a clean breast of it to his father.

Poor old Admiral Beverley collected all his son's debts, settled them up, got him a berth as overseer in one of the new South African settlements, and told Tom, the last time they met, that Gerard was writing more hopefully and reasonably than he had ever done before, and that they hoped to make a decent fellow of him yet.

The ruffled complacency of the dinner guests of that evening was restored when they heard that both the butler and footman had given indignant warning to the Somers–Brands the very next day.

'You may be quite sure,' said Sir Charles Merivale to me subsequently, 'that the butler and footman were in league, and it was one of them who took it. They got frightened when Tom suggested his experiment, and were afraid of a search coming next; so they decided to put it back. It was a clever idea of Tom's – saved any disturbance, and restored to Nellie her ring without any more fuss!'

I smiled demurely. For the 'clever idea' was a happy inspiration that I have often congratulated myself upon since then.

DORCAS DENE

Created by George R Sims
(1847–1922)

A journalist, novelist, dramatist and bohemian man-about-town, George Robert Sims enjoyed a literary career that lasted nearly fifty years. Many of his plays and musical burlesques, often adapted from French sources, were successes on the London stage. His verse, collected in an 1881 volume entitled The Dragonet Ballads, *included one poem, 'Christmas Day in the Workhouse', a biting critique of the Victorian poor laws, which was familiar enough to inspire parodies and re-workings into the twenty-first century. Both his fiction and his non-fiction, particularly his 1917 autobiography, continue to offer interesting perspectives on nineteenth- and early twentieth-century London. Sims was fascinated by crime and criminals – he reported extensively on Jack the Ripper – and he wrote his own detective fiction. His most interesting character in the genre is Dorcas Dene who appeared in twenty short stories gathered together in two volumes published in 1897 and 1898. Like other women detectives of the period, Dorcas has been driven into the business of combating crime by the need to earn money. A former actress (which helps when, as she frequently does, she adopts a disguise), she marries a painter who goes blind and can no longer work. She is then invited by their next-door neighbour, who runs a detective agency, to join him in his enterprise. The man later dies and leaves his firm to Dorcas. In the course of her varied investigations, she becomes an experienced sleuth, much admired by Scotland Yard. Sims was a skilled writer and the Dorcas Dene stories, narrated by her 'Watson', Mr Saxon, are all neatly plotted and well told.*

THE HAVERSTOCK HILL MURDER

The blinds had been down at the house in Elm Tree Road and the house shut for nearly six weeks. I had received a note from Dorcas saying that she was engaged on a case which would take her away for some little time, and that as Paul had not been very well lately she had arranged that he and her mother should accompany her. She would advise me as soon as they returned. I called once at Elm Tree Road and found it was in charge of the two servants and Toddlekins, the bulldog. The housemaid informed me that Mrs Dene had not written, so that she did not know where she was or when she would be back, but that letters which arrived for her were forwarded by her instructions to Mr Jackson of Penton Street, King's Cross.

Mr Jackson, I remembered, was the ex-police sergeant who was generally employed by Dorcas when she wanted a house watched or certain inquiries made among tradespeople. I felt that it would be unfair to go to Jackson. Had Dorcas wanted me to know where she was she would have told me in her letter.

The departure had been a hurried one. I had gone to the North in connection with a business matter of my own on a Thursday evening, leaving Dorcas at Elm Tree Road, and when I returned on Monday afternoon I found Dorcas's letter at my chambers. It was written on the Saturday, and evidently on the eve of departure.

But something that Dorcas did not tell me I learned quite accidentally from my old friend Inspector Swanage, of Scotland Yard, whom I met one cold February afternoon at Kempton Park Steeplechases.

Inspector Swanage has a much greater acquaintance with the fraternity known as 'the boys' than any other officer. He has attended race meetings for years, and 'the boys' always greet him respectfully, though they wish him further. Many a prettily-planned coup of theirs has he nipped in the bud, and many an unsuspecting greenhorn has he saved from pillage by a timely whisper that the well-dressed young gentlemen who are putting their fivers on so merrily and coming out of the enclosure with their pockets stuffed full of banknotes are men who get their living by clever swindling, and are far more dangerous than the ordinary vulgar pickpocket.

On one occasion not many years ago I found a well-known publisher at a race meeting in earnest conversation with a beautifully-dressed, grey-haired sportsman. The publisher informed me that his new acquaintance was the owner of a horse which was certain to win the next race, and that it would start at ten to one. Only, in order not to shorten the price nobody was to know the name of the horse, as the stable had three in the race. He had obligingly taken a fiver off the publisher to put on with his own money.

I told the publisher that he was the victim of a 'tale-pitcher', and that he would never see his fiver again. At that moment Inspector Swanage came on the scene, and the owner of race horses disappeared as if by magic. Swanage recognised the man instantly, and having heard my publisher's story said, 'If I have the man taken will you prosecute?' The publisher shook his head. He didn't want to send his authors mad with delight at the idea that somebody had eventually succeeded in getting a fiver the best of him. So Inspector Swanage strolled away. Half an hour later he came to us in the enclosure and said, 'Your friend's horse doesn't run, so he's given me that fiver back again for you.' And with a broad grin he handed my friend a banknote.

It was Inspector Swanage's skill and kindness on this occasion that made me always eager to have a chat with him when I saw him at a race meeting, for his conversation was always interesting.

The February afternoon had been a cold one, and soon after the commencement of racing there were signs of fog. Now a foggy afternoon is dear to the hearts of 'the boys'. It conceals their operations, and helps to cover their retreat. As the fog came up the Inspector began to look anxious, and I went up to him.

'You don't like the look of things?' I said.

'No, if this gets worse the band will begin to play – there are some very warm members of it here this afternoon. It was a day just like this last year that they held up a bookmaker going to the station, and eased him of over £500. Hullo?'

As he uttered the exclamation the Inspector pulled out his racecard and seemed to be anxiously studying it. But under his voice he said to me, 'Do you see that tall man in a fur coat talking to a bookmaker? See, he's just handed him a banknote?'

'Where? I don't see him.'

'Yonder. Do you see that old gipsy-looking woman with racecards? She has just thrust her hand through the railings and offered one to the man.'

'Yes, yes – I see him now.'

'That's Flash George. I've missed him lately, and I heard he was broke, but he's in funds again evidently by his get-up.'

'One of "the boys"?'

'Has been – but he's been on another lay lately. He was mixed up in that big jewel case – £10,000 worth of diamonds stolen from a demimondaine. He got rid of some of the jewels for the thieves, but we could never bring it home to him. But he was watched for a long time afterwards and his game was stopped. The last we heard of him he was hard up and borrowing from some of his pals. He's gone now. I'll just go and ask the bookie what he's betting to.'

The Inspector stepped across to the bookmaker and presently returned.

'He is in luck again,' he said. 'He's put a hundred ready on the favourite for this race. By the bye, how's your friend Mrs Dene getting on with her case?'

I confessed my ignorance as to what Dorcas was doing at the present moment – all I knew was that she was away.

'Oh, I thought you'd have known all about it,' said the Inspector. 'She's on the Hannaford case.'

'What, the murder?'

'Yes.'

'But surely that was settled by the police? The husband was arrested immediately after the inquest.'

'Yes, and the case against him was very strong, but we know

that Dorcas Dene has been engaged by Mr Hannaford's family, who have made up their minds that the police, firmly believing him guilty, won't look anywhere else for the murderer – of course they are convinced of his innocence. But you must excuse me – the fog looks like thickening, and may stop racing – I must go and put my men to work.'

'One moment before you go – why did you suddenly ask me how Mrs Dene was getting on? Was it anything to do with Flash George that put it in your head?'

The Inspector looked at me curiously.

'Yes,' he said, 'though I didn't expect you'd see the connection. It was a mere coincidence. On the night that Mrs Hannaford was murdered, Flash George, who had been lost sight of for some time by our people, was reported to have been seen by the Inspector who was going his rounds in the neighbourhood. He was seen about half-past two o'clock in the morning looking rather dilapidated and seedy. When the report of the murder came in, the Inspector at once remembered that he had seen Flash George in Haverstock Hill. But there was nothing in it – as the house hadn't been broken into and there was nothing stolen. You understand now why seeing Flash George carried my train of thought on to the Hannaford murder and Dorcas Dene. Goodbye.'

The Inspector hurried away and a few minutes afterwards the favourite came in alone for the second race on the card. The stewards immediately afterwards announced that racing would be abandoned on account of the fog increasing, and I made my way to the railway station and went home by the members' train.

Directly I reached home I turned eagerly to my newspaper file and read up the Hannaford murder. I knew the leading features, but every detail of it had now a special interest to me, seeing that Dorcas Dene had taken the case up.

These were the facts as reported in the Press:

Early in the morning of January 5 a maidservant rushed out of the house, standing in its own grounds on Haverstock Hill, calling 'Murder!' Several people who were passing instantly came to her and inquired what was the matter, but all she could gasp was, 'Fetch a policeman'. When the policeman arrived he followed the terrified girl into the house and was conducted to the drawing-room, where he found a lady lying in her nightdress in the centre of the room covered with blood, but still alive. He sent one of the servants for a doctor, and another to the police station to inform the superintendent. The doctor came immediately and declared that the woman was dying. He did everything that could be done for her, and presently she partially regained consciousness. The superintendent had by this time arrived, and in the presence of the doctor asked her who had injured her.

She seemed anxious to say something, but the effort was too much for her, and presently she relapsed into unconsciousness. She died two hours later, without speaking.

The woman's injuries had been inflicted with some heavy instrument. On making a search of the room the poker was found lying between the fireplace and the body. The poker was found to have blood upon it, and some hair from the unfortunate lady's head.

The servants stated that their master and mistress, Mr and Mrs Hannaford, had retired to rest at their usual time, shortly before midnight. The housemaid had seen them go up together. She had been working at a dress which she wanted for next Sunday, and sat up late, using her sewing-machine in the kitchen. It was one o'clock in the morning when she passed her master and mistress's door, and she judged by what she heard that they were quarrelling. Mr Hannaford was not in the house when the murder was discovered. The house was searched thoroughly in every direction, the first idea of the police being that he had committed suicide. The telegraph was then set to work, and at ten o'clock a man answering Mr Hannaford's description was arrested at Paddington Station, where he was taking a ticket for Uxbridge.

Taken to the police station and informed that he would be charged with murdering his wife, he appeared to be horrified, and for some time was a prey to the most violent emotion. When he had recovered himself and was made aware of the serious position in which he stood, he volunteered a statement. He was warned, but he insisted on making it. He declared that he and his wife had quarrelled violently after they had retired to rest. Their quarrel was about a purely domestic matter, but he was in an irritable, nervous condition, owing to his health, and at last he had worked himself up into such a state, that he had risen, dressed himself, and gone out into the street. That would be about two in the morning. He had wandered about in a state of nervous excitement until daybreak. At seven he had gone into a coffee house and had breakfast, and had then gone into the park and sat on a seat and fallen asleep. When he woke up it was nine o'clock. He had taken a cab to Paddington, and had intended to go to Uxbridge to see his mother, who resided there. Quarrels between himself and his wife had been frequent of late, and he was ill and wanted to get away, and he thought perhaps if he went to his mother for a day or two he might get calmer and feel better. He had been very much worried lately over business matters. He was a stock-jobber, and the market in the securities in which he had been speculating was against him.

At the conclusion of the statement, which was made in a nervous, excited manner, he broke down so completely that it was deemed desirable to send for the doctor and keep him under close observation.

Police investigations of the premises failed to find any further clue. Everything pointed to the supposition that the result of the quarrel had been an attack by the husband – possibly in a sudden fit of homicidal mania – on the unfortunate woman. The police suggestion was that the lady, terrified by her husband's behaviour, had risen in the night and run down the stairs to the drawing-room, and that he had followed her there, picked up the poker, and furiously attacked her. When she fell, apparently lifeless, he had run back to his bedroom, dressed himself, and made his escape quietly from the house. There was nothing missing so far as could be ascertained – nothing to suggest in any way that any third party, a burglar from outside or some person inside, had had anything to do with the matter.

The coroner's jury brought in a verdict of wilful murder, and the husband was charged before a magistrate and committed for trial. But in the interval his reason gave way, and, the doctors certifying that he was undoubtedly insane, he was sent to Broadmoor.

Nobody had the slightest doubt of his guilt, and it was his mother who, broken-hearted, and absolutely refusing to believe in her son's guilt, had come to Dorcas Dene and requested her to take up the case privately and investigate it. The poor old lady declared that she was perfectly certain that her son could not have been guilty of such a deed, but the police were satisfied, and would make no further investigation.

This I learnt afterwards when I went to see Inspector Swanage. All I knew when I had finished reading up the case in the newspapers was that the husband of Mrs Hannaford was in Broadmoor, practically condemned for the murder of his wife, and that Dorcas Dene had left home to try and prove his innocence.

The history of the Hannafords as given in the public Press was as follows: Mrs Hannaford was a widow when Mr Hannaford, a man of six-and-thirty, married her. Her first husband was a Mr Charles Drayson, a financier, who had been among the victims of the disastrous fire in Paris. His wife was with him in the Rue Jean Goujon that fatal night. When the fire broke out they both tried to escape together. They became separated in the crush. She was only slightly injured, and succeeded in getting out; he was less fortunate. His gold watch, a presentation one, with an inscription, was found among a mass of charred unrecognisable remains when the ruins were searched.

Three years after this tragedy the widow married Mr Hannaford. The death of her first husband did not leave her well off. It was found that he was heavily in debt, and had he lived a serious charge of fraud would undoubtedly have been preferred against him. As it was, his partner, a Mr Thomas Holmes, was arrested and sentenced to five years penal servitude in connection with a joint fraudulent transaction.

The estate of Mr Drayson went to satisfy the creditors, but Mrs Drayson, the widow, retained the house at Haverstock Hill, which he had purchased and settled on her, with all the furniture and contents, some years previously. She wished to continue living in the house when she married again, and Mr Hannaford consented, and they made it their home. Hannaford himself, though not a wealthy man, was a fairly successful stock-jobber, and until the crisis, which had brought on great anxiety and helped to break down his health, had had no financial worries. But the marriage, so it was alleged, had not been a very happy one and quarrels had been frequent. Old Mrs Hannaford was against it from the first, and to her her son always turned in his later matrimonial troubles. Now that his life had probably been spared by this mental breakdown, and he had been sent to Broadmoor, she had but one object in life – to see her son free, some day restored to reason, and with his innocence proved to the world.

* * * * * *

It was about a fortnight after my interview with Inspector Swanage, and my study of the details of the Haverstock Hill murder, that one morning I opened a telegram and to my intense delight found that it was from Dorcas Dene. It was from London, and informed me that in the evening they would be very pleased to see me at Elm Tree Road.

In the evening I presented myself about eight o'clock. Paul was alone in the drawing-room when I entered, and his face and his voice when he greeted me showed me plainly that he had benefitted greatly by the change.

'Where have you been, to look so well?' I asked. 'The South of Europe, I suppose – Nice or Monte Carlo?'

'No,' said Paul smiling, 'we haven't been nearly so far as that. But I mustn't tell tales out of school. You must ask Dorcas.'

At that moment Dorcas came in and gave me a cordial greeting.

'Well,' I said, after the first conversational preliminaries, 'who committed the Haverstock Hill murder?'

'Oh, so you know that I have taken that up, do you? I imagined it would get about through the Yard people. You see, Paul dear, how wise I was to give out that I had gone away.'

'Give out!' I exclaimed. '*Haven't* you been away then?'

'No, Paul and mother have been staying at Hastings, and I have been down whenever I have been able to spare a day, but as a matter of fact I have been in London the greater part of the time.'

'But I don't see the use of your pretending you were going away.'

'I did it on purpose. I knew the fact that old Mrs Hannaford had engaged me would get about in certain circles, and I wanted certain people to think that I had gone away to investigate some clue which I thought I had discovered. In order to baulk all possible inquirers I didn't even let the servants forward my letters. They went to Jackson, who sent them on to me.'

'Then you were really investigating in London?'

'Now shall I tell you where you heard that I was on this case?'

'Yes.'

'You heard it at Kempton Park Steeplechases, and your informant was Inspector Swanage.'

'You have seen him and he has told you.'

'No; I saw you there talking to him.'

'You saw me? You were at Kempton Park? I never saw you.'

'Yes, you did, for I caught you looking full at me. I was trying to sell some racecards just before the second race, and was holding them between the railings of the enclosure.'

'What! You were that old gipsy woman? I'm certain Swanage didn't know you.'

'I didn't want him to, or anybody else.'

'It was an astonishing disguise. But come, aren't you going to tell me anything about the Hannaford case? I've been reading it up, but I fail entirely to see the slightest suspicion against anyone but the husband. Everything points to his having committed the crime in a moment of madness. The fact that he has since gone completely out of his mind seems to me to show that conclusively.'

'It is a good job he did go out of his mind – but for that I am afraid he would have suffered for the crime, and the poor broken-hearted old mother for whom I am working would soon have followed him to the grave.'

'Then you don't share the general belief in his guilt?'

'I did at first, but I don't now.'

'You have discovered the guilty party?'

'No – not yet – but I hope to.'

'Tell me exactly all that has happened – there may still be a chance for your "assistant".'

'Yes, it is quite possible that now I may be able to avail myself of your services. You say you have studied the details of this case – let us just run through them together, and see what you think of my plan of campaign so far as it has gone. When old Mrs Hannaford came to me, her son had already been declared insane and unable to plead, and had gone to Broadmoor. That was nearly a month after the commission of the crime, so that much valuable time had been lost. At first I declined to take the matter up – the police had so thoroughly investigated the affair. The case seemed so absolutely conclusive that I told her that it would be useless for her to incur the heavy expense of a private investigation. But she pleaded so earnestly – her faith in her son was so great – and she seemed such a sweet, dear old lady, that at last she conquered my scruples, and I consented to study the case, and see if there was the slightest alternative theory to go on. I had almost abandoned hope, for there was nothing in the published reports to encourage it, when I determined to go to the fountain-head, and see the Superintendent who had had the case in hand.

'He received me courteously, and told me everything. He was certain that the husband committed the murder. There was an entire absence of motive for anyone else in the house to have done it, and the husband's flight from the house in the middle of the night was absolutely damning. I inquired if they had found anyone who had seen the husband in the street – anyone who could fix the time at which he had left the house. He replied that no such witness had been found. Then I asked if the policeman on duty that night had made any report of any suspicious characters being seen about. He said that the only person he had noticed at all was a man well known to the police – a man named Flash George. I asked what time Flash George had been seen and whereabouts, and I ascertained that it was at half-past two in the morning, and about a hundred yards below the scene of the crime, that when the policeman spoke to him he said he was coming from Hampstead, and was going to Covent Garden Market. He walked away in the direction of the Chalk Farm Road. I inquired what Flash George's record was, and ascertained that he was the associate of thieves and swindlers, and he was suspected of having disposed of some jewels, the proceeds of a robbery which had made a nine days' sensation. But the police had failed to bring the charge home to him, and the jewels had never been traced. He was also a gambler, a frequenter of racecourses and certain night-clubs of evil repute, and had not been seen about for some time previous to that evening.'

'And didn't the police make any further investigations in that direction?'

'No. Why should they? There was nothing missing from the house – not the slightest sign of an attempted burglary. All their efforts were directed to proving the guilt of the unfortunate woman's husband.'

'And you?'

'I had a different task – mine was to prove the husband's innocence. I determined to find out something more of Flash George. I shut the house up, gave out that I had gone away, and took, amongst other things, to selling cards and pencils on racecourses. The day that Flash George made his reappearance on the turf after a long absence was the day that he backed the winner of the second race at Kempton Park for a hundred pounds.'

'But surely that proves that if he had been connected with any crime it must have been one in which money was obtained. No one has attempted to associate the murder of Mrs Hannaford with robbery.'

'No. But one thing is certain – that on the night of the crime Flash George was in the neighbourhood. Two days previously he had borrowed a few pounds of a pal because he was "stony broke". When he reappears as a racing man, he has on a fur coat, is evidently in first-class circumstances, and he bets in hundred-pound notes. He is a considerably richer man after the murder of Mrs Hannaford than he was before, and he was seen within a hundred yards of the house at half-past two o'clock on the night that the crime was committed.'

'That might have been a mere accident. His sudden wealth may be the result of a lucky gamble, or a swindle of which you know nothing. I can't see that it can possibly have any bearing on the Hannaford crime, because nothing was taken from the house.'

'Quite true. But here is a remarkable fact. When he went up to the betting man he went to one who was betting close to the rails. When he pulled out that hundred-pound note I was at the rails, and I pushed my cards in between and asked him to buy one. Flash George is a "suspected character", and quite capable on a foggy day of trying to swindle a bookmaker. The bookmaker took the precaution to open that note, it being for a hundred pounds, and examined it carefully. That enabled me to see the number. I had sharpened pencils to sell, and with one of them I hastily took down the number of that note – 35421.'

'That was clever. And you have traced it?'

'Yes.'

'And has that furnished you with any clue?'

'It has placed me in possession of a most remarkable fact. The hundred-pound note which was in Flash George's possession on Kempton Park racecourse was one of a number which were paid over the counter of the Union Bank of London for a five-thousand-pound cheque over ten years ago. And that cheque was drawn by the murdered woman's husband.'

'Mr Hannaford!'

'No; her first husband – Mr Charles Drayson.'

* * * * * *

When Dorcas Dene told me that the £100 note Flash George had handed to the bookmaker at Kempton Park was one which had some years previously been paid to Mr Charles Drayson, the first husband of the murdered woman, Mrs Hannaford, I had to sit still and think for a moment.

It was curious certainly, but after all much more remarkable coincidences than that occur daily. I could not see what practical value there was in Dorcas's extraordinary discovery, because Mr Charles Drayson was dead, and it was hardly likely that his wife would have kept a £100 note of his for several years. And if she had, she had not been murdered for that, because there were no signs of the house having been broken into. The more I thought the business over the more confused I became in my attempt to establish a clue from it, and so after a minute's silence I frankly confessed to Dorcas that I didn't see where her discovery led to.

'I don't say that it leads very far by itself,' said Dorcas. 'But you must look at all the circumstances. During the night of January 5 a lady is murdered in her own drawing-room. Round about the time that the attack is supposed to have been made upon her a well-known bad character is seen close to the house. That person, who just previously has been ascertained to have been so hard up that he had been borrowing of his associates, reappears on the turf a few weeks later expensively dressed and in possession of money. He bets with a £100 note, and that £100 note I have traced to the previous possession of the murdered woman's first husband, who lost his life in the disastrous fire in Paris, while on a short visit to that capital.'

'Yes, it certainly is curious, but –'

'Wait a minute – I haven't finished yet. Of the banknotes – several of them for £100 – which were paid some years ago to Mr Charles Drayson, not one had come back to the bank before the murder.'

'Indeed!'

'Since the murder several of them have come in. Now, is it not a remarkable circumstance that during all those years £5,000 worth of banknotes should have remained out!'

'It is remarkable, but after all banknotes circulate – they may pass through hundreds of hands before returning to the bank.'

'Some may, undoubtedly, but it is highly improbable that all would under ordinary circumstances – especially notes for £100. These are sums which are not passed from pocket to pocket. As a rule they go to the bank of one of the early receivers of them, and from that bank into the Bank of England.'

'You mean that it is an extraordinary fact that for many years not one of the notes paid to Mr Charles Drayson by the Union Bank came back to the Bank of England.'

'Yes, that is an extraordinary fact, but there is a fact which is more extraordinary still, and that is that soon after the murder of Mrs Hannaford that state of things alters. It looks as though the murderer had placed the notes in circulation again.'

'It does, certainly. Have you traced back any of the other notes that have come in?'

'Yes; but they have been cleverly worked. They have nearly all been circulated in the betting ring; those that have not have come in from money-changers in Paris and Rotterdam. My own belief is that before long the whole of those notes will come back to the bank.'

'Then, my dear Dorcas, it seems to me that your course is plain, and you ought to go to the police and ask them to get the bank to circulate a list of the notes.'

Dorcas shook her head. 'No, thank you,' she said. 'I'm going to carry this case through on my own account. The police are convinced that the murderer is Mr Hannaford, who is at present in Broadmoor, and the bank has absolutely no reason to interfere. No question has been raised of the notes having been stolen. They were paid to the man who died over ten years ago, not to the woman who was murdered last January.'

'But you have traced one note to Flash George, who is a bad lot, and he was near the house on the night of the tragedy. You suspect Flash George and –'

'I do not suspect Flash George of the actual murder,' she said, 'and I don't see how he is to be arrested for being in possession of a banknote which forms no part of the police case, and which he might easily say he had received in the betting ring.'

'Then what are you going to do?'

'Follow up the clue I have. I have been shadowing Flash George all the time I have been away. I know where he lives – I know who are his companions.'

'And do you think the murderer is among them?'

'No. They are all a little astonished at his sudden good fortune. I have heard them "chip" him, as they call it, on the subject. I have carried my investigations up to a certain point and there they stop short. I am going a step further tomorrow evening, and it is in that step that I want assistance.'

'And you have come to me?' I said eagerly.

'Yes.'

'What do you want me to do?'

'Tomorrow morning I am going to make a thorough examination of the room in which the murder was committed. Tomorrow evening I have to meet a gentleman of whom I know nothing but his career and his name. I want you to accompany me.'

'Certainly; but if I am your assistant in the evening I shall expect to be your assistant in the morning – I should very much like to see the scene of the crime.'

'I have no objection. The house on Haverstock Hill is at present shut up and in charge of a caretaker, but the solicitors who are managing the late Mrs Hannaford's estate have given me permission to go over it and examine it.'

The next day at eleven o'clock I met Dorcas outside Mrs Hannaford's house, and the caretaker, who had received his instructions, admitted us. He was the gardener, and an old servant, and had been present during the police investigation. The bedroom in which Mr Hannaford and his wife slept on the fatal night was on the floor above. Dorcas told me to go upstairs, shut the door, lie down on the bed, and listen. Directly a noise in the room below attracted my attention, I was to jump up, open the door and call out.

I obeyed her instructions and listened intently, but lying on the bed I heard nothing for a long time. It must have been quite a quarter of an hour when suddenly I heard a sound as of a door opening with a cracking sound. I leapt up, ran to the balusters, and called over, 'I heard that!'

'All right, then, come down,' said Dorcas, who was standing in the hall with the caretaker.

She explained to me that she had been moving about the drawing-room with the man, and they had both made as much noise with their feet as they could. They had even opened and shut the drawing-room door, but nothing had attracted my attention. Then Dorcas had sent the man to open the front door. It had opened with the cracking sound that I had heard.

'Now,' said Dorcas to the caretaker, 'you were here when the police were coming and going – did the front door always make a sound like that?'

'Yes, madam. The door had swollen or warped, or something, and it was always difficult to open. Mrs Hannaford spoke about it once and was going to have it eased.'

'That's it, then,' said Dorcas to me. 'The probability is that it was the noise made by the opening of that front door which first attracted the attention of the murdered woman.'

'That was Hannaford going out – if his story is correct.'

'No; Hannaford went out in a rage. He would pull the door open violently, and probably bang it to. That she would understand. It was when the door opened again with a sharp crack that she listened, thinking it was her husband come back.'

'But she was murdered in the drawing- room!'

'Yes. My theory, therefore, is that after the opening of the front door she expected her husband to come upstairs. He didn't do so, and she concluded that he had gone into one of the rooms downstairs to spend the night, and she got up and came down to find him and ask him to get over his temper and come back to bed. She went into the drawing-room to see if he was there, and was struck down from behind before she had time to utter a cry. The servants heard nothing, remember.'

'They said so at the inquest – yes.'

'Now come into the drawing-room. This is where the caretaker tells me the body was found – here in the centre of the room – the poker with which the fatal blow had been struck was lying between the body and the fireplace. The absence of a cry and the position of the body show that when Mrs Hannaford opened the door she saw no one (I am, of course, presuming that the murderer was not her husband) and she came in further. But there must have been someone in the room or she couldn't have been murdered in it.'

'That is indisputable; but he might not have been in the room at the time – the person might have been hiding in the hall and followed her in.'

'To suppose that we must presume that the murderer came into the room, took the poker from the fireplace, and went out again in order to come in again. That poker was secured, I am convinced, when the intruder heard footsteps coming down the stair. He picked up the poker and then concealed himself here.'

'Then why, my dear Dorcas, shouldn't he have remained concealed until Mrs Hannaford had gone out of the room again?'

'I think she was turning to go when he rushed out and struck her down. He probably thought that she had heard the noise of the door, and might go and alarm the servants.'

'But just now you said she came in believing that her husband had returned and was in one of the rooms.'

'The intruder could hardly be in possession of her thoughts.'

'In the meantime he could have got out at the front door.'

'Yes; but if his object was robbery he would have to go without the plunder. He struck the woman down in order to have time to get what he wanted.'

'Then you think he left her here senseless while he searched the house?'

'Nobody got anything by searching the house, ma'am,' broke in the caretaker. 'The police satisfied themselves that nothing had been disturbed. Every door was locked, the plate was all complete, not a bit of jewellery or anything was missing. The servants were all examined about that, and the detectives went over every room and every cupboard to prove it wasn't no burglar broke in or anything of that sort. Besides, the windows were all fastened.'

'What he says is quite true,' said Dorcas to me, 'but something alarmed Mrs Hannaford in the night and brought her to the drawing-room in her nightdress. If it was, as I suspect, the opening of the front door, that is how the guilty person got in.'

The caretaker shook his head. 'It was the poor master as did it, ma'am, right enough. He was out of his mind.'

Dorcas shrugged her shoulders. 'If he had done it, it would have been a furious attack, there would have been oaths and cries, and the poor lady would have received a rain of blows. The medical evidence shows that death resulted from one heavy blow on the back of the skull. But let us see where the murderer could have concealed himself ready armed with the poker here in the drawing-room.'

In front of the drawing-room window were heavy curtains, and I at once suggested that curtains were the usual place of concealment on the stage and might be in real life.

As soon as I had asked the question Dorcas turned to the caretaker. 'You are certain that every article of furniture is in its place exactly as it was that night?'

'Yes; the police prepared a plan of the room for the trial, and since then by the solicitors' orders we have not touched a thing.'

'That settles the curtains then,' continued Dorcas. 'Look at the windows for yourself. In front of one, close by the curtains, is an ornamental table covered with china and glass and bric-à-brac; and in front of the other a large settee. No man could have come from behind those curtains without shifting that furniture out of his way. That would have immediately attracted Mrs Hannaford's attention and given her time to scream and rush out of the room. No, we must find some other place for the assassin. Ah – I wonder if –'

Dorcas's eyes were fixed on a large brown bear which stood nearly against the wall by the fireplace. The bear, a very fine, big specimen, was supported in its upright position by an ornamental iron pole, at the top of which was fixed an oil lamp covered with a yellow silk shade.

'That's a fine bear lamp,' exclaimed Dorcas.

'Yes,' said the caretaker, 'it's been here ever since I've been in the family's service. It was bought by the poor mistress's first husband, Mr Drayson, and he thought a lot of it. But,' he added, looking at it curiously, 'I always thought it stood closer to the wall than that. It used to – right against it.'

'Ah,' exclaimed Dorcas, 'that's interesting. Pull the curtains right back and give me all the light you can.'

As the man obeyed her directions she went down on her hands and knees and examined the carpet carefully.

'You are right,' she said. 'This has been moved a little forward, and not so very long ago – the carpet for a square of some inches is a different colour to the rest. The brown bear stands on a square mahogany stand, and the exact square now shows in the colour of the carpet that has been hidden by it. Only here is a discoloured portion and the bear does not now stand on it.'

The evidence of the bear having been moved forward from a position it had long occupied was indisputable. Dorcas got up and went to the door of the drawing-room.

'Go and stand behind that bear,' she said. 'Stand as compact as you can, as though you were endeavouring to conceal yourself.'

I obeyed, and Dorcas, standing in the drawing-room doorway, declared that I was completely hidden.

'Now,' she said, coming to the centre of the room and turning her back to me, 'reach down from where you are and see if you can pick up the shovel from the fireplace without making a noise.'

I reached out carefully and had the shovel in my hand without making a sound.

'I have it,' I said.

'That's right. The poker would have been on the same side as the shovel, and much easier to pick up quietly. Now, while my back is turned, grasp the shovel by the handle, leap out at me, and raise the shovel as if to hit me – but don't get excited and do it, because I don't want to realise the scene too completely.'

I obeyed. My footsteps were scarcely heard on the heavy-pile drawing-room carpet. When Dorcas turned round the shovel was above her head ready to strike.

'Thank you for letting me off,' she said, with a smile. Then her face becoming serious again, she exclaimed: 'The murderer of Mrs Hannaford concealed himself behind that brown bear lamp, and attacked her in exactly the way I have indicated. But why had he moved the bear two or three inches forward?'

'To conceal himself behind it.'

'Nonsense! His concealment was a sudden act. That bear is heavy – the glass chimney of the lamp would have rattled if it had been done violently and hurriedly while Mrs Hannaford was coming downstairs – that would have attracted her attention and she would have called out, "Who's there?" at the doorway, and not have come in looking about for her husband.'

Dorcas looked the animal over carefully, prodded it with her fingers, and then went behind it.

After a minute or two's close examination, she uttered a little cry and called me to her side.

She had found in the back of the bear a small straight slit. This was quite invisible. She had only discovered it by an accidentally violent thrust of her fingers into the animal's fur. Into this slit she thrust her hand, and the aperture yielded sufficiently for her to thrust her arm in. The interior of the bear was hollow, but Dorcas's hand as it went down struck against a wooden bottom. Then she withdrew her arm and the aperture closed up. It had evidently been specially prepared as a place of concealment, and only the most careful examination would have revealed it.

'Now,' exclaimed Dorcas, triumphantly, 'I think we are on a straight road! This, I believe, is where those missing banknotes lay concealed for years. They were probably placed there by Mr Drayson with the idea that someday his frauds might be discovered or he might be made a bankrupt. This was his little nest-egg, and his death in Paris before his fraud was discovered prevented him making use of them. Mrs Hannaford evidently knew nothing of the hidden treasure, or she would speedily have removed it. But someone knew, and that someone put his knowledge to practical use the night that Mrs Hannaford was murdered. The man who got in at the front door that night, got in to relieve the bear of its valuable stuffing; he moved the bear to get at the aperture, and was behind it when Mrs Hannaford came in. The rest is easy to understand.'

'But how did he get in at the front door?'

'That's what I have to find out. I am sure now that Flash George was in it. He was seen outside, and some of the notes that were concealed in the brown bear lamp have been traced to him. Who was Flash George's accomplice we may discover tonight. I think I have an idea, and if that is correct we shall have the solution of the whole mystery before dawn tomorrow morning.'

'Why do you think you will learn so much tonight?'

'Because Flash George met a man two nights ago outside the Criterion. I was selling wax matches, and followed them up, pestering them. I heard George say to his companion, whom I had never seen with him before, "Tell him Hungerford Bridge, midnight, Wednesday. Tell him to bring the lot and I'll cash up for them!"'

'And you think the "him" – ?'

'Is the man who rifled the brown bear and killed Mrs Hannaford.'

★ ★ ★ ★ ★ ★

At eleven o'clock that evening I met Dorcas Dene in Villiers Street. I knew what she would be like, otherwise her disguise would have completely baffled me. She was dressed as an Italian street musician, and was with a man who looked like an Italian organ-grinder.

Dorcas took my breath away by her first words.

'Allow me to introduce you,' she said, 'to Mr Thomas Holmes. This is the gentleman who was Charles Drayson's partner, and was sentenced to five years' penal servitude over the partnership frauds.'

'Yes,' replied the organ-grinder in excellent English. 'I suppose I deserved it for being a fool, but the villain was Drayson – he had all my money, and involved me in a fraud at the finish.'

'I have told Mr Holmes the story of our discovery,' said Dorcas. 'I have been in communication with him ever since I discovered the notes were in circulation. He knew Drayson's affairs, and he has given me some valuable information. He is with us tonight because he knew Mr Drayson's former associates, and he may be able to identify the man who knew the secret of the house at Haverstock Hill.'

'You think that is the man Flash George is to meet?'

'I do. What else can "Tell him to bring the lot and I'll cash up" mean but the rest of the banknotes?'

Shortly before twelve we got on to Hungerford Bridge – the narrow footway that runs across the Thames by the side of the railway.

I was to walk ahead and keep clear of the Italians until I heard a signal.

We crossed the bridge after that once or twice, I coming from one end and the Italians from the other, and passing each other about the centre.

At five minutes to midnight I saw Flash George come slowly along from the Middlesex side. The Italians were not far behind. A minute later an old man with a grey beard, and wearing an old Inverness cape, passed me, coming from the Surrey side. When he met Flash George the two stopped and leant over the parapet, apparently interested in the river. Suddenly I heard Dorcas's signal. She began to sing the Italian song, 'Santa Lucia'.

I had my instructions. I jostled up against the two men and begged their pardon.

Flash George turned fiercely round. At the same moment I seized the old man and shouted for help. The Italians came hastily up. Several foot passengers rushed to the scene and inquired what was the matter.

'He was going to commit suicide,' I cried. 'He was just going to jump into the water.'

The old man was struggling in my grasp. The crowd were keeping back Flash George. They believed the old man was struggling to get free to throw himself into the water.

The Italian rushed up to me.

'Ah, poor old man!' he said. 'Don't let him get away!'

He gave a violent tug to the grey beard. It came off in his hands. Then with an oath he seized the supposed would-be suicide by the throat.

'You infernal villain!' he said.

'Who is he?' asked Dorcas.

'Who is he!' exclaimed Thomas Holmes, 'why, the villain who brought me to ruin – *my precious partner – Charles Drayson!*'

As the words escaped from the supposed Italian's lips, Charles Drayson gave a cry of terror, and leaping on to the parapet, plunged into the river.

Flash George turned to run, but was stopped by a policeman who had just come up.

Dorcas whispered something in the man's ear, and the officer, thrusting his hand in the rascal's pocket, drew out a bundle of banknotes.

A few minutes later the would-be suicide was brought ashore. He was still alive, but had injured himself terribly in his fall, and was taken to the hospital.

Before he died he was induced to confess that he had taken advantage of the Paris fire to disappear. He had flung his watch down in order that it might be found as evidence of his death. He had, previously to visiting the Rue Jean Goujon, received a letter at his hotel which told him pretty plainly the game was up, and he knew that at any moment a warrant might be issued against him. After reading his name amongst the victims, he lived as best he could abroad, but after some years, being in desperate straits, he determined to do a bold thing, return to London and endeavour to get into his house and obtain possession of the money which was lying unsuspected in the interior of the brown bear lamp. He had concealed it, well knowing that at any time the crash might come, and everything belonging to him be seized. The hiding-place he had selected was one which neither his creditors nor his relatives would suspect.

On the night he entered the house, Flash George, whose acquaintance he had made in London, kept watch for him while he let himself in with his latch-key, which he had carefully preserved. Mr Hannaford's leaving the house was one of those pieces of good fortune which occasionally favour the wicked.

With his dying breath Charles Drayson declared that he had no intention of killing his wife. He feared that, having heard a noise, she had come to see what it was, and might alarm the house in her terror, and as she turned to go out of the drawing-room he struck her, intending only to render her senseless until he had secured the booty.

* * * * * *

Mr Hannaford, completely recovered and in his right mind, was in due time released from Broadmoor. The letter from his mother to Dorcas Dene, thanking her for clearing her son's character and proving his innocence of the terrible crime for which he had been practically condemned, brought tears to my eyes as Dorcas read it aloud to Paul and myself. It was touching and beautiful to a degree.

As she folded it up and put it away, I saw that Dorcas herself was deeply moved.

'These are the rewards of my profession,' she said. 'They compensate for everything.'

CONSTANCE DUNLAP

Created by Arthur B Reeve
(1880-1936)

Arthur B Reeve's varied career as an author included writing film serials which starred the escapologist Harry Houdini, novelettes for the legendary pulp magazine Weird Tales *and some of the most popular American crime fiction of the early twentieth century. His best known character was Craig Kennedy, the 'scientific detective', who appeared in dozens of short stories and novels. A professor of chemistry, Kennedy applied his knowledge of science and·his mastery of scientific gadgets to the solution of apparently baffling crimes. His adventures were narrated by his own Watson-like companion, the journalist Walter Jameson, and attracted a wide readership for many decades. Film versions of Reeve's works were made throughout the 1910s and 1920s and a TV series based on Craig Kennedy's cases was produced as late as 1952.* Constance Dunlap, Woman Detective *is a collection of interlinked stories published in 1913. The publishers advertised it as part of the 'Craig Kennedy Series', although it does not feature Reeve's most famous creation. The title character is a young woman thrown on her own resources by the crimes and eventual suicide of her weak-willed husband. In a series of adventures she demonstrates her ability to deal with a range of criminals from gunrunners and embezzlers to blackmailers and shoplifters. 'The Dope Fiends', in which Constance comes face to face with cokeheads and drug-dealers, is a fascinating story in its revelations of attitudes at the time to cocaine and those who used it. And Constance emerges, as she does from all the stories, as a woman of strong character and great intelligence.*

THE DOPE FIENDS

'I have a terrible headache,' remarked Constance Dunlap to her friend, Adele Gordon, the petite cabaret singer and dancer of the Mayfair, who had dropped in to see her one afternoon.

'You poor, dear creature,' soothed Adele. 'Why don't you go to see Dr Price? He has cured me. He's splendid – splendid.'

Constance hesitated. Dr Moreland Price was a well-known physician. All day and even at night, she knew, automobiles and cabs rolled up to his door and their occupants were, for the most part, stylishly gowned women.

'Oh, come on,' urged Adele. 'He doesn't charge as highly as people seem to think. Besides, I'll go with you and introduce you, and he'll charge only as he does the rest of us in the profession.'

Constance's head throbbed frantically. She felt that she must have some relief soon. 'All right,' she agreed, 'I'll go with you, and thank you, Adele.'

Dr Price's office was on the first floor of the fashionable Recherche Apartments, and, as she expected, Constance noted a line of motor cars before it.

They entered and were admitted to a richly furnished room, in mahogany and expensive Persian rugs, where a number of patients waited. One after another an attendant summoned them noiselessly and politely to see the doctor, until at last the turn of Constance and Adele came.

Dr Price was a youngish, middle-aged man, tall, with a sallow countenance and a self-confident, polished manner which went a long way in reassuring the patients, most of whom were ladies.

As they entered the doctor's sanctum behind the folding doors, Adele seemed to be on very good terms indeed with him.

They seated themselves in the deep leather chairs beside Dr Price's desk, and he inclined his head to listen to the story of their ailments.

'Doctor,' began Constance's introducer, 'I've brought my friend, Mrs Dunlap, who is suffering from one of those awful headaches. I thought perhaps you could give her some of that medicine that has done me so much good.'

The doctor bowed without saying anything and shifted his eyes from Adele to Constance.

'Just what seems to be the difficulty?' he inquired.

Constance told him how she felt, of her general lassitude and the big, throbbing veins in her temples.

'Ah — a woman's headaches!' he smiled, adding, 'Nothing serious, however, in this case, as far as I can see. We can fix this one all right, I think.'

He wrote out a prescription quickly and handed it to Constance.

'Of course,' he added, as he pocketed his fee, 'it makes no difference to me personally, but I would advise that you have it filled at Muller's — Miss Gordon knows the place. I think Muller's drugs are perhaps fresher than those of most druggists, and that makes a great deal of difference.'

He had risen and was politely and suavely bowing them out of another door, at the same time by pressing a button signifying to his attendant to admit the next patient.

Constance had preceded Adele, and, as she passed through the other door, she overheard the doctor whisper to her friend, 'I'm going to stop for you tonight to take a ride. I have something important I want to say to you.'

She did not catch Adele's answer, but as they left the marble and onyx, brass-grilled entrance, Adele remarked: 'That's his car — over there. Oh, but he is a reckless driver — dashes along pell-mell — but always seems to have his eye out for everything — never seems to be arrested, never in an accident.'

Constance turned in the direction of the car and was startled to see the familiar face of Drummond across the street dodging behind it. What was it now, she wondered — a divorce case, a scandal — what?

The medicine was made up into little powders, to be taken until they gave relief, and Constance folded the paper of one, poured it on the back of her tongue and swallowed a glass of water afterward.

Her head continued to throb, but she felt a sense of well-being that she had not before. Adele urged her to take another, and Constance did so.

The second powder increased the effect of the first marvellously. But Constance noticed that she now began to feel queer. She was not used to taking medicine. For a moment she felt that she was above, beyond the reach of ordinary rules and laws. She could have done any sort of physical task, she felt, no matter how difficult. She was amazed at herself, as compared to what she had been only a few moments before.

'Another one?' asked Adele finally.

Constance was by this time genuinely alarmed at the sudden unwonted effect on herself. 'N-no,' she replied dubiously, 'I don't think I want to take any more, just yet.'

'Not another?' asked Adele in surprise. 'I wish they would affect me that way. Sometimes I have to take the whole dozen before they have any effect.'

They chatted for a few minutes, and finally Adele rose.

'Well,' she remarked with a nervous twitching of her body, as if she were eager to be doing something, 'I really must be going. I can't say I feel any too well myself.'

'I think I'll take a walk with you,' answered Constance, who did not like the continued effect of the two powders. 'I feel the need of exercise – and air.'

Adele hesitated, but Constance already had her hat on. She had seen Drummond watching Dr Price's door, and it interested her to know whether he could possibly have been following Adele or someone else.

As they walked along Adele quickened her pace, until they came again to the drug store.

'I believe I'll go in and get something,' she remarked, pausing.

For the first time in several minutes Constance looked at the face of her friend. She was amazed to discover that Adele looked as if she had had a spell of sickness. Her eyes were large and glassy, her skin cold and sweaty, and she looked positively pallid and thin.

As they entered the store Muller, the druggist, bowed again and looked at Adele a moment as she leaned over the counter and whispered something to him. Without a word he went into the arcana behind the partition that cuts off the mysteries of the prescription room in every drug store from the front of the store.

When Muller returned he handed her a packet, for which she paid and which she dropped quickly into her pocketbook, hugging the pocketbook close to herself.

Adele turned and was about to hurry from the store with Constance. 'Oh, excuse me,' she said suddenly as if she had just recollected something, 'I promised a friend of mine I'd telephone this afternoon, and I have forgotten to do it. I see a pay station here.' Constance waited.

Adele returned much quicker than one would have expected she could call up a number, but Constance thought nothing of it at the time. She did notice, however, that as her friend emerged from the booth a most marvellous change had taken place in her. Her step was firm, her eye clear, her hand steady. Whatever it was, reasoned Constance, it could not have been serious to have disappeared so quickly.

It was with some curiosity as to just what she might expect that Constance went around to the famous cabaret that night. The Mayfair occupied two floors of what had been a wide brownstone house before business and pleasure had crowded the residence district further and further uptown. It was a very well-known bohemian rendezvous, where under-, demi- and upper-world rubbed elbows without friction and seemed to enjoy the novelty and be willing to pay for it.

Adele, who was one of the performers, had not arrived yet, but Constance, who had come with her mind still full of the two unexpected encounters with Drummond, was startled to see him here again. Fortunately he did not see her, and she slipped unobserved into an angle near the window overlooking the street.

Drummond had been engrossed in watching someone already there, and Constance made the best use she could of her eyes to determine who it was. The outdoor walk and a good dinner had checked her headache, and now the excitement of the chase of something, she knew not what, completed the cure.

It was not long before she discovered that Drummond was watching intently, without seeming to do so, a nervous-looking fellow whose general washed-out appearance of face was especially unattractive for some reason or other. He was very thin, very pale, and very stary about the eyes. Then, too, it seemed as if the bone in his nose was going, due perhaps to the shrinkage of the blood vessels from some cause.

Constance noticed a couple of girls whom she had seen Adele speak to on several other occasions approaching the young man.

There came an opportune lull in the music and from around the corner of her protecting angle Constance could just catch the greeting of one of the girls, 'Hello, Sleighbells! Got any snow?'

It was a remark that seemed particularly malapropos to the sultry weather, and Constance half expected a burst of laughter at the unexpected sally.

Instead, she was surprised to hear the young man reply in a very serious and matter-of-fact manner, 'Sure. Got any money, May?'

She craned her neck, carefully avoiding coming into Drummond's line of vision, and as she did so she saw two silver quarters gleam momentarily from hand to hand, and the young man passed each girl stealthily a small white paper packet.

Others came to him, both men and women. It seemed to be an established thing, and Constance noted that Drummond watched it all covertly.

'Who is that?' asked Constance of the waiter who had served her sometimes when she had been with Adele, and knew her.

'Why, they call him Sleighbells Charley,' he replied, 'a coke fiend.'

'Which means a cocaine fiend, I suppose!' she queried.

'Yes. He's a lobbygow for the grapevine system they have now of selling the dope in spite of this new law.'

'Where does he get the stuff!' she asked.

The waiter shrugged his shoulders. 'Nobody knows, I guess. I don't. But he gets it in spite of the law and peddles it. Oh, it's all adulterated – with some white stuff, I don't know what, and the price they charge is outrageous. They must make an ounce retail at five or six times the cost. Oh, you can bet that someone who is at the top is making a pile of money out of that graft, all right.'

He said it not with any air of righteous indignation, but with a certain envy.

Constance was thinking the thing over in her mind. Where did the 'coke' come from? The 'grapevine' system interested her.

'Sleighbells' seemed to have disposed of all the 'coke' he had brought with him. As the last packet went, he rose slowly, and shuffled out. Constance, who knew that Adele would not come for some time, determined to follow him. She rose quietly and, under cover of a party going out, managed to disappear without, as far as she knew, letting Drummond catch a glimpse of her. This would not only employ her time, but it was better to avoid Drummond as far as possible, at present, too, she felt.

At a distance of about half a block she followed the curiously shuffling figure. He crossed the avenue, turned and went uptown, turned again, and, before she knew it, disappeared in a drug store. She had been so engrossed in following the lobbygow that it was with a start that she realised that he had entered Muller's.

What did it all mean? Was the druggist, Muller, the man higher up? She recalled suddenly her own experience of the afternoon. Had Muller tried to palm off something on her? The more she thought of it the more sure she was that the powders she had taken had been doped.

Slowly, turning the matter over in her mind, she returned to the Mayfair. As she peered in cautiously before entering she saw that Drummond had gone. Adele had not come in yet, and she went in and sat down again in her old place.

Perhaps half an hour later, outside, she heard a car drive up with a furious rattle of gears. She looked out of the window and, as far as she could determine in the shadows, it was Dr Price. A woman got out, Adele. For a moment she stopped to talk, then Dr Price waved a gay goodbye and was off. All she could catch was a hasty, 'No; I don't think I'd better come in tonight,' from him.

As Adele entered the Mayfair she glanced about, caught sight of Constance and came and sat down by her.

It would have been impossible for her to enter unobserved, so popular was she. It was not long before the two girls whom Constance had seen dealing with 'Sleighbells' sauntered over.

'Your friend was here tonight,' remarked one to Adele.

'Which one?' laughed Adele.

'The one who admired your dancing the other night and wanted to take lessons.'

'You mean the young fellow who was selling something?' asked Constance pointedly.

'Oh, no,' returned the girl quite casually. 'That was Sleighbells,' and they all laughed.

Constance thought immediately of Drummond. 'The other one, then,' she said, 'the thick-set man who was all alone!'

'Yes; he went away afterward. Do you know him?'

'I've seen him somewhere,' evaded Constance; 'but I just can't quite place him.'

She had not noticed Adele particularly until now. Under the light she had a peculiar worn look, the same as she had had before.

The waiter came up to them. 'Your turn is next,' he hinted to Adele.

'Excuse me a minute,' she apologised to the rest of the party. 'I must fix up a bit. No,' she added to Constance, 'don't come with me.'

She returned from the dressing room a different person, and plunged into the wild dance for which the limited orchestra was already tuning up. It was a veritable riot of whirl and rhythm. Never before had Constance seen Adele dance with such abandon. As she executed the wild mazes of a newly imported dance, she held even the jaded Mayfair spellbound. And when she concluded with one daring figure and sat down, flushed and excited, the diners applauded and even shouted approval. It was an event for even the dance-mad Mayfair.

Constance did not share in the applause. At last she understood. Adele was a dope fiend, too.

She felt it with a sense of pain. Always, she knew, the fiends tried to get away alone somewhere for a few minutes to snuff some of their favourite nepenthe. She had heard before of the cocaine 'snuffers' who took a little of the deadly powder, placed it on the back of the hand, and inhaled it up the nose with a quick intake of breath. Adele was one. It was not Adele who danced. It was the dope.

Constance was determined to speak.

'You remember that man the girls spoke of?' she began.

'Yes. What of him?' asked Adele with almost a note of defiance.

'Well, I really *do* know him,' confessed Constance. 'He is a detective.'

Constance watched her companion curiously, for at the mere word she had stopped short and faced her. 'He is?' she asked quickly. 'Then that was why Dr Price –'

She managed to suppress the remark and continued her walk home without another word.

In Adele's little apartment Constance was quick to note that the same haggard look had returned to her friend's face.

Adele had reached for her pocketbook with a sort of clutching eagerness and was about to leave the room.

Constance rose. 'Why don't you give up the stuff?' she asked earnestly. 'Don't you want to?'

For a moment Adele faced her angrily. Then her real nature seemed slowly to come to the surface. 'Yes,' she murmured frankly.

'Then why don't you?' pleaded Constance.

'I haven't the power. There is an indescribable excitement to do something great, to make a mark. It's soon gone, but while it lasts, I can sing, dance, do anything – and then – every part of my body begins crying for more of the stuff again.'

There was no longer any necessity of concealment from Constance. She took a pinch of the stuff, placed it on the back of her wrist and quickly sniffed it. The change in her was magical.

ARTHUR B REEVE

From a quivering wretched girl she became a self-confident neurasthenic.

'I don't care,' she laughed hollowly now. 'Yes, I know what you are going to tell me. Soon I'll be "hunting the cocaine bug", as they call it, imagining that in my skin, under the flesh, are worms crawling, perhaps see them, see the little animals running around and biting me.'

She said it with a half-reckless cynicism. 'Oh, you don't know. There are two souls in the cocainist – one tortured by the pain of not having the stuff, the other laughing and mocking at the dangers of it. It stimulates. It makes your mind work – without effort, by itself. And it gives such visions of success, makes you feel able to do so much, and to forget. All the girls use it.'

'Where do they get it?' asked Constance 'I thought the new law prohibited it.'

'Get it?' repeated Adele. 'Why, they get it from that fellow they call "Sleighbells". They call it "snow", you know, and the girls who use it "snowbirds". The law does prohibit its sale, but...'

She paused significantly.

'Yes,' agreed Constance; 'but Sleighbells is only a part of the system after all. Who is the man at the top?'

Adele shrugged her shoulders and was silent. Still, Constance did not fail to note a sudden look of suspicion which Adele shot at her. Was Adele shielding someone?

Constance knew that someone must be getting rich from the traffic, probably selling hundreds of ounces a week and making thousands of dollars. Somehow she felt a sort of indignation at the whole thing. Who was it? Who was the man higher up?

In the morning as she was working about her little kitchenette an idea came to her. Why not hire the vacant apartment across the hall from Adele? An optician, who was a friend of hers, in the course of a recent conversation, had mentioned an invention, a model of which he had made for the inventor. She would try it.

Since, with Constance, the outlining of a plan was tantamount to the execution, it was not many hours later before she had both the apartment and the model of the invention.

Her wall separated her from the drug store and by careful calculation she determined about where came the little prescription department. Carefully, so as to arouse no suspicion, she began to bore away at the wall with various tools, until finally she had a small, almost imperceptible opening. It was tedious work, and toward the end needed great care so as not to excite suspicion. But finally she was rewarded. Through it she could see just a trace of daylight, and by squinting could see a row of bottles on a shelf opposite.

Then, through the hole, she pushed a long, narrow tube, like a putty blower. When at last she placed her eye at it, she gave a low exclamation of satisfaction. She could now see the whole of the little room.

It was a detectascope, invented by Gaillard Smith, adapter of the detectaphone, an instrument built up on the principle of the cytoscope which physicians use to explore internally down the throat. Only, in the end of the tube, instead of an ordinary lens, was placed what is known as a 'fish-eye' lens, which had a range something like nature has given the eyes of fishes, hence the name. Ordinarily cameras, because of the flatness of their lenses, have a range of only a few degrees, the greatest being scarcely more than ninety. But this lens was globular, and, like a drop of water, refracted light from all directions. When placed so that half of it caught the light it 'saw' through an angle of 180 degrees, 'saw' everything in the room instead of just that little row of bottles on the shelf opposite.

Constance set herself to watch, and it was not long before her suspicions were confirmed, and she was sure that this was nothing more than a 'coke' joint. Still she wondered whether Muller was the real source of the traffic of which Sleighbells was the messenger. She was determined to find out.

All day she watched through her detectascope. Once she saw Adele come in and buy more dope. It was with difficulty that she kept from interfering. But, she reflected, the time was not ripe. She had thought the thing out. There was no use in trying to get at it through Adele. The only way was to stop the whole curse at its source, to dam the stream. People came and went. She soon found that he was selling them packets from a box hidden in the woodwork. That much she had learned, anyhow.

Constance watched faithfully all day with only time enough taken out for dinner. It was after her return from this brief interval that she felt her heart give a leap of apprehension, as she looked again through the detectascope. There was Drummond in the back of the store talking to Muller and a woman who looked as if she might be Mrs Muller, for both seemed nervous and anxious.

As nearly as she could make out, Drummond was alternately threatening and arguing with Muller. Finally the three seemed to agree, for Drummond walked over to a typewriter on a table, took a fresh sheet of carbon paper from a drawer, placed it between two sheets of paper, and hastily wrote something.

Drummond read over what he had written. It seemed to be short, and the three apparently agreed on it. Then, in a trembling hand, Muller signed the two copies which Drummond had made, one of which Drummond himself kept and the other he sealed in an envelope and sent away by a boy. Drummond reached into his pocket and pulled out a huge roll of bills of large denomination. He counted out what seemed to be approximately half, handed it to the woman, and replaced the rest in his pocket. What it was all about Constance could only vaguely guess. She longed to know what was in the letter and why the money had been paid to the woman.

Perhaps a quarter of an hour after Drummond left Adele appeared again, pleading for more dope. Muller went back of the partition and made up a fresh paper of it from a bottle also concealed.

Constance was torn by conflicting impulses. She did not want to miss anything in the perplexing drama that was being enacted before her, yet she wished to interfere with the deadly course of Adele. Still, perhaps the girl would resent interference if she found out that Constance was spying on her. She determined to wait a little while before seeing Adele. It was only after a decided effort that she tore herself away from the detectascope and knocked on Adele's door as if she had just come in for a visit. Again she knocked, but still there was no answer. Every minute something might be happening next door. She hurried back to her post of observation.

One of the worst aspects of the use of cocaine, she knew, was the desire of the user to share his experience with someone else. The passing on of the habit, which seemed to be one of the strongest desires of the drug fiend, made him even more dangerous to society than he would otherwise have been. That thought gave Constance an idea.

She recalled also now having heard somewhere that it was a common characteristic of these poor creatures to have a passion for fast automobiling, to go on long rides, perhaps even without having the money to pay for them. That, too, confirmed the idea which she had.

As the night advanced she determined to stick to her post. What could it have been that Drummond was doing? It was no good, she felt positive.

Suddenly before her eye, glued to its eavesdropping aperture, she saw a strange sight. There was a violent commotion in the store. Blue-coated policemen seemed to swarm in from nowhere. And in the rear, directing them, appeared Drummond, holding by the arm the unfortunate Sleighbells, quaking with fear, evidently having been picked up already elsewhere by the wily detective.

Muller put up a stout resistance, but the officers easily seized him and, after a hasty but thorough search, unearthed his *cache* of the contraband drug.

As the scene unfolded, Constance was more and more bewildered after having witnessed that which preceded it, the signing of the letter and the passing of the money. Muller evidently had nothing to say about that. What did it mean?

The police were still holding Muller, and Constance had not noted that Drummond had disappeared.

'It's on the first floor – left, men,' sounded a familiar voice outside her own door. 'I know she's there. My shadow saw her buy the dope and take it home.'

Her heart was thumping wildly. It was Drummond leading his squad of raiders, and they were about to enter the apartment of Adele. They knocked, but there was no answer.

A few moments before Constance would have felt perfectly safe in saying that Adele was out. But if Drummond's man had seen her enter, might she not have been there all the time, be there still, in a stupor? She dreaded to think of what might happen if the poor girl once fell into their hands. It would be the final impulse that would complete her ruin.

Constance did not stop to reason it out. Her woman's intuition told her that now was the time to act – that there was no retreat.

She opened her own door just as the raiders had forced in the flimsy affair that guarded the apartment of Adele.

'So!' sneered Drummond, catching sight of her in the dim light of the hallway. 'You are mixed up in these violations of the new drug law, too!'

Constance said nothing. She had determined first to make Drummond display his hand.

'Well,' he ground out, 'I'm going to get these people this time. I represent the Medical Society and the Board of Health. These men have been assigned to me by the Commissioner as a dope squad. We want this girl. We have others who will give evidence; but we want this one, too.'

He said it with a bluster that even exaggerated the theatrical character of the raid itself. Constance did not stop to weigh the value of his words, but through the door she brushed quickly. Adele might need her if she was indeed there.

As she entered the little living-room she saw a sight which almost transfixed her. Adele was there – lying across a divan, motionless.

Constance bent over. Adele was cold. As far as she could determine there was not a breath or a heartbeat!

What did it mean? She did not stop to think. Instantly there flashed over her the recollection of an instrument she had read about at one of the city hospitals. It might save Adele. Before anyone knew what she was doing she had darted to the telephone

111

in the lower hall of the apartment and had called up the hospital frantically, imploring them to hurry. Adele must be saved.

Constance had no very clear idea of what happened next in the hurly-burly of events, until the ambulance pulled up at the door and the white-coated surgeon burst in carrying a heavy suitcase.

With one look at the unfortunate girl he muttered, 'Paralysis of the respiratory organs – too large a dose of the drug. You did perfectly right,' and began unpacking the case.

Constance, calm now in the crisis, stood by him and helped as deftly as could any nurse.

It was a curious arrangement of tubes and valves, with a large rubber bag, and a little pump that the doctor had brought. Quickly he placed a cap, attached to it, over the nose and mouth of the poor girl, and started the machine.

'Wh-what is it?' gasped Drummond as he saw Adele's hitherto motionless breast now rise and fall.

'A pulmotor,' replied the doctor, working quickly and carefully, 'an artificial lung. Sometimes it can revive even the medically dead. It is our last chance with this girl.'

Constance had picked up the packet which had fallen beside Adele and was looking at the white powder.

'Almost pure cocaine,' remarked the young surgeon, testing it. 'The hydrochloride, large crystals, highest quality. Usually it is adulterated. Was she in the habit of taking it this way?'

Constance said nothing. She had seen Muller make up the packet – specially now, she recalled. Instead of the adulterated dope he had given Adele the purest kind. Why? Was there some secret he wished to lock in her breast forever?

Mechanically the pulmotor pumped. Would it save her?

Constance was living over what she had already seen through the detectascope. Suddenly she thought of the strange letter and of the money.

She hurried into the drug store. Muller had already been taken away, but before the officer left in charge could interfere she picked up the carbon sheet on which the letter had been copied, turned it over and held it eagerly to the light.

She read in amazement. It was a confession. In it Muller admitted to Dr Moreland Price that he was the head of a sort of dope trust, that he had messengers out, like Sleighbells, that he had often put dope in the prescriptions sent him by the doctor, and had repeatedly violated the law and refilled such prescriptions. On its face it was complete and convincing.

Yet it did not satisfy Constance. She could not believe that Adele had committed suicide. Adele must possess some secret. What was it?

'Is – is there any change?' she asked anxiously of the young surgeon now engrossed in his work.

For answer he merely nodded to the apparently motionless form on the bed, and for a moment stopped the pulmotor.

The mechanical movement of the body ceased. But in its place was a slight tremor about the lips and mouth.

Adele moved – was faintly gasping for breath!

'Adele!' cried Constance softly in her ear. 'Adele!'

Something, perhaps a faraway answer of recognition, seemed to flicker over her face. The doctor redoubled his efforts.

'Adele – do you know me?' whispered Constance again.

'Yes,' came back faintly at last. 'There – there's something – wrong with it – they – they –'

'How? What do you mean?' urged Constance. 'Tell me, Adele.'

The girl moved uneasily. The doctor administered a stimulant and she vaguely opened her eyes, began to talk hazily, dreamily. Constance bent over to catch the faint words which would have been lost to the others.

'They – are going to – double cross the Health Department,' she murmured as if to herself, then gathering strength she went on, 'Muller and Sleighbells will be arrested and take the penalty. They have been caught with the goods, anyhow. It has all been arranged so that the detective will get his case. Money – will be paid to both of them, to Muller and the detective, to swing the case and protect him. He made me do it. I saw the detective, even danced with him and he agreed to do it. Oh, I would do anything – I am his willing tool when I have the stuff. But – this time – it was –' She rambled off incoherently.

'Who made you do it? Who told you?' prompted Constance. 'For whom would you do anything?'

Adele moaned and clutched Constance's hand convulsively. Constance did not pause to consider the ethics of questioning a half-unconscious girl. Her only idea was to get at the truth.

'Who was it?' she reiterated.

Adele turned weakly.

'Dr Price,' she murmured as Constance bent her ear to catch even the faintest sound. 'He told me – all about it – last night – in the car.'

Instantly Constance understood. Adele was the only one outside who held the secret, who could upset the carefully planned frame-up that was to protect the real head of the dope trust, who had paid liberally to save his own wretched skin.

She rose quickly and wheeled about suddenly on Drummond.

'You will convict Dr Price also,' she said in a low tone. 'This girl must not be dragged down, too. You will leave her alone, and both you and Mr Muller will hand over that money to her for her cure of the habit.'

Drummond started forward angrily, but fell back as Constance added in a lower but firmer tone, 'Or I'll have you all up on a charge of attempting murder.'

Drummond turned surlily to those of his 'dope squad' who remained:

'You can go, boys,' he said brusquely. 'There's been some mistake here.'

SARAH FAIRBANKS

Created by Mary E Wilkins
(1852–1930)

Born in Massachusetts, Mary Wilkins began her career writing for children when she was no more than a teenager herself. After the death of both her parents, she needed to find new ways to support herself and turned to producing short stories and longer fiction for an adult readership. Her tales of New England, often of marginalised characters struggling with the frustrations and constraints of their lives, were collected in volumes such as A Humble Romance *and* A New England Nun *and won her much praise, although today she is probably better known for her stories of ghosts and the supernatural. 'Luella Miller', the story of a metaphorical vampire leeching the life force out of her victims, and 'The Shadows on the Wall', in which a spirit finds an original way of haunting its former home, make regular appearances in anthologies. 'The Long Arm' was first published in* Pocket Magazine *in 1895 and later appeared in a collection of four detective stories by four different authors. Mary E Wilkins was not, however, a crime writer in any sense and Sarah Fairbanks is not a detective in the same way that most of the other characters in this book are. She is a woman suspected of a crime who is obliged to turn sleuth in order to clear her name. Disappointingly, she is unable to do so without male assistance in the shape of the professional detective Francis Dix but none the less she is a strong, determined character who refuses to submit meekly to fate. 'The Long Arm', which has been described as 'a typical Wilkins story plus a murder', is also interesting in its depiction of what is implicitly a lesbian relationship, unusual in a work of fiction from that period.*

THE LONG ARM

*(From notes written by Miss Sarah Fairbanks immediately
after the report of the Grand Jury.)*

As I take my pen to write this, I have a feeling that I am in the
witness-box – for, or against myself, which? The place of the
criminal in the dock I will not voluntarily take. I will affirm
neither my innocence nor my guilt. I will present the facts of the
case as impartially and as coolly as if I had nothing at stake. I will
let all who read this judge me as they will.

This I am bound to do, since I am condemned to something
infinitely worse than the life-cell or the gallows. I will try my
own self in lieu of judge and jury; my guilt or my innocence
I will prove to you all, if it be in mortal power. In my despair
I am tempted to say, I care not which it may be, so something
be proved. Open condemnation could not overwhelm me like
universal suspicion.

Now, first, as I have heard is the custom in the courts of law,
I will present the case. I am Sarah Fairbanks, a country school
teacher, twenty-nine years of age. My mother died when I was
twenty-three. Since then, while I have been teaching at Digby,
a cousin of my father's, Rufus Bennett, and his wife have lived
with my father. During the long summer vacation they returned
to their little farm in Vermont, and I kept house for my father.

For five years I have been engaged to be married to Henry
Ellis, a young man whom I met in Digby. My father was very
much opposed to the match, and has told me repeatedly that if I
insisted upon marrying him in his lifetime he would disinherit
me. On this account Henry never visited me at my own home;
while I could not bring myself to break off my engagement.
Finally, I wished to avoid an open rupture with my father. He
was quite an old man, and I was the only one he had left of a
large family.

I believe that parents should honour their children, as well as
children their parents; but I had arrived at this conclusion: in

nine-tenths of the cases wherein children marry against their parents' wishes, even when the parents have no just grounds for opposition, the marriages are unhappy.

I sometimes felt that I was unjust to Henry, and resolved that, if ever I suspected that his fancy turned toward any other girl, I would not hinder it, especially as I was getting older and, I thought, losing my good looks.

A little while ago, a young and pretty girl came to Digby to teach the school in the south district. She boarded in the same house with Henry. I heard that he was somewhat attentive to her, and I made up my mind I would not interfere. At the same time it seemed to me that my heart was breaking. I heard her people had money, too, and she was an only child. I had always felt that Henry ought to marry a wife with money, because he had nothing himself, and was not very strong.

School closed five weeks ago, and I came home for the summer vacation. The night before I left, Henry came to see me, and urged me to marry him. I refused again; but I never before had felt that my father was so hard and cruel as I did that night. Henry said that he should certainly see me during the vacation, and when I replied that he must not come, he was angry, and said – but such foolish things are not worth repeating. Henry has really a very sweet temper, and would not hurt a fly.

The very night of my return home, Rufus Bennett and my father had words about some maple sugar which Rufus made on his Vermont farm and sold to father, who made a good trade for it to some people in Boston. That was father's business. He had once kept a store, but had given it up, and sold a few articles that he could make a large profit on here and there at wholesale. He used to send to New Hampshire and Vermont for butter, eggs, and cheese. Cousin Rufus thought father did not allow him enough profit on the maple sugar, and in the dispute father lost his temper, and said that Rufus had given him underweight. At that, Rufus swore an oath, and seized father by the throat. Rufus's wife screamed, 'Oh, don't! don't! oh, he'll kill him!'

I went up to Rufus and took hold of his arm.

'Rufus Bennett,' said I, 'you let go my father!'

But Rufus's eyes glared like a madman's, and he would not let go. Then I went to the desk-drawer where father had kept a pistol since some houses in the village were broken into; I got out the pistol, laid hold of Rufus again, and held the muzzle against his forehead.

'You let go of my father,' said I, 'or I'll fire!'

Then Rufus let go, and father dropped like a log. He was purple in the face. Rufus's wife and I worked a long time over him to bring him to.

'Rufus Bennett,' said I, 'go to the well and get a pitcher of water.' He went, but when father had revived and got up, Rufus gave him a look that showed he was not over his rage.

'I'll get even with you yet, Martin Fairbanks, old man as you are!' he shouted out, and went into the outer room.

We got father to bed soon. He slept in the bedroom downstairs, out of the sitting-room. Rufus and his wife had the north chamber, and I had the south one. I left my door open that night, and did not sleep. I listened; no one stirred in the night. Rufus and his wife were up very early in the morning, and before nine o'clock left for Vermont. They had a day's journey, and would reach home about nine in the evening. Rufus's wife bade father goodbye, crying, while Rufus was getting their trunk downstairs, but Rufus did not go near father nor me. He ate no breakfast; his very back looked ugly when he went out of the yard.

That very day about seven in the evening, after tea, I had just washed the dishes and put them away, and went out on the north doorstep, where father was sitting, and sat down on the lowest step. There was a cool breeze there; it had been a very hot day.

'I want to know if that Ellis fellow has been to see you any lately?' said father all at once.

'Not a great deal,' I answered.

'Did he come to see you the last night you were there?' said father.

'Yes, sir,' said I, 'he did come.'

'If you ever have another word to say to that fellow while I live, I'll kick you out of the house like a dog, daughter of mine though you be,' said he. Then he swore a great oath and called God to witness. 'Speak to that fellow again, if you dare, while I live!' said he.

I did not say a word; I just looked up at him as I sat there. Father turned pale and shrank back, and put his hand to his throat, where Rufus had clutched him. There were some purple fingermarks there.

'I suppose you would have been glad if he had killed me,' father cried out.

'I saved your life,' said I.

'What did you do with that pistol?' he asked.

'I put it back in the desk-drawer.'

I got up and went around and sat on the west doorstep, which is the front one. As I sat there, the bell rang for the Tuesday evening meeting, and Phoebe Dole and Maria Woods, two old maiden ladies, dressmakers, our next-door neighbours, went past on their way to meeting. Phoebe stopped and asked if Rufus and his wife were gone. Maria went around the house. Very soon they went on, and several other people passed. When they had all gone, it was as still as death.

I sat alone a long time, until I could see by the shadows that the full moon had risen. Then I went to my room and went to bed.

I lay awake a long time, crying. It seemed to me that all hope of marriage between Henry and me was over. I could not expect him to wait for me. I thought of that other girl; I could see her pretty face wherever I looked. But at last I cried myself to sleep.

At about five o'clock I awoke and got up. Father always wanted his breakfast at six o'clock, and I had to prepare it now.

When father and I were alone, he always built the fire in the kitchen stove, but that morning I did not hear him stirring as usual, and I fancied that he must be so out of temper with me, that he would not build the fire.

I went to my closet for a dark blue calico dress which I wore to do housework in. It had hung there during all the school term.

As I took it off the hook, my attention was caught by something strange about the dress I had worn the night before. This dress was made of thin summer silk; it was green in colour, sprinkled over with white rings. It had been my best dress for two summers, but now I was wearing it on hot afternoons at home, for it was the coolest dress I had. The night before, too, I had thought of the possibility of Henry's driving over from Digby and passing the house. He had done this sometimes during the last summer vacation, and I wished to look my best if he did.

As I took down the calico dress I saw what seemed to be a stain on the green silk. I threw on the calico hastily, and then took the green silk and carried it over to the window. It was covered with spots – horrible great splashes and streaks down the front. The right sleeve, too, was stained, and all the stains were wet.

'What have I got on my dress?' said I.

It looked like blood. Then I smelled of it, and it was sickening in my nostrils, but I was not sure what the smell of blood was like. I thought I must have got the stains by some accident the night before.

'If that is blood on my dress,' I said, 'I must do something to get it off at once, or the dress will be ruined.'

It came to my mind that I had been told that bloodstains had been removed from cloth by an application of flour paste on the wrong side. I took my green silk, and ran down the back stairs, which lead – having a door at the foot – directly into the kitchen.

There was no fire in the kitchen stove, as I had thought. Everything was very solitary and still, except for the ticking of the clock on the shelf. When I crossed the kitchen to the pantry, however, the cat mewed to be let in from the shed. She had a little door of her own by which she could enter or leave the shed at will, an aperture just large enough for her Maltese body to pass at ease beside the shed door. It had a little lid, too, hung upon a leathern hinge. On my way I let the cat in; then I went into the pantry and got a bowl of flour. This I mixed with water into a stiff paste, and applied to the under surface of the stains on my dress. I then hung the dress up to dry in the dark end of a closet leading out of the kitchen, which contained some old clothes of father's.

Then I made up the fire in the kitchen stove. I made coffee, baked biscuits, and poached some eggs for breakfast.

Then I opened the door into the sitting-room and called, 'Father, breakfast is ready'. Suddenly I started. There was a red stain on the inside of the sitting-room door. My heart began to beat in my ears. 'Father!' I called out. 'Father!'

There was no answer.

'Father!' I called again, as loud as I could scream. 'Why don't you speak? What is the matter?'

The door of his bedroom stood open. I had a feeling that I saw a red reflection in there. I gathered myself together and went across the sitting-room to father's bedroom door. His little looking-glass hung over his bureau opposite his bed, which was reflected in it.

That was the first thing I saw, when I reached the door. I could see father in the looking-glass and the bed. Father was dead there; he had been murdered in the night.

* * * * * *

I think I must have fainted away, for presently I found myself on the floor, and for a minute I could not remember what had happened. Then I remembered, and an awful, unreasoning terror seized me. 'I must lock all the doors quick,' I thought; 'quick, or the murderer will come back.'

I tried to get up, but I could not stand. I sank down again. I had to crawl out of the room on my hands and knees.

I went first to the front door; it was locked with a key and a bolt. I went next to the north door, and that was locked with a key and bolt. I went to the north shed door, and that was bolted. Then I went to the little-used east door in the shed, beside which the cat had her little passage-way, and that was fastened with an iron hook. It has no latch.

The whole house was fastened on the inside. The thought

struck me like an icy hand, 'The murderer is in this house!' I rose to my feet then; I unhooked that door, and ran out of the house, and out of the yard, as for my life.

I took the road to the village. The first house, where Phoebe Dole and Maria Woods live, is across a wide field from ours. I did not intend to stop there, for they were only women, and could do nothing; but seeing Phoebe looking out of the window, I ran into the yard.

She opened the window.

'What is it?' said she. 'What is the matter, Sarah Fairbanks?'

Maria Woods came and leaned over her shoulder. Her face looked almost as white as her hair, and her blue eyes were dilated. My face must have frightened her.

'Father – father is murdered in his bed!' I said.

There was a scream, and Maria Woods's face disappeared from over Phoebe Dole's shoulder – she had fainted. I do not know whether Phoebe looked paler – she is always very pale – but I saw in her black eyes a look which I shall never forget. I think she began to suspect me at that moment.

Phoebe glanced back at Maria, but she asked me another question.

'Has he had words with anybody?' said she.

'Only with Rufus,' I said; 'but Rufus is gone.'

Phoebe turned away from the window to attend to Maria, and I ran on to the village.

A hundred people can testify what I did next – can tell how I called for the doctor and the deputy sheriff; how I went back to my own home with the horror-stricken crowd; how they flocked in and looked at poor father; but only the doctor touched him, very carefully, to see if he were quite dead; how the coroner came, and all the rest.

The pistol was in the bed beside father, but it had not been fired; the charge was still in the barrel. It was bloodstained, and there was one bruise on father's head which might have been inflicted by the pistol, used as a club. But the wound which caused his death was in his breast, and made evidently by some cutting instrument, though the cut was not a clean one; the weapon must have been dull.

They searched the house, lest the murderer should be hidden away. I heard Rufus Bennett's name whispered by one and another. Everybody seemed to know that he and father had had words the night before; I could not understand how, because I had told nobody except Phoebe Dole, who had had no time to spread the news, and I was sure that no one else had spoken of it.

They looked in the closet where my green silk dress hung, and pushed it aside to be sure nobody was concealed behind it, but they did not notice anything wrong about it. It was dark in the closet, and besides, they did not look for anything like that until later.

All these people – the deputy sheriff, and afterwards the high sheriff, and other out-of-town officers, for whom they had telegraphed, and the neighbours – all hunted their own suspicion, and that was Rufus Bennett. All believed he had come back, and killed my father. They fitted all the facts to that belief. They made him do the deed with a long, slender screwdriver, which he had recently borrowed from one of the neighbours and had not returned. They made his fingermarks, which were still on my father's throat, fit the red prints of the sitting-room door. They made sure that he had returned and stolen into the house by the east door shed, while father and I sat on the doorsteps the evening before; that he had hidden himself away, perhaps in that very closet where my dress hung, and afterwards stolen out and killed my father, and then escaped.

They were not shaken when I told them that every door was bolted and barred that morning. They themselves found all the windows fastened down, except a few which were open on account of the heat, and even these last were raised only the width of the sash, and fastened with sticks, so that they could be raised no higher. Father was very cautious about fastening the house, for he sometimes had considerable sums of money by him. The officers saw all these difficulties in the way, but they fitted them somehow to their theory, and two deputy sheriffs were at once sent to apprehend Rufus.

They had not begun to suspect me then, and not the slightest watch was kept on my movements. The neighbours were very kind, and did everything to help me, relieving me altogether of all those last offices – in this case so much sadder than usual.

An inquest was held, and I told freely all I knew, except about the bloodstains on my dress. I hardly knew why I kept that back. I had no feeling then that I might have done the deed myself, and I could not bear to convict myself, if I was innocent.

Two of the neighbours, Mrs Holmes and Mrs Adams, remained with me all that day. Towards evening, when there were very few in the house, they went into the parlour to put it in order for the funeral, and I sat down alone in the kitchen. As I sat there by the window I thought of my green silk dress, and wondered if the stains were out. I went to the closet and brought the dress out to the light. The spots and streaks had almost disappeared. I took the dress out into the shed, and scraped off the flour paste, which was quite dry; I swept up the paste, burned it in the stove, took the dress upstairs to my own closet, and hung it in its old place. Neighbours remained with me all night.

At three o'clock in the afternoon of the next day, which was Thursday, I went over to Phoebe Dole's to see about a black dress to wear at the funeral. The neighbours had urged me to have my black silk dress altered a little, and trimmed with crape.

I found only Maria Woods at home. When she saw me she gave a little scream, and began to cry. She looked as if she had already been weeping for hours. Her blue eyes were bloodshot.

'Phoebe's gone over to – Mrs Whitney's to – try on her dress,' she sobbed.

'I want to get my black silk dress fixed a little,' said I.

'She'll be home – pretty soon,' said Maria.

I laid my dress on the sofa and sat down. Nobody ever consults Maria about a dress. She sews well, but Phoebe does all the planning.

Maria Woods continued to sob like a child, holding her little soaked handkerchief over her face. Her shoulders heaved. As for me, I felt like a stone; I could not weep.

'Oh,' she gasped out finally, 'I knew – I knew! I told Phoebe – I knew just how it would be, I – knew!'

I roused myself at that.

'What do you mean?' said I.

'When Phoebe came home Tuesday night and said she heard your father and Rufus Bennett having words, I knew how it would be,' she choked out. 'I knew he had a dreadful temper.'

'Did Phoebe Dole know Tuesday night that father and Rufus Bennett had words?' said I.

'Yes,' said Maria Woods.

'How did she know?'

'She was going through your yard, the short cut to Mrs Ormsby's, to carry her brown alpaca dress home. She came right home and told me; and she overheard them.'

'Have you spoken of it to anybody but me?' said I.

Maria said she didn't know; she might have done so. Then she remembered hearing Phoebe herself speak of it to Harriet Sargent when she came in to try on her dress. It was easy to see how people knew about it.

I did not say any more, but I thought it was strange that Phoebe Dole had asked me if father had had words with anybody when she knew it all the time.

Phoebe came in before long. I tried on my dress, and she made her plan about the alterations, and the trimming. I made no suggestions. I did not care how it was done, but if I had cared it would have made no difference. Phoebe always does things her own way. All the women in the village are in a manner under Phoebe Dole's thumb. The garments are visible proofs of her force of will.

While she was taking up my black silk on the shoulder seams, Phoebe Dole said, 'Let me see – you had a green silk made at Digby three summers ago, didn't you?'

'Yes,' I said.

'Well,' said she, 'why don't you have it dyed black? Those

thin silks dye quite nice. It would make you a good dress.'

I scarcely replied, and then she offered to dye it for me herself. She had a recipe which she used with great success. I thought it was very kind of her, but did not say whether I would accept her offer or not. I could not fix my mind upon anything but the awful trouble I was in.

'I'll come over and get it tomorrow morning,' said Phoebe.

I thanked her. I thought of the stains, and then my mind seemed to wander again to the one subject. All the time Maria Woods sat weeping. Finally Phoebe turned to her with impatience.

'If you can't keep calmer, you'd better go upstairs, Maria,' said she. 'You'll make Sarah sick. Look at her! She doesn't give way – and think of the reason she's got.'

'I've got reason, too,' Maria broke out; then, with a piteous shriek, 'Oh, I've got reason.'

'Maria Woods, go out of the room!' said Phoebe. Her sharpness made me jump, half dazed as I was.

Maria got up without a word, and went out of the room, bending almost double with convulsive sobs.

'She's been dreadfully worked up over your father's death,' said Phoebe calmly, going on with the fitting. 'She's terribly nervous. Sometimes I have to be real sharp with her, for her own good.'

I nodded. Maria Woods has always been considered a sweet, weakly, dependent woman, and Phoebe Dole is undoubtedly very fond of her. She has seemed to shield her, and take care of her nearly all her life. The two have lived together since they were young girls.

Phoebe is tall, and very pale and thin; but she never had a day's illness. She is plain, yet there is a kind of severe goodness and faithfulness about her colourless face, with the smooth bands of white hair over her ears.

I went home as soon as my dress was fitted. That evening Henry Ellis came over to see me. I do not need to go into details concerning that visit. It seemed enough to say that he tendered the fullest sympathy and protection, and I accepted them. I cried a little, for the first time, and he soothed and comforted me.

Henry had driven over from Digby and tied his horse in the yard. At ten o'clock he bade me goodnight on the doorstep, and was just turning his buggy around, when Mrs Adams came running to the door.

'Is this yours?' said she, and she held out a knot of yellow ribbon.

'Why, that's the ribbon you have around your whip, Henry,' said I.

He looked at it.

'So it is,' he said. 'I must have dropped it.' He put it into his pocket and drove away.

'He didn't drop that ribbon tonight!' said Mrs Adams. 'I found it Wednesday morning out in the yard. I thought I remembered seeing him have a yellow ribbon on his whip.'

* * * * * *

When Mrs Adams told me she had picked up Henry's whip-ribbon Wednesday morning, I said nothing, but thought that Henry must have driven over Tuesday evening after all, and even come up into the yard, although the house was shut up, and I in bed, to get a little nearer to me. I felt conscience-stricken, because I could not help a thrill of happiness, when my father lay dead in the house.

My father was buried as privately and as quietly as we could bring it about. But it was a terrible ordeal. Meantime word came from Vermont that Rufus Bennett had been arrested on his farm. He was perfectly willing to come back with the officers, and indeed, had not the slightest trouble in proving that he was at his home in Vermont when the murder took place. He proved by several witnesses that he was out of the state long before my father and I sat on the steps together that evening, and that he proceeded directly to his home as fast as the train and stagecoach could carry him.

The screwdriver with which the deed was supposed to have been committed was found, by the neighbour from whom it had been borrowed, in his wife's bureau drawer. It had been returned, and she had used it to put a picture-hook in her chamber. Bennett was discharged and returned to Vermont.

Then Mrs Adams told of the finding of the yellow ribbon from Henry Ellis's whip, and he was arrested, since he was held to have a motive for putting my father out of the world. Father's opposition to our marriage was well known, and Henry was suspected also of having had an eye to his money. It was found, indeed, that my father had more money than I had known myself.

Henry owned to having driven into the yard that night, and to having missed the ribbon from his whip on his return; but one of the hostlers in the livery stables in Digby, where he kept his horse and buggy, came forward and testified to finding the yellow ribbon in the carriage-room that Tuesday night before Henry returned from his drive. There were two yellow ribbons in evidence, therefore, and the one produced by the hostler seemed to fit Henry's whip-stock the more exactly.

Moreover, nearly the exact minute of the murder was claimed to be proved by the post-mortem examination; and by the testimony of the stableman as to the hour of Henry's return and the speed of his horse, he was further cleared of suspicion; for, if the opinion of the medical experts was correct, Henry must have returned to the livery stable too soon to have committed the murder.

He was discharged, at any rate, although suspicion still clung to him. Many people believe now in his guilt – those who do not, believe in mine; and some believe we were accomplices.

After Henry's discharge, I was arrested. There was no one else left to accuse. There must be a motive for the murder; I was the only person left with a motive. Unlike the others, who were discharged after preliminary examination, I was held to the grand jury and taken to Dedham, where I spent four weeks in jail, awaiting the meeting of the grand jury.

Neither at the preliminary examination, nor before the grand jury, was I allowed to make the full and frank statement that I am making here. I was told simply to answer the questions that were put to me, and to volunteer nothing, and I obeyed.

I know nothing about law. I wished to do the best I could – to act in the wisest manner, for Henry's sake and my own. I said nothing about the green silk dress. They searched the house for all manner of things, at the time of my arrest, but the dress was not there – it was in Phoebe Dole's dye-kettle. She had come over after it one day when I was picking beans in the garden, and had taken it out of the closet. She brought it back herself, and told me this, after I had returned from Dedham.

'I thought I'd get it and surprise you,' said she. 'It's taken a beautiful black.'

She gave me a strange look – half as if she would see into my very soul, in spite of me, half as if she were in terror of what she would see there, as she spoke. I do not know just what Phoebe Dole's look meant. There may have been a stain left on that dress after all, and she may have seen it.

I suppose if it had not been for that flour-paste which I had learned to make, I should have hung for the murder of my father. As it was, the grand jury found no bill against me because there was absolutely no evidence to convict me; and I came home a free woman. And if people were condemned for their motives, would there be enough hangmen in the world?

They found no weapon with which I could have done the deed. They found no bloodstains on my clothes. The one thing which told against me, aside from my ever-present motive, was the fact that on the morning after the murder the doors and windows were fastened. My volunteering this information had of course weakened its force as against myself.

Then, too, some held that I might have been mistaken in my terror and excitement, and there was a theory, advanced by a few, that the murderer had meditated making me also a victim, and had locked the doors that he might not be frustrated in his designs, but had lost heart at the last, and had allowed me to escape, and then fled himself. Some held that he had intended

129

to force me to reveal the whereabouts of father's money, but his courage had failed him.

Father had quite a sum in a hiding-place which only he and I knew. But no search for money had been made, as far as anyone could see – not a bureau drawer had been disturbed, and father's gold watch was ticking peacefully under his pillow; even his wallet in his vest pocket had not been opened. There was a small roll of banknotes in it, and some change; father never carried much money. I suppose if father's wallet and watch had been taken, I should not have been suspected at all.

I was discharged, as I have said, from lack of evidence, and have returned to my home – free, indeed, but with this awful burden of suspicion on my shoulders. That brings me up to the present day. I returned yesterday evening. This evening Henry Ellis has been over to see me; he will not come again, for I have forbidden him to do so. This is what I said to him:

'I know you are innocent, you know I am innocent. To all the world beside we are under suspicion – I more than you, but we are both under suspicion. If we are known to be together that suspicion is increased for both of us. I do not care for myself, but I do care for you. Separated from me the stigma attached to you will soon fade away, especially if you should marry elsewhere.'

Then Henry interrupted me.

'I will never marry elsewhere,' said he.

I could not help being glad that he said it, but I was firm.

'If you should see some good woman whom you could love, it will be better for you to marry elsewhere,' said I.

'I never will!' he said again. He put his arms around me, but I had strength to push him away.

'You never need, if I succeed in what I undertake before you meet the other,' said I. I began to think he had not cared for that pretty girl who boarded in the same house after all.

'What is that?' he said. 'What are you going to undertake?'

'To find my father's murderer,' said I.

Henry gave me a strange look; then, before I could stop him, he took me fast in his arms and kissed my forehead.

'As God is my witness, Sarah, I believe in your innocence,' he said; and from that minute I have felt sustained and fully confident of my power to do what I had undertaken.

My father's murderer I will find. Tomorrow I begin my search. I shall first make an exhaustive examination of the house, such as no officer in the case has yet made, in the hope of finding a clue. Every room I propose to divide into square yards, by line and measure, and every one of these square yards I will study as if it were a problem in algebra.

I have a theory that it is impossible for any human being to enter any house, and commit in it a deed of this kind, and not leave behind traces which are the known quantities in an algebraic equation to those who can use them.

There is a chance that I shall not be quite unaided. Henry has promised not to come again until I bid him, but he is to send a detective here from Boston – one whom he knows. In fact, the man is a cousin of his, or else there would be small hope of our securing him, even if I were to offer him a large price.

The man has been remarkably successful in several cases, but his health is not good; the work is a severe strain upon his nerves, and he is not driven to it from any lack of money. The physicians have forbidden him to undertake any new case, for a year at least, but Henry is confident that we may rely upon him for this.

I will now lay aside this and go to bed. Tomorrow is Wednesday; my father will have been dead seven weeks. Tomorrow morning I will commence the work, in which, if it be in human power, aided by a higher wisdom, I shall succeed.

* * * * * *

(*The pages which follow are from Miss Fairbanks's journal, begun after the conclusion of the notes already given to the reader.*)

Wednesday night. – I have resolved to record carefully each day the progress I make in my examination of the house. I began today at the bottom – that is, with the room least likely to contain any clue, the parlour. I took a chalk-line and a yard-stick, and divided the floor into square yards, and every one of these squares I examined on my hands and knees. I found in this way literally nothing on the carpet but dust, lint, two common white pins, and three inches of blue sewing-silk.

At last I got the dustpan and brush, and yard by yard swept the floor. I took the sweepings in a white pasteboard box out into the yard in the strong sunlight, and examined them. There was nothing but dust and lint and five inches of brown woollen thread – evidently a ravelling of some dress material. The blue silk and the brown thread are the only possible clues which I found today, and they are hardly possible. Rufus's wife can probably account for them.

Nobody has come to the house all day. I went down to the store this afternoon to get some necessary provisions, and people stopped talking when I came in. The clerk took my money as if it were poison.

Thursday night. – Today I have searched the sitting-room, out of which my father's bedroom opens. I found two bloody footprints on the carpet which no one had noticed before – perhaps because the carpet itself is red and white. I used a microscope which I had in my school work. The footprints, which are close to the bedroom door, pointing out into the sitting-room, are both from the right foot; one is brighter than the other, but both are faint. The foot was evidently either bare or clad only in a stocking – the prints are so widely spread. They are wider than my father's shoes. I tried one in the brightest print.

I found nothing else new in the sitting-room. The bloodstains on the doors which have been already noted are still there. They had not been washed away, first by order of the sheriff, and next by mine. These stains are of two kinds; one looks as if made by a bloody garment brushing against it; the other, I should say, was made in the first place by the grasp of a bloody hand, and then brushed over with a cloth. There are none of these marks upon the door leading to the bedroom – they are on the doors leading into the front entry and the china closet. The china closet is really a pantry, although I use it only for my best dishes and preserves.

Friday night. – Today I searched the closet. One of the shelves, which is about as high as my shoulders, was bloodstained. It looked to me as if the murderer might have caught hold of it to steady himself. Did he turn faint after his dreadful deed? Some tumblers of jelly were ranged on that shelf and they had not been disturbed. There was only that bloody clutch on the edge.

I found on this closet floor, under the shelves, as if it had been rolled there by a careless foot, a button, evidently from a man's clothing. It is an ordinary black enamelled metal trousers-button; it had evidently been worn off and clumsily sewn on again, for a quantity of stout white thread is still clinging to it. This button must have belonged either to a single man or to one with an idle wife.

If one black button had been sewn on with white thread, another is likely to be. I may be wrong, but I regard this button as a clue.

The pantry was thoroughly swept – cleaned, indeed, by Rufus's wife, the day before she left. Neither my father nor Rufus could have dropped it there, and they never had occasion to go to that closet. The murderer dropped the button.

I have a white pasteboard box which I have marked 'clues'. In it I have put the button.

This afternoon Phoebe Dole came in. She is very kind. She had re-cut the dyed silk, and she fitted it to me. Her great shears clicking in my ears made me nervous. I did not feel like stopping to think about clothes. I hope I did not appear ungrateful, for she is the only soul beside Henry who has treated me as she did before this happened.

Phoebe asked me what I found to busy myself about, and I replied, 'I am searching for my father's murderer'. She asked me if I thought I should find a clue, and I replied, 'I think so'. I had found the button then, but I did not speak of it. She said Maria was not very well.

I saw her eyeing the stains on the doors, and I said I had not washed them off, for I thought they might yet serve a purpose in detecting the murderer. She looked closely at those on the entry-door – the brightest ones – and said she did not see how they could help, for there were no plain fingermarks there, and she should think they would make me nervous.

'I'm beyond being nervous,' I replied.

Saturday. – Today I have found something which I cannot understand. I have been at work in the room where my father came to his dreadful end. Of course some of the most startling evidences have been removed. The bed is clean, and the carpet washed, but the worst horror of it all clings to that room. The spirit of murder seemed to haunt it. It seemed to me at first that I could not enter that room, but in it I made a strange discovery.

My father, while he carried little money about his person, was in the habit of keeping considerable sums in the house; there is no bank within ten miles. However, he was wary; he had a hiding-place which he had revealed to no one but myself. He had a small stand in his room near the end of his bed. Under this stand, or rather under the top of it, he had tacked a large leather wallet. In this he kept all his spare money. I remember how his eyes twinkled when he showed it to me.

'The average mind thinks things have either got to be in or on,' said my father. 'They don't consider there's ways of getting around gravitation and calculation.'

In searching my father's room I called to mind that saying of his, and his peculiar system of concealment, and then I made my discovery. I have argued that in a search of this kind I ought not only to search for hidden traces of the criminal, but for everything which had been for any reason concealed. Something which my father himself had hidden, something from his past history, may furnish a motive for someone else.

The money in the wallet under the table, some five hundred dollars, had been removed and deposited in the bank. Nothing more was to be found there. I examined the bottom of the bureau, and the undersides of the chair seats. There are two chairs in the room, besides the cushioned rocker – green-painted wooden chairs, with flag seats. I found nothing under the seats.

Then I turned each of the green chairs completely over, and examined the bottoms of the legs. My heart leaped when I found a bit of leather tacked over one. I got the tack-hammer and drew the tacks. The chair leg had been hollowed out, and for an inch the hole was packed tight with cotton. I began picking out the cotton, and soon I felt something hard. It proved to be an old-fashioned gold band, quite wide and heavy, like a wedding ring.

I took it over to the window and found this inscription on the inside: 'Let love abide for ever'. There were two dates – one in August, forty years ago, and the other in August of the present year.

I think the ring had never been worn; while the first part of the inscription is perfectly clear, it looks old, and the last is evidently freshly cut.

This could not have been my mother's ring. She had only her wedding ring, and that was buried with her. I think my father must have treasured up this ring for years; but why? What does it mean? This can hardly be a clue; this can hardly lead to the discovery of a motive, but I will put it in the box with the rest.

Sunday night. – Today, of course, I did not pursue my search. I did not go to church. I could not face old friends that could not face me. Sometimes I think that everybody in my native village believes in my guilt. What must I have been in my general appearance and demeanour all my life? I have studied myself in the glass, and tried to discover the possibilities of evil that they must see in my face.

This afternoon about three o'clock, the hour when people here have just finished their Sunday dinner, there was a knock on the north door. I answered it, and a strange young man stood there with a large book under his arm. He was thin and cleanly shaved, with a clerical air.

'I have a work here to which I would like to call your attention,' he began; and I stared at him in astonishment, for why should a book agent be peddling his wares upon the Sabbath?

His mouth twitched a little.

'It's a Biblical Cyclopædia,' said he.

'I don't think I care to take it,' said I.

'You are Miss Sarah Fairbanks, I believe?'

'That is my name,' I replied stiffly.

'Mr Henry Ellis, of Digby, sent me here,' he said next. 'My name is Dix – Francis Dix.'

Then I knew it was Henry's first cousin from Boston – the detective who had come to help me. I felt the tears coming to my eyes.

'You are very kind to come,' I managed to say.

'I am selfish, not kind,' he returned, 'but you had better let me come in, or any chance of success in my book agency is lost, if the neighbours see me trying to sell it on a Sunday. And, Miss Fairbanks, this is a *bona fide* agency. I shall canvass the town.'

He came in. I showed him all that I have written, and he read it carefully. When he had finished he sat still for a long time, with his face screwed up in a peculiar meditative fashion.

'We'll ferret this out in three days at the most,' said he finally, with a sudden clearing of his face and a flash of his eyes at me.

'I had planned for three years, perhaps,' said I.

'I tell you, we'll do it in three days,' he repeated. 'Where can I get board while I canvass for this remarkable and interesting book under my arm? I can't stay here, of course, and there is no hotel. Do you think the two dressmakers next door, Phoebe Dole and the other one, would take me in?'

I said they had never taken boarders.

'Well, I'll go over and enquire,' said Mr Dix; and he had gone, with his book under his arm, almost before I knew it.

Never have I seen anyone act with the strange noiseless soft speed that this man does. Can he prove me innocent in three days? He must have succeeded in getting board at Phoebe Dole's, for I saw him go past to meeting with her this evening. I feel sure he will be over very early tomorrow morning.

* * * * * *

Monday night. – The detective came as I expected. I was up as soon as it was light, and he came across the dewy fields, with his Cyclopædia under his arm. He had stolen out from Phoebe Dole's back door.

He had me bring my father's pistol; then he bade me come with him out into the backyard. 'Now, fire it,' he said, thrusting the pistol into my hands. As I have said before, the charge was still in the barrel.

'I shall arouse the neighbourhood,' I said.

'Fire it,' he ordered.

I tried; I pulled the trigger as hard as I could.

'I can't do it,' I said.

'And you are a reasonably strong woman, too, aren't you?'

I said I had been considered so. Oh, how much I heard about the strength of my poor woman's arms, and their ability to strike that murderous weapon home!

Mr Dix took the pistol himself, and drew a little at the trigger.

'I could do it,' he said, 'but I won't. It would arouse the neighbourhood.'

'This is more evidence against me,' I said despairingly. 'The murderer had tried to fire the pistol and failed.'

'It is more evidence against the murderer,' said Mr Dix.

We went into the house, where he examined my box of clues long and carefully. Looking at the ring, he asked whether there was a jeweller in this village, and I said there was not. I told him that my father oftener went on business to Acton, ten miles away, than elsewhere.

He examined very carefully the button which I had found in the closet, and then asked to see my father's wardrobe. That was soon done. Beside the suit in which father was laid away there was one other complete one in the closet in his room. Besides that, there were in this closet two overcoats, an old black frock coat, a pair of pepper-and-salt trousers, and two black vests. Mr Dix examined all the buttons; not one was missing.

There was still another old suit in the closet off the kitchen. This was examined, and no button found wanting.

'What did your father do for work the day before he died?' he then asked.

I reflected and said that he had unpacked some stores which had come down from Vermont, and done some work out in the garden.

'What did he wear?'

'I think he wore the pepper-and-salt trousers and the black vest. He wore no coat, while at work.'

Mr Dix went quietly back to father's room and his closet, I following. He took out the grey trousers and the black vest, and examined them closely.

'What did he wear to protect these?' he asked.

'Why, he wore overalls!' I said at once. As I spoke I remembered seeing father go around the path to the yard, with those blue overalls drawn up high under his arms.

'Where are they?'

'Weren't they in the kitchen closet?'

'No.'

We looked again, however, in the kitchen closet; we searched the shed thoroughly. The cat came in through her little door, as we stood there, and brushed around our feet. Mr Dix stooped and stroked her. Then he went quickly to the door, beside which her little entrance was arranged, unhooked it, and stepped out. I was following him, but he motioned me back.

'None of my boarding mistress's windows commands us,' he said, 'but she might come to the back door.'

I watched him. He passed slowly around the little winding footpath, which skirted the rear of our house and extended faintly through the grassy fields to the rear of Phoebe Dole's. He stopped, searched a clump of sweetbriar, went on to an old well, and stopped there. The well had been dry many a year, and was choked up with stones and rubbish. Some boards are laid over it, and a big stone or two, to keep them in place.

Mr Dix, glancing across at Phoebe Dole's back door, went down on his knees, rolled the stones away, then removed the boards and peered down the well. He stretched far over the brink, and reached down. He made many efforts; then he got up and came to me, and asked me to get for him an umbrella with a crooked handle, or something that he could hook into clothing.

I brought my own umbrella, the silver handle of which formed an exact hook. He went back to the well, knelt again, thrust in the umbrella and drew up, easily enough, what he had been fishing for. Then he came bringing it to me.

'Don't faint,' he said, and took hold of my arm. I gasped when I saw what he had – my father's blue overalls, all stained and splotched with blood!

I looked at them, then at him.

'Don't faint,' he said again. 'We're on the right track. This is where the button came from – see, see!' He pointed to one of the straps of the overalls, and the button was gone. Some white thread clung to it. Another black metal button was sewed on roughly with the same white thread that I found on the button in my box of clues.

'What does it mean?' I gasped out. My brain reeled.

'You shall know soon,' he said. He looked at his watch. Then he laid down the ghastly bundle he carried. 'It has puzzled you to know how the murderer went in and out and yet kept the doors locked, has it not?' he said.

'Yes.'

'Well, I am going out now. Hook that door after me.'

He went out, still carrying my umbrella. I hooked the door. Presently I saw the lid of the cat's door lifted, and his hand and arm thrust through. He curved his arm up towards the hook, but it came short by half a foot. Then he withdrew his arm, and thrust in my silver-handled umbrella. He reached the door-hook easily enough with that.

Then he hooked it again. That was not so easy. He had to work a long time. Finally he accomplished it, unhooked the door again, and came in.

'That was how!' I said.

'No, it was not,' he returned. 'No human being, fresh from such a deed, could have used such patience as that to fasten the door after him. Please hang your arm down by your side.'

I obeyed. He looked at my arm, then at his own.

'Have you a tape measure?' he asked.

I brought one out of my work-basket. He measured his arm, then mine, and then the distance from the cat-door to the hook.

'I have two tasks for you today and tomorrow,' he said. 'I shall come here very little. Find all your father's old letters, and read them. Find a man or woman in this town whose arm is six inches longer than yours. Now I must go home, or my boarding mistress will get curious.'

He went through the house to the front door, looked all ways to be sure no eyes were upon him, made three strides down the yard, and was pacing soberly up the street, with his Cyclopædia under his arm.

I made myself a cup of coffee, then I went about obeying his instructions. I read old letters all the forenoon; I found packages in trunks in the garret; there were quantities in father's desk. I have selected several to submit to Mr Dix. One of them treats of an old episode in father's youth, which must have years since ceased to interest him. It was concealed after his favourite fashion – tacked under the bottom of his desk. It was written forty years ago, by Maria Woods, two years before my father's marriage – and it was a refusal of an offer of his hand. It was written in the stilted fashion of that day; it might have been copied from a 'Complete Letter-writer'.

My father must have loved Maria Woods as dearly as I love Henry, to keep that letter so carefully all these years. I thought he cared for my mother. He seemed as fond of her as other men of their wives, although I did use to wonder if Henry and I would ever get to be quite so much accustomed to each other.

Maria Woods must have been as beautiful as an angel when she was a girl. Mother was not pretty; she was stout, too, and awkward, and I suppose people would have called her rather slow and dull. But she was a good woman, and tried to do her duty.

Tuesday night. – This evening was my first opportunity to obey the second of Mr Dix's orders. It seemed to me the best way to compare the average length of arms was to go to the prayer-meeting. I could not go about the town with my tape measure, and demand of people that they should hold out their arms. Nobody knows how I dreaded to go to the meeting, but I went, and I looked not at my neighbours' cold altered faces, but at their arms.

I discovered what Mr Dix wished me to, but the discovery can avail nothing, and it is one he could have made himself. Phoebe Dole's arm is fully seven inches longer than mine. I never noticed it before, but she has an almost abnormally long arm. But why should Phoebe Dole have unhooked that door?

She made a prayer – a beautiful prayer. It comforted even me a little. She spoke of the tenderness of God in all the troubles of life, and how it never failed us.

When we were all going out I heard several persons speak of Mr Dix and his Biblical Cyclopædia. They decided that he was a theological student, book-canvassing to defray the expenses of his education.

Maria Woods was not at the meeting. Several asked Phoebe how she was, and she replied, 'Not very well'.

It is very late. I thought Mr Dix might be over tonight, but he has not been here.

Wednesday. – I can scarcely believe what I am about to write. Our investigations seem to point all to one person, and that person – It is incredible! I will not believe it.

Mr Dix came as before, at dawn. He reported, and I reported. I showed Maria Woods's letter. He said he had driven to Acton, and found that the jeweller there had engraved the last date in the ring about six weeks ago.

'I don't want to seem rough, but your father was going to get married again,' said Mr Dix.

'I never knew him to go near any woman since mother died,' I protested.

'Nevertheless, he had made arrangements to be married,' persisted Mr Dix.

'Who was the woman?'

He pointed at the letter in my hand.

'Maria Woods!'

He nodded.

I stood looking at him – dazed. Such a possibility had never entered my head.

He produced an envelope from his pocket, and took out a little card with blue and brown threads neatly wound upon it.

'Let me see those threads you found,' he said.

I got the box and we compared them. He had a number of pieces of blue sewing-silk and brown woollen ravellings, and they matched mine exactly.

'Where did you find them?' I asked.

'In my boarding mistress's piece-bag.'

I stared at him.

'What does it mean?' I gasped out.

'What do you think?'

'It is impossible!'

★ ★ ★ ★ ★ ★

Wednesday, continued. – When Mr Dix thus suggested to me the absurd possibility that Phoebe Dole had committed the murder, he and I were sitting in the kitchen. He was near the table; he laid a sheet of paper upon it, and began to write. The paper is before me.

'First,' said Mr Dix, and he wrote rapidly as he talked, 'Whose arm is of such length that it might unlock a certain door of this house from the outside? – Phoebe Dole's.

'Second, who had in her piece-bag bits of the same threads and ravellings found upon your parlour floor, where she had not by your knowledge entered? – Phoebe Dole.

'Third, who interested herself most strangely in your bloodstained green silk dress, even to dyeing it? – Phoebe Dole.

'Fourth, who was caught in a lie, while trying to force the guilt of the murder upon an innocent man? – Phoebe Dole.'

Mr Dix looked at me. I had gathered myself together. 'That

proves nothing,' I said. 'There is no motive in her case.'

'There is a motive.'

'What is it?'

'Maria Woods shall tell you this afternoon.'

He then wrote:

'Fifth, who was seen to throw a bundle down the old well, in the rear of Martin Fairbanks's house, at one o'clock in the morning? – Phoebe Dole.'

'Was she – seen?' I gasped.

Mr Dix nodded. Then he wrote.

'Sixth, who had a strong motive, which had been in existence many years ago? – Phoebe Dole.'

Mr Dix laid down his pen, and looked at me again.

'Well, what have you to say?' he asked.

'It is impossible!'

'Why?'

'She is a woman.'

'A man could have fired that pistol, as she tried to do.'

'It would have taken a man's strength to kill with the kind of weapon that was used,' I said.

'No, it would not. No great strength is required for such a blow.'

'But she is a woman!'

'Crime has no sex.'

'But she is a good woman – a church member. I heard her pray yesterday afternoon. It is not in character.'

'It is not for you, nor for me, nor for any mortal intelligence, to know what is or is not in character,' said Mr Dix.

He arose and went away. I could only stare at him in a half-dazed manner.

Maria Woods came this afternoon, taking advantage of Phoebe's absence on a dressmaking errand. Maria has aged ten years in the last few weeks. Her hair is white, her cheeks are fallen in, her pretty colour is gone.

'May I have the ring he gave me forty years ago?' she faltered.

I gave it to her; she kissed it and sobbed like a child. 'Phoebe took it away from me before,' she said, 'but she shan't this time.'

Maria related with piteous sobs the story of her long subordination to Phoebe Dole. This sweet child-like woman had always been completely under the sway of the other's stronger nature. The subordination went back beyond my father's original proposal to her; she had, before he made love to her as a girl, promised Phoebe she would not marry; and it was Phoebe who, by representing to her that she was bound by this solemn promise, had led her to write a letter to my father declining his offer, and sending back the ring.

'And after all, we were going to get married, if he had not died,' she said. 'He was going to give me this ring again, and he had had the other date put in. I should have been so happy!'

She stopped and stared at me with horror-stricken enquiry.

'What was Phoebe Dole doing in your backyard at one o'clock that night?' she cried.

'What do you mean?' I returned.

'I saw Phoebe come out of your back shed door at one o'clock that very night. She had a bundle in her arms. She went along the path about as far as the old well, then she stooped down, and seemed to be working at something. When she got up she didn't have the bundle. I was watching at our back door. I thought I heard her go out a little while before, and went downstairs, and found that door unlocked. I went in quick, and up to my chamber, and into my bed, when she started home across the fields. Pretty soon I heard her come in, then I heard the pump going. She slept downstairs; she went on to her bedroom. What was she doing in your backyard that night?'

'You must ask her,' said I. I felt my blood running cold.

'I've been afraid to,' moaned Maria Woods. 'She's been dreadful strange lately. I wish that book agent was going to stay at our house.'

Maria Woods went home in about an hour. I got a ribbon for her, and she has my poor father's ring concealed in her withered bosom. Again, I cannot believe this.

Thursday. – It is all over, Phoebe Dole has confessed! I do

not know now in exactly what way Mr Dix brought it about
– how he accused her of her crime. After breakfast I saw them
coming across the fields; Phoebe came first, advancing with rapid
strides like a man, Mr Dix followed, and my father's poor old
sweetheart tottered behind, with her handkerchief at her eyes.
Just as I noticed them the front doorbell rang; I found several
people there, headed by the high sheriff. They crowded into the
sitting-room just as Phoebe Dole came rushing in, with Mr Dix
and Maria Woods.

'I did it!' Phoebe cried out to me. 'I am found out, and I have
made up my mind to confess. She was going to marry your father
– I found it out. I stopped it once before. This time I knew I
couldn't unless I killed him. She's lived with me in that house
for over forty years. There are other ties as strong as the marriage
one, that are just as sacred. What right had he to take her away
from me and break up my home?

'I overheard your father and Rufus Bennett having words. I
thought folks would think he did it. I reasoned it all out. I had
watched your cat go in that little door, I knew the shed door
hooked, I knew how long my arm was; I thought I could undo
it. I stole over here a little after midnight. I went all around the
house to be sure nobody was awake. Out in the front yard I
happened to think my shears were tied on my belt with a ribbon,
and I untied them. I thought I put the ribbon in my pocket – it
was a piece of yellow ribbon – but I suppose I didn't, because they
found it afterwards, and thought it came off your young man's
whip.

'I went round to the shed door, unhooked it, and went in.
The moon was light enough. I got out your father's overalls from
the kitchen closet; I knew where they were. I went through the
sitting-room to the parlour.

'In there I slipped off my dress and skirts and put on the
overalls. I put a handkerchief over my face, leaving only my eyes
exposed. I crept out then into the sitting-room; there I pulled off
my shoes and went into the bedroom.

'Your father was fast asleep; it was such a hot night, the clothes were thrown back and his chest was bare. The first thing I saw was that pistol on the stand beside his bed. I suppose he had had some fear of Rufus Bennett coming back, after all. Suddenly I thought I'd better shoot him. It would be surer and quicker; and if you were aroused I knew that I could get away, and everybody would suppose that he had shot himself.

'I took up the pistol and held it close to his head. I had never fired a pistol, but I knew how it was done. I pulled, but it would not go off. Your father stirred a little – I was mad with horror – I struck at his head with the pistol. He opened his eyes and cried out; then I dropped the pistol, and took these' – Phoebe Dole pointed to the great shining shears hanging at her waist – 'for I am strong in my wrists. I only struck twice, over his heart.

'Then I went back into the sitting-room. I thought I heard a noise in the kitchen – I was full of terror then – and slipped into the sitting-room closet. I felt as if I were fainting, and clutched the shelf to keep from falling.

'I felt that I must go upstairs to see if you were asleep, to be sure you had not waked up when your father cried out. I thought if you had I should have to do the same by you. I crept upstairs to your chamber. You seemed sound asleep, but, as I watched, you stirred a little; but instead of striking at you I slipped into your closet. I heard nothing more from you. I felt myself wet with blood. I caught something hanging in your closet, and wiped myself over with it. I knew by the feeling it was your green silk. You kept quiet, and I saw you were asleep, so crept out of the closet, and down the stairs, got my clothes and shoes, and, out in the shed, took off the overalls and dressed myself. I rolled up the overalls, and took a board away from the old well and threw them in as I went home. I thought if they were found it would be no clue to me. The handkerchief, which was not much stained, I put to soak that night, and washed it out next morning, before Maria was up. I washed my hands and arms carefully that night, and also my shears.

'I expected Rufus Bennett would be accused of the murder, and, maybe, hung. I was prepared for that, but I did not like to think I had thrown suspicion upon you by staining your dress. I had nothing against you. I made up my mind I'd get hold of that dress – before anybody suspected you – and dye it black. I came in and got it, as you know. I was astonished not to see any more stains on it. I only found two or three little streaks that scarcely anybody would have noticed. I didn't know what to think. I suspected, of course, that you had found the stains and got them off, thinking they might bring suspicion upon you.

'I did not see how you could possibly suspect me in any case. I was glad when your young man was cleared. I had nothing against him. That is all I have to say.'

I think I must have fainted away then. I cannot describe the dreadful calmness with which that woman told this – that woman with the good face, whom I had last heard praying like a saint in meeting. I believe in demoniacal possession after this.

When I came to, the neighbours were around me, putting camphor on my head, and saying soothing things to me, and the old friendly faces had returned. But I wish I could forget!

They have taken Phoebe Dole away – I only know that. I cannot bear to talk any more about it when I think there must be a trial, and I must go!

Henry has been over this evening. I suppose we shall be happy after all, when I have had a little time to get over this. He says I have nothing more to worry about. Mr Dix has gone home. I hope Henry and I may be able to repay his kindness some day.

★ ★ ★ ★ ★ ★

A month later. I have just heard that Phoebe Dole has died in prison. This is my last entry. May God help all other innocent women in hard straights as He has helped me!

HAGAR THE GYPSY

Created by Fergus Hume
(1859–1932)

Fergus Hume was the author of the most popular crime novel of the Victorian era. The Mystery of a Hansom Cab, *was set in Melbourne, Australia, where it was first published (by Hume himself) in 1886. The following year it was published in London and became a huge success, far outselling* A Study in Scarlet, *Conan Doyle's first Sherlock Holmes novel, which also appeared in 1887. Sadly for him, Hume had sold the English rights in his novel for a mere £50. After moving to England from Australia, he continued to write fiction for the rest of his life, publishing more than 120 novels and volumes of short stories over the next forty-five years, although none of them achieved anything like the sales of his debut. One of these books was the 1898 collection* Hagar of the Pawn-Shop. *Hagar is a Romany woman who inherits a Lambeth pawn-shop and is drawn into the lives of her customers. She finds that many of them need her problem-solving talents to right wrongs done to them or throw light on mysterious crimes. Lively and resourceful, Hagar is one of the most interesting female detectives of the era. In 1898, and for many decades to come, it was very unusual for a Romany or Gypsy character to appear in popular fiction as anything other than either a vagabond of doubtful morals or a downright villain. By contrast, Hagar is not only attractive and quick-witted, she also possesses a strict sense of duty and a determination to act honestly at all times. The tales in which she appears are some of the most distinctive crime stories of the 1890s.*

THE FIFTH CUSTOMER AND THE COPPER KEY

The several adventures in which she had been engaged begot in Hagar a thirst for the romantic. To find that strange stories were attached to many pawned articles; to ascertain such histories of the past; to follow up their conclusions in the future – these things greatly pleased the girl, and gave her an interest in a somewhat dull life. She began to perceive that there was more romance in modern times than latter-day sceptics are willing to admit. Tropical scenery, ancient inns, ruined castles, are not necessary to engender romance. It is of the human heart, of human life; and even in the dingy Lambeth pawn-shop it blossomed and bloomed like some rare flower thrusting itself upward betwixt the arid city stones. Romance came daily to the gipsy girl, even in her prosaic business existence.

Out of a giant tooth, an unburied bone, a mighty footprint, Cuvier could construct a marvellous and prehistoric world. In like manner, from some trifle upon which she lent money, Hagar would deduce tales as fantastic as the Arabian Nights, as adventurous as the story of Gil Blas. Of such sort was the romance brought about by the pawning of the copper key.

The man who pawned it was in appearance like some Eastern mage; and the key itself, with its curious workmanship, green with verdigris, might have served to unlock the tower of Don Roderick. Its owner entered the shop one morning shortly before noon, and at the sight of his wrinkled face, and the venerable white beard which swept his breast, Hagar felt that he was a customer out of the common. With a gruff salutation, he threw down a paper parcel, which clanged on the counter.

'Look at that,' said he, sharply. 'I wish to pawn it.'

In no wise disturbed by his discourtesy, Hagar opened the package, and found therein a roll of linen; this, when unwound, revealed a slender copper key of no great size. The wards at the lower end were nearly level with the stem of the key itself, as they consisted merely of five or six prickles of copper encircling at irregular intervals the round stem. The handle, however, was ornate and curious, being shaped like a bishop's crozier, while within the crook of the pastoral staff design the letters 'CR' were interwoven in an elaborate monogram. Altogether, this key – apparently very ancient – was a beautiful piece of workmanship, but of no value save to a dealer in rarities. Hagar examined it carefully, shook her head, and tossed it on the counter.

'I wouldn't give you five shillings on it,' said she, contemptuously; 'it is worth nothing.'

'Bah, girl! You do not know what you are talking about. Look at the workmanship.'

'Very fine, no doubt; but –'

'And the monogram, you blind bat!' interrupted the old man. '"CR" – that stands for Carolus Rex.'

'Oh,' said Hagar, picking up the key again, and taking it to the light of the window; 'it is an historic key, then?'

'Yes. It is said to be the key of the box in which the First Charles kept the treasonous papers which ultimately cost him his head. Oh, you may look! The key is authentic enough. It has been in the Danetree family for close on two hundred and fifty years.'

'And are you a Danetree?'

'No; I am Luke Parsons, the steward of the family.'

'Indeed!' said Hagar, with a piercing glance. 'Then how comes the key into your possession?'

'I don't recognise your right to ask such questions,' said Parsons, in an angry tone. 'The key came into my possession honestly.'

'Very probably; but I should like to know how. Do not get in a rage, Mr Parsons,' added Hagar, hastily; 'we pawnbrokers have to be very particular, you know.'

'I don't know,' snapped the customer; 'but if your curiosity must be satisfied, the key came to me from my father Mark, a former steward of the Danetrees. It was given to him by the then head of the family some sixty years ago.'

'What are all these figures graven on the stem?' asked Hagar, noting a number of hieroglyphic marks.

'Ordinary Arabic numerals,' retorted Parsons. 'What they mean I know no more than you do. If I did I should be rich,' he added, to himself.

'Ah! there is some secret connected with these figures?' said Hagar, overhearing.

'If there is, you won't find it out,' replied the old man, ungraciously; 'and it is none of your business, anyhow! What you have to do is to lend money on the key.'

Hagar hesitated. The article, notwithstanding its workmanship, its age, and its historical associations, was worth very little. Had its interest consisted of these merely, she would not have taken the key in pawn. But the row of mysterious figures decided her. Here was a secret, connected – as was probable from the remark of the old man – with a hidden treasure. Remembering her experience with the cryptogram of the Florentine Dante, Hagar determined to retain the key, and, if possible, to discover the secret.

'If you are really in want of money, I will let you have a pound on it,' she said, casting a glance at the threadbare clothes of her customer.

'If I did not need money, I should not have blundered into your spider's web,' he retorted. 'A pound will do; make out the ticket in the name of Luke Parsons, The Lodge, Danetree Hall, Buckton, Kent.'

In silence Hagar did as she was bid; in silence she gave him ticket and money; and in silence he walked out of the shop. When alone she took up the key, and began to examine the figures without loss of time. The learning of many secrets had created in her a burning desire to learn more. If ingenuity and perseverance could do it, Hagar was bent upon discovering the secret of the copper key.

This mysterious object was so covered with verdigris that she was unable to decipher the marks. With her usual promptness, Hagar got the necessary materials, and cleaned the key thoroughly. The figures – those, as Parsons had said, of Arabic numerals – then appeared clearer, and Hagar noted that they extended the whole length of the copper stem. Taking paper and pencil, she copied them out carefully, with the following result:

'20211814115251256205255 – H – 38518212.'

'An odd jumble of figures!' said Hagar, staring at the result of her labours. 'I wonder what they mean.'

Unversed in the science of unravelling cryptograms, she was unable to answer her own question; and after an hour of profitless investigation, which made her head ache, she numbered the key according to the numeral of the ticket, and put it away. But the oddity of the affair, the strange circumstance of the figures with the letter 'H' stranded among them, often made her reflective, and she was devoured by curiosity – that parent of all great discoveries – to know what key and figures meant. Nevertheless, for all her thought no explanation of the problem presented itself. To her the secret of the key was the secret of the Sphinx – as mysterious, as unguessable.

Then it occurred to her that there might be some story, or legend, or tradition attached to this queer key, which might throw some light on the mystery of the figures. If she learnt the story, it was not improbable that she might gain a hint therefrom. At all events, Parsons had spoken of concealed riches connected with the reading of the cypher. To attempt to unravel the problem without knowing the reason for which the figures were engraved was, vulgarly speaking, putting the cart before the horse. Hagar determined that the cart should be in its proper place, viz., at the tail of the animal. In other words, she resolved first to learn the legend of the key, and afterwards attempt a reading of the riddle. To get at the truth, it was necessary to see Parsons.

No sooner had Hagar made up her mind to this course than she resolved to carry out her plan. Leaving Bolker to mind the shop, she went off down to Kent – to the Lodge, Buckton, that address which Parsons had given to be written on the ticket. With her she took the key, in case it might be wanted, and shortly after midday she alighted at a little rural station.

Oh, it was sweet to be once more in the country, to wander through green lanes o'er-arched with bending hazels, to smell the perfume of Kentish orchards, to run across the springy turf of wide moors golden with gorse! Such a fair expanse was stretched out at the back of the station, and across it – as Hagar was informed by an obliging porter – Danetree Hall was to be found. At the gates thereof, in a pretty and quaint lodge, dwelt surly Mr Parsons, and thither went Hagar; but in truth she almost forgot her errand in the delights of the country.

Her gipsy blood sang in her veins as she ran across the green sward, and her heart leaped in her bosom for very lightness. She forgot the weary Lambeth pawn-shop; she thought not of Eustace Lorn; she did not let her mind dwell upon the return of Goliath and her subsequent disinheritance; all she knew was that she was a Romany lass, a child of the road, and had entered again into her kingdom. In such a happy vein she saw the red roofs of Danetree Hall rising above the trees of a great park; and almost immediately she arrived at the great iron gates, behind which, on one side of a stately avenue, she espied the lodge wherein dwelt Parsons.

He was sitting outside smoking a pipe, morose even in the golden sunlight, with the scent of flowers in his nostrils, the music of the birds in his ears. On seeing Hagar peering between the bars of the gate he started up, and literally rushed towards her.

'Pawn-shop girl!' he growled, like an angry bear. 'What do you want?'

'Civility in the first place; rest in the second!' retorted Hagar, coolly. 'Let me in, Mr Parsons. I have come to see you about that copper key.'

'You've lost it?' shouted the gruff creature.

'Not I; it's in my pocket. But I wish to know its story.'

'Why?' asked Parsons, opening the gates with manifest reluctance.

Without replying Hagar marched past him, into his garden, and the porch of his house. Finally she took her seat in the chair

Parsons had vacated. The old man seemed rather pleased with her ungracious behaviour, which matched so well with his own; and after closing the gates he came to stare at her brilliant face.

'You're a handsome woman, and a bold one,' said he, slowly. 'Come inside, and tell me why you wish to know the story of the key.'

Accepting the invitation with civility, Hagar followed her eccentric host into a prim little parlour furnished in the ugly fashion of the early Victorian era. Chairs and sofa were of mahogany and horsehair; a round table, with gilt-edged books lying thereon at regular intervals, occupied the centre of the apartment, and the gilt-framed mirror over the fireplace was swathed in green gauze. Copperplate prints of the Queen and the Prince Consort decorated the crudely-papered walls, and the well-worn carpet was of a dark-green hue sprinkled with bouquets of red flowers. Altogether a painfully ugly room, which made anyone gifted with artistic aspirations shudder. Hagar, whose eye was trained to beauty, shuddered duly, and then took her seat on the most comfortable of the ugly chairs.

'Why do you want to know the story of the key?' asked Parsons, throwing his bulky figure on the slippery sofa.

'Because I wish to read the riddle of the key.'

Parsons started up, and his face grew red with anger. 'No, no! You shall not – you must not! Never will I make her rich!'

'Make who rich?' asked Hagar, astonished at this outburst.

'Marion Danetree – the proud hussy! My son loves her, but she disdains him. He is breaking his heart, while she laughs. If that picture were found she would be rich, and despise my poor Frank the more.'

'The picture? What picture?'

'Why, the one that is hidden,' said Parsons in surprise. 'The clue to the hiding-place is said to be concealed in the figures on the key. If you find the picture, it will sell for thirty thousand pounds, which would go to that cruel Miss Danetree.'

'I don't quite understand,' said Hagar, rather bewildered. 'Would you mind telling me the story from the beginning?'

154

'As you please,' replied the old man, moodily. 'I'll make it as short as I can. Squire Danetree, the grandfather of the present lady, who is the only representative of the family, was very rich, and a friend of George the Fourth. Like all the Danetrees, he was a scamp, and squandered the property of the family in entertainments during the Regency. He sold all the pictures of the Hall save one, *The Nativity*, by Andrea del Castagno, a famous Florentine painter of the Renaissance. The King offered thirty thousand pounds for this gem, as he wished to buy it for the nation. Danetree refused, as he had some compunction at robbing his only son, and wished to leave him the picture as the only thing saved out of the wreck. But as time went on, and money became scarce, he determined to sell this last valuable. Then the picture disappeared.'

'How did it disappear?'

'My father hid it,' replied Parsons, coolly. 'It was not known at the time, but the old man confessed on his death-bed that, determined to save the family from ruin, he had concealed the picture while Squire Danetree was indulging in his mad orgies in London. When my father confessed, the spendthrift squire was dead, and he wished the son – the present Miss Danetree's father – to possess the picture and to sell it, in order to restore the fortunes of the family.'

'Well, did he not tell where the picture was hidden?'

'No; he died on the point of revealing the secret,' said Parsons. 'All he could say was "The key! the key!" Then I knew that the hiding-place was indicated by the row of figures graven on the stem of the copper key. I tried to make out the meaning; so did my son; so did Squire Danetree and his daughter. But all to no purpose. None can read the riddle.'

'But why did you pawn the key?'

'It wasn't for money, you may be sure of that!' snapped the old man – 'or I should not have taken a paltry pound for it. No, I pawned it to put it beyond my son's reach. He was always poring over it, so I thought he might guess the meaning and find the picture.'

'And why not? Don't you want it found?'

Parsons's face assumed a malignant expression. 'No!' said he, sharply – 'for then Frank would be foolish enough to give the picture to Miss Danetree – to the woman who despises him. If you guess the riddle, don't tell him, as I don't want to make the proud jade rich.'

'I can't guess the riddle,' replied Hagar hopelessly. 'Your story does not aid me in the least.'

While thus speaking, her eyes wandered to the wall at the back of the glum old steward. Thereon she saw in a frame of black wood one of those hideous samplers which our grandmothers were so fond of working. It was a yellow square, embroidered – or rather stitched – with the alphabet in diverse colours, and also an array of numerals up to twenty-six. Hagar idly wondered why the worker had stopped at that particular number; and then she noticed that the row of figures was placed directly under the row of letters. At once the means of reading the key riddle flashed on her brain. The cypher was exceedingly simple. All that had to be done was to substitute letters for the figures. Hagar uttered an ejaculation which roused old Parsons from his musings.

'What's the matter?' said he, turning his head: 'what are you looking at, girl? Oh,' he added, following her gaze, 'that sampler; 'twas done by my mother; a rare hand at needlework she was! But never mind her just now. I want to know about that riddle.'

'I can't guess it,' said Hagar, keeping her own counsel, for reasons to be revealed hereafter. 'Do you wish your key back? I have it here.'

'No; I don't want my son to get it, and make that proud wench rich by guessing the riddle. Keep the key till I call for it. What! Are you going? Have a drink of milk?'

The offer was hospitably made, but Hagar declined it, as she had no desire to break bread with this malignant old man. Making a curt excuse, she took her leave, and within the hour she was on her way back to London, with a clue to the cypher in her brain. The sampler had revealed the secret; for without doubt it was from his wife's needlework that the Parsons of sixty years before had got the idea of constructing his cryptogram. In the sampler the figures were placed thus:

A B C D E F G H I J K L M N O P Q R S T U V W X Y Z
1 2 3 4 5 6 7 8 9 10 11 12 13 14 15 16 17 18 19 20 21 22 23 24 25 26

and Parsons had simply substituted figures for letters. The thing was so plain that Hagar wondered why, with the key-sampler staring him in the face, the steward had not succeeded in reading the riddle.

When back in the shop, she applied her test to the figures on the key, and found out the meaning thereof. Then she considered what was the best course to pursue. Clearly it was not wise to tell Parsons, as he hated Miss Danetree, and if he found the picture through Hagar's aid he might either hide it again or destroy it. Should she tell Miss Danetree herself, or Frank Parsons, the despised lover? After some consideration the girl wrote to the latter, asking him to call on her at the shop. She felt rather a sympathy with his plight after hearing his father's story, and wished to judge for herself if he was an eligible suitor for Miss Danetree's hand. If she liked him, and found him worthy, Hagar was resolved to tell him how to find the picture, and by doing so thus aid him to gain the hand of the disdainful beauty. If, on the other hand, she did not care for him, Hagar concluded to reveal her discovery to Miss Danetree herself. Her resolution thus being taken, she waited quietly for the arrival of the steward's son.

When he presented himself, Hagar liked him very much indeed, for three reasons. In the first place, he was handsome – a sure passport to a woman's favour; in the second, he had a fine frank nature, and a tolerably intelligent brain; in the third, he was deeply in love with Marion Danetree. This last reason influenced Hagar as much as anything, for she was at a romantic age, and took a deep interest in love and lovers.

'It is most extraordinary that my father should have pawned

the key,' said Frank, when Hagar had told her story, less the explanation of the riddle.

'It may be extraordinary, Mr Parsons, but it is very lucky – for you.'

'I don't see it,' said Frank, raising his eyebrows. 'Why?'

'Why,' replied Hagar, drawing the key out of her pocket, 'because I have discovered the secret.'

'What! Do you know what that line of figures means?'

'Yes. When I paid my visit to your father, I saw an article in his room which gave me a clue. I worked out the cypher, and now I know where the picture is hidden.'

Young Parsons sprang to his feet with glowing eyes. 'Where – oh, where?' he almost shouted. 'Tell me, quick!'

'For you to tell Miss Danetree, no doubt,' said Hagar, coolly.

At once his enthusiasm died away, and he sat down, with a frown on his face. 'What do you know about Miss Danetree?' he asked, sharply.

'All that your father told me, Mr Parsons. You love her, but she does not love you; and for that your father hates her.'

'I know he does,' said the young man, sighing, 'and very unjustly. I will be frank with you, Miss Stanley.'

'I think it is best for you to be so, as I hold your fate in my hands.'

'You hold – fate! What do you mean?'

Hagar shrugged her shoulders in pity at his obtuseness. 'Why,' she said, quietly, 'this picture is worth thirty thousand pounds, and Miss Danetree is worth nothing except that ruined Hall. If I tell you where to find that picture, you will be able to restore her fortunes, and make her a comparatively rich woman. Now you cannot read the cypher; I can; and so – you see!'

Young Parsons laughed outright at her comprehensive view of the situation, although he blushed a little at the same time, and gave an indignant denial to the hinted motive which prompted Hagar's speech. 'I am not a fortune-hunter,' he said, bluntly; 'if I learn the whereabouts of Castagno's *Nativity*, I shall certainly tell Mar – I mean Miss Danetree. But as for trading on that knowledge to make her marry me against her will, I'd rather die than act so basely!'

'Ah, my dear young man, I am afraid you have no business instincts,' said Hagar, dryly. 'I thought you loved the lady.'

'You are determined to get at the truth, I see. Yes; I do love her.'

'And she loves you?'

Parsons hesitated, and blushed again at this downright questioning. 'Yes; I think she does – a little,' he said, at length.

'H'm! That means she loves you a great deal.'

'Well,' said the young man, slyly, 'you are a woman, and should be able to read a woman's character. Don't you think so?'

'Perhaps. But you forget that I have not seen this particular woman – or rather angel, as I suppose you call her.'

'You are a queer girl!'

'And you – a lovesick young man!' rejoined Hagar, mimicking his tone. 'But time passes; tell me about your wooing.'

'There is little to tell,' rejoined Frank, dolefully. 'My father is, as you know, the steward of the Danetree family; but as they were ruined by the Regency squire, his duties are now light enough. Miss Danetree is the last of the race, and all that remains to her is the Hall, the few acres which surround it, and a small income from the rents of two outlying farms. I was brought up from childhood with Marion – I must call her so, as it is the name which comes easiest to my lips – and I loved her always. She loves me also.'

'Then why will she not marry you?'

'Because she is poor and I am poor. Oh, my position as son of her steward would not stand in the way could I support her as my wife. But my father always refused to let me learn a profession or a trade, or even to earn my own livelihood, as he desired me to succeed him as the steward of the Danetree property. In the old days the post was a good one; but now it is worth nothing.'

'And your father dislikes Miss Danetree.'

'Yes, because he thinks she scorns me – which she does not. But she will not let me tell him the truth until there is a chance of our marriage.'

'Well,' said Hagar, producing the paper on which was written the line of figures, 'I am about to give you that chance. This cypher is quite easy; figures have been substituted for letters – that is all. A is set down as one, B as two, and so on.'

'I don't quite understand.'

'I will show you. These figures must be divided into numbers, and a letter set over each. Now, the first number is twenty, and the twentieth letter of the alphabet is T. The twenty-first letter is U. Then come the eighteenth and the fourteenth letters. What are they?'

Frank counted. 'R and N,' he said, after a pause. 'Ah! I see the first word is T, U, R, N – that is turn!'

'Exactly; represented by numbers, 20, 21, 18, 14. Now you understand, so I need not explain further. Here is the cypher written out.'

Young Parsons took up the paper and read as follows:

```
T  u  r  n  k  e  y  l  e  f  t  e  y  e
20 21 18 14 11 5 25 12 5  6 20 5 25 5

         8  c  h  e  r  u  b
         H  3  8  5 18 21  2
```

'Turn key left eye eighth cherub!' repeated Parsons, in puzzled tones. 'I have no doubt that you have solved the problem correctly; but, I do not know what the sentence means.'

'Well,' said Hagar, rather sharply, 'it means, I should think, that the left eye of some cherub's head is a keyhole, into which is to be thrust the copper key upon which the figures are engraved. Doubtless, by turning the key the wall will open, and the picture will be discovered.'

'What a clever girl you are!' cried Parsons, in admiration.

'I use my brains, that is all,' said Hagar, coolly. 'I'm afraid you don't. However, are there a number of sculptured cherubs in Danetree Hall?'

'Yes; there is a room called "The Cherubs' Room", from a

number of carved heads. How did you guess that there was more than one?'

'Because the letter "H" corresponds with the figure eight; so no doubt there are more than eight heads. All you have to do is to take this copper key, put it into the left eye of the eighth cherub, and find the picture. Then you can marry Miss Danetree, and the pair of you can live on the thirty thousand pounds. If she is as clever as you, you'll need it all.'

Quite impervious to Hagar's irony, Frank Parsons took his leave with many admiring words and protestations of gratitude. When he found the picture he promised to let Hagar know, and to invite her to Danetree Hall to see it. Then he departed, and it was only when she was left alone that Hagar reflected she had not got back the pound lent on the key. But she consoled herself with the reflection that she could demand it when the hidden picture was discovered. Principal and interest was what she required; for Hagar was nothing if not business-like.

That same evening Frank was seated in the prim little parlour with his dour father. He had been up to the Hall, and had proved the truth of Hagar's reading by discovering the picture; also he had seen Marion Danetree, and told her of the good fortune which was coming. She would be able to buy back the lost acres of the family, to restore and refurnish the old house, to take up her position again in the county, and reign once more as the lady of Danetree Hall. All this Frank told his father, and the old man's brow grew black as night.

'You have made her rich!' he muttered – 'that proud girl who looks upon you as dirt beneath her feet.'

Frank smiled. He had not told his father the termination of the interview with Marion; nor did he intend to do so at present.

'We'll talk of Marion and her pride tomorrow,' he said, rising; 'I am going to bed just now; but you know how I discovered the picture, and how it has been restored to the Danetrees as grandfather wished.'

When his son left the room, Luke Parsons sat with folded hands and a dull pain in his heart. It was gall and wormwood to him that the woman who rejected Frank should acquire wealth and regain her position through the aid of the man she despised. Oh, if he could only hide the picture, or even destroy it! – anything rather than that proud Marion Danetree should be placed on an eminence to look down on his bright boy. To rob her of this newly-found wealth – to take away the picture – Parsons felt that he would commit even a crime.

And why should he not? Frank had left the key on the table – the copper key which was to be placed in the left eye of the cherub. Parsons knew well enough – from the explanation of his son – how the key was to be used; how his father had designed the hiding-place of the Castagno picture. The lock and key which had belonged to the First Charles had been given to the old man by his master. He had placed the first behind the cherub, with the keyhole in the left eye, so as to keep the panel or portion of the wall in its place; and on the second he had graven the numbers indicating the locality. Parsons rose to his feet and stretched out his hand for the copper key. When he touched it, all his scruples vanished. He made up his mind then and there to go up that night to the Hall and destroy the picture. Then Marion Danetree would no longer be rich, or benefit by the secret which Frank had discovered. It will be seen that Mr Parsons never thought of Hagar's share in the reading of the cypher.

As steward he had keys of all the doors in the Hall, and was able easily to gain admission at whatever hour he chose. He chose to enter now, and with a lantern in his hand, and a clasp-knife hidden in his pocket, he went on his errand of destruction. Unlocking a small side door under the greater terrace, he passed along the dark underground passages, ascending to the upper floor, and in a short space of time he found himself in 'The Cherubs' Room'.

It was a large and lofty apartment, panelled with oak darkened by time and carved with fruit and flowers and foliage after the mode of Grinling Gibbons. Between each panel there was a beautifully-carven cherub's head, with curly hair, and wings placed crosswise under the chin. The moonlight streaming in through the wide and uncurtained windows showed all these things clearly to the wild eyes of the old man; and he made haste to fulfil his task before the moon should set and leave him in darkness. Swinging the lantern so that its yellow light should illuminate the walls, Parsons counted the cherubs' heads between the panels, starting from the door, and was rewarded by finding the one he sought. The left eye of this face was pierced, and into it he inserted the slender copper stem of the key. There was a cracking sound as he turned it, and then the whole of the panel swung outward to the left. On the back of this he beheld the picture of Andrea del Castagno. The sight of it was so unexpected that he started back with a cry, and let fall the lantern, which was immediately extinguished. However, this mattered little, as he had ample light in the rays of the summer moon. In the white radiance he relighted his candle, and then, betwixt the yellow glare of the one and the chill glimmer of the other, he examined the gem of art which, in the interests of mistaken pride, he proposed to destroy. It was beautiful beyond description.

Under a lowly roof of thatched straw lay the Divine Child, stretching up His little hands to the Holy Mother. With arms crossed upon her breast in ecstatic adoration, Mary bent over Him worshiping; and in the dim obscurity of the humble dwelling could be seen the tall form and reverend head of Joseph. Above spread the dark blue of the night sky, broken by golden dashes of colour, in which were seen the majestic forms of wide-winged angels looking earthward. At the top of the picture there was a blaze of light radiating from the Godhead, and in the arrowy beam streaming downward floated the white spectre of the Holy Dove. The marvellous beauty of the picture lay in the dispersion and disposition of the various lights: that mild lustre which emanated from the Form of the Child, the aureole hovering round the bowed head of Mary; the glory of the golden atmosphere surrounding the angels; and, highest and most wonderful of all, the fierce white light which showered down, blinding the terrible, from the unseen Deity. The picture was majestic, sublime: a dream of lovely piety, a masterpiece of art.

For the moment Parsons was spellbound before this wonderful

creation which he intended to destroy. Almost he was tempted to forego his evil purpose, and to spare the beautiful vision which spread itself so gloriously before trial. But the thought of Marion and her scorn, of Frank and his hopeless love, decided him. With a look of hatred he opened the knife, and raised the blade to slash the picture.

'Stop!'

With a cry, Parsons dropped the knife and wheeled round at that imperious command. At the further end of the room, candle in hand, stood the tall form of a woman. She wore a dressing-gown hastily thrown over her shoulders; her hair was loose, her feet were bare; and she approached the steward noiselessly and swiftly. It was Marion Danetree, and her eyes were full of anger.

'What are you doing here at this time of night?' she demanded haughtily of the sullen old man. 'I heard a cry and the noise of a fall, and I came down.'

'I want to spoil that picture,' said Parsons between his teeth.

'Destroy Castagno's *Nativity*? Take away my only chance of restoring the family fortunes? You are mad.'

'No; I am Frank's father. You despise him; you hate him. Through him you have found the picture; but now – ' He picked up the knife again.

'Wait a moment!' said Marion, comprehending Parsons's motive; 'if you destroy that picture, you prevent my marriage with Frank.'

'What?' – the knife crashed on the floor – 'are you going to marry my boy?'

'Yes. Did not Frank tell you? When we discovered the picture together this afternoon, he asked me to be his wife. I consented only too gladly.'

'But – but I thought you despised him!'

'Despise him? I love him better than all the world! Go away, Mr Parsons, and thank God that He sent me to prevent you committing a crime. I shall bring that picture to Frank as my dowry. He shall take my name, and there will once more be a Squire Danetree at the Hall.'

'O Miss Danetree – Marion – forgive me!' cried Parsons, quite broken down.

'I forgive you; it was love for Frank made you think of this folly. But go – go! it is not seemly that you should be here at this hour of the night.'

Parsons closed up the panel in silence, locked it, and turned to go. But as he passed her he held out his hand.

'What is this?' asked Marion, smiling.

'My gift to you – my marriage gift – the copper key which has brought you a husband and a fortune.'

JUDITH LEE

Created by Richard Marsh
(1857–1915)

Judith Lee is one of the most original characters to be found in the crime stories of the Edwardian era. When she made her first appearance in The Strand Magazine *in 1911 the editor of that periodical, Herbert Greenhough-Smith, described her as 'the fortunate possessor of a gift which gives her a place apart in detective fiction'. Judith Lee has the ability to read lips and, it sometimes seems, she can go nowhere without seeing people discussing wicked plots and outrageous crimes, blithely unaware that their words have been understood by the young woman on the far side of the room. The story I have chosen for this volume is taken from early in her career when her peculiar talent is all that saves her from an unfounded accusation that she is herself a thief. Judith Lee was the creation of Richard Marsh, one of the most interesting and prolific writers of genre fiction in the late nineteenth and early twentieth centuries. Marsh is best known for* The Beetle, *a tale of supernatural horror. First published in 1897, the same year as Bram Stoker's* Dracula, *this is an account of a shape-shifting devotee of ancient Egyptian gods who stalks the fog-shrouded streets of late Victorian London. It was a great commercial success, outselling Stoker's work, and was made into a silent film in 1919, two years before Count Dracula made his debut on a cinema screen. Other horror novels followed, as well as crime fiction* (Philip Bennion's Death, The Datchet Diamonds) *and collections of uncanny short stories with titles like* The Seen and the Unseen *and* Both Sides of the Veil. *Marsh's work appeared in most of the well-known periodicals of the day.*

EAVESDROPPING AT INTERLAKEN

I have sometimes thought that this gift of mine for reading words as they issue from people's lips places me, with or without my will, in the position of the eavesdropper. There have been occasions on which, before I knew it, I have been made cognisant of conversations, of confidences, which were meant to be sacred; and, though such knowledge has been acquired through no fault of mine, I have felt ashamed, just as if I had been listening at a key-hole, and I have almost wished that the power which Nature gave me, and which years of practice have made perfect, was not mine at all. On the other hand, there have been times when I was very glad indeed that I was able to play the part of eavesdropper. As, to very strict purists, this may not sound a pleasant confession to make, I will give an instance of the kind of thing I mean.

I suppose I was about seventeen; I know I had just put my hair up, which had grown to something like a decent length since it had come in contact with the edge of that doughty Scottish chieftain's – MacGregor's – knife. My mother was not very well. My father was reluctant to leave her. It looked as if the summer holiday which had been promised me was in peril, when two acquaintances, Mr and Mrs Travers, rather than that I should lose it altogether, offered to take me under their wing. They were going for a little tour in Switzerland, proposing to spend most of their time at Interlaken, and my parents, feeling that I should be perfectly safe with them, accepted their proffered chaperonage.

Everything went well until we got to Interlaken. There they met some friends who were going on a climbing expedition, and, as Mr and Mrs Travers were both keen mountaineers, they were very eager to join them. I was the only difficulty in their way. They could not say exactly how long they would be absent, but probably a week; and what was to become of me in that great hotel there all alone? They protested that it would be quite impossible to leave me; they would have to give up that climb; and I believe they would have done so if what seemed to be a solution of the difficulty had not turned up.

The people in the hotel were for the most part very sociable folk, as people in such places are apt to be. Among other persons whose acquaintance we had made was a middle-aged widow, a Mrs Hawthorne. When she heard of what Mr and Mrs Travers wanted to do, and how they could not do it because of me, she volunteered, during their absence, to occupy their place as my chaperon, assuring them that every possible care should be taken of me.

In the hotel were stopping a brother and sister, a Mr and Miss Sterndale. With them I had grown quite friendly. Mr Sterndale I should have set down as twenty-five or twenty-six, and his sister as a year or two younger. From the day on which I had first seen them they had shown an inclination for my society; and, to speak quite frankly, on different occasions Mr Sterndale had paid me what seemed to me to be delicate little attentions which were very dear to my maiden heart. I had some difficulty in inducing people to treat me as if I were grown up. After a few minutes' conversation even perfect strangers would ask me how old I was, and when I told them they were apt to assume an attitude towards me as if I were the merest child, of which I disapproved.

What attracted me to Mr Sterndale was that, from the very first, he treated me with deference, as if I were at least as old as he was.

On the third day after Mr and Mrs Travers had left Mrs Hawthorne came to me with a long face and a letter in her hand.

'My dear, I cannot tell you how annoyed I am, but I shall have to go to England at once – today. And whatever will become of you?'

It seemed that her only sister was dangerously ill, and that she was implored to go to her as soon as she could. Of course, she would have to go. I told her that it did not matter in the least about me; Mr and Mrs Travers would be back in a day or two, and now that I knew so many people in the hotel, who were all of them disposed to be friendly, I should be perfectly all right until they came. She must not allow any consideration for me to keep her for a moment from obeying her sister's call. She left for London that afternoon; but, so far from everything being perfectly all right with me after she had gone, the very next day my troubles began.

They began in the morning. I was sitting on the terrace with a book. Mr Sterndale had been talking to me. Presently his sister came through an open French window from the lounge. Her brother went up to her; I sat still. She was at the other end of the terrace, and when she saw me she nodded and smiled. When her brother came up to her, he said something which, as his back was towards me, of course I did not catch; but her answer to him, which was very gently uttered, I saw quite distinctly; all the while she was speaking she was smiling at me.

'She has a red morocco jewel-case sort of a thing on the corner of her mantel-shelf; I put it under the bottom tray. With the exception of that gold locket which she is always wearing it's the only decent thing in it; it's full of childish trumpery.'

That was what Miss Sterndale said to her brother, and I saw her say it with rather curious feelings. What had he asked her? To what could she be referring? I had 'a red morocco jewel-case sort of a thing', and it stood on a corner of my mantel-shelf. I also had a gold locket, which, if I was not, as she put it, always wearing, I did wear pretty often. Certainly it was the only article in my jewel-case which was worth very much; and with a horrid sort of qualm I owned to myself that the rest of the contents might come under the definition of 'childish trumpery'. She said she had put something under the bottom tray. What bottom tray? Whose bottom tray? There were trays in my jewel-case; she could not possibly have meant that she had put anything under one of them. The idea was too preposterous. And yet, if we had not been going to St Beatenberg, I think I should have gone straight up to my bedroom to see. I do not know how it was; the moment before I had been perfectly happy; there was not a grain of suspicion in the air, nor in my mind; then all of a sudden I felt quite curious. Could there be two persons in the house possessed of 'a red morocco jewel-case sort of a thing', which stood on a corner of the mantel-shelf, in which was a gold locket and a rather mixed collection of childish trumpery I wondered. If I was the only person in the house who owned such a treasure, what did she mean by saying that she had put something under the bottom tray? The case was locked; I had locked it myself before leaving the room, of that I was sure. Had she unlocked it – with what key? She could not have broken it open. Was the something which she had put under the bottom tray a present which was meant to be a surprise to me?

The evening before, we had arranged to make an excursion to St Beatenberg on the Lake of Thun – five or six of us. I was dressed ready to start when Miss Sterndale came through that French window. She also was ready, and her brother. Presently the others appeared. I was feeling a little confused; I could not think of an excuse which would give me an opportunity of examining my jewel-case. Anyhow, I kept trying to tell myself it was absurd. I wished I could not see what people were saying merely by watching their lips. What Miss Sterndale had said to her brother had nothing at all to do with me. I had unintentionally heard something which I had not been meant to hear, and I was being properly punished for my pains.

My day at St Beatenberg was spoilt, though I kept telling myself that it was all my own fault, and nobody else's. Everyone was gay, and full of fun and laughter – everyone but me. My mood was so obviously out of tune with theirs that they commented on it.

'What is the matter with you, Miss Lee?' asked Mrs Dalton; 'you look as if you were not enjoying yourself one little bit.'

I did not like to say that I was not; as a matter of fact, when they rallied me I said that I was – but it was not true.

When I got back to the hotel and was in my bedroom, I went straight up to that 'red morocco jewel-case sort of a thing' and looked at it. It was locked, just as I had left it. Clearly I had been worrying myself all day long about nothing at all. Still, I got my keys and opened it; there was nothing to show that the contents had been touched. I lifted the two trays – and I gasped. I do not know how else to describe it – something seemed all at once to be choking me, so that it was with an effort that I breathed. In the jewel-case, under the bottom tray, was a pendant – a beautiful circular diamond pendant, of the size, perhaps, of a five-shilling piece. It was not mine; I never had anything so beautiful in my life. Where did it come from? Could Miss Sterndale have put it there? Was that the meaning of her words?

I took the pendant out. It was a beauty; it could not be a present from the Sterndales, from either the sister or the brother. They must have known that I could not accept such a gift as that from strangers. And then, what a queer way of making a present – and such a present!

As I looked at it I began to have a very uncomfortable feeling that I had seen it before, or one very like it, on someone in the house. My head, or my brain, or something, seemed to be so muddled that at the moment I could not think who that someone was. I had washed and tidied myself before I decided that I would go down with the pendant in my hand and, at the risk of no matter what misunderstanding, ask Miss Sterndale what she meant by putting it there. So, when I had got my unruly hair into something like order, downstairs I went, and rushed into the lounge with so much impetuosity that I all but cannoned against Miss Goodridge, who was coming out.

'Good gracious, child!' she exclaimed. 'Do look where you are going. You almost knocked me over.'

The instant I saw her, and she said that, I remembered – I knew whom I had seen wearing that diamond pendant which I was holding tightly clasped in the palm of my hand. It was the person whom I had almost knocked over, Miss Goodridge herself – of course! One of the persons in the hotel whom, so far as I knew anything of them, I liked least. Miss Goodridge was a tall, angular person of perhaps quite thirty-five, who dressed and carried herself as if she were still a girl. She had been most unpleasant to me. I had no idea what I had done or said to cause her annoyance, but I had a feeling that she disliked me, and was at no pains to conceal the fact. The sight of her, and the thought that I had nearly knocked her over, quite drove the sense out of my head.

'Oh, Miss Goodridge!' I exclaimed, rather fatuously. 'You look as if something had happened.'

'Something has happened,' she replied. 'There's a thief in the house. I have been robbed. Someone has stolen my pendant – my diamond pendant.'

Someone had stolen her diamond pendant! I do not know if the temperature changed all at once, but I do know that a chill went all over me. Was that the explanation? Could it possibly be – I did not care to carry even my thought to a logical finish. I stood there as if I were moonstruck, with Miss Goodridge looking at me with angry eyes.

'What is the matter with the child?' she asked. 'I did not know you dark-skinned girls could blush, but I declare you've gone as red as a lobster.'

I do not know if she thought that lobsters were red before they were boiled. I tried to explain, to say what I wanted to say, but I appeared to be tongue-tied.

'Can't you speak?' she demanded. 'Don't glare at me as if you'd committed a murder. Anyone would think that you had been robbed instead of me. I suppose you haven't stolen my pendant?'

She drew her bow at a venture, but her arrow hit the mark.

'Oh, Miss Goodridge!' I repeated. It seemed to be all I could say.

She put her hand upon my shoulder.

'What is the matter with the girl? You young wretch! Have you been playing any tricks with that pendant of mine?'

'I – I found it,' I stammered. I held out to her my open hand with the pendant on the palm.

'You – you found it? Found what?' She looked at me and then at my outstretched hand. 'My pendant! She's got my pendant!' She snatched it from me. 'You – you young – thief! And you have the insolence to pretend you found it!'

'I did find it – I found it in my bedroom.'

'Did you really? Of all the assurance! I've always felt that you were the kind of creature with whom the less one had to do the better, but I never credited you with a taste for this sort of thing. Get out of my way! Don't you ever dare to speak to me again.'

She did not wait for me to get out of her way; she gave me a violent push and rushed right past me. It was a polished floor; if I had not come in contact with a big armchair I should have tumbled on to it. My feelings when I was left alone in the lounge were not enviable. At seventeen, even if one thinks oneself grown up, one is still only a child, and I was a stranger in a strange land, without a friend in all that great hotel, without a soul to advise me. Still, as I knew that I was absolutely and entirely innocent, I did not intend to behave as if I were guilty. I went up to my room again and dressed for dinner. I told myself over and over again as I performed my simple toilette that I would make Miss Goodridge eat her words before she had done, though at that moment I had not the faintest notion how I was going to do it.

That was a horrid dinner – not from the culinary, but from my point of view. If the dinner was horrid, in the lounge afterwards it was worse. Miss Sterndale actually had the audacity to come up to me and pretend to play the part of sympathetic friend.

'You seem to be all alone,' she began. I was all alone; I had never thought that anyone could feel so utterly alone as I did in that crowded lounge. 'Miss Lee, why do you look at me like that?' I was looking at her as if I wished her to understand that I was looking into her very soul – if she had one. Her smiling serenity of countenance was incredible to me, knowing what I knew. 'Have you had bad news from home, or from Mr and Mrs Travers, or are you unhappy because Mrs Hawthorne has gone? You seem so different. What has been the matter with you the whole of today?'

I was on the point of giving an explanation which I think might have startled her when I happened to glance across the room. At a table near the open window, Mr Sterndale was sitting with Miss Goodridge. They were having coffee. Although Miss Goodridge was sitting sideways, she continually turned her head to watch me, Mr Sterndale was sitting directly facing me. He had a cigarette in one hand, and every now and then he sipped his coffee, but most of the time he talked. But, although I could not even hear the sound of his voice, I saw what he said as distinctly as if he had been shouting in my ear. It was the sentence he was uttering which caused me to defer the explanation which I had it in my mind to give to his sister.

'Of course, the girl's a thief – I'm afraid that goes without saying.' It was that sentence which was issuing from his lips at the moment when I chanced to glance in his direction which caused the explanation I had been about to make to his sister to be deferred.

Miss Goodridge had her coffee cup up to her mouth, so I could not see what she said; but if I had been put to it I might have made a very shrewd guess by the reply he made. He took his cigarette from his lips, blew out a thin column of smoke, leaned back in his chair – and all the time he was looking smilingly at me with what he meant me to think were the eyes of a friend.

'It's all very well for you to talk. I may have had my suspicions, but it is only within the last hour or two that they have been confirmed.'

She said something which again I could not see; his reply suggested that she must have asked a question.

'I'll tell you what I mean by saying that my doubts have been confirmed. A man was passing through this afternoon with whom I have some acquaintance – the Rector of Leeds.' I wonder he did not say the Bishop of London. 'He saw – our friend – ' He made a slight inclination of his head towards me. 'At sight of her he exclaimed: "Halloa, there's that Burnett girl!" For a parson he has rather a free and easy way of speaking; he's one of your modern kind.'

I believed him!

'"Burnett girl?" I said. "But her name's Lee – Judith Lee." "Oh, she calls herself Lee now, does she? That settles it." "Settles what?" I asked, because I saw that there was something in his tone. "My dear Reggie," he said (he always calls me Reggie; I've known him for years), "at the beginning of the season that girl

174

whom you call Judith Lee was at Pontresina, staying in the same hotel as I was. She called herself Burnett then. Robberies were going on all the time, people were continually missing things. At last a Russian woman lost a valuable lot of jewellery. That settled it – Miss Burnett went.'"

Miss Goodridge turned so that her face was hidden; but, as before, his reply gave me a pretty good clue as to the question she had asked.

'Of course I mean it. Do you think I'd say a thing like that if I didn't mean it? I won't tell you all he said – it wouldn't be quite fair. But it came to this. He said that the young lady whom we have all thought so sweet and innocent –'

Miss Goodridge interposed with a remark which, in a guessing competition, I think I could have come pretty near to. He replied:

'Well, I've sometimes felt that you were rather hard on her, that perhaps you were a trifle prejudiced.'

Miss Goodridge turned her face towards me, and then I saw her words.

'I'm a better judge of feminine human nature than you suppose. The first moment I saw her I knew she was a young cat, though I admit I didn't take her to be as bad as she is. What did your clerical friend say of her, of the Miss Burnett whom we know now as Miss Lee?'

I did not wait to learn his answer – I had learnt enough. What his sister thought of my demeanour I did not care; I had been dimly conscious that she had been talking to me all the while, but what she was saying I do not know. My attention had been wholly taken up with what I did not hear. Before he began his reply to Miss Goodridge's genial inquiry I got up from my chair and marched out of the lounge, without saying a word to Miss Sterndale. When I had gone a little way I remembered that I had left my handkerchief – my best lace handkerchief – on the table by which I had been sitting. Even in the midst of my agitation I was conscious that I could not afford to lose it, so went back for it.

Miss Sterndale had joined her brother and Miss Goodridge. Two or three other people were standing by them, evidently interested in what was being said. I found my handkerchief. As I was going off with it Miss Sterndale turned round in my direction, without, however, thinking it worth her while to break off the remark she was making, taking it for granted, of course, that it was inaudible to me. I came in, as it were, for the tail end of it.

'... I am so disappointed in her; I have tried to like her, and now I fear it is only too certain that she is one of those creatures of whom the less said the better.'

That these words referred to me I had not the slightest doubt. Yet, while they were still on her lips, presuming on her conviction that they were hidden from me, she nodded and smiled as if she were wishing me a friendly goodnight.

The treachery of it! Now that I am able to look back calmly, I think it was that which galled me most. Her brother, with his gratuitous, horrible lies, had actually been pretending to make love to me – I am sure that was what he wished me to think he was doing. What a fool he must have thought me!

That was a sleepless night. It was hours before I got between the sheets, and when I did it was not to slumber. The feeling that I was so entirely alone, and that there was not a soul within miles and miles to whom I could turn for help, coupled with the consciousness that I had scarcely enough money to pay the hotel bill, and, what was even worse, that Mr and Mrs Travers had gone off with the return-half of my ticket to London, so that I could not go back home however much I might want to – these things were hard enough to bear; but they seemed to be as nothing compared to that man and woman's treachery. What was their motive, what could have induced them, was beyond my comprehension. It was a problem which I strove all night to solve. But the solution came on the morrow.

I soon knew what had happened when I went downstairs. Miss Goodridge had told her story of the pendant, and Mr Sterndale had circulated his lie about his clerical friend. Everybody shunned me. Some persons had the grace to pretend not to see me; others looked me full in the face and cut me dead. The only persons who were disposed to show any perception of my presence were the

Sterndales. As, entering the breakfast-room, I passed their table, they both smiled and nodded, but I showed no consciousness of them. As I took a seat at my own table, I saw him say to his sister:

'Our young friend seems to have got her back up – little idiot!'

Little idiot, was I? Only yesterday he had called me something else. The feeling that he was saying such things behind my back hurt me more than if he had shouted them to my face. I averted my gaze, keeping my eyes fixed on my plate. I would learn no more of what he said about me, or of what anyone said. I was conscious that life might become unendurable if I were made acquainted with the comments which people were making on me then. Yet, as I sat there with downcast face, might they not construe that as the bearing of a conscience-stricken and guilty wretch? I felt sure that that was what they were doing. But I could not help it; I would not see what they were saying.

Later in the morning matters turned out so that I did see, so that practically I had to see what the Sterndales said to each other. And perhaps, on the whole, it was fortunate for me that I did. I had spent the morning out of doors. On the terrace the Sterndales were standing close together, talking; so engrossed were they by what they were saying that they did not notice me; while, though I did not wish to look at them, something made me. That may seem to be an exaggeration. It is not – it is the truth. My wish was to have nothing more to do with them for ever and ever; but some instinct, which came I know not whence, made me turn my eyes in their direction and see what they were saying. And, as I have already said, it was well for me that I did.

They both seemed to be rather excited. He was speaking quickly and with emphasis.

'I tell you,' he was saying, as I paused to watch, 'we will do it today.'

His sister said something which, as she was standing sideways, was lost to me. He replied:

'The little idiot has cooked her own goose; there's no need for us to waste time in cooking it any more – she's done. I tell you we can strip the house of all it contains, and they'd lock her up for doing it.'

Again his sister spoke; without, because of her position, giving herself away to me. He went on again:

'There are only two things in the house worth having – I could give you a catalogue of what everyone has got. Mrs Anstruther's diamonds – the necklace is first-rate, and the rest of them aren't bad; and that American woman's pearls. Those five ropes of pearls are worth – I hope they'll be worth a good deal to us. The rest of the things you may make a present of to our young friend. The odium will fall on her – you'll see. We shall be able to depart with the only things worth having, at our distinguished leisure, without a stain upon our characters.'

He smiled – some people might have thought it a pleasant smile – to me it seemed a horrid one. That smile finished me – it reminded me of the traitor's kiss. I passed into the house still unnoticed, though I do not suppose that if I had been noticed it would have made any difference to them.

What he meant by what he had said I did not clearly understand. The only thing I quite realised was that he was still making sport of me. I also gathered that that was an amusement which he proposed to continue, though just how I did not see. Nor did I grasp the inner meaning of his allusion to Mrs Anstruther's diamonds and Mrs Newball's pearls – no doubt it was Mrs Newball he meant when he spoke of the American woman. The fine jewels of those two ladies, which they aired at every opportunity, were, as I knew perfectly well, the talk of the whole hotel. Probably that was what they meant they should be. When Mrs Anstruther had diamonds round her neck and on her bosom and in her ears and hair and round her wrists and on her fingers – I myself had seen her wear diamond rings on all the fingers of both hands and two diamond bracelets on each wrist – she was a sight to be remembered; while Mrs Newball, with her five strings of splendid pearls, which she sometimes wore all together as a necklace and sometimes twisted as bracelets round her wrists, together with a heterogeneous collection of ornaments of all sorts and kinds, made a pretty good second.

Not a person spoke to me the whole of that day. Everyone avoided me in a most ostentatious manner: and everyone, or nearly everyone, had been so friendly. It was dreadful. If I had had enough money to pay the hotel bill, as well as the return-half of my ticket home, I believe I should have left Interlaken there and then. But the choice of whether I would go or stay, as it turned out, was not to be left to me.

Depressed, miserable, homesick, devoutly wishing that I had never left home, almost resolved that I would never leave it again, I was about to go up to my room to dress for what I very well knew would only be the ghastly farce of dinner, when, as I reached the lift, a waiter came up to me and said that the manager wished to see me in his office. I did not like the man's manner; it is quite easy for a Swiss waiter to be rude, and I was on the point of telling him that at the moment I was engaged and that the manager would have to wait, when something which I thought I saw in his eye caused me to change my mind, and, with an indefinable sense of discomfort, I allowed him to show me to the managerial sanctum. I never had liked the look of that manager; I liked it less than ever when I found myself alone in his room with him. He was a youngish man, with a moustache, and hair parted mathematically in the centre. In general his bearing was too saccharine to be pleasant; he did not err in that respect just then – it was most offensive. He looked me up and down as if I were one of his employees who had done something wrong, and, without waiting for me to speak, he said:

'You are Miss Judith Lee – or you pretend that is your name?'

He spoke English very well, as most of the Swiss one meets in hotels seem to do. Nothing could have been more impertinent than his tone, unless it was the look which accompanied it. I stared at him.

'I am Miss Lee. I do not pretend that is my name; it is.'

'Very well – that is your affair, not mine. You will no longer be allowed to occupy a room in this hotel. You can go at once.'

'What do you mean?' I asked. The man was incredible.

'You know very well what I mean. Don't you try that sort of thing with me. You have stolen an article of jewellery belonging to a guest in my hotel. She is a very kind-hearted lady, and she is not willing to hand you over to the police. You owe me some money; here's your bill. Are you going to pay it?'

He handed me a long strip of paper which was covered with figures. One glance at the total was enough to tell me that I had not enough money. Mrs Travers was acting as my banker. She had left me with ample funds to serve as pocket-money till she returned, but with nothing like enough money to pay that bill.

'Mrs Travers will pay you when she comes back, either tomorrow or the day after.'

'Will she?' The sneer with which he said it! 'How am I to know that you're not at the same game together?'

'The same game! What do you mean? How dare you look at me like that, and talk to me as if I were one of your servants!'

'I'm not going to talk to you at all, my girl; I'm going to do. I'm not going to allow a person who robs my guests to remain in my house under any pretext whatever. Your luggage, such as it is, will remain here until my bill is paid.' He rang a bell which was on the table by which he was standing. The waiter entered who had showed me there. He was a big man, with a square, dark face. 'This young woman must go at once. If she won't leave of her own accord we must put her out, by the back door. Now, my girl – out you go!'

The waiter approached me. He spoke to me as he might have done to a dog.

'Now, then, come along.'

He actually put his hand upon my shoulder. Another second, and I believe he would have swung me round and out of the room. But just as he touched me the door was opened and someone came rushing in – Mrs Anstruther, in a state of the greatest excitement.

'My diamonds have been stolen!' she cried. 'Someone has stolen my diamonds!'

'Your diamonds?' The manager looked at her and then at me. 'I trust, madam, you are mistaken?'

'I'm not mistaken.' She sank on to a chair. She was a big woman of about fifty, and, at the best of times, was scant of breath. Such was her agitation that just then she could scarcely breathe at all. 'As if I could be mistaken about a thing like that! I went up to my bedroom – to dress for dinner – and I unlocked my trunk – I always keep it locked; I took out my jewel-case – and unlocked that – and my diamonds were gone. They've been stolen! – stolen! – stolen!'

She repeated the word 'stolen' three times over, as if the heinousness of the fact required to be emphasised by repetition. The manager was evidently uneasy, which even I felt was not to be wondered at.

'This is a very serious matter, Mrs Anstruther –'

She cut him short.

'Serious? Do you think I need you to tell me that it's serious? You don't know how serious. Those diamonds are worth thousands and thousands of pounds – more than the whole of your twopenny-halfpenny hotel – and they've been stolen. From my trunk, in my bedroom, in your hotel, they've been stolen!'

The way she hurled the words at him! He looked at me, and he asked:

'What do you know about this?'

What did I know? In the midst of my confusion and distress I was asking myself what I did know. Before I could speak the door was opened again and Mrs Newball came in. And not Mrs Newball only, but six or seven other women, some of them accompanied by men – their husbands and their brothers. And they all told the same tale. Something had been stolen from each: from Mrs Newball her five strings of pearls, from Mrs This and Miss That the article of jewellery which was valued most. I am convinced that that manager, or his room, or probably his hotel, had never witnessed such a scene before. They were all as excited as could be, and they were all talking at once, and every second or two, someone else kept coming in with some fresh tale of a dreadful loss. How that man kept his head at all was, and is, a mystery to me. At last he reduced them to something like silence, and in the presence of them all he said to me – pointing at me with his finger, as if I were a thing to be pointed at:

'It is you who have done this! You!'

Someone exclaimed in the crowd: 'I saw her coming out of Mrs Anstruther's room.'

The manager demanded: 'Who spoke? Who was it said that?'

A slight, faded, fair-haired woman came out into the public gaze.

'I am Mrs Anstruther's maid. I was going along to her room when I saw this young lady come out of the door. Whether she saw me or not I can't say; she might have done, because she ran off as fast as ever she could. I wondered what she was doing there, and when my mistress came I told her what I had seen, and that's what made her open her trunk.'

'What Perkins says is quite true,' corroborated Mrs Anstruther. 'She did tell me, and that made me uneasy; I had heard something about a diamond pendant having been stolen last night, so I opened my jewel-case, and my diamonds were gone.'

'Mine was the diamond pendant which was stolen by this creature last night,' interposed Miss Goodridge. 'She came to my room and took it out of my trunk. Since she did that it seems not impossible that she has played the same trick on other people today. If she has, she must have had a pretty good haul, because I don't believe there is a person in the hotel who hasn't lost something.'

The manager spoke to an under-strapper:

'Have this young woman's luggage searched at once, in the presence of witnesses, and let me know the result as soon as you possibly can.'

As the under-strapper went out I noticed for the first time that Mr Sterndale was present with the rest, and almost at the same instant his sister came in. She looked about her as if wondering what was the cause of all the fuss. Then she went up to her brother, and he whispered something to her, and she whispered something to him. Only three or four words in each case, but my heart gave a leap in my bosom – I mean that, really, because it did feel as if it actually had jumped – courage came into me, and strength, and something better than hope: certainty; because they had delivered themselves into my hands. I was never more thankful that I had the power of eavesdropping – you can call it eavesdropping, if you like! – than I was at that moment. Only a second before I had been fearing that I was in a tight place, from which there was no way out; which would mean something for me from which my very soul seemed to shrink. But God had given me a gift, a talent, which I had striven with all my might to improve ten, twenty fold, and that would deliver me from the wiles of those two people, even when hope of deliverance there seemed none. I feel confident that I held myself straighter, that trouble went from my face as it had done from my heart, and that, though each moment the case against me seemed to be growing blacker and blacker, I grew calmer and more self-possessed. I knew I had only to wait till the proper moment came, and the toils in which they thought they had caught me would prove to be mere nothings; they would be caught, and I should be free.

All the same, until that moment for which I was waiting came, it was not nice for me – standing there amidst all those excited people, between two porters, who kept close to either side of me, as if I were a prisoner and they had me in charge; though I dare say it was as well that they did keep as close to me as they did, because I fancy that some of the injured guests at that hotel would have liked to give me a practical demonstration of what their feelings towards me were.

That under-strapper came back in a surprisingly short space of time with a hand-bag – a brown bag, which I recognised to be my own.

The agitated guests crowded round him like a swarm of bees. He had difficulty in forcing his way through them. The manager did his best to keep them in something like order – first with a show of mildness.

'Ladies, gentlemen – gently, gently, if you please.' Then, with sudden ferocity: 'Stand back, there! If you will not stand back, if you will not make room, how can anything be done? Keep these people back!'

To whom this order was addressed was not quite clear. Thus admonished, the people kept themselves back – at least, sufficiently to enable that under-strapper to pass with my bag to the table. The manager said to him:

'Go to the other side; what have you in that bag?' When, as he said this, his guests evinced an inclination to press forward, he threw out his arms on either side of him and positively shouted:

'Will you not keep back? If you will keep back, everything shall be done in order before you all. I ask you only to be a little sensible. If there is so much confusion, we shall not know what we are doing. I beg of you that you will be calm.'

If they were not precisely calm, the people did show some slight inclination to behave with an approach to common sense. They permitted the bag to be placed on the table, and the manager to open it, having first put some questions to the young man who brought it in.

'Where did you find this bag?'

'In her room.' I was the 'her' which he made clear by pointing his finger straight at me.

'Was anyone else present in the room at the time you found it? Did you find anything else?'

'There were three other persons present in the room. That bag was the first thing I touched. When I opened it and saw what was inside, I thought that, for the present, that would be enough. I think you also will be of my opinion when you see what it contains.'

Then the manager opened the bag. He looked inside, then he turned it upside down and allowed the whole contents to fall out on to the table. Of all the extraordinary collections! I believe there were articles belonging to every person in the hotel. When you came to think of it, it was amazing how they had been gathered together – in what could only have been a short space of time – without the gatherer being detected. As for the behaviour

of the guests of the hotel, it was like Bedlam broken loose. They
pressed forward all together, ejaculating, exclaiming, snatching at
this and that, as each saw some personal belonging,

'Keep back! Keep back!' shouted the manager. 'Will you not
keep back?' As he positively roared at them they did shrink back
as if a trifle startled. 'If you will only have a little patience each
lady shall have what belongs to her – if it is here.'

Mrs Anstruther's voice was heard above the hubbub: 'Are my
diamonds there?' Then Mrs Newball's: 'And my pearls?'

The under-strapper was examining the miscellaneous collection
which my bag had contained with all those women breaking
into continual exclamations, watching him with hungry eyes. He
announced the result of his examination.

'No; Mrs Anstruther's diamonds do not appear to be here, nor
Mrs Newball's pearls; there is nothing here which at all resembles
them.'

The manager held out towards me a minatory finger;
everyone seemed to have developed a sudden mania for pointing,
particularly at me.

'You! Where have you put Mrs Newball's pearls and Mrs
Anstruther's diamonds? Better make a clean breast of it, and no
longer play the hypocrite. We will find them, if you do not tell us
where they are, be sure of it. Now tell us at once.'

How he thundered at me! It was most embarrassing, or it would
have been if I had not been conscious that I held the key of the
situation in my hand. As it was, I minded his thunder scarcely a
little bit, though I always have hated being shouted at. I was very
calm – certainly the calmest person there – which, of course, was
not saying very much.

'I can tell you where they are, if that is what you mean.'

'You know that is what I mean. Tell us at once! At once!'

He banged his fist upon the table so that that miscellaneous
collection trembled. I did not tremble, though perhaps it was his
intention that I should. I was growing calmer and calmer.

'In the first place, let me inform you that if you suppose I
put those things in my bag – the bag is certainly mine – or had

anything to do with their getting there, you are mistaken.'

My words, and perhaps my manner, created a small diversion. 'What impudence!' 'What assurance!' 'Did you ever see anything like it?' 'So young and so brazen!' 'The impudent baggage!' Those were some of the things which they said, which were very nice for me to have to listen to. But I was sure, from a glimpse I had caught of Mr and Miss Sterndale, that they were not quite at their ease, and that was such a comfort.

'No lies!' thundered the manager, whose English became a little vulgar. 'No foolery! No stuck-up rubbish! Tell us the truth – where are these ladies' jewels?'

'I propose to tell you the truth, if you will have a little patience.' I returned him look for look; I was not the least afraid of him. 'I am going to give you a little surprise.' I was so conscious of that that I was beginning to feel almost amused. 'I have a power of which I think none of you has any conception, especially two of you. I know what people are saying although I do not hear them; like the deaf and dumb, who know what a person is saying by merely watching his lips.'

There were some very rude interruptions, to which I paid no notice whatever. An elderly man whom I had never seen before, and who spoke with an air of authority, advised them to give me a hearing. They did let me go on.

I told them what I had seen Miss Sterndale say to her brother on the balcony the morning before. It was some satisfaction to see the startled look which came upon the faces of both the brother and the sister. They made some very noisy and uncivil comments, but, as I could see how uncomfortable they were feeling, I let them make them. I went on. I told how unhappy I had been all day, and how, when I returned, I found under the bottom tray of my jewel-case the diamond pendant. How, astounded, I went down to ask Miss Sterndale why she had put it there, and how, encountering Miss Goodridge bewailing her loss, utterly taken aback, I held out to her her pendant in a manner which, I admitted, might very easily have seemed suspicious.

By this time the manager's room was in a delightful state of din. Mr and Miss Sterndale were both of them shouting together, declaring that it was shocking that such a creature as I was should be allowed to make such monstrous insinuations. I believe, if it had not been for that grey-haired man who had suddenly assumed a position of authority, that Miss Sterndale would have made a personal assault on me. She seemed half beside herself with rage – and, I was quite sure, with something else as well.

I continued – in spite of the Sterndales. I could see that I was creating a state of perplexity in the minds of my hearers which might very shortly induce them to take up an entirely different attitude towards me. I told of the brief dialogue which had taken place between the sister and brother that very morning. And then you should have seen how the Sterndales stormed and raged.

'It seems to me,' observed the grey-haired man to Mr Sterndale, 'that you protest too much, sir. If this young lady is all the things you say she is, presently you will have every opportunity of proving it. Since she is one young girl among all us grown-ups, it is only right and decent that we should hear what she has to say for herself. We can condemn her afterwards – that part will be easy.'

So I went on again. There was very little to add. They knew almost as much of the rest as I did. Someone had effected a wholesale clearance of pretty nearly every valuable which the house contained. I did not pretend to be certain, but I thought it extremely probable that it was Miss Sterndale who had done this, while her brother kept the owners occupied in other directions. At this point glances were exchanged. I afterwards learned that Mr Sterndale had organised a party for an excursion on the Lake of Brienz, which had been joined by nearly everyone in the place with the exception of Miss Sterndale, who was supposed to have gone for a solitary expedition up the Schynnige Platte. When Miss Sterndale saw those glances, as I have no doubt she did, she commenced to storm and rage again, and continued to the end. I do not think, even then, she guessed what was coming; but she was already more uncomfortable than she had expected to be, and I could see that her brother felt the same.

His face was white and set; he looked like a man who was trying to think of the best way in which to confront a desperate situation.

I went on to explain, quite calmly, that as, owing to the machinations of Mr Sterndale and his sister, everyone in the house had come to look upon me as a thief, their evident intention was to allow suspicion to be centred on me, and that that was why they put those things in my bag.

'But what were they going to gain by that?' asked the grey-haired man, rather pertinently. His question was echoed in a chorus by the rest – particularly, I noticed, by the Sterndales, who laid emphasis on the transparent absurdity of what I was saying.

'If you will allow me to continue, I will soon make it perfectly clear to you what they were going to gain. If you remember, when Mr Sterndale was talking to his sister on the balcony this morning, I saw him say to her that there were only two things in the house worth having.'

Here Mr Sterndale burst into a very hurricane of adjectives. The grey-haired man addressed him with rather unlooked-for vigour.

'Silence, sir! Allow Miss Lee to continue.'

Mr Sterndale was silent. I fancy he was rather cowed by what he saw in the speaker's eyes. I did continue.

'The only two things which, according to Mr Sterndale, were worth having were Mrs Anstruther's diamonds and Mrs Newball's pearls. If they put the whole of the rest of the stolen things into my bag it would be taken for granted that I was the thief, and they would be able to continue in unsuspected possession of the two things which were worth much more than all the rest put together.'

The moment I stopped the clamour began again.

'And where do you suggest, young lady,' asked the grey-haired man, 'that those two articles are?'

'I will tell you.' I looked at Miss Sterndale and then at her brother. I believe they would both have liked to have killed and eaten me. They can scarcely have been sure, even then, of what I was going to say, but I could see that they were devoured by anxiety and fear. 'I have told you that I can see what people are saying by merely watching their lips. When Miss Sterndale came into the room she whispered something to her brother, in so faint a whisper that her words could have been scarcely audible even to themselves; but I saw their faces, and I knew what they had said as plainly as if they had shouted it. He told her that he had Mrs Anstruther's diamonds in the pocket of the jacket he has on.'

I paused. The first expression on Mr Sterndale's face was one of blank astonishment. Then he broke into Billingsgate abuse of me.

'You infernal liar! You two-faced cat! You dirty little witch! I'm not going to stay in this room to be insulted by a miserable creature –'

He made for the door. 'Stop him!' I cried. As he reached the door it was thrown back almost in his face, and who should come into the room but Mr and Mrs Travers. How glad I was to see them! 'Stop him!' I cried to Mr Travers. 'Stop that man!' And Mr Travers stopped him. 'Put your hand into the pocket of his jacket and take out what he has there.'

Mr Travers, knowing nothing of what had been taking place, must have been rather at a loss as to what I might mean by such a request; but he did as I told him, all the same. Mr Sterndale struggled; he did his best to protect himself and his pocket; but he was rather a small man, and Mr Travers was a giant, both in stature and in strength. In a very few seconds he was staring at the contents of his hand.

'From the look of things, this gentleman's pocket seems to be stuffed with diamonds. Here's a diamond necklace.'

He held one up in the air. Heavy weight though she was, I believe that Mrs Anstruther sprang several inches from the floor.

'It's my necklace!' she screamed.

'And where are my pearls?' demanded Mrs Newball.

'Miss Sterndale whispered to her brother that your pearls were inside the bodice of her dress.'

The words were scarcely out of my lips before Mrs Newball sprang at Miss Sterndale, and there ensued a really painful scene. Had she not been restrained, I dare say she would have torn Miss Sterndale's clothes right off her. As it was, someone opened her bodice, and the pearls were produced.

The scene which followed was like pandemonium on a small scale. It seemed as if everyone had gone stark, staring mad. Guests, manager, and staff were all shouting together. I know that Mrs Travers had her arm round me, and I was happier than – only a few minutes before – I thought that I should ever feel again.

We did not prosecute the Sterndales – which turned out not to be their name, and they were proved not to be sister and brother. Law in Switzerland does not move too quickly; the formalities to be observed are numerous. I did not very much want to have to remain in Switzerland for an indefinite period, at my own expense, to give evidence in a case in which I was not in the faintest degree interested. The others, the guests in the hotel, did not want to do that anymore than I did. Their property was restored to them – that was what they wanted.

They would have liked to punish the thieves, but not at the cost of so much inconvenience to themselves. So far as we were concerned, the criminals got off scot-free; but, none the less, they did not escape the vengeance of the law. That night they were arrested at Interlaken on another charge. It seemed that they were the perpetrators of that robbery in the hotel at Pontresina which, according to Mr Sterndale, his apocryphal clerical friend had laid at my door. They had passed there as Mr and Mrs Burnett, and were found guilty and sentenced to a long term of imprisonment. I have not seen or heard anything of that pseudonymous brother and sister since. I hope I never shall.

To find out what people are saying to each other in confidence, when they suppose themselves to be out of the reach of curious ears, may be very like eavesdropping. If it is, I am very glad that, on various occasions in my life, I have been enabled to be an eavesdropper in that sense. Had I not, at Interlaken, had the power which made of me an eavesdropper, I might have been branded as a criminal, and my happiness, my whole life, have been destroyed for ever.

DIANA MARBURG, 'THE ORACLE OF MADDOX STREET'

Created by LT Meade (1844–1914) and Robert Eustace (1854–1943)

She appeared in only a handful of stories, first published in Pearson's Magazine *in 1902, but Diana Marburg is one of the most interesting and offbeat women detectives of the period. A palmist by profession, with an interest in the occult and what she calls 'strange mysteries of the unseen world', she is invited to use her expertise in solving crimes. Although palm-reading plays its part in the Diana Marburg stories, the explanations and motives for the wrongdoings in them are rooted very firmly in the natural world rather than the realm of the supernatural. One tale provides an early example of the use of fingerprints (the first UK Fingerprint Bureau was only established in Scotland Yard the year before the story's publication); another contains arguably the most ingenious, if wildly implausible, method of murder in all of Edwardian crime fiction. There is no murder in 'Sir Penn Caryll's Engagement', only fraud and deception, but the perpetrators certainly display plenty of ingenuity in the means they employ to carry out their scam. Whether it is plausible or not is up to the individual reader to decide. Diana Marburg was created by the same writing partnership that produced Florence Cusack (see p. 48). LT Meade was a feminist, novelist and founder-editor in 1887 of* Atalanta, *a well-known magazine for girls. She was an almost ridiculously productive writer who published more than 300 books in her lifetime. Robert Eustace was the pen name of an English doctor named Eustace Robert Barton who collaborated with several other writers, including, later in his career, Dorothy L Sayers. Meade and Eustace were also responsible for several other memorable characters who appeared in the magazines of the period, including a femme fatale and supervillain named Madame Sara and John Bell, an investigator of the supernatural.*

SIR PENN CARYLL'S ENGAGEMENT

Sir Penn Caryll's engagement was the talk of all his friends. He was a man of about forty, of good family, fairly rich, and boasting of two nice country seats. He also kept a racing stable and added thereby considerably to his income. Sir Penn was so good-looking, so cheery and gay of heart, that he was a great favourite, and more than one eager mother thought of him as an excellent husband for her daughter, and more than one pretty girl looked at him with eyes of favour.

Nevertheless Sir Penn had proved himself impervious to the charms of all fair women, until a certain day when a bright-eyed Tasmanian girl, who went by the name of Esther Haldane, brought him to her feet. The girl in question was only nineteen, was to all appearances poor, and seemed to have no relations in London, except a brother, who was considered by those who knew best to be a somewhat questionable possession. Karl Haldane was a man without apparent profession, and with no certain income, and there was little doubt that he and his sister lived, before the engagement, more or less as adventurers.

After Sir Penn declared his attachment to Miss Haldane, however, he placed his country seat in Sussex at her disposal, putting her under the charge of his aunt, a certain Mrs Percival, and going there himself at intervals. The wedding was to take place early in July. Sir Penn received the congratulations of his friends, and Miss Haldane was thought one of the luckiest girls of the day.

The time was the fourth of May. I was dining alone and was somewhat surprised when Sir Penn's card was brought to me with a request scribbled in writing that I would see him without a moment's delay. I hurried at once into his presence. His face was as a rule remarkable for its serenity, and I was startled when I observed the change in it.

'I fear you are not well,' I said. 'I hope there is nothing wrong.'

'I am afraid there is,' he replied. 'May I tell you the object of my visit?'

I asked him to seat himself, and prepared to listen with attention.

'I have decided to ask you to help me,' he said abruptly. 'An ordinary detective would be worse than useless. I have been brought into contact lately with the most extraordinary and uncanny phenomenon, and unless matters are put right without delay, I shall find myself in a serious financial difficulty. You may be certain I would not say these things to you without grave reason, and I must ask for the utmost secrecy on your part.'

'Of course,' I replied.

He bent forward and looked at me keenly.

'Have you ever, in all your experience of occult matters, come across a case of thought-reading in which you were satisfied that imposture was absolutely excluded, and that the thoughts of one person were really conveyed to the brain of another? Do such things exist in this world of reality?'

I paused before replying.

'You ask me a strange question, Sir Penn, and if you want my true opinion I do think such things possible.'

'You think so? Who, then, can be safe? Now listen to my own personal experience. You know, of course, that I am the owner of a number of racehorses. Horse-racing is an expensive game, and my expenses are principally met by successful speculation on my horses. Now, of course, there are many secrets in a stable, such as which is the best horse for a certain race, or the capacity of any other horse. These things have to be kept from the outside world. The most important of all our secrets are obtained by what we call "trials".

'I will briefly explain. We have, say, half a dozen horses, and we wish to know which is the best for a certain distance. The horses are led out and mounted, and the trial gallop takes place. Now the horse that wins the race may not by any means be the best of the half-dozen horses that we wish to prove, for if such were the case anyone watching the trial would at once know our secret. So to keep the matter dark the various saddles are weighted with different weights, giving heavier loads for some horses to carry than others. In this manner we can not only calculate which is the best horse, but can keep the information from outsiders. For a slightly weighted bad horse will beat a heavily weighted good one.

'No one but the trainer and myself know what weights are applied to the saddles, and the whole thing is done just at the last moment before the horses start. After the trial only my trainer and myself know which is the best horse. We then discuss what we will do and which horse I shall support in the betting market. Is that clear to you?'

'Perfectly,' I replied.

'You doubtless also comprehend that if these matters were known to an outsider, he could profit immensely by backing my best horse, and could prevent me getting my money on at a good price.'

'I understand.'

'Then pray listen. For some time I have been certain that secrets with regard to the weights in the saddles have eked out, to my own immense loss and to the great gain of someone else. On looking carefully into the matter, I find that the bookmakers in London, through whom the fiend who is trying to ruin me must execute his commissions, have information with regard to the horses almost immediately after the trial takes place at Lewes.

'Now I will tell you of the last case. A trial took place of my horses on the twentieth of April on the Downs at eleven o'clock in the morning. On that occasion even my trainer did not know the weights that they carried. In order to make things quite safe I kept the knowledge altogether to myself. The people who witnessed the race were my aunt, Mrs Percival, Miss Esther Haldane, the young lady to whom I have the honour of being engaged, I myself and my trainer. My bay horse Victor won the trial, though he was not first by any means in the race. We four talked the matter over on the Downs; we then walked home quietly all together. On reaching home at twelve o'clock I wired to my agent in cipher to invest heavily on Victor, whose price was twenty to one.

'That same afternoon, I received the astounding information that he was first favourite at three to one, a large commission already having been executed. Now this commission was executed at Tattersalls, in London, at half-past eleven, actually within half an hour after the trial was known, and also half an hour before any of us reached home from the Downs. The thing is astounding, for even if anyone did secretly watch the trial it would be impossible, without knowing the weights, to tell which was the best horse. That knowledge was only known to us four, and to no one else in the world. You have, therefore, this fact to face. A certain piece of information is known to four people on an open Down in Sussex at ten minutes past eleven, and yet that information is acted on in London twenty minutes later. There is no question of my trainer playing me false, as he could not possibly communicate the information in the time I have mentioned, and I have come to the conclusion that some extraordinary thought-transference is the only thing to fall back upon.'

I was silent for a moment, then I said suddenly:

'Do you happen to remember, Sir Penn, if the sun was shining on that last occasion?'

'Why?' he asked, in some surprise.

'Because there would be just the possibility of your trainer heliographing the information.'

'That is a clever suggestion,' he exclaimed, 'but it won't do. It happened to be a cloudy day.'

'Then for the moment I see no solution,' I replied. 'May I ask if you know anyone who has ever threatened to read your thoughts?'

'Certainly I do. Karl Haldane, my future wife's brother, who calls himself a clairvoyant. To be plain with you, Miss Marburg, I have no particular fancy for Mr Karl Haldane; but there is no doubt he is extremely clever, and Esther is devotedly attached to him. He certainly would be the last man who would try to ruin me. We must try to get at the solution in some other way.'

'Nevertheless, may I ask you a question or two?' I said. 'Was Mr

196

Haldane at your house when the affair you have just mentioned took place?'

'No, he had been staying with us, but he left early that morning.'

'I should like to see him,' I said, after a pause.

Sir Penn's eyes brightened.

'You are wrong in suspecting for a moment that Haldane has anything to do with the matter,' he said. 'Nevertheless if you like to meet him, you can: I am particularly anxious to introduce you to Esther. I have a big party down at Lewes just now. A trial of my horses for the Derby takes place early next week. Will you come to my place and be present at the trial? Can you do so?'

'Of course I will come. I would throw over any engagement for such an important, and I must say, to me, interesting case.'

'Will you come tomorrow? I will meet you by the four o'clock train.'

I promised to do so, and after thanking me warmly Sir Penn took his leave. Truly a queer case had now been put into my hands. Sir Penn was regarded amongst all his friends as a practical man; nevertheless, in his difficulties he consulted me, the occultist and believer in thought reading. One thing certainly was evident, either what had happened was a genuine case of thought transference, or a very subtle form of fraud. The latter seemed truly to be impossible.

When I reached Lewes the next day Sir Penn was waiting for me. On arriving at Court Prospect, the name of his beautiful house, I found a large party assembled in the hall. Mrs Percival, Sir Penn's aunt, was present, and was dispensing tea. I had met her before, and she came forward now and greeted me kindly.

'It is very good of you to come, Miss Marburg,' she said, 'and I have delighted more than one person present by saying I am sure you will give a séance while you are with us. Oh! Of course I quite believe in palmistry, and Mr Haldane, one of the best clairvoyants I have ever known, will arrive this evening. We shall doubtless have a most interesting time. Have you yet met Mr Haldane?'

'No.'

'Then I shall have the pleasure of introducing two kindred spirits. Ah! Esther, my dear, come here.'

A slim, remarkably graceful girl rose from her seat at a little distance. She strolled leisurely towards us. I am tall, but Miss Haldane was half a head taller. Mrs Percival made the necessary introduction. Miss Haldane looked at me slowly. All her movements were slow. She then opened her magnificent eyes a trifle wider than their wont and held out her hand.

'I am glad to see you,' she said in a cordial tone.

She did not utter another word, but went back to her seat. I stood silent where she had left me. I no longer wondered at Sir Penn's infatuation. It was not the beauty of the girl that so impressed me; she was beautiful, for all her features were good; but from a strict standpoint there were prettier girls in the room. No, Miss Haldane's beauty lay in the extraordinary and almost wicked magnetism of her eyes. Those eyes knew too much. I did not think they looked good – they saw too deeply beneath the surface. Even I, callous to most things of that sort, felt my heart beat uncomfortably fast after Miss Haldane's extraordinary and penetrating glance.

'You look tired, Miss Marburg,' said Mrs Percival. 'Won't you have some tea?'

She handed me a cup which I took mechanically. I was still thinking of Miss Haldane and her eyes. I felt quite sure that no one could see her without thinking of her eyes alone, the rest of her beautifully moulded face, graceful pose and slim young figure being all forgotten in the effect that the eyes produced.

In the drawing-room just before dinner I was introduced to Miss Haldane's brother. To my astonishment he was in every respect her opposite. He was a fair haired, stoutly built, ugly man. He was not only ugly but his expression was absolutely unpleasant. Nevertheless, he too had his charms. When he spoke you forgot the ugly features, the sunken eyes, the leer round the mouth. His voice was good, nay, beautiful. His intellect was undoubtedly powerful, and he had a sympathising manner which appealed more or less to all those to whom he spoke. He happened to be my neighbour at dinner on that first evening, and before the meal came to an end I had arrived at the conclusion that he was a most remarkable and most interesting man.

On the next day several of the guests took their departure, and Esther Haldane and I found ourselves alone. We went for a walk together on the Downs and afterwards sat in the cosy boudoir where she made tea for me.

'You must allow me to congratulate you,' I said suddenly. 'You are a very lucky girl.'

'What do you mean?' she asked.

'Need you ask? You have won the affections of Sir Penn Caryll. You are about to marry him. I have known him since I was a child. You are in luck, Miss Haldane. You are going to marry a good man.'

She fixed her eyes on me, the pupils dilating until they looked black; then, very slowly, the lovely eyes filled with tears. She dropped on her knees beside me.

'You are a clairvoyante,' she said; 'so, for that matter, is Karl. I am afraid of Karl, and very little would make me afraid of you. Will you look at my hand?'

She held it out as she spoke. I examined it attentively. I saw, to my regret, many bad points. The Mount of Mercury was sunken, the heart-line was chained, and Jupiter was remarkable for his absence. All these things proclaimed this girl, according to my creed, to be unscrupulous, even cruel. She did not look cruel, and I had no reason up to the present to doubt her honour. Nevertheless, I dropped her hand with a sigh. It was quite an unusual one for a girl to possess.

'What is the matter?' she asked. 'Am I so very bad?'

'I have seen more promising hands,' I answered.

'Tell me what you see?'

'Do you really wish to know?'

'Yes.'

'Forewarned is forearmed,' I said, after a moment's pause. 'Your circumstances are happy, Miss Haldane, and there is no reason why you should not lead a good and honourable life to the end of the chapter. Nevertheless, your hand points to a certain unscrupulousness in your character. For instance, I should not care to submit you to a very great money temptation.'

'Oh, you are horrible!' she cried. Her face grew very white. 'You frighten me; you talk nonsense, and yet, and yet it is nonsense that Karl believes in.'

She began to rub the offending palm.

'I am going to my room,' she said. 'Your words have worried me.'

Her manner was somewhat that of a spoilt child. I smiled to myself, but an unaccountable weight of suspicion and dread was hanging over me. Why should I believe anything evil of a beautiful girl like Esther Haldane? What object could she have in injuring the man whom she was about to marry? I felt ashamed of my own suspicions; nevertheless they would not quite go away.

On the next day the trial of Sir Penn's horses would take place, and on that evening just when dinner was coming to an end, Miss Haldane raised her voice and called across to her brother, who was sitting at the other end of the table.

'Karl,' she cried, 'Sir Penn has been asking if you will not give us a séance this evening. You have been very disagreeable not to do so before. You will oblige, I think I may say, all the company. Will you not consent on this occasion?'

The ladies bowed and smiled, and the men bent forward to watch what Haldane would do. I thought – or was I mistaken? – that he gave his sister a sudden glance of understanding. Then he said with that slow sort of drawl which now and then characterised him:

'I shall have much pleasure in doing what the company wish.'

Sir Penn expressed his satisfaction, and there was a chorus of approval from one and all.

When we met in the drawing-room Haldane came to the front.

'Ladies and gentlemen,' he said, 'I have been asked to give tonight a demonstration of thought transference. This I am willing to do on a condition. I want you all to be absolutely satisfied that there is no deception. I will therefore leave the room in company with someone now present, who shall remain with me until I return.

'While I am away, a certain sentence employing intelligible words shall be decided upon by two persons in the room. All the company may know the sentence if they so will, but it is essential that two should do so in order that there may be a witness that my interpretation of the said sentence is correct. The two persons who know the sentence will stand with their backs towards me at one end of the room; I will stand with my back towards them at the other. And if those two people faithfully think of that sentence, and of that sentence alone, I promise to read their thoughts and to say what it is. Do you all consider that fair?'

'Certainly,' said Sir Penn, 'and I will bet you ten pounds, Haldane, that you fail.'

'Done, Sir Penn,' was the answer.

A discussion as to who should be the person to accompany Mr Haldane outside the room, and to choose the sentence within the room, immediately ensued.

'In view of my wager, ladies and gentlemen,' cried Sir Penn, 'I think I may claim the right to be one of those to choose the sentence. As to my partner, I will leave the choice to yourselves.'

I could see by Sir Penn's manner that he was determined to clear up the terrible suspicion that was haunting him.

'I will be your partner, if I may,' said Miss Haldane, and she went up to Sir Penn, and laid her hand on his arm.

He seemed to hesitate for a minute; then he looked into her eyes, and said softly:

'As you wish.'

Sir Penn then turned to me.

'Miss Marburg,' he said, 'may I ask you to accompany Mr Haldane from the room?'

'With pleasure,' I replied. I felt interested and excited, and was determined that no trickery should be played if I could prevent it.

Karl Haldane and I repaired to the library, and in exactly ten minutes' time returned to the drawing-room. There was a dead silence. Sir Penn and Miss Haldane stood at the further end of the room. Karl Haldane at once took up his position, with his back towards them. Being, as it were, in the position of umpire, I determined to watch the experiment with the utmost vigilance, and accordingly I crossed the room to where Sir Penn and Miss Haldane were standing. I stood near them and took care to watch them both. They were absolutely still. Miss Haldane's hands were locked in front of her, her features were as quiet as though she were sitting for her photograph; her face was whiter than usual, and her strange eyes had a staring look. I thought the expression of the eyes unnatural – she looked as though she were about to cry.

Fully five minutes passed, and then Mr Haldane called out in a clear, musical voice:

'I have received the impression. Judge, please, if I am correct. I presume I must thank Sir Penn for this copybook sentence. It is as follows:

'"If you are using your powers for fraudulent purposes, beware!"

'Am I right, Sir Penn?'

The Baronet's reply was to come forward, open his pocket-book and hand the clairvoyant a banknote for ten pounds. There was quite a sensation in the room.

Later that same evening Sir Penn found an opportunity of seeing me alone.

'What do you think of this affair?' he asked.

'I cannot tell you what I think of it at present,' was my answer. 'I am certain there is an explanatory cause, although what it is I cannot say. Let me think over everything most carefully. Mr Haldane leaves tomorrow, does he not?'

'Yes, thank goodness, by an early train. I don't like the man and I cannot pretend that I do. I wish with all my heart he were not Esther's brother. But let us turn to something more important. Tomorrow the trial of my horses takes place. I propose that you and Mrs Percival and Miss Haldane and myself go to see it. I have a colt named Fritz, who is in for the Derby, and I think I know what he can do. If the trial goes as I expect, Fritz will be the winner. The result of tomorrow's trial must be kept absolutely a secret until I can operate in the market. If I find that the information again gets out – well, I shall cease to keep racehorses.'

'I will do my very best for you, Sir Penn,' I answered.

When he had left me I went to my room – there I sat down and prepared to think out the enigma. Hour after hour went by, and my busy brain felt on fire. Each moment I became more and more certain that some fraud was being worked by Mr Haldane, but he could scarcely manage this without an accomplice, and terrible as the idea was, if there really was foul play, his sister must stand in that position towards him. Her hand betrayed her. What her motive was it was impossible to tell, but her hand made crime a contingency not too remote to contemplate.

As I thought and thought I became certain that if only I could discover the key to that evening's performance, I should have also the key to the entire position. I recalled the scene vividly. Miss Haldane's curious and rigid attitude; the peculiar expression in her eyes. I thought of all the ordinary methods of communication – hand language – lip language. Both were out of the question. Yet the means must have been very sure in order to communicate the exact wording of the sentence.

Through what channel of the senses could it have passed? Was there any movement? I fixed my memory again, centring my whole thoughts upon it. The eyes! Esther Haldane's eyes had always struck me as wonderful – nay more, as odd. They looked very odd as I gazed at them while the clairvoyant at the other end of the room was thinking out the sentence. She had blinked several times, too, as if about to cry.

I arose from my chair. A strange idea had struck me. I lit my candle and went down through the silent house. I entered the drawing-room. When I got there I quickly examined the exact places where Haldane and his sister had stood. From the place where Miss Haldane stood her eyes by means of a big mirror could be seen by Haldane. As I thought over this fact the dim outline of a terrible plot began to reveal itself. The human eyes are always naturally winking. Only a code, such as the Morse Telegraphic Code, was necessary. A long closing of the lids for a dash, a short one for a dot, and any communication was possible and could not be detected by the closest observer.

I left the drawing-room, and crossing over to the library took down a volume of the *Encyclopaedia Britannica*, and carefully copied the letter signs of the Morse Telegraphic Code. I then returned to my room.

During breakfast I watched Miss Haldane, and as I did so the simplicity of the wicked scheme, evidently evolved both by her brother and herself, was borne in upon me. She looked particularly handsome this morning, but also nervous and anxious.

The guests who were still staying in the house took their departure after breakfast, amongst those to leave being Karl Haldane. I saw him go up to his sister and kiss her. As he was leaving the room she turned very white, so white that I wondered if she were going to faint.

'Are you ill?' I said. 'Does it trouble you so much to part from your brother?'

'We are very much attached,' she said, her lips quivering.

'I have remarked that,' I answered.

She flashed an excited glance at me.

'Who would not be?' she continued. 'Has he not fascinated you? There is no woman who comes in contact with him who does not love him.'

At that instant Sir Penn came into the room. He went up to her, and laid his hand affectionately on her shoulder.

'We are due on the Downs at eleven,' he said. 'Miss Marburg is coming with us.'

'Are you?' asked Miss Haldane.

The information certainly gave her no pleasure.

'I should like to see the horses,' was my answer.

Nothing more was said. Mrs Percival came into the room, the conversation became general, and at about a quarter to eleven we four started for our walk. It was a glorious morning, sunny and warm. Nevertheless, our conversation flagged, and we walked on for some time in silence.

At length we reached the racing ground, and Sir Penn showed us a good position to witness the trial, in which some dozen horses were to take part. Mr Martin, the trainer, and our four selves took up our position at the intended winning post on a little rise amongst some furze bushes. Sir Penn drew out his watch.

'It is exactly midday,' he said.

'Here they come!' cried Miss Haldane excitedly, and in a few moments, with a thunder of hoofs, the animals galloped past.

'Just what I thought, Martin,' said the baronet. 'If Fritz doesn't bring home the Blue Riband this year he is certain to be in the first three.'

'And if he is, you will be richer than ever,' said Miss Haldane, laying her hand on his arm. 'Do go, Miss Marburg, to look at the probable winner of the Derby. Take Miss Marburg to see Fritz, won't you, Penn?'

Sir Penn and the trainer moved up to where the horses were being pulled up. As Sir Penn did so he turned to me.

'Will you come?' he asked. 'Won't you come too, Esther?'

'No,' she replied. 'I am feeling tired. I will stay with Mrs Percival.'

'Do, my dear,' said the elder lady. 'We will both sit down on this knoll of grass and wait for you, Penn, and for Miss Marburg.'

I slowly followed Sir Penn, but when I had gone a few steps, I turned aside and pretended to be plucking some small flowers that grew on the edge of the common. My heart was beating almost to suffocation. I feared that Miss Haldane would observe me, and that I should lose a possible opportunity. But she had evidently forgotten my existence. Mrs Percival had opened a newspaper and was beginning to read. Sir Penn and the trainer were more than a hundred yards away. I stood on her left. She rose slowly to her feet and gazed out steadily across the Down in the direction of an old ruined barn some six hundred yards off.

I quickly took out pencil and paper and, keeping my eyes fixed on hers, marked the movement of the long and short closure of her lids. That slip of paper I have still, and this is the copy as I took it down:

FRITZWONTRIAL

Without a moment's pause or giving myself time to think I rushed up to her side.

'What are you doing?' I cried.

My voice startled her. She flashed round, fury in her eyes.

'Fritz won trial,' I said, as I deciphered the dots and dashes from the code.

She stared wildly at me for one moment, then suddenly falling on her knees she burst into a passion of tears. At this instant Sir Penn came up.

'Esther!' he cried. 'Miss Marburg, whatever is the matter?'

I turned to him.

'This is the matter,' I answered. 'The plot is discovered. Send a couple of stable lads to prevent anyone from leaving that barn, and bring whoever is there here at once.'

In a moment the word was given, and Sir Penn turned to Miss Haldane. She still knelt on the grass, her face covered, the tears flowing between her fingers. Sir Penn's face turned white as death. I saw that he guessed the worst. The girl to whom he was engaged, and whom he loved with all his heart, had betrayed him. Nothing else greatly mattered at that moment.

'Look!' I cried.

Two boys on their horses had just headed off the figure of a man who was running with all his might towards the railway station. It was, I could see at a glance, Mr Karl Haldane. A moment later he was brought to the spot where we stood. His face was also white, but very hard and determined-looking.

'Come, Esther, old girl,' he said, speaking in an almost rough tone, and pulling the weeping girl to her feet. 'You did your best. We must all fail at times. I presume,' he added, 'that Esther and I have failed, but will you explain why you sent two men to interfere with my liberty, Sir Penn?'

'I think I can best explain,' was my answer.

I then proceeded, in the presence of Esther and Karl Haldane, to give step by step the means I had taken to discover their secret. When I had finished speaking there was silence. After a pause, which was the most impressive I ever endured, Esther Haldane approached Sir Penn.

'You can, of course, arrest both me and my husband,' she said.

'Good heavens!' he exclaimed. 'Your husband?'

'Yes, Karl Haldane is my husband. I have played you the meanest trick a woman can play a man. I tried first to win your love, secondly to win your money. I succeeded in the first. I failed in the latter. All that I have done I have done for my husband, the only man on God's earth whom I really love. I love him so well that I can even go under for him. You can take what steps you please to punish us both. Come, Karl, our game is up.'

LADY MOLLY

Created by Baroness Emma Orczy
(1865–1947)

The daughter of a Hungarian aristocrat, Baroness Emma Orczy was born on the family estate in Tarnaörs, northern Hungary. A peasant uprising in 1868 forced her parents to move to Budapest and she was later educated in Paris and Brussels. The family settled in London when she was in her teens and she studied art at Heatherley's School of Art in Chelsea. It was there that she met her husband Montague Barstow and her first published work was a collection of Hungarian folk tales which he illustrated. Her first historical novel was published in 1899. Her most famous character, Sir Percy Blakeney aka 'The Scarlet Pimpernel', a daring English adventurer who rescues people from the guillotine in Revolutionary France, made his debut in a play in 1903 and went on to appear in a long series of novels and short stories. Baroness Orczy created two very distinctive detectives in the Edwardian era. One was 'The Old Man in the Corner' who solves seemingly insoluble mysteries whilst barely stirring from his seat in a London teashop. He and the lady journalist Polly Burton, who records the mysteries on which the old man throws light, first appeared in The Royal Magazine *in 1901 and later in three collections of short stories. Baroness Orczy's other detective creation was Lady Molly Robertson-Kirk, a young woman who has reached a position of authority in Scotland Yard nearly a decade before women in real life were even allowed to join the police. As narrated by her adoring sidekick, Mary Granard, Lady Molly's adventures are very much of their time but they are still great fun to read.*

THE WOMAN IN THE BIG HAT

1

Lady Molly always had the idea that if the finger of Fate had pointed to Mathis' in Regent Street, rather than to Lyons', as the most advisable place for us to have a cup of tea that afternoon, Mr Culledon would be alive at the present moment.

My dear lady is quite sure – and needless to say that I share her belief in herself – that she would have anticipated the murderer's intentions, and thus prevented one of the most cruel and callous of crimes which were ever perpetrated in the heart of London.

She and I had been to a matinée of *Trilby*, and were having tea at Lyons', which is exactly opposite Mathis' Vienna café in Regent Street. From where we sat we commanded a view of the street and of the café, which had been very crowded during the last hour.

We had lingered over our toasted muffin until past six, when our attention was drawn to the unusual commotion which had arisen both outside and in the brilliantly lighted place over the road.

We saw two men run out of the doorway, and return a minute or two later in company with a policeman. You know what is the inevitable result of such a proceeding in London. Within three minutes a crowd had collected outside Mathis'. Two or three more constables had already assembled, and had some difficulty in keeping the entrance clear of intruders.

But already my dear lady, keen as a pointer on the scent, had hastily paid her bill, and, without waiting to see if I followed her or not, had quickly crossed the road, and the next moment her graceful form was lost in the crowd.

I went after her, impelled by curiosity, and presently caught sight of her in close conversation with one of our own men. I have always thought that Lady Molly must have eyes at the back of her head, otherwise how could she have known that I stood behind her now? Anyway, she beckoned to me, and together we entered Mathis', much to the astonishment and anger of the less fortunate crowd.

The usually gay little place was indeed sadly transformed. In one corner the waitresses, in dainty caps and aprons, had put their heads together, and were eagerly whispering to one another whilst casting furtive looks at the small group assembled in front of one of those pretty alcoves, which, as you know, line the walls all round the big tea-room at Mathis'.

Here two of our men were busy with pencil and notebook, whilst one fair-haired waitress, dissolved in tears, was apparently giving them a great deal of irrelevant and confused information.

Chief Inspector Saunders had, I understood, been already sent for; the constables, confronted with this extraordinary tragedy, were casting anxious glances towards the main entrance, whilst putting the conventional questions to the young waitress. And in the alcove itself, raised from the floor of the room by a couple of carpeted steps, the cause of all this commotion, all this anxiety, and all these tears, sat huddled up on a chair, with arms lying straight across the marble-topped table, on which the usual paraphernalia of afternoon tea still lay scattered about. The upper part of the body, limp, backboneless, and awry, half propped up against the wall, half falling back upon the outstretched arms, told quite plainly its weird tale of death.

Before my dear lady and I had time to ask any questions, Saunders arrived in a taxicab. He was accompanied by the medical officer, Dr Townson, who at once busied himself with the dead man, whilst Saunders went up quickly to Lady Molly.

'The chief suggested sending for you,' he said quickly; 'he was 'phoning you when I left. There's a woman in this case, and we shall rely on you a good deal.'

'What has happened?' asked my dear lady, whose fine eyes were glowing with excitement at the mere suggestion of work.

'I have only a few stray particulars,' replied Saunders, 'but the chief witness is that yellow-haired girl over there. We'll find out what we can from her directly Dr Townson has given us his opinion.'

The medical officer, who had been kneeling beside the dead man, now rose and turned to Saunders. His face was very grave.

'The whole matter is simple enough, so far as I am concerned,' he said. 'The man has been killed by a terrific dose of morphia – administered, no doubt, in this cup of chocolate,' he added, pointing to a cup in which there still lingered the cold dregs of the thick beverage.

'But when did this occur?' asked Saunders, turning to the waitress.

'I can't say,' she replied, speaking with obvious nervousness. 'The gentleman came in very early with a lady, somewhere about four. They made straight for this alcove. The place was just beginning to fill, and the music had begun.'

'And where is the lady now?'

'She went off almost directly. She had ordered tea for herself and a cup of chocolate for the gentleman, also muffins and cakes. About five minutes afterwards, as I went past their table, I heard her say to him. "I am afraid I must go now, or Jay's will be closed, but I'll be back in less than half an hour. You'll wait for me, won't you?"'

'Did the gentleman seem all right then?'

'Oh, yes,' said the waitress. 'He had just begun to sip his chocolate, and merely said "S'long" as she gathered up her gloves and muff and then went out of the shop.'

'And she has not returned since?'

'No.'

'When did you first notice there was anything wrong with this gentleman?' asked Lady Molly.

'Well,' said the girl with some hesitation, 'I looked at him once or twice as I went up and down, for he certainly seemed to have fallen all of a heap. Of course, I thought that he had gone to sleep, and I spoke to the manageress about him, but she thought that I ought to leave him alone for a bit. Then we got very busy, and I paid no more attention to him, until about six o'clock, when most afternoon tea customers had gone, and we were beginning to get the tables ready for dinners. Then I certainly did think there was something wrong with the man. I called to the manageress, and we sent for the police.'

'And the lady who was with him at first, what was she like? Would you know her again?' queried Saunders.

'I don't know,' replied the girl; 'you see, I have to attend to such crowds of people of an afternoon, I can't notice each one. And she had on one of those enormous mushroom hats; no one could have seen her face – not more than her chin – unless they looked right under the hat.'

'Would you know the hat again?' asked Lady Molly.

'Yes – I think I should,' said the waitress. 'It was black velvet and had a lot of plumes. It was enormous,' she added, with a sigh of admiration and of longing for the monumental headgear.

During the girl's narrative one of the constables had searched the dead man's pockets. Among other items, he had found several letters addressed to Mark Culledon, Esq., some with an address in Lombard Street, others with one in Fitzjohn's Avenue, Hampstead. The initials MC, which appeared both in the hat and on the silver mount of a letter-case belonging to the unfortunate gentleman, proved his identity beyond a doubt.

A house in Fitzjohn's Avenue does not, somehow, suggest a bachelor establishment. Even whilst Saunders and the other men were looking through the belongings of the deceased, Lady Molly had already thought of his family – children, perhaps a wife, a mother – who could tell?

What awful news to bring to an unsuspecting, happy family, who might even now be expecting the return of father, husband, or son, at the very moment when he lay murdered in a public place, the victim of some hideous plot or feminine revenge!

As our amiable friends in Paris would say, it jumped to the eyes that there was a woman in the case – a woman who had worn a gargantuan hat for the obvious purpose of remaining unidentifiable when the question of the unfortunate victim's companion that afternoon came up for solution. And all these facts to put before an expectant wife or an anxious mother!

As, no doubt, you have already foreseen, Lady Molly took

the difficult task on her own kind shoulders. She and I drove together to Lorbury House, Fitzjohn's Avenue, and on asking of the manservant who opened the door if his mistress were at home, we were told that Lady Irene Culledon was in the drawing-room.

Mine is not a story of sentiment, so I am not going to dwell on that interview, which was one of the most painful moments I recollect having lived through.

Lady Irene was young – not five-and-twenty, I should say – *petite* and frail-looking, but with a quiet dignity of manner which was most impressive. She was Irish, as you know, the daughter of the Earl of Athyville, and, it seems, had married Mr Mark Culledon in the teeth of strenuous opposition on the part of her family, which was as penniless as it was aristocratic, whilst Mr Culledon had great prospects and a splendid business, but possessed neither ancestors nor high connections. She had only been married six months, poor little soul, and from all accounts must have idolised her husband.

Lady Molly broke the news to her with infinite tact, but there it was! It was a terrific blow – wasn't it? – to deal to a young wife – now a widow; and there was so little that a stranger could say in these circumstances. Even my dear lady's gentle voice, her persuasive eloquence, her kindly words, sounded empty and conventional in the face of such appalling grief.

2

Of course, everyone expected that the inquest would reveal something of the murdered man's inner life – would, in fact, allow the over-eager public to get a peep into Mr Mark Culledon's secret orchard, wherein walked a lady who wore abnormally large velvet hats, and who nourished in her heart one of those terrible grudges against a man which can only find satisfaction in crime.

Equally, of course, the inquest revealed nothing that the public did not already know. The young widow was extremely reticent on the subject of her late husband's life, and the servants had all been fresh arrivals when the young couple, just home from their honeymoon, organised their new household at Lorbury House.

There was an old aunt of the deceased – a Mrs Steinberg – who lived with the Culledons, but who at the present moment was very ill. Someone in the house – one of the younger servants, probably – very foolishly had told her every detail of the awful tragedy. With positively amazing strength, the invalid thereupon insisted on making a sworn statement, which she desired should be placed before the coroner's jury. She wished to bear solemn testimony to the integrity of her late nephew, Mark Culledon, in case the personality of the mysterious woman in the big hat suggested to evilly disposed minds any thought of scandal.

'Mark Culledon was the one nephew whom I loved,' she stated with solemn emphasis. 'I have shown my love for him by bequeathing to him the large fortune which I inherited from the late Mr Steinberg. Mark was the soul of honour, or I should have cut him out of my will as I did my other nephews and nieces. I was brought up in a Scotch home, and I hate all this modern fastness and smartness, which are only other words for what I call profligacy.'

Needless to say, the old lady's statement, solemn though it was, was of no use whatever for the elucidation of the mystery which surrounded the death of Mr Mark Culledon. But as Mrs Steinberg had talked of 'other nephews', whom she had cut out of her will in favour of the murdered man, the police directed inquiries in those various quarters.

Mr Mark Culledon certainly had several brothers and sisters, also cousins, who at different times – usually for some peccadillo or other – seemed to have incurred the wrath of the strait-laced old lady. But there did not appear to have been any ill-feeling in the family owing to this. Mrs Steinberg was sole mistress of her fortune. She might just as well have bequeathed it *in toto* to some hospital as to one particular nephew whom she favoured, and the various relations were glad, on the whole, that the money was going to remain in the family rather than be cast abroad.

The mystery surrounding the woman in the big hat deepened as the days went by. As you know, the longer the period of time which elapses between a crime and the identification of the criminal, the greater chance the latter has of remaining at large.

In spite of strenuous efforts and close questionings of every one of the employees at Mathis', no one could give a very accurate description of the lady who had tea with the deceased on that fateful afternoon.

The first glimmer of light on the mysterious occurrence was thrown, about three weeks later, by a young woman named Katherine Harris, who had been parlour-maid at Lorbury House when first Mr and Lady Irene Culledon returned from their honeymoon.

I must tell you that Mrs Steinberg had died a few days after the inquest. The excitement had been too much for her enfeebled heart. Just before her death she had deposited £250 with her banker, which sum was to be paid over to any person giving information which would lead to the apprehension and conviction of the murderer of Mr Mark Culledon.

This offer had stimulated everyone's zeal, and, I presume, had aroused Katherine Harris to a realisation of what had all the while been her obvious duty.

Lady Molly saw her in the chief's private office, and had much ado to disentangle the threads of the girl's confused narrative. But the main point of Harris's story was that a foreign lady had once called at Lorbury House, about a week after the master and mistress had returned from their honeymoon. Lady Irene was out at the time, and Mr Culledon saw the lady in his smoking-room.

'She was a very handsome lady,' explained Harris, 'and was beautifully dressed.'

'Did she wear a large hat?' asked the chief.

'I don't remember if it was particularly large,' replied the girl.

'But you remember what the lady was like?' suggested Lady Molly.

'Yes, pretty well. She was very, very tall, and very good-looking.'

'Would you know her again if you saw her?' rejoined my dear lady.

'Oh, yes; I think so,' was Katherine Harris's reply.

Unfortunately, beyond this assurance the girl could say nothing very definite. The foreign lady seems to have been closeted with Mr Culledon for about an hour, at the end of which time Lady Irene came home.

The butler being out that afternoon it was Harris who let her mistress in, and as the latter asked no questions, the girl did not volunteer the information that her master had a visitor. She went back to the servants' hall, but five minutes later the smoking-room bell rang, and she had to run up again. The foreign lady was then in the hall alone, and obviously waiting to be shown out. This Harris did, after which Mr Culledon came out of his room, and, in the girl's own graphic words, 'he went on dreadful'.

'I didn't know I 'ad done anything so very wrong,' she explained, 'but the master seemed quite furious, and said I wasn't a proper parlour-maid, or I'd have known that visitors must not be shown in straight away like that. I ought to have said that I didn't know if Mr Culledon was in; that I would go and see. Oh, he did go on at me!' continued Katherine Harris, volubly. 'And I suppose he complained to the mistress, for she give me notice the next day.'

'And you have never seen the foreign lady since?' concluded Lady Molly.

'No; she never come while I was there.'

'By the way, how did you know she was foreign? Did she speak like a foreigner?'

'Oh, no,' replied the girl. 'She did not say much – only asked for Mr Culledon – but she looked French like.'

This unanswerable bit of logic concluded Katherine's statement. She was very anxious to know whether, if the foreign lady was hanged for murder, she herself would get the £250.

On Lady Molly's assurance that she certainly would, she departed in apparent content.

3

'Well! we are no nearer than we were before,' said the chief, with an impatient sigh, when the door had closed behind Katherine Harris.

'Don't you think so?' rejoined Lady Molly, blandly.

'Do you consider that what we have heard just now has helped us to discover who was the woman in the big hat?' retorted the chief, somewhat testily.

'Perhaps not,' replied my dear lady, with her sweet smile; 'but it may help us to discover who murdered Mr Culledon.'

With which enigmatical statement she effectually silenced the chief, and finally walked out of his office, followed by her faithful Mary.

Following Katherine Harris's indications, a description of the lady who was wanted in connection with the murder of Mr Culledon was very widely circulated, and within two days of the interview with the ex-parlour-maid another very momentous one took place in the same office.

Lady Molly was at work with the chief over some reports, whilst I was taking shorthand notes at a side desk, when a card was brought in by one of the men, and the next moment, without waiting either for permission to enter or to be more formally announced, a magnificent apparition literally sailed into the dust-covered little back office, filling it with an atmosphere of Parma violets and Russia leather.

I don't think that I had ever seen a more beautiful woman in my life. Tall, with a splendid figure and perfect carriage, she vaguely reminded me of the portraits one sees of the late Empress of Austria. This lady was, moreover, dressed to perfection, and wore a large hat adorned with a quantity of plumes.

The chief had instinctively risen to greet her, whilst Lady Molly, still and placid, was eyeing her with a quizzical smile.

'You know who I am, sir,' began the visitor as soon as she had sunk gracefully into a chair; 'my name is on that card. My appearance, I understand, tallies exactly with that of a woman who is supposed to have murdered Mark Culledon.'

She said this so calmly, with such perfect self-possession, that I literally gasped. The chief, too, seemed to have been metaphorically lifted off his feet. He tried to mutter a reply.

'Oh, don't trouble yourself, sir!' she interrupted him, with a smile. 'My landlady, my servant, my friends have all read the description of the woman who murdered Mr Culledon. For the past twenty-four hours I have been watched by your police, therefore I have come to you of my own accord, before they came to arrest me in my flat. I am not too soon, am I?' she asked, with that same cool indifference which was so startling, considering the subject of her conversation.

She spoke English with a scarcely perceptible foreign accent, but I quite understood what Katherine Harris had meant when she said that the lady looked 'French like'. She certainly did not look English, and when I caught sight of her name on the card, which the chief had handed to Lady Molly, I put her down at once as Viennese. Miss Elizabeth Löwenthal had all the charm, the grace, the elegance, which one associates with Austrian women more than with those of any other nation.

No wonder the chief found it difficult to tell her that, as a matter of fact, the police were about to apply for a warrant that very morning for her arrest on a charge of wilful murder .

'I know – I know,' she said, seeming to divine his thoughts; 'but let me tell you at once, sir, that I did not murder Mark Culledon. He treated me shamefully, and I would willingly have made a scandal just to spite him; he had become so respectable and strait-laced. But between scandal and murder there is a wide gulf. Don't you think so, madam?' she added, turning for the first time towards Lady Molly.

'Undoubtedly,' replied my dear lady, with the same quizzical smile.

'A wide gulf which, no doubt, Miss Elizabeth Löwenthal will best be able to demonstrate to the magistrate tomorrow,' rejoined the chief, with official sternness of manner.

I thought that, for the space of a few seconds, the lady lost her self-assurance at this obvious suggestion – the bloom on her cheeks seemed to vanish, and two hard lines appeared between her fine eyes. But, frightened or not, she quickly recovered herself, and said quietly:

'Now, my dear sir, let us understand one another. I came here for that express purpose. I take it that you don't want your police to look ridiculous any more than I want a scandal. I don't want detectives to hang about round my flat, questioning my neighbours and my servants. They would soon find out that I did not murder Mark Culledon, of course; but the atmosphere of the police would hang round me, and I – I prefer Parma violets,' she added, raising a daintily perfumed handkerchief to her nose.

'Then you have come to make a statement?' asked the chief.

'Yes,' she replied; 'I'll tell you all I know. Mr Culledon was engaged to marry me; then he met the daughter of an earl, and thought he would like her better as a wife than a simple Miss Löwenthal. I suppose I should be considered an undesirable match for a young man who has a highly respectable and snobbish aunt, who would leave him all her money only on the condition that he made a suitable marriage. I have a voice, and I came over to England two years ago to study English, so that I might sing in oratorio at the Albert Hall. I met Mark on the Calais-Dover boat, when he was returning from a holiday abroad. He fell in love with me, and presently he asked me to be his wife. After some demur, I accepted him; we became engaged, but he told me that our engagement must remain a secret, for he had an old aunt from whom he had great expectations, and who might not approve of his marrying a foreign girl, who was without connections and a professional singer. From that moment I mistrusted him, nor was I very astonished when gradually his affection for me seemed to cool. Soon after, he informed me, quite callously, that he had changed his mind, and was going to marry some swell English lady. I didn't care much, but I wanted to punish him by making a scandal, you understand. I went to his house just to worry him, and finally I decided to bring an action for breach of promise against him. It would have upset him, I know; no doubt his aunt would have cut him out of her will. That is all I wanted, but I did not care enough about him to murder him.'

Somehow her tale carried conviction. We were all of us obviously impressed. The chief alone looked visibly disturbed, and I could read what was going on in his mind.

'As you say, Miss Löwenthal,' he rejoined, 'the police would have found all this out within the next few hours. Once your connection with the murdered man was known to us, the record of your past and his becomes an easy one to peruse. No doubt, too,' he added insinuatingly, 'our men would soon have been placed in possession of the one undisputable proof of your complete innocence with regard to that fateful afternoon spent at Mathis' café.'

'What is that?' she queried blandly.

'An alibi.'

'You mean, where I was during the time that Mark was being murdered in a teashop?'

'Yes,' said the chief.

'I was out for a walk,' she replied quietly.

'Shopping, perhaps?'

'No.'

'You met someone who would remember the circumstance — or your servants could say at what time you came in?'

'No,' she repeated dryly; 'I met no one, for I took a brisk walk on Primrose Hill. My two servants could only say that I went out at three o'clock that afternoon and returned after five.'

There was silence in the little office for a moment or two. I could hear the scraping of the pen with which the chief was idly scribbling geometrical figures on his blotting pad.

Lady Molly was quite still. Her large, luminous eyes were fixed on the beautiful woman who had just told us her strange story, with its unaccountable sequel, its mystery which had deepened with the last phrase which she had uttered. Miss Löwenthal, I felt sure, was conscious of her peril. I am not sufficiently a psychologist to know whether it was guilt or merely fear which was distorting the handsome features now, hardening the face and causing the lips to tremble.

Lady Molly scribbled a few words on a scrap of paper, which she then passed over to the chief. Miss Löwenthal was making visible efforts to steady her nerves.

'That is all I have to tell you,' she said, in a voice which sounded dry and harsh. 'I think I will go home now.'

But she did not rise from her chair, and seemed to hesitate as if fearful lest permission to go were not granted her.

To her obvious astonishment – and, I must add, to my own – the chief immediately rose and said, quite urbanely:

'I thank you very much for the helpful information which you have given me. Of course, we may rely on your presence in town for the next few days, may we not?'

She seemed greatly relieved, and all at once resumed her former charm of manner and elegance of attitude. The beautiful face was lit up by a smile.

The chief was bowing to her in quite a foreign fashion, and in spite of her visible reassurance she eyed him very intently. Then she went up to Lady Molly and held out her hand.

My dear lady took it without an instant's hesitation. I, who knew that it was the few words hastily scribbled by Lady Molly which had dictated the chief's conduct with regard to Miss Löwenthal, was left wondering whether the woman I loved best in all the world had been shaking hands with a murderess.

4

No doubt you will remember the sensation which was caused by the arrest of Miss Löwenthal, on a charge of having murdered Mr Mark Culledon, by administering morphia to him in a cup of chocolate at Mathis' café in Regent Street.

The beauty of the accused, her undeniable charm of manner, the hitherto blameless character of her life, all tended to make the public take violent sides either for or against her, and the usual budget of amateur correspondence, suggestions, recriminations and advice poured into the chief's office in titanic proportions.

I must say that, personally, all my sympathies went out to Miss Löwenthal. As I have said before, I am no psychologist, but I had seen her in the original interview at the office, and I could not get rid of an absolutely unreasoning certitude that the beautiful Viennese singer was innocent.

The magistrate's court was packed, as you may well imagine, on that first day of the inquiry; and, of course, sympathy with the accused went up to fever pitch when she staggered into the dock, beautiful still, despite the ravages caused by horror, anxiety, fear, in face of the deadly peril in which she stood.

The magistrate was most kind to her; her solicitor was unimpeachably assiduous; even our fellows, who had to give evidence against her, did no more than their duty, and were as lenient in their statements as possible.

Miss Löwenthal had been arrested in her flat by Danvers, accompanied by two constables. She had loudly protested her innocence all along, and did so still, pleading 'Not guilty' in a firm voice.

The great points in favour of the arrest were, firstly, the undoubted motive of disappointment and revenge against a faithless sweetheart, then the total inability to prove any kind of alibi, which, under the circumstances, certainly added to the appearance of guilt.

The question of where the fatal drug was obtained was more difficult to prove. It was stated that Mr Mark Culledon was director of several important companies, one of which carried on business as wholesale druggists.

Therefore it was argued that the accused, at different times and under some pretext or other, had obtained drugs from Mr Culledon himself. She had admitted to having visited the deceased at his office in the City, both before and after his marriage.

Miss Löwenthal listened to all this evidence against her with a hard, set face, as she did also to Katherine Harris's statement about her calling on Mr Culledon at Lorbury House, but she brightened up visibly when the various attendants at Mathis' café were placed in the box.

A very large hat belonging to the accused was shown to the witnesses, but, though the police upheld the theory that that was the headgear worn by the mysterious lady at the café on that fateful afternoon, the waitresses made distinctly contradictory statements with regard to it.

Whilst one girl swore that she recognised the very hat, another was equally positive that it was distinctly smaller than the one she recollected, and when the hat was placed on the head of Miss Löwenthal, three out of the four witnesses positively refused to identify her.

Most of these young women declared that though the accused, when wearing the big hat, looked as if she might have been the lady in question, yet there was a certain something about her which was different.

With that vagueness which is a usual and highly irritating characteristic of their class, the girls finally parried every question by refusing to swear positively either for or against the identity of Miss Löwenthal.

'There's something that's different about her somehow,' one of the waitresses asserted positively.

'What is it that's different?' asked the solicitor for the accused, pressing his point.

'I can't say,' was the perpetual, maddening reply.

Of course, the poor young widow had to be dragged into the case, and here, I think, opinions and even expressions of sympathy were quite unanimous.

The whole tragedy had been inexpressibly painful to her, of course, and now it must have seemed doubly so. The scandal which had accumulated round her late husband's name must have added the poignancy of shame to that of grief. Mark Culledon had behaved as callously to the girl whom clearly he had married from interested, family motives, as he had to the one whom he had heartlessly cast aside.

Lady Irene, however, was most moderate in her statements.

There was no doubt that she had known of her husband's previous entanglement with Miss Löwenthal, but apparently had not thought fit to make him accountable for the past. She did not know that Miss Löwenthal had threatened a breach of promise action against her husband.

Throughout her evidence she spoke with absolute calm and dignity, and looked indeed a strange contrast, in her closely fitting tailor-made costume of black serge and tiny black toque, to the more brilliant woman who stood in the dock.

The two great points in favour of the accused were, firstly, the vagueness of the witnesses who were called to identify her, and, secondly, the fact that she had undoubtedly begun proceedings for breach of promise against the deceased. Judging by the latter's letters to her, she would have had a splendid case against him, which fact naturally dealt a severe blow to the theory as to motive for the murder.

On the whole, the magistrate felt that there was not a sufficiency of evidence against the accused to warrant his committing her for trial; he therefore discharged her, and, amid loud applause from the public, Miss Löwenthal left the court a free woman.

Now, I know that the public did loudly, and, to my mind, very justly, blame the police for that arrest, which was denounced as being as cruel as it was unjustifiable. I felt as strongly as anybody on the subject, for I knew that the prosecution had been instituted in defiance of Lady Molly's express advice, and in distinct contradiction to the evidence which she had collected. When, therefore, the chief asked my dear lady to renew her efforts in that mysterious case, it was small wonder that her enthusiasm did not respond to his anxiety. That she would do her duty was beyond a doubt, but she had very naturally lost her more fervent interest in the case.

The mysterious woman in the big hat was still the chief subject of leading articles in the papers, coupled with that of the ineptitude of the police who could not discover her. There were caricatures and picture post-cards in all the shop windows of a gigantic hat covering the whole figure of its wearer, only the feet, and a very long and pointed chin, protruding from beneath the enormous brim. Below was the device, 'Who is she? Ask the police?'

One day – it was the second since the discharge of Miss Löwenthal – my dear lady came into my room beaming. It was the first time I had seen her smile for more than a week, and already I had guessed what it was that had cheered her.

'Good news, Mary,' she said gaily. 'At last I've got the chief to let me have a free hand. Oh, dear! what a lot of argument it takes to extricate that man from the tangled meshes of red tape!'

'What are you going to do?' I asked.

'Prove that my theory is right as to who murdered Mark Culledon,' she replied seriously; 'and as a preliminary we'll go and ask his servants at Lorbury House a few questions.'

It was then three o'clock in the afternoon. At Lady Molly's bidding, I dressed somewhat smartly, and together we went off in a taxi to Fitzjohn's Avenue.

Lady Molly had written a few words on one of her cards, urgently requesting an interview with Lady Irene Culledon. This she handed over to the man-servant who opened the door at Lorbury House. A few moments later we were sitting in the cosy boudoir. The young widow, high-bred and dignified in her tight-fitting black gown, sat opposite to us, her white hands folded demurely before her, her small head, with its very close coiffure, bent in closest attention towards Lady Molly.

'I most sincerely hope, Lady Irene,' began my dear lady, in her most gentle and persuasive voice, 'that you will look with all possible indulgence on my growing desire – shared, I may say, by all my superiors at Scotland Yard – to elucidate the mystery which still surrounds your late husband's death.'

Lady Molly paused, as if waiting for encouragement to proceed. The subject must have been extremely painful to the young widow; nevertheless she responded quite gently:

'I can understand that the police wish to do their duty in the matter; as for me, I have done all, I think, that could be expected of me. I am not made of iron, and after that day in the police court –'

She checked herself, as if afraid of having betrayed more emotion than was consistent with good breeding, and concluded more calmly:

'I cannot do any more.'

'I fully appreciate your feelings in the matter,' said Lady Molly, 'but you would not mind helping us – would you? – in a passive way, if you could, by some simple means, further the cause of justice.'

'What is it you want me to do?' asked Lady Irene.

'Only to allow me to ring for two of your maids and to ask them a few questions. I promise you that they shall not be of such a nature as to cause you the slightest pain.'

For a moment I thought that the young widow hesitated, then, without a word, she rose and rang the bell.

'Which of my servants did you wish to see?' she asked, turning to my dear lady as soon as the butler entered in answer to the bell.

'Your own maid and your parlour-maid, if I may,' replied Lady Molly.

Lady Irene gave the necessary orders, and we all sat expectant and silent until, a minute or two later, two girls entered the room. One wore a cap and apron, the other, in neat black dress and dainty lace collar, was obviously the lady's maid.

'This lady,' said their mistress, addressing the two girls, 'wishes to ask you a few questions. She is a representative of the police, so you had better do your best to satisfy her with your answers.'

'Oh!' rejoined Lady Molly pleasantly – choosing not to notice the tone of acerbity with which the young widow had spoken, nor the unmistakable barrier of hostility and reserve which her words had immediately raised between the young servants and the 'representative of the police' – 'what I am going to ask these two young ladies is neither very difficult nor very unpleasant. I merely want their kind help in a little comedy which will have to be played this evening, in order to test the accuracy of certain statements made by one of the waitresses at Mathis' teashop with regard to the terrible tragedy which has darkened this house. You will do that much, will you not?' she added, speaking directly to the maids.

No one can be so winning or so persuasive as my dear lady. In a moment I saw the girls' hostility melting before the sunshine of Lady Molly's smile.

'We'll do what we can, ma'am,' said the maid.

'That's a brave, good girl!' replied my lady. 'You must know that the chief waitress at Mathis' has, this very morning, identified the woman in the big hat who, we all believe, murdered your late master. Yes!' she continued, in response to a gasp of astonishment which seemed to go round the room like a wave, 'the girl seems quite positive, both as regards the hat and the woman who wore it. But, of course, one cannot allow a human life to be sworn away without bringing every possible proof to bear on such a statement, and I am sure that everyone in this house will understand that we don't want to introduce strangers more than we can help into this sad affair, which already has been bruited abroad too much.'

She paused a moment; then, as neither Lady Irene nor the maids made any comment, she continued:

'My superiors at Scotland Yard think it their duty to try and confuse the witness as much as possible in her act of identification. They desire that a certain number of ladies wearing abnormally large hats should parade before the waitress. Among them will be, of course, the one whom the girl has already identified as being the mysterious person who had tea with Mr Culledon at Mathis' that afternoon.

'My superiors can then satisfy themselves whether the waitress is or is not so sure of her statement that she invariably picks out again and again one particular individual amongst a number of others or not.'

'Surely,' interrupted Lady Irene, dryly, 'you and your superiors do not expect my servants to help in such a farce?'

'We don't look upon such a proceeding as a farce, Lady Irene,' rejoined Lady Molly, gently. 'It is often resorted to in the interests

227

of an accused person, and we certainly would ask the cooperation of your household.'

'I don't see what they can do.'

But the two girls did not seem unwilling. The idea appealed to them, I felt sure; it suggested an exciting episode, and gave promise of variety in their monotonous lives.

'I am sure both these young ladies possess fine big hats,' continued Lady Molly with an encouraging smile.

'I should not allow them to wear ridiculous headgear,' retorted Lady Irene, sternly.

'I have the one your ladyship wouldn't wear, and threw away,' interposed the young parlour-maid. 'I put it together again with the scraps I found in the dusthole.'

There was just one instant of absolute silence, one of those magnetic moments when Fate seems to have dropped the spool on which she was spinning the threads of a life, and is just stooping in order to pick it up.

Lady Irene raised a black-bordered handkerchief to her lips, then said quietly:

'I don't know what you mean, Mary. I never wear big hats.'

'No, my lady,' here interposed the lady's maid; 'but Mary means the one you ordered at Sanchia's and only wore the once – the day you went to that concert.'

'Which day was that?' asked Lady Molly, blandly.

'Oh! I couldn't forget that day,' ejaculated the maid; 'her ladyship came home from the concert – I had undressed her, and she told me that she would never wear her big hat again – it was too heavy. That same day Mr Culledon was murdered.'

'That hat would answer our purpose very well,' said Lady Molly, quite calmly. 'Perhaps Mary will go and fetch it, and you had better go and help her put it on.'

The two girls went out of the room without another word, and there were we three women left facing one another, with that awful secret, only half-revealed, hovering in the air like an intangible spectre.

'What are you going to do, Lady Irene?' asked Lady Molly,

after a moment's pause, during which I literally could hear my own heart beating, whilst I watched the rigid figure of the widow in deep black crape, her face set and white, her eyes fixed steadily on Lady Molly.

'You can't prove it!' she said defiantly.

'I think we can,' rejoined Lady Molly, simply; 'at any rate, I mean to try. I have two of the waitresses from Mathis' outside in a cab, and I have already spoken to the attendant who served you at Sanchia's, an obscure milliner in a back street near Portland Road. We know that you were at great pains there to order a hat of certain dimensions and to your own minute description; it was a copy of one you had once seen Miss Löwenthal wear when you met her at your late husband's office. We can prove that meeting, too. Then we have your maid's testimony that you wore that same hat once, and once only, the day, presumably, that you went out to a concert – a statement which you will find it difficult to substantiate – and also the day on which your husband was murdered.'

'Bah! the public will laugh at you!' retorted Lady Irene, still defiantly. 'You would not dare to formulate so monstrous a charge!'

'It will not seem monstrous when justice has weighed in the balance the facts which we can prove. Let me tell you a few of these, the result of careful investigation. There is the fact that you knew of Mr Culledon's entanglement with Miss Elizabeth Löwenthal, and did your best to keep it from old Mrs Steinberg's knowledge, realising that any scandal round her favourite nephew would result in the old lady cutting him – and therefore you – out of her will. You dismissed a parlour-maid for the sole reason that she had been present when Miss Löwenthal was shown into Mr Culledon's study. There is the fact that Mrs Steinberg had so worded her will that, in the event of her nephew dying before her, her fortune would devolve on you; the fact that, with Miss Löwenthal's action for breach of promise against your husband, your last hope of keeping the scandal from the old lady's ears had effectually vanished. You saw the fortune eluding your grasp;

you feared Mrs Steinberg would alter her will. Had you found the means, and had you dared, would you not rather have killed the old lady? But discovery would have been certain. The other crime was bolder and surer. You have inherited the old lady's millions, for she never knew of her nephew's earlier peccadillos.

'All this we can state and prove, and the history of the hat, bought, and worn one day only, that same memorable day, and then thrown away.'

A loud laugh interrupted her – a laugh that froze my very marrow.

'There is one fact you have forgotten, my lady of Scotland Yard,' came in sharp, strident accents from the black-robed figure, which seemed to have become strangely spectral in the fast gathering gloom which had been enveloping the luxurious little boudoir. 'Don't omit to mention the fact that the accused took the law into her own hands.'

And before my dear lady and I could rush to prevent her, Lady Irene Culledon had conveyed something – we dared not think what – to her mouth.

'Find Danvers quickly, Mary!' said Lady Molly, calmly. 'You'll find him outside. Bring a doctor back with you.'

Even as she spoke Lady Irene, with a cry of agony, fell senseless in my dear lady's arms.

The doctor, I may tell you, came too late. The unfortunate woman evidently had a good knowledge of poisons. She had been determined not to fail; in case of discovery, she was ready and able to mete out justice to herself.

I don't think the public ever knew the real truth about the woman in the big hat. Interest in her went the way of all things. Yet my dear lady had been right from beginning to end. With unerring precision she had placed her dainty finger on the real motive and the real perpetrator of the crime – the ambitious woman who had married solely for money, and meant to have that money even at the cost of one of the most dastardly murders that have ever darkened the criminal annals of this country.

I asked Lady Molly what it was that first made her think of

Lady Irene as the possible murderess. No one else for a moment had thought her guilty.

'The big hat,' replied my dear lady with a smile. 'Had the mysterious woman at Mathis' been tall, the waitresses would not, one and all, have been struck by the abnormal size of the hat. The wearer must have been petite, hence the reason that under a wide brim only the chin would be visible. I at once sought for a small woman. Our fellows did not think of that, because they are men.'

You see how simple it all was!

MADELYN MACK

Created by Hugh Cosgro Weir
(1884-1934)

Madelyn Mack is probably the most flamboyant and eccentric of all the female detectives of the period, and the one with the most resemblance to Sherlock Holmes. Like Holmes, she works as a private consulting detective, although her city is New York rather than London. Her creator goes to great lengths to emphasise her genius as a criminologist and she attracts much admiring attention for her startling deductive abilities. Also like Holmes, she has her Watson in the journalist Nora Noraker who narrates the stories. She has her addictions – she carries a locket around her neck which holds cola berries to keep her awake for days at a stretch when she is on a particularly demanding case. And she has her musical tastes – she is a collector of gramophone records, some of which she privately commissions from famous performers. She was the brainchild of an Illinois-born writer, advertising guru and magazine publisher named Hugh Cosgro Weir and first appeared in a volume of short stories entitled Miss Madelyn Mack, Detective, *published in 1914. The book was originally dedicated to a woman named Mary Holland, a pioneering fingerprint expert from Chicago whom Weir knew. Holland worked as a detective and Madelyn Mack was probably based, very loosely, on her. At one time Weir wrote screenplays for the burgeoning American movie business and several of the Madelyn Mack stories were made into short films starring Alice Joyce, a popular actress of the silent era. Weir's interest in the cinema continued and, at the time of his death, aged only 50, he was the editor of* The New Movie Magazine.

THE MAN WITH NINE LIVES

1

Now that I seek a point of beginning in the curious comradeship between Madelyn Mack and myself, the weird problems of men's knavery that we have confronted together come back to me with almost a shock.

Perhaps the events which crowd into my memory followed each other too swiftly for thoughtful digest at the time of their occurrence. Perhaps only a sober retrospect can supply a properly appreciative angle of view.

Madelyn Mack! What newspaper reader does not know the name? Who, even among the most casual followers of public events, does not recall the young woman who found the missing heiress, Virginia Denton, after a three months' disappearance; who convicted 'Archie' Irwin, chief of the 'fire bug trust'; who located the absconder, Wolcott, after a pursuit from Chicago to Khartoum; who solved the riddle of the double Peterson murder; who – but why continue the enumeration of Miss Mack's achievements? They are of almost household knowledge, at least that portion which, from one cause or another, has found their way into the newspaper columns. Doubtless those admirers of Miss Mack, whose opinions have been formed through the press chronicles of her exploits, would be startled to know that not one in ten of her cases has ever been recorded outside of her own file cases. And many of them – the most sensational from a newspaper viewpoint – will never be!

It is the woman, herself, however, who has seemed to me always a greater mystery than any of the problems to whose unravelling she has brought her wonderful genius. In spite of the deluge of printer's ink that she has inspired, I question if it has been given to more than a dozen persons to know the true Madelyn Mack.

I do not refer, of course, to her professional career. The salient points of that portion of her life, I presume, are more or less generally known – the college girl confronted suddenly with the necessity of earning her own living; the epidemic of mysterious 'shop-lifting' cases chronicled in the newspaper she was studying for employment advertisements; her application to the New York department stores, that had been victimised, for a place on their detective staffs, and their curt refusal; her sudden determination to undertake the case as a freelance, and her remarkable success, which resulted in the conviction of the notorious Madame Bousard, and which secured for Miss Mack her first position as assistant house-detective with the famous Niegel dry-goods firm. I sometimes think that this first case, and the realisation which it brought her of her peculiar talent, is Madelyn's favourite – that its place in her memory is not even shared by the recovery of Mrs Niegel's fifty-thousand-dollar pearl necklace, stolen a few months after the employment of the college girl detective at the store, and the reward for which, incidentally, enabled the ambitious Miss Mack to open her own office.

Next followed the Bergner kidnapping case, which gave Madelyn her first big advertising broadside, and which brought the beginning of the steady stream of business that resulted, after three years, in her Fifth Avenue suite in the Maddox Building, where I found her on that – to me – memorable afternoon when a sapient Sunday editor dispatched me for an interview with the woman who had made so conspicuous a success in a man's profession.

I can see Madelyn now, as I saw her then – my first close-range view of her. She had just returned from Omaha that morning, and was planning to leave for Boston on the midnight express. A suitcase and a fat portfolio of papers lay on a chair in a corner. A young woman stenographer was taking a number of letters at an almost incredible rate of dictation. Miss Mack finished the last paragraph as she rose from a flat-top desk to greet me.

I had vaguely imagined a masculine-appearing woman, curt of voice, sharp of feature, perhaps dressed in a severe, tailor-made gown. I saw a young woman of maybe twenty-five, with

234

red and white cheeks, crowned by a softly waved mass of dull gold hair, and a pair of vivacious, grey-blue eyes that at once made one forget every other detail of her appearance. There was a quality in the eyes which for a long time I could not define. Gradually I came to know that it was the spirit of optimism, of joy in herself, and in her life, and in her work, the exhilaration of doing things. And there was something contagious in it. Almost unconsciously you found yourself believing in her and in her sincerity.

Nor was there a suggestion foreign to her sex in my appraisal. She was dressed in a simply embroidered white shirt-waist and white broadcloth skirt. One of Madelyn's few peculiarities is that she always dresses either in complete white or complete black. On her desk was a jar of white chrysanthemums.

'How do I do it?' she repeated, in answer to my question, in a tone that was almost a laugh.

'Why – just by hard work, I suppose. Oh, there isn't anything wonderful about it! You can do almost anything, you know, if you make yourself really think you can! I am not at all unusual or abnormal. I work out my problems just as I would work out a problem in mathematics, only instead of figures I deal with human motives. A detective is always given certain known factors, and I keep building them up, or subtracting them, as the case may be, until I know that the answer must be correct.

'There are only two real rules for a successful detective, hard work and common sense – not uncommon sense such as we associate with our old friend, Sherlock Holmes, but common, business sense. And, of course, imagination! That may be one reason why I have made what you call a success. A woman, I think, always has a more acute imagination than a man!'

'Do you then prefer women operatives on your staff?' I asked.

She glanced up with something like a twinkle from the jade paper-knife in her hands.

'Shall I let you into a secret? All of my staff, with the exception of my stenographer, are men. But I do most of my work in person. The factor of imagination can't very well be used second, or third, or fourth handed. And then, if I fail, I can only blame Madelyn Mack! Someday,' – the gleam in her grey-blue eyes deepened – 'someday I hope to reach a point where I can afford to do only consulting work or personal investigation. The business details of an office staff, I am afraid, are a bit too much of routine for me!'

The telephone jingled. She spoke a few crisp sentences into the receiver, and turned. The interview was over.

When I next saw her, three months later, we met across the body of Morris Anthony, the murdered bibliophile. It was a chance discovery of mine which Madelyn was good enough to say suggested to her the solution of the affair, and which brought us together in the final melodramatic climax in the grim mansion on Washington Square, when I presume my hysterical warning saved her from the fangs of Dr Lester Randolph's hidden cobra. In any event, our acquaintanceship crystallised gradually into a comradeship, which revolutionised two angles of my life.

Not only did it bring to me the stimulus of Madelyn Mack's personality, but it gave me exclusive access to a fund of newspaper 'copy' that took me from scant-paid Sunday 'features' to a 'space' arrangement in the city room, with an income double that which I had been earning. I have always maintained that in our relationship Madelyn gave all, and I contributed nothing. Although she invariably made instant disclaimer, and generally ended by carrying me up to the 'Rosary', her chalet on the Hudson, as a cure for what she termed my attack of the 'blues', she was never able to convince me that my protest was not justified!

It was at the 'Rosary' where Miss Mack found haven from the stress of business. She had copied its design from an ivy-tangled Swiss chalet that had attracted her fancy during a summer vacation ramble through the Alps, and had built it on a jagged bluff of the river at a point near enough to the city to permit of fairly convenient motoring, although, during the first years of our friendship, when she was held close to the commercial grindstone, weeks often passed without her being able to snatch a day there. In the end, it was the gratitude of Chalmers Walker for her remarkable work which cleared his chorus-girl wife from the seemingly unbreakable coil of circumstantial evidence in the murder of Dempster, the theatrical broker, that enabled Madelyn to realise her long-cherished dream of setting up as a consulting expert. Although she still maintained an office in town, it was confined to one room and a small reception hall, and she limited her attendance there to two days of the week. During the remainder of the time, when not engaged directly on a case, she seldom appeared in the city at all. Her flowers and her music – she was passionately devoted to both – appeared to content her effectually.

I charged her with growing old, to which she replied with a shrug. I upbraided her as a cynic, and she smiled inscrutably. But the manner of her life was not changed. In a way I envied her. It was almost like looking down on the world and watching tolerantly its mad scramble for the rainbow's end. The days I snatched at the 'Rosary', particularly in the summer, when Madelyn's garden looked like nothing so much as a Turner picture, left me with almost a repulsion for the grind of Park Row. But a workaday newspaper woman cannot indulge the dreams of a genius whom fortune has blessed. Perhaps this was why Madelyn's invitations came with a frequency and a subtleness that could not be resisted. Somehow they always reached me when I was in just the right receptive mood.

It was late on a Thursday afternoon of June, the climax of a racking five days for me under the blistering Broadway sun, that Madelyn's motor caught me at the *Bugle* office, and Madelyn insisted on bundling me into the tonneau without even a suitcase.

'We'll reach the Rosary in time for a fried chicken supper,' she promised. 'What you need is four or five days' rest where you can't smell the asphalt.'

'You fairy godmother!' I breathed as I snuggled down on the cushions.

Neither of us knew that already the crimson trail of crime was twisting toward us – that within twelve hours we were to be pitchforked from a quiet weekend's rest into the vortex of tragedy.

2

We had breakfasted late and leisurely. When at length we had finished, Madelyn had insisted on having her phonograph brought to the rose-garden, and we were listening to Sturveysant's matchless rendering of 'The Jewel Song' – one of the three records for which Miss Mack had sent the harpist her check for two hundred dollars the day before.

I had taken the occasion to read her a lazy lesson on extravagance. The beggar had probably done the work in less than two hours!

As the plaintive notes quivered to a pause, Susan, Madelyn's housekeeper, crossed the garden, and laid a little stack of letters and the morning papers on a rustic table by our bench. Madelyn turned to her correspondence with a shrug.

'From the divine to the prosaic!'

Susan sniffed with the freedom of seven years of service.

'I heard one of them fiddling chaps at Hammerstein's last week who could beat that music with his eyes closed!'

Madelyn stared at her sorrowfully.

'At your age – Hammerstein's!'

Susan tossed her prim rows of curls, glanced contemptuously at the phonograph by way of retaliation, and made a dignified retreat. In the doorway she turned.

'Oh, Miss Madelyn, I am baking one of your old-fashioned strawberry shortcakes for lunch!'

'Really?' Madelyn raised a pair of sparkling eyes. 'Susan, you're a dear!'

A contented smile wreathed Susan's face even to the tips of her precise curls. Madelyn's gaze crossed to me.

'What are you chuckling over, Nora?'

'From a psychological standpoint, the pair of you have given me two interesting studies,' I laughed. 'A single sentence compensates Susan for a week of your glumness!'

Madelyn extended a hand toward her mail.

'And what is the other feature that appeals to your dissecting mind?'

'Fancy a world-known detective rising to the point of enthusiasm at the mention of strawberry shortcake!'

'Why not? Even a detective has to be human once in a while!' Her eyes twinkled. 'Another point for my memoirs, Miss Noraker!'

As her gaze fell to the half-opened letter in her hand, my eyes travelled across the garden to the outlines of the chalet, and I breathed a sigh of utter content. Broadway and Park Row seemed very, very far away. In a momentary swerving of my gaze, I saw that a line as clear cut as a pencil-stroke had traced itself across Miss Mack's forehead.

The suggestion of lounging indifference in her attitude had vanished like a wind-blown veil. Her glance met mine suddenly. The twinkle I had last glimpsed in her eyes had disappeared. Silently she pushed a square sheet of close, cramped writing across the table to me.

'My Dear Madam:

'When you read this, it is quite possible that it will be a letter from a dead man.

'I have been told by no less an authority than my friend, Cosmo Hamilton, that you are a remarkable woman. While I will say at the outset that I have little faith in the analytical powers of the feminine brain, I am prepared to accept Hamilton's judgement.

'I cannot, of course, discuss the details of my problem in correspondence.

'As a spur to quick action, I may say, however, that, during the past five months, my life has been attempted no fewer than eight different times, and I am convinced that the ninth attempt, if made, will be successful. The curious part of it lies in the fact that I am absolutely unable to guess the reason for the persistent vendetta. So far as I know, there is no person in the world who should desire my removal. And yet I have been shot at from ambush on four occasions, thugs have rushed me once,

239

a speeding automobile has grazed me twice, and this evening I found a cunning little dose of cyanide of potassium in my favourite cherry pie!

'All of this, too, in the shadow of a New Jersey skunk farm! It is high time, I fancy, that I secure expert advice. Should the progress of the mysterious vendetta, by any chance, render me unable to receive you personally, my niece, Miss Muriel Jansen, I am sure, will endeavour to act as a substitute.

'Respectfully Yours,

'Wendell Marsh.'

'Three Forks Junction, NJ,

'June 16.'

At the bottom of the page a lead pencil had scrawled the single line in the same cramped writing:

'For God's sake, hurry!'

Madelyn retained her curled-up position on the bench, staring across at a bush of deep crimson roses.

'Wendell Marsh?' She shifted her glance to me musingly. 'Haven't I seen that name somewhere lately?' (Madelyn pays me the compliment of saying that I have a card-index brain for newspaper history!)

'If you have read the Sunday supplements,' I returned drily, with a vivid remembrance of Wendell Marsh as I had last seen him, six months before, when he crossed the gang-plank of his steamer, fresh from England, his face browned from the Atlantic winds. It was a face to draw a second glance – almost gaunt, self-willed, with more than a hint of cynicism. (Particularly when his eyes met the waiting press group!) Someone had once likened him to the pictures of Oliver Cromwell.

'Wendell Marsh is one of the greatest newspaper copy-makers that ever dodged an interviewer,' I explained. 'He hates reporters like an upstate farmer hates an automobile, and yet has a flock of them on his trail constantly. His latest exploit to catch the spotlight was the purchase of the Bainford relics in London. Just before that he published a three-volume history on *The World's Great Cynics*. Paid for the publication himself.'

Then came a silence between us, prolonging itself. I was trying, rather unsuccessfully, to associate Wendell Marsh's half-hysterical letter with my mental picture of the austere millionaire...

'For God's sake, hurry!'

What wrenching terror had reduced the ultra-reserved Mr Marsh to an appeal like this? As I look back now I know that my wildest fancy could not have pictured the ghastliness of the truth.

Madelyn straightened abruptly.

'Susan, will you kindly tell Andrew to bring around the car at once? If you will find the New Jersey automobile map, Nora, we'll locate Three Forks Junction.'

'You are going down?' I asked mechanically.

She slipped from the bench.

'I am beginning to fear,' she said irrelevantly, 'that we'll have to defer our strawberry shortcake!'

3

The sound eye of Daniel Peddicord, liveryman by avocation, and sheriff of Merino County by election, drooped over his florid left cheek. Mr Peddicord took himself and his duties to the tax-payers of Merino County seriously.

Having lowered his sound eye with befitting official dubiousness, while his glass eye stared guilelessly ahead, as though it took absolutely no notice of the procedure, Mr Peddicord jerked a fat, red thumb toward the winding stairway at the rear of the Marsh hall.

'I reckon as how Mr Marsh is still up there, Miss Mack. You see, I told 'em not to disturb the body until –'

Our stares brought the sentence to an abrupt end. Mr Peddicord's sound eye underwent a violent agitation.

'You don't mean that you haven't – heard?'

The silence of the great house seemed suddenly oppressive. For the first time I realised the oddity of our having been received by an ill-at-ease policeman instead of by a member of the family. I was abruptly conscious of the incongruity between Mr Peddicord's awkward figure and the dim, luxurious background.

Madelyn gripped the chief's arm, bringing his sound eye circling around to her face.

'Tell me what has happened!'

Mr Peddicord drew a huge red handkerchief over his forehead.

'Wendell Marsh was found dead in his library at eight o'clock this morning! He had been dead for hours.'

Tick-tock! Tick-tock! Through my daze beat the rhythm of a tall, gaunt clock in the corner. I stared at it dully. Madelyn's hands had caught themselves behind her back, her veins swollen into sharp blue ridges. Mr Peddicord still gripped his red handkerchief.

'It sure is queer you hadn't heard! I reckoned as how that was what had brought you down. It – it looks like murder!'

In Madelyn's eyes had appeared a greyish glint like cold steel.

'Where is the body?'

'Upstairs in the library. Mr Marsh had worked –'

'Will you kindly show me the room?'

I do not think we noted at the time the crispness in her tones, certainly not with any resentment. Madelyn had taken command of the situation quite as a matter of course.

'Also, will you have my card sent to the family?'

Mr Peddicord stuffed his handkerchief back into a rear trousers' pocket. A red corner protruded in jaunty abandon from under his blue coat.

'Why, there ain't no family – at least none but Muriel Jansen.' His head cocked itself cautiously up the stairs. 'She's his niece, and I reckon now everything here is hers. Her maid says as how she is clear bowled over. Only left her room once since – since it happened. And that was to tell me as how nothing was to be disturbed.' Mr Peddicord drew himself up with the suspicion of a frown. 'Just as though an experienced officer wouldn't know that much!'

Madelyn glanced over her shoulder to the end of the hall. A hatchet-faced man in russet livery stood staring at us with wooden eyes.

Mr Peddicord shrugged.

'That's Peters, the butler. He's the chap what found Mr Marsh.'

I could feel the wooden eyes following us until a turn in the stairs blocked their range.

A red-glowing room – oppressively red. Scarlet-frescoed walls, deep red draperies, cherry-upholstered furniture, Turkish-red rugs, rows on rows of red-bound books. Above, a great, flat glass roof, open to the sky from comer to corner, through which the splash of the sun on the rich colours gave the weird semblance of a crimson pool almost in the room's exact centre. Such was Wendell Marsh's library – as eccentrically designed as its master.

It was the wreck of a room that we found. Shattered vases littered the floor – books were ripped savagely apart – curtains were hanging in ribbons – a heavy leather rocker was splintered.

The wreckage might have marked the death-struggle of giants. In the midst of the destruction, Wendell Marsh was twisted on his back. His face was shrivelled, his eyes were staring. There was no hint of a wound or even a bruise. In his right hand was gripped an object partially turned from me.

I found myself stepping nearer, as though drawn by a magnet. There is something hypnotic in such horrible scenes! And then I barely checked a cry.

Wendell Marsh's dead fingers held a pipe – a strangely carved, red sandstone bowl, and a long, glistening stem.

Sheriff Peddicord noted the direction of my glance.

'Mr Marsh got that there pipe in London, along with those other relics he brought home. They do say as how it was the first pipe ever smoked by a white man. The Indians of Virginia gave it to a chap named Sir Walter Raleigh. Mr Marsh had a new stem put to it, and his butler says he smoked it every day. Queer, ain't it, how some folks' tastes do run?'

The sheriff moistened his lips under his scraggly yellow moustache.

'Must have been some fight what done this!' His head included the wrecked room in a vague sweep.

Madelyn strolled over to a pair of the ribboned curtains, and fingered them musingly.

'But that isn't the queerest part.' The chief glanced at Madelyn expectantly. 'There was no way for anyone else to get out – or in!'

Madelyn stooped lower over the curtains. They seemed to fascinate her. 'The door?' she hazarded absently. 'It was locked?'

'From the inside. Peters and the footman saw the key when they broke in this morning... Peters swears he heard Mr Marsh turn it when he left him writing at ten o'clock last night.'

'The windows?'

'Fastened as tight as a drum – and, if they wasn't, it's a matter of a good thirty foot to the ground.'

'The roof, perhaps?'

'A cat might get through it – if every part wasn't clamped as tight as the windows.'

Mr Peddicord spoke with a distinct inflection of triumph. Madelyn was still staring at the curtains.

'Isn't it rather odd,' I ventured, 'that the sounds of the struggle, or whatever it was, didn't alarm the house?'

Sheriff Peddicord plainly regarded me as an outsider. He answered my question with obvious shortness.

'You could fire a blunderbuss up here and no one would be the wiser. They say as how Mr Marsh had the room made sound-proof. And, besides, the servants have a building to themselves, all except Miss Jansen's maid, who sleeps in a room next to her at the other end of the house.'

My eyes circled back to Wendell Marsh's knotted figure – his shrivelled face – horror-frozen eyes – the hand gripped about the fantastic pipe. I think it was the pipe that held my glance. Of all incongruities, a pipe in the hand of a dead man!

Maybe it was something of the same thought that brought

Madelyn of a sudden across the room. She stooped, straightened the cold fingers, and rose with the pipe in her hand.

A new stem had obviously been added to it, of a substance which I judged to be jessamine. At its end, teethmarks had bitten nearly through. The stone bowl was filled with the cold ashes of half-consumed tobacco. Madelyn balanced it musingly.

'Curious, isn't it, Sheriff, that a man engaged in a life-or-death struggle should cling to a heavy pipe?'

'Why – I suppose so. But the question, Miss Mack, is what became of that there other man? It isn't natural as how Mr Marsh could have fought with himself.'

'The other man?' Madelyn repeated mechanically. She was stirring the rim of the dead ashes.

'And how in tarnation was Mr Marsh killed?'

Madelyn contemplated a dust-covered finger.

'Will you do me a favour, Sheriff?'

'Why, er – of course.'

'Kindly find out from the butler if Mr Marsh had cherry pie for dinner last night!'

The sheriff gulped.

'Che-cherry pie? '

Madelyn glanced up impatiently.

'I believe he was very fond of it.'

The sheriff shuffled across to the door uncertainly. Madelyn's eyes flashed to me.

'You might go, too, Nora.'

For a moment I was tempted to flat rebellion. But Madelyn affected not to notice the fact. She is always so aggravatingly sure of her own way! With what I tried to make a mood of aggrieved silence, I followed the sheriff's blue-coated figure. As the door closed, I saw that Madelyn was still balancing Raleigh's pipe.

From the top of the stairs Sheriff Peddicord glanced across at me suspiciously.

'I say, what I would like to know is what became of that there other man!'

4

A wisp of a black-gowned figure, peering through a dormer window at the end of the second-floor hall, turned suddenly as we reached the landing. A white, drawn face, suggesting a tired child, stared at us from under a frame of dull-gold hair, drawn low from a careless part. I knew at once it was Muriel Jansen, for the time, at least, mistress of the house of death.

'Has the coroner come yet, Sheriff?'

She spoke with one of the most liquid voices I have ever heard. Had it not been for her bronze hair, I would have fancied her at once of Latin descent. The fact of my presence she seemed scarcely to notice, not with any suggestion of aloofness, but rather as though she had been drained even of the emotion of curiosity.

'Not yet, Miss Jansen. He should be here now.'

She stepped closer to the window, and then turned slightly.

'I told Peters to telegraph to New York for Dr Dench when he summoned you. He was one of Uncle's oldest friends. I – I would like him to be here when – when the coroner makes his examination.'

The sheriff bowed awkwardly.

'Miss Mack is upstairs now.'

The pale face was staring at us again with raised eyebrows.

'Miss Mack? I don't understand.' Her eyes shifted to me.

'She had a letter from Mr Marsh by this morning's early post,' I explained. 'I am Miss Noraker. Mr Marsh wanted her to come down at once. She didn't know, of course – couldn't know – that – that he was – dead!'

'A letter from – Uncle?' A puzzled line gathered in her face.

I nodded.

'A distinctly curious letter. But – Miss Mack would perhaps prefer to give you the details.'

The puzzled line deepened. I could feel her eyes searching mine intently.

'I presume Miss Mack will be down soon,' I volunteered. 'If you wish, however, I will tell her –'

'That will hardly be necessary. But – you are quite sure – a letter?'

'Quite sure,' I returned, somewhat impatiently.

And then, without warning, her hands darted to her head, and she swayed forward. I caught her in my arms with a side-view of Sheriff Peddicord staring, open-mouthed.

'Get her maid!' I gasped.

The sheriff roused into belated action. As he took a cumbersome step toward the nearest door, it opened suddenly. A gaunt, middle-aged woman, in a crisp white apron, digested the situation with cold, grey eyes. Without a word, she caught Muriel Jansen in her arms.

'She has fainted,' I said rather vaguely. 'Can I help you?'

The other paused with her burden.

'When I need you, I'll ask you!' she snapped, and banged the door in our faces.

In the wake of Sheriff Peddicord, I descended the stairs. A dozen question marks were spinning through my brain. Why had Muriel Jansen fainted? Why had the mention of Wendell Marsh's letter left such an atmosphere of bewildered doubt? Why had the dragon-like maid – for such I divined her to be – faced us with such hostility? The undercurrent of hidden secrets in the dim, silent house seemed suddenly intensified.

With a vague wish for fresh air and the sun on the grass, I sought the front veranda, leaving the sheriff in the hall, mopping his face with his red handkerchief.

A carefully tended yard of generous distances stretched an inviting expanse of graded lawn before me. Evidently Wendell Marsh had provided a discreet distance between himself and his neighbours. The advance guard of a morbid crowd was already shuffling about the gate. I knew that it would not be long, too, before the press-siege would begin.

I could picture frantic city editors pitchforking their star men New Jerseyward. I smiled at the thought. The *Bugle*, the slave-driver that presided over my own financial destinies, was assured of a generous 'beat' in advance. The next train from New York was not due until late afternoon.

From the staring line about the gate, the figure of a well-set-up young man in blue serge detached itself with swinging step.

'A reporter?' I breathed, incredulous.

With a glance at me, he ascended the steps, and paused at the door, awaiting an answer to his bell. My stealthy glances failed to place him among the 'stars' of New York newspaperdom. Perhaps he was a local correspondent. With smug expectancy, I awaited his discomfiture when Peters received his card. And then I rubbed my eyes. Peters was stepping back from the door, and the other was following him with every suggestion of assurance.

I was still gasping when a maid, broom in hand, zigzagged toward my end of the veranda. She smiled at me with a pair of friendly black eyes.

'Are you a detective?'

'Why?' I parried.

She drew her broom idly across the floor.

'I – I always thought detectives different from other people.'

She sent a rivulet of dust through the railing, with a side glance still in my direction.

'Oh, you will find them human enough,' I laughed, 'outside of detective stories!'

She pondered my reply doubtfully.

'I thought it about time Mr Truxton was appearing!' she ventured suddenly.

'Mr Truxton?'

'He's the man that just came – Mr Homer Truxton. Miss Jansen is going to marry him!'

A light broke through my fog.

'Then he is not a reporter?'

'Mr Truxton? He's a lawyer.' The broom continued its dilatory course. 'Mr Marsh didn't like him – so they say!'

I stepped back, smoothing my skirts. I have learned the cardinal rule of Madelyn never to pretend too great an interest in the gossip of a servant.

The maid was mechanically shaking out a rug.

'For my part, I always thought Mr Truxton far and away the pick of Miss Jansen's two steadies. I never could understand what she could see in Dr Dench! Why, he's old enough to be her –'

In the doorway, Sheriff Peddicord's bulky figure beckoned.

'Don't you reckon as how it's about time we were going back to Miss Mack?' he whispered.

'Perhaps,' I assented rather reluctantly.

From the shadows of the hall, the sheriff's sound eye fixed itself on me belligerently.

'I say, what I would like to know is what became of that there other man!'

As we paused on the second landing the well-set-up figure of Mr Homer Truxton was bending toward a partially opened door. Beyond his shoulder, I caught a fleeting glimpse of a pale face under a border of rumpled dull-gold hair. Evidently Muriel Jansen had recovered from her faint. The door closed abruptly, but not before I had seen that her eyes were red with weeping.

Madelyn was sunk into a red-backed chair before a huge, flat-top desk in the corner of the library, a stack of Wendell Marsh's red-bound books, from a wheel-cabinet at her side, bulked before her. She finished the page she was reading – a page marked with a broad blue pencil – without a hint that she had heard us enter.

Sheriff Peddicord stared across at her with a disappointment that was almost ludicrous. Evidently Madelyn was falling short of his conception of the approved attitudes for a celebrated detective!

'Are you a student of Elizabethan literature, Sheriff?' she asked suddenly.

The sheriff gurgled weakly.

'If you are, I am quite sure you will be interested in Mr Marsh's collection. It is the most thorough on the subject that I have ever seen. For instance, here is a volume on the inner court life of Elizabeth – perhaps you would like me to read you this random passage?'

The sheriff drew himself up with more dignity than I thought he possessed.

'We are investigating a crime, Miss Mack!'

Madelyn closed the book with a sigh.

'So we are! May I ask what is your report from the butler?'

'Mr Marsh did not have cherry pie for dinner last night!' the sheriff snapped.

'You are quite confident?'

And then abruptly the purport of the question flashed to me.

'Why, Mr Marsh, himself, mentioned the fact in his letter!' I burst out.

Madelyn's eyes turned to me reprovingly.

'You must be mistaken, Nora.'

With a lingering glance at the books on the desk, she rose. Sheriff Peddicord moved toward the door, opened it, and faced about with an abrupt clearing of his throat.

'Begging your pardon. Miss Mack, have – have you found any clues in the case?'

Madelyn had paused again at the ribboned curtains.

'Clues? The man who made Mr Marsh's death possible, Sheriff, was an expert chemist, of Italian origin, living for some time in London – and he died three hundred years ago!'

From the hall we had a fleeting view of Sheriff Peddicord's face, flushed as red as his handkerchief, and then it and the handkerchief disappeared.

I whirled on Madelyn sternly.

'You are carrying your absurd joke, Miss Mack, altogether too –'

I paused, gulping in my turn. It was as though I had stumbled from the shadows into an electric glare.

Madelyn had crossed to the desk, and was gently shifting the dead ashes of Raleigh's pipe into an envelope. A moment she sniffed at its bowl, peering down at the crumpled body at her feet.

'The pipe!' I gasped. 'Wendell Marsh was poisoned with the pipe!'

Madelyn sealed the envelope slowly.

'Is that fact just dawning on you, Nora?'

'But the rest of it – what you told the –'

Madelyn thrummed on the bulky volume of Elizabethan history.

'Some day, Nora, if you will remind me, I will give you the material for what you call a Sunday "feature" on the historic side of murder as a fine art!'

5

In a curtain-shadowed nook of the side veranda Múriel Jansen was awaiting us, pillowed back against a bronze-draped chair, whose colours almost startlingly matched the gold of her hair. Her resemblance to a tired child was even more pronounced than when I had last seen her.

I found myself glancing furtively for signs of Homer Truxton, but he had disappeared.

Miss Jansen took the initiative in our interview with a nervous abruptness, contrasting oddly with her hesitancy at our last meeting.

'I understand. Miss Mack, that you received a letter from my uncle asking your presence here. May I see it?'

The eagerness of her tones could not be mistaken.

From her wrist-bag Madelyn extended the square envelope of the morning post, with its remarkable message. Twice Muriel Jansen's eyes swept slowly through its contents. Madelyn watched her with a little frown. A sudden tenseness had crept into the air, as though we were all keying ourselves for an unexpected climax. And then, like a thunder-clap, it came.

'A curious communication,' Madelyn suggested. 'I had hoped you might be able to add to it?'

The tired face in the bronze-draped chair stared across the lawn.

'I can. The most curious fact of your communication, Miss Mack, is that Wendell Marsh did not write it!'

Never have I admired more keenly Madelyn's remarkable poise. Save for an almost imperceptible indrawing of her breath, she gave no hint of the shock which must have stunned her as it did me. I was staring with mouth agape. But, then, I presume you have discovered by this time that I was not designed for a detective!

Strangely enough, Muriel Jansen gave no trace of wonder in her announcement. Her attitude suggested a sense of detachment from the subject as though suddenly it had lost its interest. And yet, less than an hour ago, it had prostrated her in a swoon.

'You mean the letter is a forgery?' asked Madelyn quietly.

'Quite obviously.'

'And the attempts on Mr Marsh's life to which it refers?'

'There have been none. I have been with my uncle continuously for six months. I can speak definitely.'

Miss Jansen fumbled in a white-crocheted bag.

'Here are several specimens of Mr Marsh's writing. I think they should be sufficient to convince you of what I say. If you desire others –'

I was gulping like a truant schoolgirl as Madelyn spread on her lap the three notes extended to her. Casual business and personal references they were, none of more than half a dozen lines. Quite enough, however, to complete the sudden chasm at our feet – quite enough to emphasise a bold, aggressive penmanship, almost perpendicular, without the slightest resemblance to the cramped, shadowy writing of the morning's astonishing communication.

Madelyn rose from her chair, smoothing her skirts thoughtfully. For a moment she stood at the railing, gazing down upon a trellis of yellow roses, her face turned from us. For the first time in our curious friendship, I was actually conscious of a feeling of pity for her! The blank wall which she faced seemed so abrupt – so final!

Muriel Jansen shifted her position slightly.

'Are you satisfied, Miss Mack?'

'Quite.' Madelyn turned, and handed back the three notes. 'I presume this means that you do not care for me to continue the case?'

I whirled in dismay. I had never thought of this possibility.

'On the contrary, Miss Mack, it seems to me an additional reason why you should continue!'

I breathed freely again. At least we were not to be dismissed with the abruptness that Miss Jansen's maid had shown! Madelyn bowed rather absently.

'Then if you will give me another interview, perhaps this afternoon –'

Miss Jansen fumbled with the lock of her bag.

For the first time her voice lost something of its directness.

'Have – have you any explanation of this astonishing – forgery?'

Madelyn was staring out toward the increasing crowd at the gate. A sudden ripple had swept through it.

'Have you ever heard of a man by the name of Orlando Julio, Miss Jansen?'

My own eyes, following the direction of Madelyn's gaze, were brought back sharply to the veranda. For the second time, Muriel Jansen had crumpled back in a faint.

As I darted toward the servants' bell Madelyn checked me. Striding up the walk were two men with the unmistakable air of physicians. At Madelyn's motioning hand they turned toward us.

The foremost of the two quickened his pace as he caught sight of the figure in the chair. Instinctively I knew that he was Dr Dench – and it needed no profound analysis to place his companion as the local coroner.

With a deft hand on Miss Jansen's heartbeats, Dr Dench raised a ruddy, brown-whiskered face inquiringly toward us.

'Shock!' Madelyn explained. 'Is it serious?'

The hand on the wavering breast darted toward a medicine case, and selected a vial of brownish liquid. The gaze above it continued its scrutiny of Madelyn's slender figure.

Dr Dench was of the rugged, German type, steel-eyed, confidently sure of movement, with the physique of a splendidly muscled animal. If the servant's tattle was to be credited, Muriel Jansen could not have attracted more opposite extremes in her suitors.

The coroner – a rusty-suited man of middle age, in quite obvious professional awe of his companion – extended a glass of water. Miss Jansen wearily opened her eyes before it reached her lips.

Dr Dench restrained her sudden effort to rise. 'Drink this, please!' There was nothing but professional command in his voice. If he loved the grey-pallored girl in the chair, his emotions were under superb control.

Madelyn stepped to the background, motioning me quietly.

'I fancy I can leave now safely. I am going back to town.'

'Town?' I echoed.

'I should be back by the latter part of the afternoon. Would it inconvenience you to wait here?'

'But, why on earth – ' I began.

'Will you tell the butler to send around the car? Thanks!'

When Madelyn doesn't choose to answer questions she ignores them. I subsided as gracefully as possible. As her machine whirled under the porte cochère, however, my curiosity again overflowed my restraint.

'At least, who is Orlando Julio?' I demanded.

Madelyn carefully adjusted her veil.

'The man who provided the means for the death of Wendell Marsh!' And she was gone.

I swept another glance at the trio on the side veranda, and with what I tried to convince myself was a philosophical shrug, although I knew perfectly well it was merely a pettish fling, sought a retired corner of the rear drawing room, with my pad and pencil.

After all, I was a newspaper woman, and it needed no elastic imagination to picture the scene in the city room of the *Bugle* if I failed to send a proper accounting of myself.

A few minutes later a tread of feet, advancing to the stairs, told me that the coroner and Dr Dench were ascending for the belated examination of Wendell Marsh's body. Miss Jansen had evidently recovered, or been assigned to the ministrations of her maid. Once Peters, the wooden-faced butler, entered ghostily to inform me that luncheon would be served at one, but effaced himself almost before my glance returned to my writing.

I partook of the meal in the distinguished company of Sheriff Peddicord. Apparently Dr Dench was still busied in his gruesome task upstairs, and it was not surprising that Miss Jansen preferred her own apartments.

However much the sheriff's professional poise might have been jarred by the events of the morning, his appetite had not been affected. His attention was too absorbed in the effort to do justice to the Marsh hospitality to waste time in table talk.

He finished his last spoonful of strawberry ice-cream with a heavy sigh of contentment, removed the napkin, which he had tucked under his collar, and, as though mindful of the family's laundry bills, folded it carefully and wiped his lips with his red handkerchief. It was not until then that our silence was interrupted.

Glancing cautiously about the room, and observing that the butler had been called kitchenward, to my amazement he essayed a confidential wink.

'I say,' he ventured enticingly, leaning his elbow on the table, 'what I would like to know is what became of that there other man!'

'Are you familiar with the Fourth Dimension, Sheriff?' I returned solemnly. I rose from my chair, and stepped toward him confidentially in my turn. 'I believe that a thorough study of that subject would answer your question.'

It was three o'clock when I stretched myself in my corner of the drawing-room, and stuffed the last sheets of my copy paper into a special-delivery-stamped envelope.

My story was done. And Madelyn was not there to blue-pencil the Park Row adjectives! I smiled rather gleefully as I patted my hair, and leisurely addressed the envelope. The city editor would be satisfied, if Madelyn wasn't!

As I stepped into the hall, Dr Dench, the coroner, and Sheriff Peddicord were descending the stairs. Evidently the medical examination had been completed. Under other circumstances the three expressions before me would have afforded an interesting study in contrasts – Dr Dench trimming his nails with professional stoicism, the coroner endeavouring desperately to copy the other's sang-froid, and the sheriff buried in an owl-like solemnity.

Dr Dench restored his knife to his pocket.

'You are Miss Mack's assistant, I understand?'

I bowed.

'Miss Mack has been called away. She should be back, however, shortly.'

I could feel the doctor's appraising glance dissecting me with much the deliberateness of a surgical operation. I raised my eyes suddenly, and returned his stare. It was a virile, masterful face – and, I had to admit, coldly handsome!

Dr Dench snapped open his watch.

'Very well then, Miss, Miss –'

'Noraker!' I supplied crisply.

The blond beard inclined the fraction of an inch.

'We will wait.'

'The autopsy?' I ventured. 'Has it –'

'The result of the autopsy I will explain to – Miss Mack!'

I bit my lip, felt my face flush as I saw that Sheriff Peddicord was trying to smother a grin, and turned with a rather unsuccessful shrug.

Now, if I had been of a vindictive nature, I would have opened my envelope and inserted a retaliating paragraph that would have returned the snub of Dr Dench with interest. I flatter myself that I consigned the envelope to the Three Forks post office, in the rear of the Elite Dry Goods Emporium, with its contents unchanged.

As a part recompense, I paused at a corner drug store, and permitted a young man with a gorgeous pink shirt to make me a chocolate ice-cream soda. I was bent over an asthmatic straw when, through the window, I saw Madelyn's car skirt the curb.

I rushed out to the sidewalk, while the young man stared dazedly after me. The chauffeur swerved the machine as I tossed a dime to the Adonis of the fountain.

Madelyn shifted to the end of the seat as I clambered to her side. One glance was quite enough to show that her town-mission, whatever it was, had ended in failure. Perhaps it was the consciousness of this fact that brought my eyes next to her blue turquoise locket. It was open. I glared accusingly.

'So you have fallen back on the cola stimulant again, Miss Mack?'

She nodded glumly, and perversely slipped into her mouth another of the dark, brown berries, on which I have known her to keep up for forty-eight hours without sleep, and almost without food.

For a moment I forgot even my curiosity as to her errand.

'I wish the duty would be raised so high you couldn't get those things into the country!'

She closed her locket, without deigning a response. The more volcanic my outburst, the more glacial Madelyn's coldness – particularly on the cola topic. I shrugged in resignation. I might as well have done so in the first place!

I straightened my hat, drew my handkerchief over my flushed face, and coughed questioningly. Continued silence. I turned in desperation.

'Well?' I surrendered.

'Don't you know enough, Nora Noraker, to hold your tongue?'

My pent-up emotions snapped.

'Look here, Miss Mack, I have been snubbed by Dr Dench and the coroner, grinned at by Sheriff Peddicord, and I am not going to be crushed by you! What is your report – good, bad, or indifferent?'

Madelyn turned from her stare into the dust-yellow road.

'I have been a fool, Nora – a blind, bigoted, self-important fool!'

I drew a deep breath.

'Which means –'

From her bag Madelyn drew the envelope of dead tobacco

ashes from the Marsh library, and tossed it over the side of the car.
I sank back against the cushions.

'Then the tobacco after all —'

'Is nothing but tobacco — harmless tobacco!'

'But the pipe — I thought the pipe —'

'That's just it! The pipe, my dear girl, killed Wendell Marsh!
But I don't know how! I don't know how!'

'Madelyn,' I said severely, 'you are a woman, even if you are
making your living at a man's profession! What you need is a
good cry!'

6

Dr Dench, pacing back and forth across the veranda, knocked
the ashes from an amber-stemmed meerschaum, and advanced
to meet us as we alighted. The coroner and Sheriff Peddicord
were craning their necks from wicker chairs in the background.
It was easy enough to surmise that Dr Dench had parted from
them abruptly in the desire for a quiet smoke to marshal his
thoughts.

'Fill your pipe again if you wish,' said Madelyn. 'I don't mind.'

Dr Dench inclined his head, and dug the mouth of his
meerschaum into a fat leather pouch. A spiral of blue smoke soon
curled around his face. He was one of that type of men to whom
a pipe lends a distinction of studious thoughtfulness.

With a slight gesture he beckoned in the direction of the
coroner.

'It is proper, perhaps, that Dr Williams in his official capacity
should be heard first.'

Through the smoke of his meerschaum, his eyes were searching
Madelyn's face. It struck me that he was rather puzzled as to just
how seriously to take her.

The coroner shuffled nervously. At his elbow Sheriff Peddicord
fumbled for his red handkerchief.

'We have made a thorough examination of Mr Marsh's body,
Miss Mack, a most thorough examination —'

'Of course, he was not shot, nor stabbed, nor strangled, nor sandbagged?' interrupted Madelyn crisply.

The coroner glanced at Dr Dench uncertainly. The latter was smoking with an inscrutable face.

'Nor poisoned!' finished the coroner with a quick breath.

A blue smoke curl from Dr Dench's meerschaum vanished against the sun. The coroner jingled a handful of coins in his pocket. The sound jarred on my nerves oddly. Not poisoned! Then Madelyn's theory of the pipe –

My glance swerved in her direction. Another blank wall – the blankest in this riddle of blank walls!

But the bewilderment I had expected in her face I did not find. The black dejection I had noticed in the car had dropped like a whisked-off cloak. The tired lines had been erased as by a sponge. Her eyes shone with that tense glint which I knew came only when she saw a befogged way swept clear before her.

'You mean that you found no trace of poison?' she corrected.

The coroner drew himself up.

'Under the supervision of Dr Dench, we have made a most complete probe of the various organs – lungs, stomach, heart –'

'And brain, I presume?'

'Brain? Certainly not!'

'And you?' Madelyn turned toward Dr Dench. 'You subscribe to Dr Williams' opinion?'

Dr Dench removed his meerschaum.

'From our examination of Mr Marsh's body, I am prepared to state emphatically that there is no trace of toxic condition of any kind!'

'Am I to infer then that you will return a verdict of – natural death?'

Dr Dench stirred his pipe-ashes.

'I was always under the impression, Miss Mack, that the verdict in a case of this kind must come from the coroner's jury.'

Madelyn pinned back her veil, and removed her gloves.

'There is no objection to my seeing the body again?'

The coroner stared.

'Why, er – the undertaker has it now. I don't see why he should object, if you wish –'

Madelyn stepped to the door. Behind her, Sheriff Peddicord stirred suddenly.

'I say, what I would like to know, gents, is what became of that there other man!'

It was not until six o'clock that I saw Madelyn again, and then I found her in Wendell Marsh's red library. She was seated at its late tenant's huge desk. Before her were a vial of whitish grey powder, a small, rubber, inked roller, a half a dozen sheets of paper, covered with what looked like smudges of black ink, and Raleigh's pipe. I stopped short, staring.

She rose with a shrug.

'Fingerprints,' she explained laconically. 'This sheet belongs to Miss Jansen; the next to her maid; the third to the butler, Peters; the fourth to Dr Dench; the fifth to Wendell Marsh, himself. It was my first experiment in taking the "prints" of a dead man. It was – interesting.'

'But what has that to do with a case of this kind?' I demanded.

Madelyn picked up the sixth sheet of smudged paper.

'We have here the fingerprints of Wendell Marsh's murderer!'

I did not even cry my amazement. I suppose the kaleidoscope of the day had dulled my normal emotions. I remember that I readjusted a loose pin in my waist before I spoke.

'The murderer of Wendell Marsh!' I repeated mechanically. 'Then he was poisoned?'

Madelyn's eyes opened and closed without answer.

I reached over to the desk, and picked up Mr Marsh's letter of the morning post at Madelyn's elbow.

'You have found the man who forged this?'

'It was *not* forged!'

In my daze I dropped the letter to the floor.

'You have discovered then the other man in the death-struggle that wrecked the library?'

'There was no other man!'

Madelyn gathered up her possessions from the desk. From the

edge of the row of books she lifted a small, red-bound volume, perhaps four inches in width, and then with a second thought laid it back.

'By the way, Nora, I wish you would come back here at eight o'clock. If this book is still where I am leaving it, please bring it to me! I think that will be all for the present.'

'All?' I gasped. 'Do you realise that –'

Madelyn moved toward the door.

'I think eight o'clock will be late enough for your errand,' she said without turning.

The late June twilight had deepened into a sombre darkness when, my watch showing ten minutes past the hour of my instructions, I entered the room on the second floor that had been assigned to Miss Mack and myself. Madelyn at the window was staring into the shadow-blanketed yard.

'Well?' she demanded.

'Your book is no longer in the library!' I said crossly.

Madelyn whirled with a smile.

'Good! And now if you will be so obliging as to tell Peters to ask Miss Jansen to meet me in the rear drawing-room, with any of the friends of the family she desires to be present, I think we can clear up our little puzzle.'

7

It was a curious group that the graceful Swiss clock in the bronze drawing-room of the Marsh house stared down upon as it ticked its way past the half hour after eight. With a grave, rather insistent bow, Miss Mack had seated the other occupants of the room as they answered her summons. She was the only one of us that remained standing.

Before her were Sheriff Peddicord, Homer Truxton, Dr Dench, and Muriel Jansen. Madelyn's eyes swept our faces for a moment in silence, and then she crossed the room and closed the door.

'I have called you here,' she began, 'to explain the mystery of Mr Marsh's death.' Again her glance swept our faces. 'In many respects it has provided us with a peculiar, almost a unique problem.

'We find a man, in apparently normal health, dead. The observer argues at once foul play; and yet on his body is no hint of wound or bruise. The medical examination discovers no trace of poison. The autopsy shows no evidence of crime. Apparently we have eliminated all forms of unnatural death.

'I have called you here because the finding of the autopsy is incorrect, or rather incomplete. We are not confronted by natural death – but by a crime. And I may say at the outset that I am not the only person to know this fact. My knowledge is shared by one other in this room.'

Sheriff Peddicord rose to his feet and rather ostentatiously stepped to the door and stood with his back against it. Madelyn smiled faintly at the movement.

'I scarcely think there will be an effort at escape, Sheriff,' she said quietly.

Muriel Jansen was crumpled back into her chair, staring. Dr Dench was studying Miss Mack with the professional frown he might have directed at an abnormality on the operating table. It was Truxton who spoke first in the fashion of the impulsive boy.

'If we are not dealing with natural death, how on earth then was Mr Marsh killed?'

Madelyn whisked aside a light covering from a stand at her side, and raised to view Raleigh's red sandstone pipe. For a moment she balanced it musingly.

'The three-hundred-year-old death tool of Orlando Julio,' she explained. 'It was this that killed Wendell Marsh!'

She pressed the bowl of the pipe into the palm of her hand. 'As an instrument of death, it is almost beyond detection. We examined the ashes, and found nothing but harmless tobacco. The organs of the victim showed no trace of foul play.'

She tapped the long stem gravely.

'But the examination of the organs did not include the brain. And it is through the brain that the pipe strikes, killing first the mind in a nightmare of insanity, and then the body. That accounts for the wreckage that we found – the evidences apparently of two men engaged in a desperate struggle. The wreckage was the work of only one man – a maniac in the moment before death. The drug with which we are dealing drives its victim into an insane fury before his body succumbs. I believe such cases are fairly common in India.'

'Then Mr Marsh was poisoned after all?' cried Truxton. He was the only one of Miss Mack's auditors to speak.

'No, not poisoned! You will understand as I proceed. The pipe, you will find, contains apparently but one bowl and one channel, and at a superficial glance is filled only with tobacco. In reality, there is a lower chamber concealed beneath the upper bowl, to which extends a second channel. This secret chamber is charged with a certain compound of Indian hemp and dhatura leaves, one of the most powerful brain stimulants known to science – and one of the most dangerous if used above a certain strength. From the lower chamber it would leave no trace, of course, in the ashes above.

'Between the two compartments of the pipe is a slight connecting opening, sufficient to allow the hemp beneath to be ignited gradually by the burning tobacco. When a small quantity of the compound is used, the smoker is stimulated as by no other drug, not even opium. Increase the quantity above the danger point, and mark the result. The victim is not poisoned in the strict sense of the word, but literally smothered to death by the fumes!'

In Miss Mack's voice was the throb of the student before the Creation of the master.

'I should like this pipe, Miss Jansen, if you ever care to dispose of it!'

The girl was still staring woodenly.

'It was Orlando Julio, the medieval poisoner,' she gasped, 'that Uncle described –'

'In his seventeenth chapter of *The World's Great Cynics*,' finished Madelyn. 'I have taken the liberty of reading the chapter in manuscript form. Julio, however, was not the discoverer of the drug. He merely introduced it to the English public. As a matter of fact, it is one of the oldest stimulants of the East. It is easy to assume that it was not as a stimulant that Julio used it, but as a baffling instrument of murder. The mechanism of the pipe was his own invention, of course. The smoker, if not in the secret, would be completely oblivious to his danger. He might even use the pipe in perfect safety – until its lower chamber was loaded!'

Sheriff Peddicord, against the door, mopped his face with his red handkerchief, like a man in a daze. Dr Dench was still studying Miss Mack with his intent frown. Madelyn swerved her angle abruptly.

'Last night was not the first time the hemp-chamber of Wendell Marsh's pipe had been charged. We can trace the effect of the drug on his brain for several months – hallucinations, imaginative enemies seeking his life, incipient insanity. That explains his astonishing letter to me. Wendell Marsh was not a man of nine lives, but only one. The perils which he described were merely fantastic figments of the drug. For instance, the episode of the poisoned cherry pie. There was no pie at all served at the table yesterday.

'The letter to me was not a forgery. Miss Jansen, although you were sincere enough when you pronounced it such. The complete change in your uncle's handwriting was only another effect of the drug. It was this fact, in the end, which led me to the truth. You did not perceive that the dates of your notes and mine were six months apart! I knew that some terrific mental shock must have occurred in the meantime.

'And then, too, the ravages of a drug-crazed victim were at once suggested by the curtains of the library. They were not simply torn, but fairly chewed to pieces!'

A sudden tension fell over the room. We shifted nervously, rather avoiding one another's eyes. Madelyn laid the pipe back on the stand. She was quite evidently in no hurry to continue. It was Truxton again who put the leading question of the moment.

'If Mr Marsh was killed as you describe, Miss Mack, who killed him?'

Madelyn glanced across at Dr Dench.

'Will you kindly let me have the red leather book that you took from Mr Marsh's desk this evening, Doctor?'

The physician met her glance steadily.

'You think it – necessary?'

'I am afraid I must insist.'

For an instant Dr Dench hesitated. Then, with a shrug, he reached into a coat pocket and extended the red-bound volume, for which Miss Mack had dispatched me on the fruitless errand to the library. As Madelyn opened it we saw that it was not a printed volume, but filled with several hundred pages of close, cramped writing. Dr Dench's gaze swerved to Muriel Jansen as Miss Mack spoke.

'I have here the diary of Wendell Marsh, which shows us that he had been in the habit of seeking the stimulant of Indian hemp, or "hasheesh" for some time, possibly as a result of his retired, sedentary life and his close application to his books. Until his purchase of the Bainford relics, however, he had taken the stimulant in the comparatively harmless form of powdered leaves or "bhang", as it is termed in the Orient. His acquisition of Julio's drug-pipe, and an accidental discovery of its mechanism, led him to adopt the compound of hemp and dhatura, prepared for smoking – in India called "charas". No less an authority than Captain EN Windsor, bacteriologist of the Burmese government, states that it is directly responsible for a large percentage of the lunacy of the Orient. Wendell Marsh, however, did not realise his danger, nor how much stronger the latter compound is than the form of the drug to which he had been accustomed.

'Dr Dench endeavoured desperately to warn him of his peril, and free him from the bondage of the habit as the diary records, but the victim was too thoroughly enslaved. In fact, the situation had reached a point just before the final climax when it could no longer be concealed. The truth was already being suspected by the older servants. I assume this was why you feared my investigations in the case, Miss Jansen.'

Muriel Jansen was staring at Madelyn in a sort of dumb appeal.

'I can understand and admire Dr Dench's efforts to conceal the fact from the public – first, in his supervision of the inquest, which might have stumbled on the truth, and then in his removal of the betraying diary, which I left purposely exposed in the hope that it might inspire such an action. Had it not been removed, I might have suspected another explanation of the case – in spite of certain evidence to the contrary!'

Dr Dench's face had gone white.

'God! Miss Mack, do you mean that after all it was not suicide?'

'It was not suicide,' said Madelyn quietly. She stepped across toward the opposite door.

'When I stated that my knowledge that we are not dealing with natural death was shared by another person in this room, I might have added that it was shared by still a third person – not in the room!'

With a sudden movement she threw open the door before her. From the adjoining ante-room lurched the figure of Peters, the butler. He stared at us with a face grey with terror, and then crumpled to his knees. Madelyn drew away sharply as he tried to catch her skirts.

'You may arrest the murderer of Wendell Marsh, Sheriff!' she said gravely. 'And I think perhaps you had better take him outside.'

She faced our bewildered stares as the drawing-room door closed behind Mr Peddicord and his prisoner. From her stand she again took Raleigh's sandstone pipe, and with it two sheets of paper, smudged with the prints of a human thumb and fingers.

'It was the pipe in the end which led me to the truth, not only as to the method but the identity of the assassin,' she explained. 'The hand, which placed the fatal charge in the concealed chamber, left its imprint on the surface of the bowl. The fingers, grimed with the dust of the drug, made an impression which I would have at once detected had I not been so occupied with what I might find inside that I forgot what I might find outside! I am very much afraid that I permitted myself the great blunder of the modern detective – lack of thoroughness.

'Comparison with the fingerprints of the various agents in the case, of course, made the next step a mere detail of mathematical comparison. To make my identity sure, I found that my suspect possessed not only the opportunity and the knowledge for the crime, but the motive.

'In his younger days Peters was a chemist's apprentice; a fact which he utilised in his master's behalf in obtaining the drugs which had become so necessary a part of Mr Marsh's life. Had Wendell Marsh appeared in person for so continuous a supply, his identity would soon have made the fact a matter of common gossip. He relied on his servant for his agent, a detail which he mentions several times in his diary, promising Peters a generous bequest in his will as a reward. I fancy that it was the dream of this bequest, which would have meant a small fortune to a man in his position, that set the butler's brain to work on his treacherous plan of murder.'

* * * * * *

Miss Mack's dull gold hair covered the shoulders of her white peignoir in a great, thick braid. She was propped in a nest of pillows, with her favourite romance, *The Three Musketeers*, open at the historic siege of Porthos in the wine cellar. We had elected to spend the night at the Marsh house.

Madelyn glanced up as I appeared in the doorway of our room.

'Allow me to present a problem to your analytical skill, Miss Mack,' I said humbly. 'Which man does your knowledge of feminine psychology say Muriel Jansen will reward – the gravely protecting physician, or the boyishly admiring Truxton?'

'If she were thirty,' retorted Madelyn, yawning, 'she would be wise enough to choose Dr Dench. But, as she is only twenty-two, it will be Truxton.'

With a sigh, she turned again to the swashbuckling exploits of the gallant Porthos.

VIOLET STRANGE

Created by Anna Katharine Green
(1846-1935)

First published in 1878, The Leavenworth Case *was one of the earliest of all American detective novels. Its author was Anna Katharine Green, a Brooklyn-born writer who turned to fiction after failing to make much of a mark as a poet. Her story of a rich man's murder and its investigation by a detective from the New York Metropolitan Police Force named Ebenezer Gryce proved popular and significant in the later development of crime fiction. (Agatha Christie was later to cite it as an influence on her when she was beginning her career.) In the course of a long life, Green went on to write more than thirty other mystery novels including such titles as* A Strange Disappearance, Behind Closed Doors *and* The Step on the Stair. *A number of these featured Ebenezer Gryce, who thus became one of the first series characters in detective fiction, and Green also created a prototype Miss Marple in Amelia Butterworth, a nosy spinster with an eye for crime. In 1915, in her late sixties, Green published a volume of short stories,* The Golden Slipper and Other Stories, *which introduced another character to her readers. Violet Strange is an attractive young woman, a debutante who is at home amongst the upper echelons of New York society. She also leads a secret life as a professional sleuth, investigating crimes of all kinds to provide herself with an income of which her father knows nothing. The Violet Strange stories may not be as pioneering as the longer fiction Green wrote decades earlier but they are all well-written and entertaining reads.*

AN INTANGIBLE CLUE

'Not I.'

'Not studied the case which for the last few days has provided the papers with such conspicuous headlines?'

'I do not read the papers. I have not looked at one in a whole week.'

'Miss Strange, your social engagements must be of a very pressing nature just now?'

'They are.'

'And your business sense in abeyance?'

'How so?'

'You would not ask if you had read the papers.'

To this she made no reply save by a slight toss of her pretty head. If her employer felt nettled by this show of indifference, he did not betray it save by the rapidity of his tones as, without further preamble and possibly without real excuse, he proceeded to lay before her the case in question. 'Last Tuesday night a woman was murdered in this city; an old woman, in a lonely house where she has lived for years. Perhaps you remember this house? It occupies a not inconspicuous site in Seventeenth Street – a house of the olden time?'

'No, I do not remember.'

The extreme carelessness of Miss Strange's tone would have been fatal to her socially; but then, she would never have used it socially. This they both knew, yet he smiled with his customary indulgence.

'Then I will describe it.'

She looked around for a chair and sank into it. He did the same.

'It has a fanlight over the front door.'

She remained impassive.

'And two old-fashioned strips of parti-coloured glass on either side.'

'And a knocker between its panels which may bring money some day.'

'Oh, you do remember! I thought you would, Miss Strange.'

'Yes. Fanlights over doors are becoming very rare in New York.'

'Very well, then. That house was the scene of Tuesday's tragedy. The woman who has lived there in solitude for years was foully murdered. I have since heard that the people who knew her best have always anticipated some such violent end for her. She never allowed maid or friend to remain with her after five in the afternoon; yet she had money – some think a great deal – always in the house.'

'I am interested in the house, not in her.'

'Yet, she was a character – as full of whims and crotchets as a nut is of meat. Her death was horrible. She fought – her dress was torn from her body in rags. This happened, you see, before her hour for retiring; some think as early as six in the afternoon. And' – here he made a rapid gesture to catch Violet's wandering attention – 'in spite of this struggle; in spite of the fact that she was dragged from room to room – that her person was searched – and everything in the house searched – that drawers were pulled out of bureaus – doors wrenched off of cupboards – china smashed upon the floor – whole shelves denuded and not a spot from cellar to garret left unransacked, no direct clue to the perpetrator has been found – nothing that gives any idea of his personality save his display of strength and great cupidity. The police have even deigned to consult me – an unusual procedure – but I could find nothing, either. Evidences of fiendish purpose abound – of relentless search – but no clue to the man himself. It's uncommon, isn't it, not to have any clue?'

'I suppose so.' Miss Strange hated murders and it was with difficulty she could be brought to discuss them. But she was not going to be let off; not this time.

'You see,' he proceeded insistently, 'it's not only mortifying to the police but disappointing to the press, especially as few reporters believe in the No-thoroughfare business. They say, and we cannot but agree with them, that no such struggle could take place and no such repeated goings to and fro through the house

271

without some vestige being left by which to connect this crime with its daring perpetrator.'

Still she stared down at her hands – those little hands so white and fluttering, so seemingly helpless under the weight of their many rings, and yet so slyly capable.

'She must have queer neighbours,' came at last, from Miss Strange's reluctant lips. 'Didn't they hear or see anything of all this?'

'She has no neighbours – that is, after half-past five o'clock. There's a printing establishment on one side of her, a deserted mansion on the other side, and nothing but warehouses back and front. There was no one to notice what took place in her small dwelling after the printing house was closed. She was the most courageous or the most foolish of women to remain there as she did. But nothing except death could budge her. She was born in the room where she died; was married in the one where she worked; saw husband, father, mother, and five sisters carried out in turn to their graves through the door with the fanlight over the top – and these memories held her.'

'You are trying to interest me in the woman. Don't.'

'No, I'm not trying to interest you in her, only trying to explain her. There was another reason for her remaining where she did so long after all residents had left the block. She had a business.'

'Oh!'

'She embroidered monograms for fine ladies.'

'She did? But you needn't look at me like that. She never embroidered any for me.'

'No? She did first-class work. I saw some of it. Miss Strange, if I could get you into that house for ten minutes – not to see her but to pick up the loose intangible thread which I am sure is floating around in it somewhere – wouldn't you go?'

Violet slowly rose – a movement which he followed to the letter.

'Must I express in words the limit I have set for myself in our affair?' she asked. 'When, for reasons I have never thought

272

myself called upon to explain, I consented to help you a little now and then with some matter where a woman's tact and knowledge of the social world might tell without offence to herself or others, I never thought it would be necessary for me to state that temptation must stop with such cases, or that I should not be asked to touch the sordid or the bloody. But it seems I was mistaken, and that I must stoop to be explicit. The woman who was killed on Tuesday might have interested me greatly as an embroiderer, but as a victim, not at all. What do you see in me, or miss in me, that you should drag me into an atmosphere of low-down crime?'

'Nothing, Miss Strange. You are by nature, as well as by breeding, very far removed from everything of the kind. But you will allow me to suggest that no crime is low-down which makes imperative demand upon the intellect and intuitive sense of its investigator. Only the most delicate touch can feel and hold the thread I've just spoken of, and you have the most delicate touch I know.'

'Do not attempt to flatter me. I have no fancy for handling befouled spider webs. Besides, if I had – if such elusive filaments fascinated me – how could I, well-known in person and name, enter upon such a scene without prejudice to our mutual compact?'

'Miss Strange' – she had reseated herself, but so far he had failed to follow her example (an ignoring of the subtle hint that her interest might yet be caught, which seemed to annoy her a trifle) – 'I should not even have suggested such a possibility had I not seen a way of introducing you there without risk to your position or mine. Among the boxes piled upon Mrs Doolittle's table – boxes of finished work, most of them addressed and ready for delivery – was one on which could be seen the name of – shall I mention it?'

'Not mine? You don't mean mine? That would be too odd – too ridiculously odd. I should not understand a coincidence of that kind; no, I should not, notwithstanding the fact that I have lately sent out such work to be done.'

'Yet it was your name, very clearly and precisely written – your whole name, Miss Strange. I saw and read it myself.'

'But I gave the order to Madame Pirot on Fifth Avenue. How came my things to be found in the house of this woman of whose horrible death we have been talking?'

'Did you suppose that Madame Pirot did such work with her own hands? – or even had it done in her own establishment? Mrs Doolittle was universally employed. She worked for a dozen firms. You will find the biggest names on most of her packages. But on this one – I allude to the one addressed to you – there was more to be seen than the name. These words were written on it in another hand: Send without opening. This struck the police as suspicious; sufficiently so, at least, for them to desire your presence at the house as soon as you can make it convenient.'

'To open the box?'

'Exactly.'

The curl of Miss Strange's disdainful lip was a sight to see.

'You wrote those words yourself,' she coolly observed. 'While someone's back was turned, you whipped out your pencil and –'

'Resorted to a very pardonable subterfuge highly conducive to the public's good. But never mind that. Will you go?'

Miss Strange became suddenly demure.

'I suppose I must,' she grudgingly conceded. 'However obtained, a summons from the police cannot be ignored even by Peter Strange's daughter.'

Another man might have displayed his triumph by smile or gesture; but this one had learned his role too well. He simply said:

'Very good. Shall it be at once? I have a taxi at the door.'

But she failed to see the necessity of any such hurry. With sudden dignity she replied:

'That won't do. If I go to this house it must be under suitable conditions. I shall have to ask my brother to accompany me.'

'Your brother!'

'Oh, he's safe. He – he knows.'

'Your brother knows?' Her visitor, with less control than usual, betrayed very openly his uneasiness.

'He does and – approves. But that's not what interests us now, only so far as it makes it possible for me to go with propriety to that dreadful house.'

A formal bow from the other and the words:

'They may expect you, then. Can you say when?'

'Within the next hour. But it will be a useless concession on my part,' she pettishly complained. 'A place that has been gone over by a dozen detectives is apt to be brushed clean of its cobwebs, even if such ever existed.'

'That's the difficulty,' he acknowledged; and did not dare to add another word; she was at that particular moment so very much the great lady, and so little his confidential agent.

He might have been less impressed, however, by this sudden assumption of manner, had he been so fortunate as to have seen how she employed the three-quarters of an hour's delay for which she had asked.

She read those neglected newspapers, especially the one containing the following highly coloured narration of this ghastly crime:

'A door ajar – an empty hall – a line of sinister-looking blotches marking a guilty step diagonally across the flagging – silence – and an unmistakable odour repugnant to all humanity – such were the indications which met the eyes of Officer O'Leary on his first round last night, and led to the discovery of a murder which will long thrill the city by its mystery and horror.

'Both the house and the victim are well known.' Here followed a description of the same and of Mrs Doolittle's manner of life in her ancient home, which Violet hurriedly passed over to come to the following:

'As far as one can judge from appearances, the crime happened in this wise: Mrs Doolittle had been in her kitchen, as the tea-kettle found singing on the stove goes to prove, and was coming back through her bedroom, when the wretch, who had stolen in by the front door which, to save steps, she was unfortunately in the habit of leaving on the latch till all possibility of customers for the day was over, sprang upon her from behind and dealt her a swinging blow with the poker he had caught up from the hearthstone.

'Whether the struggle which ensued followed immediately upon this first attack or came later, it will take medical experts to determine. But, whenever it did occur, the fierceness of its character is shown by the grip taken upon her throat and the traces of blood which are to be seen all over the house. If the wretch had lugged her into her workroom and thence to the kitchen, and thence back to the spot of first assault, the evidences could not have been more ghastly. Bits of her clothing, torn off by a ruthless hand, lay scattered over all these floors. In her bedroom, where she finally breathed her last, there could be seen mingled with these a number of large but worthless glass beads; and close against one of the base-boards, the string which had held them, as shown by the few remaining beads still clinging to it. If in pulling the string from her neck he had hoped to light upon some valuable booty, his fury at his disappointment is evident. You can almost see the frenzy with which he flung the would-be necklace at the wall, and kicked about and stamped upon its rapidly rolling beads.

'Booty! That was what he was after; to find and carry away the poor needlewoman's supposed hoardings. If the scene baffles description − if, as some believe, he dragged her yet living from spot to spot, demanding information as to her places of concealment under threat of repeated blows, and, finally baffled, dealt the finishing stroke and proceeded on the search alone, no greater devastation could have taken place in this poor woman's house or effects. Yet such was his precaution and care for himself that he left no fingerprint behind him nor any other token which could lead to personal identification. Even though his footsteps could be traced in much the order I have mentioned, they were of so indeterminate and shapeless a character as to convey little to the intelligence of the investigator.

'That these smears (they could not be called footprints) not only crossed the hall but appeared in more than one place on the staircase proves that he did not confine his search to the lower storey; and perhaps one of the most interesting features of the case lies in the indications given by these marks of the raging course he took through these upper rooms. As the accompanying diagram will show [we omit the diagram] he went first into the large front chamber, thence to the rear where we find two rooms, one unfinished and filled with accumulated stuff most of which he left lying loose upon the floor, and the other plastered, and containing a window opening upon an alleyway at the side, but empty of all furniture and without even a carpet on the bare boards.

'Why he should have entered the latter place, and why, having entered he should have crossed to the window, will be plain to those who have studied the conditions. The front chamber windows were tightly shuttered, the attic ones cumbered with boxes and shielded from approach by old bureaus and discarded chairs. This one only was free and, although darkened by the proximity of the house neighbouring it across the alley, was the only spot on the storey where sufficient light could be had at this late hour for the examination of any object of whose value he was doubtful. That he had come across such an object and had brought it to this window for some such purpose is very satisfactorily demonstrated by the discovery of a worn-out wallet of ancient make lying on the floor directly in front of this window – a proof of his cupidity but also proof of his ill-luck. For this wallet, when lifted and opened, was found to contain two hundred or more dollars in old bills, which, if not the full hoard of their industrious owner, was certainly worth the taking by one who had risked his neck for the sole purpose of theft.

'This wallet, and the flight of the murderer without it, give to this affair, otherwise simply brutal, a dramatic interest which will be appreciated not only by the very able detectives already hot upon the chase, but by all other inquiring minds anxious to solve a mystery of which so estimable a woman has been the unfortunate victim. A problem is presented to the police –'

There Violet stopped.

When, not long after, the superb limousine of Peter Strange stopped before the little house in Seventeenth Street, it caused a veritable sensation, not only in the curiosity-mongers lingering on the sidewalk, but to the two persons within – the officer on guard and a belated reporter.

Though dressed in her plainest suit, Violet Strange looked much too fashionable and far too young and thoughtless to be observed, without emotion, entering a scene of hideous and brutal crime. Even the young man who accompanied her promised to bring a most incongruous element into this atmosphere of guilt and horror, and, as the detective on guard whispered to the man beside him, might much better have been left behind in the car.

But Violet was great for the proprieties and young Arthur followed her in.

Her entrance was a *coup de theatre*. She had lifted her veil in crossing the sidewalk and her interesting features and general air of timidity were very fetching. As the man holding open the door noted the impression made upon his companion, he muttered with sly facetiousness:

'You think you'll show her nothing; but I'm ready to bet a fiver that she'll want to see it all and that you'll show it to her.'

The detective's grin was expressive, notwithstanding the shrug with which he tried to carry it off.

And Violet? The hall into which she now stepped from the most vivid sunlight had never been considered even in its palmiest days as possessing cheer even of the stately kind. The ghastly green light infused through it by the coloured glass on either side of the doorway seemed to promise yet more dismal things beyond.

'Must I go in there?' she asked, pointing, with an admirable simulation of nervous excitement, to a half-shut door at her left. 'Is there where it happened? Arthur, do you suppose that there is where it happened?'

'No, no, Miss,' the officer made haste to assure her. 'If you are Miss Strange' (Violet bowed), 'I need hardly say that the woman was struck in her bedroom. The door beside you leads into the parlour, or as she would have called it, her work-room.

You needn't be afraid of going in there. You will see nothing but the disorder of her boxes. They were pretty well pulled about. Not all of them though,' he added, watching her as closely as the dim light permitted. 'There is one which gives no sign of having been tampered with. It was done up in wrapping paper and is addressed to you, which in itself would not have seemed worthy of our attention had not these lines been scribbled on it in a man's handwriting: "Send without opening".'

'How odd!' exclaimed the little minx with widely opened eyes and an air of guileless innocence. 'Whatever can it mean? Nothing serious I am sure, for the woman did not even know me. She was employed to do this work by Madame Pirot.'

'Didn't you know that it was to be done here?'

'No. I thought Madame Pirot's own girls did her embroidery for her.'

'So that you were surprised –'

'Wasn't I!'

'To get our message.'

'I didn't know what to make of it.'

The earnest, half-injured look with which she uttered this disclaimer did its appointed work. The detective accepted her for what she seemed and, oblivious to the reporter's satirical gesture, crossed to the work-room door, which he threw wide open with the remark:

'I should be glad to have you open that box in our presence. It is undoubtedly all right, but we wish to be sure. You know what the box should contain?'

'Oh, yes, indeed; pillowcases and sheets, with a big S embroidered on them.'

'Very well. Shall I undo the string for you?'

'I shall be much obliged,' said she, her eye flashing quickly about the room before settling down upon the knot he was deftly loosening.

Her brother, gazing indifferently in from the doorway, hardly noticed this look; but the reporter at his back did, though he failed to detect its penetrating quality.

'Your name is on the other side,' observed the detective as he drew away the string and turned the package over.

The smile which just lifted the corner of her lips was not in answer to this remark, but to her recognition of her employer's handwriting in the words under her name: Send without opening. She had not misjudged him.

'The cover you may like to take off yourself,' suggested the officer, as he lifted the box out of its wrapper.

'Oh, I don't mind. There's nothing to be ashamed of in embroidered linen. Or perhaps that is not what you are looking for?'

No one answered. All were busy watching her whip off the lid and lift out the pile of sheets and pillowcases with which the box was closely packed.

'Shall I unfold them?' she asked.

The detective nodded.

Taking out the topmost sheet, she shook it open. Then the next and the next till she reached the bottom of the box. Nothing of a criminating nature came to light. The box as well as its contents was without mystery of any kind. This was not an unexpected result of course, but the smile with which she began to refold the pieces and throw them back into the box, revealed one of her dimples which was almost as dangerous to the casual observer as when it revealed both.

'There,' she exclaimed, 'you see! Household linen exactly as I said. Now may I go home?'

'Certainly, Miss Strange.'

The detective stole a sly glance at the reporter. She was not going in for the horrors then after all.

But the reporter abated nothing of his knowing air, for while she spoke of going, she made no move towards doing so, but continued to look about the room till her glances finally settled on a long, dark curtain shutting off an adjoining room.

'There's where she lies, I suppose,' she feelingly exclaimed. 'And not one of you knows who killed her. Somehow, I cannot understand that. Why don't you know when that's what you're hired for?' The innocence with which she uttered this was astonishing. The detective began to look sheepish and the reporter turned aside to hide his smile. Whether in another moment either would have spoken no one can say, for, with a mock consciousness of having said something foolish, she caught up her parasol from the table and made a start for the door.

But, of course, she looked back.

'I was wondering,' she recommenced, with a half-wistful, half-speculative air, 'whether I should ask to have a peep at the place where it all happened.'

The reporter chuckled behind the pencil-end he was chewing, but the officer maintained his solemn air, for which act of self-restraint he was undoubtedly grateful when in another minute she gave a quick impulsive shudder not altogether assumed, and vehemently added: 'But I couldn't stand the sight; no, I couldn't! I'm an awful coward when it comes to things like that. Nothing in all the world would induce me to look at the woman or her room. But I should like – ' here both her dimples came into play though she could not be said exactly to smile – 'just one little look upstairs, where he went poking about so long without any fear it seems of being interrupted. Ever since I've read about it I have seen, in my mind, a picture of his wicked figure sneaking from room to room, tearing open drawers and flinging out the contents of closets just to find a little money – a little, little money! I shall not sleep tonight just for wondering how those high-up attic rooms really look.'

Who could dream that back of this display of mingled childishness and audacity there lay hidden purpose, intellect, and a keen knowledge of human nature. Not the two men who listened to this seemingly irresponsible chatter. To them she was a child to be humoured and humour her they did. The dainty feet which had already found their way to that gloomy staircase were allowed to ascend, followed it is true by those of the officer who did not dare to smile back at the reporter because of the brother's watchful and none too conciliatory eye.

At the stair head she paused to look back.

'I don't see those horrible marks which the papers describe as running all along the lower hall and up these stairs.'

'No, Miss Strange; they have gradually been rubbed out, but you will find some still showing on these upper floors.'

'Oh! oh! where? You frighten me – frighten me horribly! But – but – if you don't mind, I should like to see.'

Why should not a man on a tedious job amuse himself? Piloting her over to the small room in the rear, he pointed down at the boards. She gave one look and then stepped gingerly in.

'Just look!' she cried; 'a whole string of marks going straight from door to window. They have no shape, have they – just blotches? I wonder why one of them is so much larger than the rest?'

This was no new question. It was one which everybody who went into the room was sure to ask, there was such a difference in the size and appearance of the mark nearest the window. The reason – well, minds were divided about that, and no one had a satisfactory theory. The detective therefore kept discreetly silent.

This did not seem to offend Miss Strange. On the contrary it gave her an opportunity to babble away to her heart's content.

'One, two, three, four, five, six,' she counted, with a shudder at every count. 'And one of them bigger than the others.' She might have added, 'It is the trail of one foot, and strangely, intermingled at that,' but she did not, though we may be quite sure that she noted the fact. 'And where, just where did the old wallet fall? Here? Or here?'

She had moved as she spoke, so that in uttering the last 'here', she stood directly before the window. The surprise she received there nearly made her forget the part she was playing. From the character of the light in the room, she had expected, on looking out, to confront a nearby wall, but not a window in that wall. Yet that was what she saw directly facing her from across the old-fashioned alley separating this house from its neighbour; twelve unshuttered and uncurtained panes through which she caught a darkened view of a room almost as forlorn and devoid of furniture as the one in which she then stood.

When quite sure of herself, she let a certain portion of her surprise appear.

'Why, look!' she cried, 'if you can't see right in next door! What a lonesome-looking place! From its desolate appearance I should think the house quite empty.'

'And it is. That's the old Shaffer homestead. It's been empty for a year.'

'Oh, empty!' And she turned away, with the most inconsequent air in the world, crying out as her name rang up the stair, 'There's Arthur calling. I suppose he thinks I've been here long enough. I'm sure I'm very much obliged to you, officer. I really shouldn't have slept a wink tonight, if I hadn't been given a peep at these rooms, which I had imagined so different'. And with one additional glance over her shoulder, that seemed to penetrate both windows and the desolate space beyond, she ran quickly out and down in response to her brother's reiterated call.

'Drive quickly! – as quickly as the law allows, to Hiram Brown's office in Duane Street.'

Arrived at the address named, she went in alone to see Mr Brown. He was her father's lawyer and a family friend.

Hardly waiting for his affectionate greeting, she cried out quickly. 'Tell me how I can learn anything about the old Shaffer house in Seventeenth Street. Now, don't look so surprised. I have very good reasons for my request and – and – I'm in an awful hurry.'

'But –'

'I know, I know; there's been a dreadful tragedy next door to it; but it's about the Shaffer house itself I want some information. Has it an agent, a –'

'Of course it has an agent, and here is his name.'

Mr Brown presented her with a card on which he had hastily written both name and address.

She thanked him, dropped him a mocking curtsey full of charm, whispered 'Don't tell father', and was gone.

Her manner to the man she next interviewed was very

different. As soon as she saw him she subsided into her usual society manner. With just a touch of the conceit of the successful debutante, she announced herself as Miss Strange of Seventy-second Street. Her business with him was in regard to the possible renting of the Shaffer house. She had an old lady friend who was desirous of living downtown.

In passing through Seventeenth Street, she had noticed that the old Shaffer house was standing empty and had been immediately struck with the advantages it possessed for her elderly friend's occupancy. Could it be that the house was for rent? There was no sign on it to that effect, but – etc.

His answer left her nothing to hope for.

'It is going to be torn down,' he said.

'Oh, what a pity!' she exclaimed. 'Real colonial, isn't it! I wish I could see the rooms inside before it is disturbed. Such doors and such dear old-fashioned mantelpieces as it must have! I just dote on the Colonial. It brings up such pictures of the old days; weddings, you know, and parties; all so different from ours and so much more interesting.'

Is it the chance shot that tells? Sometimes. Violet had no especial intention in what she said save as a prelude to a pending request, but nothing could have served her purpose better than that one word, wedding. The agent laughed and giving her his first indulgent look remarked genially:

'Romance is not confined to those ancient times. If you were to enter that house today you would come across evidences of a wedding as romantic as any which ever took place in all the seventy odd years of its existence. A man and a woman were married there the day before yesterday who did their first courting under its roof forty years ago. He has been married twice and she once in the interval; but the old love held firm and now at the age of sixty and over they have come together to finish their days in peace and happiness. Or so we will hope.'

'Married! Married in that house and on the day that –'

She caught herself up in time. He did not notice the break.

'Yes, in memory of those old days of courtship, I suppose.

284

They came here about five, got the keys, drove off, went through the ceremony in that empty house, returned the keys to me in my own apartment, took the steamer for Naples, and were on the sea before midnight. Do you not call that quick work as well as highly romantic?'

'Very.' Miss Strange's cheek had paled. It was apt to when she was greatly excited. 'But I don't understand,' she added, the moment after. 'How could they do this and nobody know about it? I should have thought it would have got into the papers.'

'They are quiet people. I don't think they told their best friends. A simple announcement in the next day's journals testified to the fact of their marriage, but that was all. I would not have felt at liberty to mention the circumstances myself, if the parties were not well on their way to Europe.'

'Oh, how glad I am that you did tell me! Such a story of constancy and the hold which old associations have upon sensitive minds! But –'

'Why, Miss? What's the matter? You look very much disturbed.'

'Don't you remember? Haven't you thought? Something else happened that very day and almost at the same time on that block. Something very dreadful –'

'Mrs Doolittle's murder?'

'Yes. It was as near as next door, wasn't it? Oh, if this happy couple had known –'

'But fortunately they didn't. Nor are they likely to, till they reach the other side. You needn't fear that their honeymoon will be spoiled that way.'

'But they may have heard something or seen something before leaving the street. Did you notice how the gentleman looked when he returned you the keys?'

'I did, and there was no cloud on his satisfaction.'

'Oh, how you relieve me!' One – two dimples made their appearance in Miss Strange's fresh, young cheeks. 'Well! I wish them joy. Do you mind telling me their names? I cannot think of them as actual persons without knowing their names.'

'The gentleman was Constantin Amidon; the lady, Marian

Shaffer. You will have to think of them now as Mr and Mrs Amidon.'

'And I will. Thank you, Mr Hutton, thank you very much. Next to the pleasure of getting the house for my friend, is that of hearing this charming bit of news.'

She held out her hand and, as he took it, remarked:

'They must have had a clergyman and witnesses.'

'Undoubtedly.'

'I wish I had been one of the witnesses,' she sighed sentimentally.

'They were two old men.'

'Oh, no! Don't tell me that.'

'Fogies; nothing less.'

'But the clergyman? He must have been young. Surely there was someone there capable of appreciating the situation?'

'I can't say about that; I did not see the clergyman.'

'Oh, well! it doesn't matter.' Miss Strange's manner was as nonchalant as it was charming. 'We will think of him as being very young.'

And with a merry toss of her head she flitted away.

But she sobered very rapidly upon entering her limousine.

'Hello!'

'Ah, is that you?'

'Yes, I want a Marconi sent.'

'A Marconi?'

'Yes, to the *Cretic*, which left dock the very night in which we are so deeply interested.'

'Good. Whom to? The Captain?'

'No, to a Mrs Constantin Amidon. But first be sure there is such a passenger.'

'Mrs! What idea have you there?'

'Excuse my not stating over the telephone. The message is to be to this effect. Did she at any time immediately before or after her marriage to Mr Amidon get a glimpse of anyone in the adjoining house? No remarks, please. I use the telephone because I am not ready to explain myself. If she did, let her send a written description to you of that person as soon as she reaches the Azores.'

'You surprise me. May I not call or hope for a line from you early tomorrow?'

'I shall be busy till you get your answer.'

He hung up the receiver. He recognised the resolute tone.

But the time came when the pending explanation was fully given to him. An answer had been returned from the steamer, favourable to Violet's hopes. Mrs Amidon had seen such a person and would send a full description of the same at the first opportunity. It was news to fill Violet's heart with pride; the filament of a clue which had led to this great result had been so nearly invisible and had felt so like nothing in her grasp.

To her employer she described it as follows:

'When I hear or read of a case which contains any baffling features, I am apt to feel some hidden chord in my nature thrill to one fact in it and not to any of the others. In this case the single fact which appealed to my imagination was the dropping of the stolen wallet in that upstairs room. Why did the guilty man drop it? And why, having dropped it, did he not pick it up again? But one answer seemed possible. He had heard or seen something at the spot where it fell which not only alarmed him but sent him in flight from the house.'

'Very good; and did you settle to your own mind the nature of that sound or that sight?'

'I did.' Her manner was strangely businesslike. No show of dimples now. 'Satisfied that if any possibility remained of my ever doing this, it would have to be on the exact place of this occurrence or not at all, I embraced your suggestion and visited the house.'

'And that room no doubt.'

'And that room. Women, somehow, seem to manage such things.'

'So I've noticed, Miss Strange. And what was the result of your visit? What did you discover there?'

'This: that one of the blood spots marking the criminal's steps through the room was decidedly more pronounced than the rest; and, what was even more important, that the window out of which I was looking had its counterpart in the house on the opposite side of the alley. In gazing through the one I was gazing through the other; and not only that, but into the darkened area of the room beyond. Instantly I saw how the latter fact might be made to explain the former one. But before I say how, let me ask if it is quite settled among you that the smears on the floor and stairs mark the passage of the criminal's footsteps!'

'Certainly; and very bloody feet they must have been too. His shoes – or rather his one shoe – for the proof is plain that only the right one left its mark – must have become thoroughly saturated to carry its traces so far.'

'Do you think that any amount of saturation would have done this? Or, if you are not ready to agree to that, that a shoe so covered with blood could have failed to leave behind it some hint of its shape, some imprint, however faint, of heel or toe? But nowhere did it do this. We see a smear – and that is all.'

'You are right, Miss Strange; you are always right. And what do you gather from this?'

She looked to see how much he expected from her, and, meeting an eye not quite as free from ironic suggestion as his words had led her to expect, faltered a little as she proceeded to say:

'My opinion is a girl's opinion, but such as it is you have the right to have it. From the indications mentioned I could draw but this conclusion: that the blood which accompanied the criminal's footsteps was not carried through the house by his shoes –– he wore no shoes; he did not even wear stockings; probably he had none. For reasons which appealed to his judgement, he went about his wicked work barefoot; and it was the blood from his own veins and not from those of his victim which made the trail we have followed with so much interest. Do you forget those broken beads – how he kicked them about and stamped upon them in his fury? One of them pierced the ball of his foot, and that so sharply that it not only spurted blood but kept on bleeding with every step he took. Otherwise, the trail would have been lost after his passage up the stairs.'

'Fine!' There was no irony in the bureau-chief's eye now. 'You are progressing, Miss Strange. Allow me, I pray, to kiss your hand. It is a liberty I have never taken, but one which would greatly relieve my present stress of feeling.'

She lifted her hand toward him, but it was in gesture, not in recognition of his homage.

'Thank you,' said she, 'but I claim no monopoly on deductions so simple as these. I have not the least doubt that not only yourself but every member of the force has made the same. But there is a little matter which may have escaped the police, may even have escaped you. To that I would now call your attention since through it I have been enabled, after a little necessary groping, to reach the open. You remember the one large blotch on the upper floor where the man dropped the wallet? That blotch, more or less commingled with a fainter one, possessed great significance for me from the first moment I saw it. How came his foot to bleed so much more profusely at that one spot than at any other? There could be but one answer: because here a surprise met him – a surprise so startling to him in his present state of mind that he gave a quick spring backward, with the result that his wounded foot came down suddenly and forcibly instead of easily as in his previous wary tread. And what was the surprise? I made it my business to find out, and now I can tell you that it was the sight of a woman's face staring upon him from the neighbouring house which he had probably been told was empty. The shock disturbed his judgement. He saw his crime discovered – his guilty secret read, and fled in unreasoning panic. He might better have held on to his wits. It was this display of fear which led me to search after its cause, and consequently to discover that at this especial hour more than one person had been in the Shaffer house; that, in fact, a marriage had been celebrated there under circumstances as romantic as any we read of in books, and that this marriage, privately carried out, had been followed by an immediate voyage of the happy couple on one of the White Star steamers. With the rest you are conversant. I do not need to say anything about what has followed the sending of that Marconi.'

'But I am going to say something about your work in this matter, Miss Strange. The big detectives about here will have to look sharp if –'

'Don't, please! Not yet.' A smile softened the asperity of this interruption. 'The man has yet to be caught and identified. Till that is done I cannot enjoy anyone's congratulations. And you will see that all this may not be so easy. If no one happened to meet the desperate wretch before he had an opportunity to retie his shoelaces, there will be little for you or even for the police to go upon but his wounded foot, his undoubtedly carefully prepared alibi, and later, a woman's confused description of a face seen but for a moment only and that under a personal excitement precluding minute attention. I should not be surprised if the whole thing came to nothing.'

But it did not. As soon as the description was received from Mrs Amidon (a description, by the way, which was unusually clear and precise, owing to the peculiar and contradictory features of the man), the police were able to recognise him among the many suspects always under their eye. Arrested, he pleaded, just as Miss Strange had foretold, an alibi of a seemingly unimpeachable character; but neither it, nor the plausible explanation with which he endeavoured to account for a freshly healed scar amid the callouses of his right foot, could stand before Mrs Amidon's unequivocal testimony that he was the same man she had seen in Mrs Doolittle's upper room on the afternoon of her own happiness and of that poor woman's murder.

The moment when, at his trial, the two faces again confronted each other across a space no wider than that which had separated them on the dread occasion in Seventeenth Street, is said to have been one of the most dramatic in the annals of that ancient court room.

MISS NORA VAN SNOOP

Created by Clarence Rook
(1862–1915)

Born in Kent and educated at Oxford, Clarence Rook became a journalist and worked on a variety of newspapers and periodicals in the 1890s, from The Illustrated London News *to* The Idler, *the magazine founded by the humourist Jerome K Jerome. The work for which he is best known is* The Hooligan Nights, *first published in 1899, which purports to tell the story of 'Young Alf', a hoodlum from Lambeth, mostly in his own words. (The book is subtitled 'Being the Life and Opinions of a Young and Impertinent Criminal Recounted by Himself and Set Forth by Clarence Rook'.) In all likelihood, Young Alf's adventures were largely invented by Rook. He may have had contacts among London's street gangs but his book has some suspicious resemblances to other, undoubtedly fictional tales of the city's slums such as Arthur Morrison's* Tales of Mean Streets. The Hooligan Nights *may not be the direct reportage it claims to be but it is certainly well written and still deserves to be read. Once praised by George Bernard Shaw as 'a very clever fellow', Rook also wrote much else, including a volume of sketches of London life (*London Sidelights*), a guide to Switzerland and a number of short stories. One of the latter was 'The Stir Outside the Café Royal' which first appeared in* The Harmsworth Magazine *in September 1898. This is not a conventional detective story, in that it contains no great mystery to which a solution is discovered, but it deserves its place in this anthology because of its resourceful heroine Nora Van Snoop who is also shrewd enough to outwit a supposed master criminal.*

THE STIR OUTSIDE THE CAFÉ ROYAL

Colonel Mathurin was one of the aristocrats of crime; at least Mathurin was the name under which he had accomplished a daring bank robbery in Detroit which had involved the violent death of the manager, though it was generally believed by the police that the Rossiter who was at the bottom of some long firm frauds in Melbourne was none other than Mathurin under another name, and that the designer and chief gainer in a sensational murder case in the Midlands was the same mysterious and ubiquitous personage.

But Mathurin had for some years successfully eluded pursuit; indeed, it was generally known that he was the most desperate among criminals, and was determined never to be taken alive. Moreover, as he invariably worked through subordinates who knew nothing of his whereabouts and were scarcely acquainted with his appearance, the police had but a slender clue to his identity.

As a matter of fact, only two people beyond his immediate associates in crime could have sworn to Mathurin if they had met him face to face. One of them was the Detroit bank manager whom he had shot with his own hand before the eyes of his fiancée. It was through the other that Mathurin was arrested, extradited to the States, and finally made to atone for his life of crime. It all happened in a distressingly commonplace way, so far as the average spectator was concerned. But the story, which I have pieced together from the details supplied – firstly, by a certain detective sergeant whom I met in a tavern hard by Westminster; and secondly, by a certain young woman named Miss Van Snoop – has an element of romance, if you look below the surface.

It was about half-past one o'clock, on a bright and pleasant day, that a young lady was driving down Regent Street in a hansom which she had picked up outside her boarding house near Portland Road Station. She had told the cabman to drive slowly, as she was nervous behind a horse; and so she had leisure to scan, with the curiosity of a stranger, the strolling crowd that at nearly all hours of the day throngs Regent Street. It was a sunny morning, and everybody looked cheerful. Ladies were shopping, or looking in at the shop windows. Men about town were collecting an appetite for lunch; flower girls were selling 'nice vi'lets, sweet vi'lets, penny a bunch'; and the girl in the cab leaned one arm on the apron and regarded the scene with alert attention. She was not exactly pretty, for the symmetry of her features was discounted by a certain hardness in the set of the mouth. But her hair, so dark as to be almost black, and her eyes of greyish blue set her beyond comparison with the commonplace.

Just outside the Café Royal there was a slight stir, and a temporary block in the foot traffic. A brougham was setting down, behind it was a victoria, and behind that a hansom; and as the girl glanced round the heads of the pair in the brougham, she saw several men standing on the steps. Leaning back suddenly, she opened the trapdoor in the roof.

'Stop here,' she said, 'I've changed my mind.'

The driver drew up by the kerb, and the girl skipped out.

'You shan't lose by the change,' she said, handing him half-a-crown.

There was a tinge of American accent in the voice; and the cabman, pocketing the half-crown with thanks, smiled.

'They may talk about that McKinley tariff,' he soliloquised as he crawled along the kerb towards Piccadilly Circus, 'but it's better 'n free trade – lumps!'

Meanwhile the girl walked slowly back towards the Café Royal, and, with a quick glance at the men who were standing there, entered. One or two of the men raised their eyebrows; but the girl was quite unconscious, and went on her way to the luncheon-room.

'American, you bet,' said one of the loungers. 'They'll go anywhere and do anything.'

Just in front of her as she entered was a tall, clean-shaven man, faultlessly dressed in glossy silk hat and frock coat, with a flower in his button-hole. He looked around for a moment in search of a convenient table. As he hesitated, the girl hesitated; but when the waiter waved him to a small table laid for two, the girl immediately sat down behind him at the next table.

'Excuse me, madam,' said the waiter, 'this table is set for four; would you mind –'

'I guess,' said the girl, 'I'll stay where I am.' And the look in her eyes, as well as a certain sensation in the waiter's palm, ensured her against further disturbance.

The restaurant was full of people lunching, singly or in twos, in threes and even larger parties; and many curious glances were directed to the girl who sat at a table alone and pursued her way calmly through the menu. But the girl appeared to notice no one. When her eyes were off her plate they were fixed straight ahead – on the back of the man who had entered in front of her. The man, who had drunk a half-bottle of champagne with his lunch, ordered a liqueur to accompany his coffee. The girl, who had drunk an aerated water, leaned back in her chair and wrinkled her brows. They were very straight brows that seemed to meet over her nose when she wrinkled them in perplexity. Then she called a waiter.

'Bring me a sheet of notepaper, please,' she said, 'and my bill.'

The waiter laid the sheet of paper before her, and the girl proceeded, after a few moments thought, to write a few lines in pencil upon it. When this was done, she folded the sheet carefully, and laid it in her purse. Then, having paid her bill, she returned her purse to her dress pocket, and waited patiently.

In a few minutes the clean-shaven man at the next table settled his bill and made preparations for departure. The girl at the same time drew on her gloves, keeping her eyes immovably upon her neighbour's back. As the man rose to depart, and passed the table at which the girl had been sitting, the girl was looking into the mirror upon the wall, and patting her hair. Then she turned and followed the man out of the restaurant, while a pair at an adjacent table remarked to one another that it was a rather curious coincidence for a man and woman to enter and leave at the same moment when they had no apparent connection.

But what happened outside was even more curious.

The man halted for a moment upon the steps at the entrance. The porter, who was in conversation with a policeman, turned, whistle in hand.

'Hansom, sir?' he asked.

'Yes,' said the clean-shaven man.

The porter was raising his whistle to his lips when he noticed the girl behind.

'Do you wish for a cab, madam?' he asked, and blew upon his whistle.

As he turned again for an answer, he plainly saw the girl, who was standing close behind the clean-shaven man, slip her hand under his coat, and snatch from his hip pocket something which she quickly transferred to her own.

'Well, I'm –' began the clean-shaven man, swinging round and feeling in his pocket.

'Have you missed anything, sir?' said the porter, standing full in front of the girl to bar her exit.

'My cigarette-case is gone,' said the man, looking from one side to another.

'What's this?' said the policeman, stepping forward.

'I saw the woman's hand in the gentleman's pocket, plain as a pikestaff,' said the porter.

'Oh, that's it, is it?' said the policeman, coming close to the girl. 'I thought as much.'

'Come now,' said the clean-shaven man, 'I don't want to make a fuss. Just hand back that cigarette-case, and we'll say no more about it.'

'I haven't got it,' said the girl. 'How dare you? I never touched your pocket.'

The man's face darkened.

'Oh, come now!' said the porter.

'Look here, that won't do,' said the policeman, 'you'll have to come along of me. Better take a four-wheeler, eh, sir?'

For a knot of loafers, seeing something interesting in the wind, had collected round the entrance.

A four-wheeler was called, and the girl entered, closely followed by the policeman and the clean-shaven man.

'I was never so insulted in my life,' said the girl.

Nevertheless, she sat back quite calmly in the cab, as though she was perfectly ready to face this or any other situation, while the policeman watched her closely to make sure that she did not dispose in any surreptitious way of the stolen article.

At the police station hard by, the usual formalities were gone through, and the clean-shaven man was constituted prosecutor. But the girl stoutly denied having been guilty of any offence.

The inspector in charge looked doubtful.

'Better search her,' he said.

And the girl was led off to a room for an interview with the female searcher.

The moment the door closed the girl put her hand into her pocket, pulled out the cigarette-case, and laid it upon the table.

'There you are,' she said. 'That will fix matters so far.'

The woman looked rather surprised.

'Now,' said the girl, holding out her arms, 'feel in this other pocket, and find my purse.'

The woman picked out the purse.

'Open it and read the note on the bit of paper inside.'

On the sheet of paper which the waiter had given her, the girl had written these words, which the searcher read in a muttered undertone:

'I am going to pick this man's pocket as the best way of getting him into a police station without violence. He is Colonel Mathurin, alias Rossiter, alias Connell, and he is wanted in Detroit, New York, Melbourne, Colombo, and London. Get four men to pin him unawares, for he is armed and desperate. I am a member of the New York detective force – Nora Van Snoop.'

'It's all right,' said Miss Van Snoop, quickly, as the searcher looked up at her after reading the note. 'Show that to the boss – right away.'

CLARENCE ROOK

The searcher opened the door. After whispered consultation the inspector appeared, holding the note in his hand.

'Now then, be spry,' said Miss Van Snoop. 'Oh, you needn't worry! I've got my credentials right here,' and she dived into another pocket.

'But do you know – can you be sure,' said the inspector, 'that this is the man who shot the Detroit bank manager?'

'Great heavens! Didn't I see him shoot Will Stevens with my own eyes! And didn't I take service with the police to hunt him out?'

The girl stamped her foot, and the inspector left. For two, three, four minutes, she stood listening intently. Then a muffled shout reached her ears. Two minutes later the inspector returned.

'I think you're right,' he said. 'We have found enough evidence on him to identify him. But why didn't you give him in charge before to the police?'

'I wanted to arrest him myself,' said Miss Van Snoop, 'and I have. Oh, Will! Will!'

Miss Van Snoop sank into a cane-bottomed chair, laid her head upon the table, and cried. She had earned the luxury of hysterics. In half an hour she left the station, and, proceeding to a post office, cabled her resignation to the head of the detective force in New York.

HILDA WADE

Created by Grant Allen
(1848–1899)

Although largely forgotten today, Grant Allen was a popular and versatile writer who published books, both non-fiction and fiction, on a wide variety of subjects and in a number of different genres. His best known and most notorious book, The Woman Who Did, *appeared in 1895 and attracted controversy because of its portrait of an independent woman who defies convention to live as a single mother. Allen's feminist sympathies were also in evidence in many of his short stories. For* The Strand Magazine *he created Lois Cayley, a Cambridge-educated 'New Woman' who is left almost penniless after the deaths of her mother and her stepfather. Undeterred, she sets out on a series of adventures which take her halfway round the world and involve her in the solution of crimes which she needs all her wit and intelligence to expose. Hilda Wade is another young woman of brilliant gifts. Her almost photographic memory is astonishing and her powers of deduction remarkable. She works as a nurse at the same hospital as her admirer, Dr Cumberledge, who is the narrator of the stories in which she features. Nursing is not her vocation. It is the means by which she can get close to the man she believes to be responsible for the death of her father.* Hilda Wade: A Woman with Tenacity of Purpose *is a novel, or (more accurately) a collection of interlinked stories, which takes Allen's heroine and her would-be lover from their London hospital to the remoter regions of southern Africa in her quest for justice. Grant Allen died before he could finish it and the last chapter was completed by his friend and neighbour Arthur Conan Doyle.*

THE EPISODE OF THE NEEDLE THAT DID NOT MATCH

'Sebastian is a great man,' I said to Hilda Wade, as I sat one afternoon over a cup of tea she had brewed for me in her own little sitting-room. It is one of the alleviations of a hospital doctor's lot that he may drink tea now and again with the Sister of his ward. 'Whatever else you choose to think of him, you must admit he is a very great man.'

I admired our famous Professor, and I admired Hilda Wade: 'twas a matter of regret to me that my two admirations did not seem in return sufficiently to admire one another. 'Oh, yes,' Hilda answered, pouring out my second cup; 'he is a very great man. I never denied that. The greatest man, on the whole, I think, that I have ever come across.'

'And he has done splendid work for humanity,' I went on, growing enthusiastic.

'Splendid work! Yes, splendid! (Two lumps, I believe?) He has done more, I admit, for medical science than any other man I ever met.'

I gazed at her with a curious glance. 'Then why, dear lady, do you keep telling me he is cruel?' I inquired, toasting my feet on the fender. 'It seems contradictory.'

She passed me the muffins, and smiled her restrained smile.

'Does the desire to do good to humanity in itself imply a benevolent disposition?' she answered, obliquely.

'Now you are talking in paradox. Surely, if a man works all his life long for the good of mankind, that shows he is devoured by sympathy for his species.'

'And when your friend Mr Bates works all his life long at observing, and classifying ladybirds, I suppose that shows he is devoured by sympathy for the race of beetles!'

I laughed at her comical face, she looked at me so quizzically. 'But then,' I objected, 'the cases are not parallel. Bates kills and collects his ladybirds; Sebastian cures and benefits humanity.'

Hilda smiled her wise smile once more, and fingered her apron.

'Are the cases so different as you suppose?' she went on, with her quick glance. 'Is it not partly accident? A man of science, you see, early in life, takes up, half by chance, this, that, or the other particular form of study. But what the study is in itself, I fancy, does not greatly matter; do not mere circumstances as often as not determine it? Surely it is the temperament, on the whole, that tells: the temperament that is or is not scientific.'

'How do you mean? You *are* so enigmatic!'

'Well, in a family of the scientific temperament, it seems to me, one brother may happen to go in for butterflies – may he not? – and another for geology, or for submarine telegraphs. Now, the man who happens to take up butterflies does not make a fortune out of his hobby – there is no money in butterflies; so we say, accordingly, he is an unpractical person, who cares nothing for business, and who is only happy when he is out in the fields with a net, chasing emperors and tortoise-shells. But the man who happens to fancy submarine telegraphy most likely invents a lot of new improvements, takes out dozens of patents, finds money flow in upon him as he sits in his study, and becomes at last a peer and a millionaire; so then we say, What a splendid business head he has got, to be sure, and how immensely he differs from his poor wool-gathering brother, the entomologist, who can only invent new ways of hatching out wire-worms! Yet all may really depend on the first chance direction which led one brother as a boy to buy a butterfly net, and sent the other into the school laboratory to dabble with an electric wheel and a cheap battery.'

'Then you mean to say it is chance that has made Sebastian?'

Hilda shook her pretty head. 'By no means. Don't be so stupid. We both know Sebastian has a wonderful brain. Whatever was the work he undertook with that brain in science, he would carry it out consummately. He is a born thinker. It is like this, don't you know.' She tried to arrange her thoughts. 'The particular branch of science to which Mr Hiram Maxim's mind happens to have been directed was the making of machine-guns – and he slays his thousands. The particular branch to which Sebastian's mind happens to have been directed was medicine – and he cures as many as Mr Maxim kills. It is a turn of the hand that makes all the difference.'

'I see,' I said. 'The aim of medicine happens to be a benevolent one.'

'Quite so; that's just what I mean. The aim is benevolent; and Sebastian pursues that aim with the single-minded energy of a lofty, gifted, and devoted nature – but not a good one!'

'Not good?'

'Oh, no. To be quite frank, he seems to me to pursue it ruthlessly, cruelly, unscrupulously. He is a man of high ideals, but without principle. In that respect he reminds one of the great spirits of the Italian Renaissance – Benvenuto Cellini and so forth – men who could pore for hours with conscientious artistic care over the detail of a hem in a sculptured robe, yet could steal out in the midst of their disinterested toil to plunge a knife in the back of a rival.'

'Sebastian would not do that,' I cried. 'He is wholly free from the mean spirit of jealousy.'

'No, Sebastian would not do that. You are quite right there; there is no tinge of meanness in the man's nature. He likes to be first in the field; but he would acclaim with delight another man's scientific triumph – if another anticipated him; for would it not mean a triumph for universal science? – and is not the advancement of science Sebastian's religion? But... he would do almost as much, or more. He would stab a man without remorse, if he thought that by stabbing him he could advance knowledge.'

I recognised at once the truth of her diagnosis. 'Nurse Wade,' I cried, 'you are a wonderful woman! I believe you are right; but – how did you come to think of it?'

A cloud passed over her brow. 'I have reason to know it,' she answered, slowly. Then her voice changed. 'Take another muffin.'

I helped myself and paused. I laid down my cup, and gazed at her. What a beautiful, tender, sympathetic face! And yet, how able! She stirred the fire uneasily. I looked and hesitated. I had often wondered why I never dared ask Hilda Wade one question

301

that was nearest my heart. I think it must have been because I respected her so profoundly. The deeper your admiration and respect for a woman, the harder you find it in the end to ask her. At last I *almost* made up my mind. 'I cannot think,' I began, 'what can have induced a girl like you, with means and friends, with brains and' – I drew back, then I plumped it out – 'beauty, to take to such a life as this – a life which seems, in many ways, so unworthy of you!'

She stirred the fire more pensively than ever, and rearranged the muffin-dish on the little wrought-iron stand in front of the grate. 'And yet,' she murmured, looking down, 'what life can be better than the service of one's kind? You think it a great life for Sebastian!'

'Sebastian! He is a man. That is different; quite different. But a woman! Especially *you*, dear lady, for whom one feels that nothing is quite high enough, quite pure enough, quite good enough. I cannot imagine how –'

She checked me with one wave of her gracious hand. Her movements were always slow and dignified. 'I have a Plan in my life,' she answered earnestly, her eyes meeting mine with a sincere, frank gaze; 'a Plan to which I have resolved to sacrifice everything. It absorbs my being. Till that Plan is fulfilled – ' I saw the tears were gathering fast on her lashes. She suppressed them with an effort. 'Say no more,' she added, faltering. 'Infirm of purpose! I *will* not listen.'

I leant forward eagerly, pressing my advantage. The air was electric. Waves of emotion passed to and fro. 'But surely,' I cried, 'you do not mean to say –'

She waved me aside once more. 'I will not put my hand to the plough, and then look back,' she answered, firmly. 'Dr Cumberledge, spare me. I came to Nathaniel's for a purpose. I told you at the time what that purpose was – in part: to be near Sebastian. I want to be near him... for an object I have at heart. Do not ask me to reveal it; do not ask me to forego it. I am a woman, therefore weak. But I need your aid. Help me, instead of hindering me.'

'Hilda,' I cried, leaning forward, with quiverings of my heart, 'I will help you in whatever way you will allow me. But let me at any rate help you with the feeling that I am helping one who means in time –'

At that moment, as unkindly fate would have it, the door opened, and Sebastian entered.

'Nurse Wade,' he began, in his iron voice, glancing about him with stern eyes, 'where are those needles I ordered for that operation? We must be ready in time before Nielsen comes… Cumberledge, I shall want you.'

The golden opportunity had come and gone. It was long before I found a similar occasion for speaking to Hilda.

Every day after that the feeling deepened upon me that Hilda was there to watch Sebastian. *Why*, I did not know; but it was growing certain that a life-long duel was in progress between these two – a duel of some strange and mysterious import.

The first approach to a solution of the problem which I obtained came a week or two later. Sebastian was engaged in observing a case where certain unusual symptoms had suddenly supervened. It was a case of some obscure affection of the heart. I will not trouble you here with the particular details. We all suspected a tendency to aneurism. Hilda Wade was in attendance, as she always was on Sebastian's observation cases. We crowded round, watching. The Professor himself leaned over the cot with some medicine for external application in a basin. He gave it to Hilda to hold. I noticed that as she held it her fingers trembled, and that her eyes were fixed harder than ever upon Sebastian. He turned round to his students. 'Now this,' he began, in a very unconcerned voice, as if the patient were a toad, 'is a most unwonted turn for the disease to take. It occurs very seldom. In point of fact, I have only observed the symptom once before; and then it was fatal. The patient in that instance' – he paused dramatically – 'was the notorious poisoner, Dr Yorke-Bannerman.'

As he uttered the words, Hilda Wade's hands trembled more than ever, and with a little scream she let the basin fall, breaking it into fragments.

Sebastian's keen eyes had transfixed her in a second. 'How did you manage to do that?' he asked, with quiet sarcasm, but in a tone full of meaning.

'The basin was heavy,' Hilda faltered. 'My hands were trembling – and it somehow slipped through them. I am not... quite myself... not quite well this afternoon. I ought not to have attempted it.'

The Professor's deep-set eyes peered out like gleaming lights from beneath their overhanging brows. 'No; you ought not to have attempted it,' he answered, withering her with a glance. 'You might have let the thing fall on the patient and killed him. As it is, can't you see you have agitated him with the flurry? Don't stand there holding your breath, woman: repair your mischief. Get a cloth and wipe it up, and give *me* the bottle.'

With skilful haste he administered a little sal volatile and nux vomica to the swooning patient; while Hilda set about remedying the damage. 'That's better,' Sebastian said, in a mollified tone, when she had brought another basin. There was a singular note of cloaked triumph in his voice. 'Now, we'll begin again... I was just saying, gentlemen, before this accident, that I had seen only *one* case of this peculiar form of the tendency before; and that case was the notorious' – he kept his glittering eyes fixed harder on Hilda than ever – 'the notorious Dr Yorke-Bannerman.'

I was watching Hilda, too. At the words, she trembled violently all over once more, but with an effort restrained herself. Their looks met in a searching glance. Hilda's air was proud and fearless: in Sebastian's, I fancied I detected, after a second, just a tinge of wavering.

'You remember Yorke-Bannerman's case,' he went on. 'He committed a murder –'

'Let *me* take the basin!' I cried, for I saw Hilda's hands giving way a second time, and I was anxious to spare her.

'No, thank you,' she answered low, but in a voice that was full of suppressed defiance. 'I will wait and hear this out. I *prefer* to stop here.'

As for Sebastian, he seemed now not to notice her, though

I was aware all the time of a sidelong glance of his eye, parrot-wise, in her direction. 'He committed a murder,' he went on, 'by means of aconitine – then an almost unknown poison; and, after committing it, his heart being already weak, he was taken himself with symptoms of aneurism in a curious form, essentially similar to these; so that he died before the trial – a lucky escape for him.'

He paused rhetorically once more; then he added in the same tone: 'Mental agitation and the terror of detection no doubt accelerated the fatal result in that instance. He died at once from the shock of the arrest. It was a natural conclusion. Here we may hope for a more successful issue.'

He spoke to the students, of course, but I could see for all that that he was keeping his falcon eye fixed hard on Hilda's face. I glanced aside at her. She never flinched for a second. Neither said anything directly to the other; still, by their eyes and mouths, I knew some strange passage of arms had taken place between them. Sebastian's tone was one of provocation, of defiance, I might almost say of challenge. Hilda's air I took rather for the air of calm and resolute, but assured, resistance. He expected her to answer; she said nothing. Instead of that, she went on holding the basin now with fingers that *would* not tremble. Every muscle was strained. Every tendon was strung. I could see she held herself in with a will of iron.

The rest of the episode passed off quietly. Sebastian, having delivered his bolt, began to think less of Hilda and more of the patient. He went on with his demonstration. As for Hilda, she gradually relaxed her muscles, and, with a deep-drawn breath, resumed her natural attitude. The tension was over. They had had their little skirmish, whatever it might mean, and had it out; now, they called a truce over the patient's body.

When the case had been disposed of, and the students dismissed, I went straight into the laboratory to get a few surgical instruments I had chanced to leave there. For a minute or two, I mislaid my clinical thermometer, and began hunting for it behind a wooden partition in the corner of the room by the place for washing test-tubes. As I stooped down, turning over the various objects about the tap in my search, Sebastian's voice came to me. He had paused outside the door, and was speaking in his calm, clear tone, very low, to Hilda. 'So *now* we understand one another, Nurse Wade,' he said, with a significant sneer. 'I know whom I have to deal with!'

'And *I* know, too,' Hilda answered, in a voice of placid confidence.

'Yet you are not afraid?'

'It is not *I* who have cause for fear. The accused may tremble, not the prosecutor.'

'What! You threaten?'

'No; I do not threaten. Not in words, I mean. My presence here is in itself a threat, but I make no other. You know now, unfortunately, *why* I have come. That makes my task harder. But I will *not* give it up. I will wait and conquer.'

Sebastian answered nothing. He strode into the laboratory alone, tall, grim, unbending, and let himself sink into his easy chair, looking up with a singular and somewhat sinister smile at his bottles of microbes. After a minute he stirred the fire, and bent his head forward, brooding. He held it between his hands, with his elbows on his knees, and gazed moodily straight before him into the glowing caves of white-hot coal in the fireplace. That sinister smile still played lambent around the corners of his grizzled moustaches.

I moved noiselessly towards the door, trying to pass behind him unnoticed. But, alert as ever, his quick ears detected me. With a sudden start, he raised his head and glanced round. 'What! You here?' he cried, taken aback. For a second he appeared almost to lose his self-possession.

'I came for my clinical,' I answered, with an unconcerned air. 'I have somehow managed to mislay it in the laboratory.'

My carefully casual tone seemed to reassure him. He peered about him with knit brows. 'Cumberledge,' he asked at last, in a suspicious voice, 'did you hear that woman?'

'The woman in 93? Delirious?'

'No, no. Nurse Wade?'

'Hear her?' I echoed, I must candidly admit with intent to deceive. 'When she broke the basin?'

His forehead relaxed. 'Oh! it is nothing,' he muttered, hastily. 'A mere point of discipline. She spoke to me just now, and I thought her tone unbecoming in a subordinate... Like Korah and his crew, she takes too much upon her... We must get rid of her, Cumberledge; we must get rid of her. She is a dangerous woman!'

'She is the most intelligent nurse we have ever had in the place, sir,' I objected, stoutly.

He nodded his head twice. 'Intelligent – *je vous l'accorde;* but dangerous – dangerous!'

Then he turned to his papers, sorting them out one by one with a preoccupied face and twitching fingers. I recognised that he desired to be left alone, so I quitted the laboratory.

I cannot quite say *why,* but ever since Hilda Wade first came to Nathaniel's my enthusiasm for Sebastian had been cooling continuously. Admiring his greatness still, I had doubts as to his goodness. That day I felt I positively mistrusted him. I wondered what his passage of arms with Hilda might mean. Yet, somehow, I was shy of alluding to it before her.

One thing, however, was clear to me now – this great campaign that was being waged between the nurse and the Professor had reference to the case of Dr Yorke-Bannerman.

For a time, nothing came of it; the routine of the hospital went on as usual. The patient with the suspected predisposition to aneurism kept fairly well for a week or two, and then took a sudden turn for the worse, presenting at times most unwonted symptoms. He died unexpectedly. Sebastian, who had watched him every hour, regarded the matter as of prime importance. 'I'm glad it happened here,' he said, rubbing his hands. 'A grand opportunity. I wanted to catch an instance like this before that fellow in Paris had time to anticipate me. They're all on the lookout. Von Strahlendorff, of Vienna, has been waiting for just such a patient for years. So have I. Now fortune has favoured me. Lucky for us he died! We shall find out everything.'

We held a post-mortem, of course, the condition of the blood being what we most wished to observe; and the autopsy revealed some unexpected details. One remarkable feature consisted in a certain undescribed and impoverished state of the contained bodies which Sebastian, with his eager zeal for science, desired his students to see and identify. He said it was likely to throw much light on other ill-understood conditions of the brain and nervous system, as well as on the peculiar faint odour of the insane, now so well recognised in all large asylums. In order to compare this abnormal state with the aspect of the healthy circulating medium, he proposed to examine a little good living blood side by side with the morbid specimen under the microscope. Nurse Wade was in attendance in the laboratory, as usual. The Professor, standing by the instrument, with one hand on the brass screw, had got the diseased drop ready arranged for our inspection beforehand, and was gloating over it himself with scientific enthusiasm. 'Grey corpuscles, you will observe,' he said, 'almost entirely deficient. Red, poor in number, and irregular in outline. Plasma, thin. Nuclei, feeble. A state of body which tells severely against the due rebuilding of the wasted tissues. Now compare with typical normal specimen.' He removed his eye from the microscope, and wiped a glass slide with a clean cloth as he spoke. 'Nurse Wade, we know of old the purity and vigour of your circulating fluid. You shall have the honour of advancing science once more. Hold up your finger.'

Hilda held up her forefinger unhesitatingly. She was used to such requests; and, indeed, Sebastian had acquired by long experience the faculty of pinching the fingertip so hard, and pressing the point of a needle so dexterously into a minor vessel, that he could draw at once a small drop of blood without the subject even feeling it.

The Professor nipped the last joint between his finger and thumb for a moment till it was black at the end; then he turned to the saucer at his side, which Hilda herself had placed there, and chose from it, cat-like, with great deliberation and selective care, a particular needle. Hilda's eyes followed his every movement as closely and as fearlessly as ever. Sebastian's hand was raised, and he was just about to pierce the delicate white skin, when, with a sudden, quick scream of terror, she snatched her hand away hastily.

The Professor let the needle drop in his astonishment. 'What did you do that for?' he cried, with an angry dart of the keen eyes. 'This is not the first time I have drawn your blood. You *knew* I would not hurt you.'

Hilda's face had grown strangely pale. But that was not all. I believe I was the only person present who noticed one unobtrusive piece of sleight-of-hand which she hurriedly and skilfully executed. When the needle slipped from Sebastian's hand, she leant forward even as she screamed, and caught it, unobserved, in the folds of her apron. Then her nimble fingers closed over it as if by magic, and conveyed it with a rapid movement at once to her pocket. I do not think even Sebastian himself noticed the quick forward jerk of her eager hands, which would have done honour to a conjurer. He was too much taken aback by her unexpected behaviour to observe the needle.

Just as she caught it, Hilda answered his question in a somewhat flurried voice. 'I – I was afraid,' she broke out, gasping. 'One gets these little accesses of terror now and again. I – I feel rather weak. I don't think I will volunteer to supply any more normal blood this morning.'

Sebastian's acute eyes read her through, as so often. With a trenchant dart he glanced from her to me. I could see he began to suspect a confederacy. 'That will do,' he went on, with slow deliberateness. 'Better so. Nurse Wade, I don't know what's beginning to come over you. You are losing your nerve – which is fatal in a nurse. Only the other day you let fall and broke a basin at a most critical moment; and now, you scream aloud on a trifling apprehension.' He paused and glanced around him. 'Mr Callaghan,' he said, turning to our tall, red-haired Irish student, '*Your* blood is good normal, and YOU are not hysterical.' He selected another needle with studious care. 'Give me your finger.'

As he picked out the needle, I saw Hilda lean forward again, alert and watchful, eyeing him with a piercing glance; but, after a second's consideration, she seemed to satisfy herself, and fell back without a word. I gathered that she was ready to interfere, had occasion demanded. But occasion did not demand; and she held her peace quietly.

The rest of the examination proceeded without a hitch. For a minute or two, it is true, I fancied that Sebastian betrayed a certain suppressed agitation – a trifling lack of his accustomed perspicuity and his luminous exposition. But, after meandering for a while through a few vague sentences, he soon recovered his wonted calm; and as he went on with his demonstration, throwing himself eagerly into the case, his usual scientific enthusiasm came back to him undiminished. He waxed eloquent (after his fashion) over the 'beautiful' contrast between Callaghan's wholesome blood, 'rich in the vivifying architectonic grey corpuscles which rebuild worn tissues', and the effete, impoverished, unvitalised fluid which stagnated in the sluggish veins of the dead patient. The carriers of oxygen had neglected their proper task; the granules whose duty it was to bring elaborated food-stuffs to supply the waste of brain and nerve and muscle had forgotten their cunning. The bricklayers of the bodily fabric had gone out on strike; the weary scavengers had declined to remove the useless by-products. His vivid tongue, his picturesque fancy, ran away with him. I had never heard him talk better or more incisively before; one could feel sure, as he spoke, that the arteries of his own acute and teeming brain at that moment of exaltation were by no means deficient in those energetic and highly vital globules on whose reparative worth he so eloquently descanted. 'Sure, the Professor makes annywan see right inside wan's own vascular system,' Callaghan whispered aside to me, in unfeigned admiration.

The demonstration ended in impressive silence. As we streamed out of the laboratory, aglow with his electric fire, Sebastian held me back with a bent motion of his shrivelled forefinger. I stayed behind unwillingly. 'Yes, sir?' I said, in an interrogative voice.

The Professor's eyes were fixed intently on the ceiling. His look was one of rapt inspiration. I stood and waited. 'Cumberledge,' he said at last, coming back to earth with a start, 'I see it more plainly each day that goes. We must get rid of that woman.'

'Of Nurse Wade?' I asked, catching my breath.

He roped the grizzled moustache, and blinked the sunken eyes. 'She has lost nerve,' he went on, 'lost nerve entirely. I shall suggest that she be dismissed. Her sudden failures of stamina are most embarrassing at critical junctures.'

'Very well, sir,' I answered, swallowing a lump in my throat. To say the truth, I was beginning to be afraid on Hilda's account. That morning's events had thoroughly disquieted me.

He seemed relieved at my unquestioning acquiescence. 'She is a dangerous edged-tool; that's the truth of it,' he went on, still twirling his moustache with a preoccupied air, and turning over his stock of needles. 'When she's clothed and in her right mind, she is a valuable accessory – sharp and trenchant like a clean, bright lancet; but when she allows one of these causeless hysterical fits to override her tone, she plays one false at once – like a lancet that slips, or grows dull and rusty.' He polished one of the needles on a soft square of new chamois-leather while he spoke, as if to give point and illustration to his simile.

I went out from him, much perturbed. The Sebastian I had once admired and worshipped was beginning to pass from me; in his place I found a very complex and inferior creation. My idol had feet of clay. I was loth to acknowledge it.

I stalked along the corridor moodily towards my own room. As I passed Hilda Wade's door, I saw it half ajar. She stood a little within, and beckoned me to enter.

I passed in and closed the door behind me. Hilda looked at me with trustful eyes. Resolute still, her face was yet that of a hunted creature. 'Thank Heaven, I have *one* friend here, at least!' she said, slowly seating herself. 'You saw me catch and conceal the needle?'

'Yes, I saw you.'

She drew it forth from her purse, carefully but loosely wrapped up in a small tag of tissue-paper. 'Here it is!' she said, displaying it. 'Now, I want you to test it.'

'In a culture?' I asked; for I guessed her meaning.

She nodded. 'Yes, to see what that man has done to it.'

'What do you suspect?'

She shrugged her graceful shoulders half imperceptibly.

'How should I know? Anything!'

I gazed at the needle closely. 'What made you distrust it?' I inquired at last, still eyeing it.

She opened a drawer, and took out several others. 'See here,' she said, handing me one; '*these* are the needles I keep in antiseptic wool – the needles with which I always supply the Professor. You observe their shape – the common surgical patterns. Now, look at *this* needle, with which the Professor was just going to prick my finger! You can see for yourself at once it is of bluer steel and of a different manufacture.'

'That is quite true,' I answered, examining it with my pocket lens, which I always carry. 'I see the difference. But how did you detect it?'

'From his face, partly; but partly, too, from the needle itself. I had my suspicions, and I was watching him closely. Just as he raised the thing in his hand, half concealing it, so, and showing only the point, I caught the blue gleam of the steel as the light glanced off it. It was not the kind I knew. Then I withdrew my hand at once, feeling sure he meant mischief.'

'That was wonderfully quick of you!'

'Quick? Well, yes. Thank Heaven, my mind works fast; my perceptions are rapid. Otherwise – ' she looked grave. 'One second more, and it would have been too late. The man might have killed me.'

'You think it is poisoned, then?'

Hilda shook her head with confident dissent. 'Poisoned? Oh, no. He is wiser now. Fifteen years ago, he used poison. But science has made gigantic strides since then. He would not needlessly expose himself today to the risks of the poisoner.'

'Fifteen years ago he used poison?'

She nodded, with the air of one who knows. 'I am not speaking at random,' she answered. 'I say what I know. Someday I will explain. For the present, it is enough to tell you I know it.'

'And what do you suspect now?' I asked, the weird sense of her strange power deepening on me every second.

She held up the incriminated needle again.

'Do you see this groove?' she asked, pointing to it with the tip of another.

I examined it once more at the light with the lens. A longitudinal groove, apparently ground into one side of the needle, lengthwise, by means of a small grinding-stone and emery powder, ran for a quarter of an inch above the point. This groove seemed to me to have been produced by an amateur, though he must have been one accustomed to delicate microscopic manipulation; for the edges under the lens showed slightly rough, like the surface of a file on a small scale: not smooth and polished, as a needle-maker would have left them. I said so to Hilda.

'You are quite right,' she answered. 'That is just what it shows. I feel sure Sebastian made that groove himself. He could have bought grooved needles, it is true, such as they sometimes use for retaining small quantities of lymphs and medicines; but we had none in stock, and to buy them would be to manufacture evidence against himself, in case of detection. Besides, the rough, jagged edge would hold the material he wished to inject all the better, while its saw-like points would tear the flesh, imperceptibly, but minutely, and so serve his purpose.'

'Which was?'

'Try the needle, and judge for yourself. I prefer you should find out. You can tell me tomorrow.'

'It was quick of you to detect it!' I cried, still turning the suspicious object over. 'The difference is so slight.'

'Yes; but you tell me my eyes are as sharp as the needle. Besides, I had reason to doubt; and Sebastian himself gave me the clue by selecting his instrument with too great deliberation. He had put it there with the rest, but it lay a little apart; and as he picked it up gingerly, I began to doubt. When I saw the blue gleam, my doubt was at once converted into certainty. Then his eyes, too, had the look which I know means victory. Benign or baleful, it goes with

313

his triumphs. I have seen that look before, and when once it lurks scintillating in the luminous depths of his gleaming eyeballs, I recognise at once that, whatever his aim, he has succeeded in it.'

'Still, Hilda, I am loth –'

She waved her hand impatiently. 'Waste no time,' she cried, in an authoritative voice. 'If you happen to let that needle rub carelessly against the sleeve of your coat you may destroy the evidence. Take it at once to your room, plunge it into a culture, and lock it up safe at a proper temperature – where Sebastian cannot get at it – till the consequences develop.'

I did as she bid me. By this time, I was not wholly unprepared for the result she anticipated. My belief in Sebastian had sunk to zero, and was rapidly reaching a negative quantity.

At nine the next morning, I tested one drop of the culture under the microscope. Clear and limpid to the naked eye, it was alive with small objects of a most suspicious nature, when properly magnified. I knew those hungry forms. Still, I would not decide offhand on my own authority in a matter of such moment. Sebastian's character was at stake – the character of the man who led the profession. I called in Callaghan, who happened to be in the ward, and asked him to put his eye to the instrument for a moment. He was a splendid fellow for the use of high powers, and I had magnified the culture 300 diameters. 'What do you call those?' I asked, breathless.

He scanned them carefully with his experienced eye. 'Is it the microbes ye mean?' he answered. 'An' what 'ud they be, then, if it wasn't the bacillus of pyaemia?'

'Blood-poisoning!' I ejaculated, horror-struck.

'Aye; blood-poisoning: that's the English of it.'

I assumed an air of indifference. 'I made them that myself,' I rejoined, as if they were mere ordinary experimental germs; 'but I wanted confirmation of my own opinion. You're sure of the bacillus?'

'An' haven't I been keeping swarms of those very same bacteria under close observation for Sebastian for seven weeks past? Why, I know them as well as I know me own mother.'

'Thank you,' I said. 'That will do.' And I carried off the microscope, bacilli and all, into Hilda Wade's sitting-room. 'Look yourself!' I cried to her.

She stared at them through the instrument with an unmoved face. 'I thought so,' she answered shortly. 'The bacillus of pyaemia. A most virulent type. Exactly what I expected.'

'You anticipated that result?'

'Absolutely. You see, blood-poisoning matures quickly, and kills almost to a certainty. Delirium supervenes so soon that the patient has no chance of explaining suspicions. Besides, it would all seem so very natural! Everybody would say: "She got some slight wound, which microbes from some case she was attending contaminated." You may be sure Sebastian thought out all that. He plans with consummate skill. He had designed everything.'

I gazed at her, uncertain. 'And what will you *do*?' I asked. 'Expose him?'

She opened both her palms with a blank gesture of helplessness. 'It is useless!' she answered. 'Nobody would believe me. Consider the situation. *You* know the needle I gave you was the one Sebastian meant to use – the one he dropped and I caught – *because* you are a friend of mine, and because you have learned to trust me. But who else would credit it? I have only my word against his – an unknown nurse's against the great Professor's. Everybody would say I was malicious or hysterical. Hysteria is always an easy stone to fling at an injured woman who asks for justice. They would declare I had trumped up the case to forestall my dismissal. They would set it down to spite. We can do nothing against him. Remember, on his part, the utter absence of overt motive.'

'And you mean to stop on here, in close attendance on a man who has attempted your life?' I cried, really alarmed for her safety.

'I am not sure about that,' she answered. 'I must take time to think. My presence at Nathaniel's was necessary to my Plan. The Plan fails for the present. I have now to look round and reconsider my position.'

'But you are not safe here now,' I urged, growing warm. 'If

Sebastian really wishes to get rid of you, and is as unscrupulous as you suppose, with his gigantic brain he can soon compass his end. What he plans he executes. You ought not to remain within the Professor's reach one hour longer.'

'I have thought of that, too,' she replied, with an almost unearthly calm. 'But there are difficulties either way. At any rate, I am glad he did not succeed this time. For, to have killed me now, would have frustrated my Plan' – she clasped her hands – 'my Plan is ten thousand times dearer than life to me!'

'Dear lady!' I cried, drawing a deep breath, 'I implore you in this strait, listen to what I urge. Why fight your battle alone? Why refuse assistance? I have admired you so long – I am so eager to help you. If only you will allow me to call you –'

Her eyes brightened and softened. Her whole bosom heaved. I felt in a flash she was not wholly indifferent to me. Strange tremors in the air seemed to play about us. But she waved me aside once more. 'Don't press me,' she said, in a very low voice. 'Let me go my own way. It is hard enough already, this task I have undertaken, without *your* making it harder... Dear friend, dear friend, you don't quite understand. There are *two* men at Nathaniel's whom I desire to escape – because they both alike stand in the way of my Purpose.' She took my hands in hers. 'Each in a different way,' she murmured once more. 'But each I must avoid. One is Sebastian. The other – ' she let my hand drop again, and broke off suddenly. 'Dear Hubert,' she cried, with a catch, 'I cannot help it: forgive me!'

It was the first time she had ever called me by my Christian name. The mere sound of the word made me unspeakably happy.

Yet she waved me away. 'Must I go?' I asked, quivering.

'Yes, yes: you must go. I cannot stand it. I must think this thing out, undisturbed. It is a very great crisis.'

That afternoon and evening, by some unhappy chance, I was fully engaged in work at the hospital. Late at night a letter arrived for me. I glanced at it in dismay. It bore the Basingstoke postmark. But, to my alarm and surprise, it was in Hilda's hand. What could this change portend? I opened it, all tremulous.

'DEAR HUBERT, – ' I gave a sigh of relief. It was no longer 'Dear Dr Cumberledge' now, but 'Hubert'. That was something gained, at any rate. I read on with a beating heart. What had Hilda to say to me?

'DEAR HUBERT , – By the time this reaches you, I shall be far away, irrevocably far, from London. With deep regret, with fierce searchings of spirit, I have come to the conclusion that, for the Purpose I have in view, it would be better for me at once to leave Nathaniel's. Where I go, or what I mean to do, I do not wish to tell you. Of your charity, I pray, refrain from asking me. I am aware that your kindness and generosity deserve better recognition. But, like Sebastian himself, I am the slave of my Purpose. I have lived for it all these years, and it is still very dear to me. To tell you my plans would interfere with that end. Do not, therefore, suppose I am insensible to your goodness... Dear Hubert, spare me – I dare not say more, lest I say too much. I dare not trust myself. But one thing I *must* say. I am flying from *you* quite as much as from Sebastian. Flying from my own heart, quite as much as from my enemy. Someday, perhaps, if I accomplish my object, I may tell you all. Meanwhile, I can only beg of you of your kindness to trust me. We shall not meet again, I fear, for years. But I shall never forget you – you, the kind counsellor, who have half turned me aside from my life's Purpose. One word more, and I should falter. – In very great haste, and amid much disturbance, yours ever affectionately and gratefully,

'HILDA.'

It was a hurried scrawl in pencil, as if written in a train. I felt utterly dejected. Was Hilda, then, leaving England?

Rousing myself after some minutes, I went straight to Sebastian's rooms, and told him in brief terms that Nurse Wade had disappeared at a moment's notice, and had sent a note to tell me so.

He looked up from his work, and scanned me hard, as was his wont. 'That is well,' he said at last, his eyes glowing deep; 'she was getting too great a hold on you, that young woman!'

'She retains that hold upon me, sir,' I answered curtly.

'You are making a grave mistake in life, my dear Cumberledge,' he went on, in his old genial tone, which I had almost forgotten. 'Before you go further, and entangle yourself more deeply, I think it is only right that I should undeceive you as to this girl's true position. She is passing under a false name, and she comes of a tainted stock... Nurse Wade, as she chooses to call herself, is a daughter of the notorious murderer, Yorke-Bannerman.'

My mind leapt back to the incident of the broken basin. Yorke-Bannerman's name had profoundly moved her. Then I thought of Hilda's face. Murderers, I said to myself, do not beget such daughters as that. Not even accidental murderers, like my poor friend Le Geyt. I saw at once the *primâ facie* evidence was strongly against her. But I had faith in her still. I drew myself up firmly, and stared him back full in the face. 'I do not believe it,' I answered, shortly.

'You do not believe it? I tell you it is so. The girl herself as good as acknowledged it to me.'

I spoke slowly and distinctly. 'Dr Sebastian,' I said, confronting him, 'let us be quite clear with one another. I have found you out. I know how you tried to poison that lady. To poison her with bacilli which *I* detected. I cannot trust your word; I cannot trust your inferences. Either she is not Yorke-Bannerman's daughter at all, or else... Yorke-Bannerman was *not* a murderer...' I watched his face closely. Conviction leaped upon me. 'And someone else was,' I went on. 'I might put a name to him.'

With a stern white face, he rose and opened the door. He pointed to it slowly. 'This hospital is not big enough for you and me abreast,' he said, with cold politeness. 'One or other of us must go. Which, I leave to your good sense to determine.'

Even at that moment of detection and disgrace, in one man's eyes, at least, Sebastian retained his full measure of dignity.

ACKNOWLEDGEMENTS

Firstly, I would like to thank Ion Mills, Claire Watts, Clare Quinlivan, Ellie Lavender, Jenna Gordon and everybody at Oldcastle Books for their help while I was compiling this book and their hard work in bringing it into print. Thanks also to Elsa Mathern for the splendid cover design and to Jayne Lewis and Steven Mair for the proofreading and copy-editing skills which enabled them to pick up mistakes in my original manuscript which would have otherwise gone uncorrected. I am grateful, as always, to my family for their encouragement – in particular to my sister Lucinda and to my mother Eileen, to whom the book is dedicated. Thanks also to my family in Germany – Wolfgang, Lorna and Milena Lüers. Finally, I would not have been able to complete this anthology – or indeed any of the other books I have had published over the last fifteen years – without the unstinting love and support I receive every day from my wife, Eve.